VIRAL

Other Books by Kevin E. Ready:

—

A New Chance (2020)

All the Angels Were Jewish (2016)

Gaia Weeps - The Crisis of Global Warming (1998)

The Big One (1997)

The Holy Koran - Modern English Translation (editor) (2014)

Credit Sense: How to Borrow Money and Manage Debt (1989)

—

and with **Cap Parlier:**

TWA 800 - Accident or Incident? (1998)

—

and writing as Sarah Sarnoff

The Disambiguation of Susan (2014)

VIRAL

by
KEVIN E.READY

SAINT GAUDENS PRESS
Phoenix, Arizona & Santa Barbara, California

See other great books available from Saint Gaudens Press
http://www.SaintGaudensPress.com

Saint Gaudens Press
Post Office Box 405
Solvang, CA 93464-0405

**Saint Gaudens, Saint Gaudens Press
and the Winged Liberty colophon
are trademarks of Saint Gaudens Press**

**This edition Copyright © 2020 Kevin E. Ready
All rights reserved.**

**Print edition ISBN: 978-0-943039-57-2
eBook ISBN: 978-0-943039-58-9
Library of Congress Catalog Number: 2020937146**

Printed in the United States of America

10 8 6 4 2 3 5 7 9 1

This is a work of fiction. No character is intended to depict any real person, living or dead. Certain entities, including business, charitable, religious and educational institutions and even some famous families, are depicted for purposes of providing a proper setting for the reader to understand, enjoy and relate to the fictional story. The policies, activities and people associated with these entities, as depicted in this story, are also fictionalized. Other names, characters and incidents are the products of the author's imagination and bear no relationship to real events, or persons living or deceased.

—

In accordance with the Copyright Act of 1976 [PL 94-553; 90 Stat. 2541] and the Digital Millennium Copyright Act of 1998 (DMCA) [PL 105-304; 112 Stat. 2860], the scanning, uploading, or electronic sharing of any part of this book without the permission of the publisher constitutes unlawful piracy and theft of the author's intellectual property. If you wish to use material from this book (other than for review purposes), prior written permission must be obtained by contacting the publisher at: editorial@saintgaudenspress.com. Thank you for your support of the author's rights.

Dedication

This novel is dedicated to front-line medical workers and first responders who serve so selflessly. The author has tried to include some of their stories in his book, but has probably failed to convey the true bravery and commitment to service we see them display in real life.

Acknowledgement

The author gratefully acknowledges the assistance in the preparation of this book by his stalwart editors, Marcia Follensbee and Cap Parlier. Thanks is also given for the advice and encouragement given by Joe Glazer, Paula Frantz, Kevin Ready, Jr., Pam Piccone, Pam Oslie, and Anna Ready. Special thanks is given to Olga Ready for her encouragement and having put up the author's multi-year failure to balance a normal life with the craft of authoring books.

Prologue

Private Albert Martin Gitchell was a twenty-six-year-old U.S. Army cook, a draftee, stationed at Camp Funston, an outlying training camp near Fort Riley, Kansas. There, in early 1918, thousands of draftees were being readied to be sent into World War I. Demands for sleeping quarters for the incoming horde of draftees outpaced barracks construction, and most of Camp Funston was a tent city. Soldiers ate and slept in huge canvas tents despite the cold winter weather in northern Kansas.

On Monday, March 11, 1918, Albert Gitchell awoke with a horrible fever and sore throat. Albert put on his uniform, but instead of heading to the mess tent to serve food, as he had done the previous day, he went down to the large tent with a huge red cross on it, the infirmary. With a fever over 103°F, Gitchell was sent to a neighboring tent where soldiers with potentially contagious diseases were housed. A few hours after Albert was admitted, Corporal Lee Drake, who had been served dinner by Albert the night before, came in with similar symptoms. Shortly, Albert's Service Company non-commissioned officer, Sergeant Adolph Hurby, joined them in the convalescent tent.

By noon Tuesday, there were over a hundred soldiers with the same symptoms. They all had horribly high fever, a marked blue color to their skin from the difficulty breathing with their ferocious coughs, and lung congestion. The contagion spread to the main Fort Riley base, and by the end of the week, there were over 500 sick. By the end of the month, the number had risen to over a thousand. Two weeks after Private Gitchell got sick, the first civilian cases arose. In late March, U.S. Public Health Service (PHS) officers reported a dire outbreak of the flu at the Haskell Institute, an Indian school in Lawrence, Kansas, ninety miles east of Fort Riley on the main road and railroad line to Fort Riley. Haskell was a boarding school where the Indian children were housed in large open dormitories similar to an Army barracks. Eighteen Indian children at the Haskell Institute were ill with influenza, and three persons died, including a young female teacher. Records show that nearly fifty of the soldiers at Fort Riley died that first Spring.

Albert Gitchell was not among the dead. Albert survived and died fifty years to the week later at a Veterans' Home in South Dakota. Patient Zero for the 1918 "Spanish" Flu Pandemic, recorded for history as Albert Martin Gitchell, lived to the age of seventy-six. He was fortunate.

Shortly after the start of influenza at Fort Riley, troop trains hurriedly sent troops to the East Coast for transport overseas, and spread the flu to dozens of military bases and nearby cities. Then, the troopships brought the influenza virus to Europe, and the pandemic was off and running. France, Italy, England, Germany, and the rest of Europe succumbed. With a war on, wartime censors withheld news of the great contagion. As the only major country not involved in the war, Spain allowed word of the disastrous disease to be written about in newspapers, making it seem to the world that the disease must undoubtedly have started in Spain, hence the misnaming of the pandemic.

Eventually, 43,000 U.S. soldiers died from the flu, more than died of battle wounds in the Great War. But that figure pales in comparison to the 675,000 civilians in the United States who died. Worldwide, the death toll in 1918 through 1919 is placed by the World Health Organization (WHO) at 60 million deaths. Some scholars believe the absolute devastation that occurred in some African and Asian countries would justify a figure of from 75 to 100 million deaths. British colonial authorities in India estimated 20 Million had died in India alone. Crowded cities like Bangalore and Bombay were hit the hardest.

In America, major cities like Philadelphia had to set up schedules for picking up bodies of flu victims on the streets of the city. Nurses, doctors, and health care workers were walloped inordinately. One of the bizarre outcomes of the 1918-1919 Influenza Pandemic was the concentration of deaths in the age group from teenagers to mid-'30s. Unlike normal flu seasons where the deaths are mostly felt among the very young and the elderly, this pandemic hit the healthy young adults the hardest. The best explanation of this phenomenon is that those with the strongest, healthiest immune system had their bodies overreact to the unique new virus, flooding the lungs with fluids produced by their lymphatic system to fight the disease.

Of course, the world in 1918 was far different than today. There were no antibiotics to fight off the secondary bacterial pneumonia infections, which often were the cause of death. The general level of healthcare in those years was nowhere near the current level. Back then, there was not even a consensus among medical scholars as to what agent caused the flu. Was it bacteria? In the Journal of the American Medical Association in April 1919, there was a significant discussion of the various bacteria found in flu victims, searching for a cause. A novel concept of a minute viral organism was speculated upon by some, but was not universally accepted. The British Medical Journal in November 1918 presciently stated that "there can be no question that the virus of influenza is a living organism . . . it is possibly beyond the range of microscopic vision." But, whether they knew the cause or not, they had nothing like the vaccine capability we have today.

Today, we can identify the very genetic code of the influenza virus. In several months, we can concoct a variety of different vaccines to counter the influenza strains that circulate. We categorize the genetic code of the strains by their HA factor and NA factor and name the strains accordingly, H_N_. The H1N1 strain that caused the 1918 pandemic is still around but seems to have genetically shifted to be less lethal. Or perhaps we have just become more immune to it. Most readers of this book have been exposed to the same influenza H1N1 virus strain that killed so many millions of people a hundred years ago. But, new strains of influenza circulate from time to time and cause illness and death. They often pass to humans through domestic animals, poultry, and swine. Some speculate that Private Gitchell might have acquired his influenza virus when he handled a hog carcass delivered by a Kansas farmer to cook at the mess tent at Camp Funston.

The current vogue in reporting of pandemic dangers in the news media are reports of the avian flu virus and the coronavirus, or rather viruses, as there are several known to exist. In the several recorded cases when the avian influenza strains have crossed over and infected humans, the death rate has been horrific. In a few countries, over half of those certified as getting the avian flu have died. At this writing, the novel coronavirus is spreading around the world, and the final outcome is still unknown. World health officials are watching these strains closely.

For all the advantages we have today over our forebears in 1918 in dealing with the viruses, we have one significant detriment. Back then, cross country train rides took ten days or more, and multi-week transoceanic steamship voyages were the quickest method of world travel and the quickest way to spread contagion. It took nearly six months for the infection to spread to its greatest level in Europe in late 1918. Elsewhere in the world, the full impact was not felt until 1919. Some remoter areas were not hit until 1920.

Today, the same type of infection as 1918, or worse, could arrive by airliner in mere hours from the farthest corner of the planet. And, as wonderful as our scientific expertise to create vaccines is, the fact remains that even once we identify a virus strain that it takes many months to culture the virus, formulate the vaccine, test it and then produce the hundreds of millions of doses of vaccine needed to protect the populace.

So, even with our prodigious expertise at making influenza vaccines, there is still a very good likelihood that a pandemic might take place today before we have the ability to fight it. One medical expert conjectured that enough vaccine to fight an influenza pandemic could be manufactured in just 20 to 30 weeks to fight a viral disease that could spread worldwide in 20 to 30 hours. We need only look at coronavirus to see that relationship.

———

Chapter 1

Nursing School Dormitory
Shebeen al Kom City
Minufiya Governorate, North Central Egypt
5:00 AM Local Time February 26th

Miriam Mansoor woke with a start, thinking someone had called her name. As she often did in the nursing college dorm, it took her a moment to orient herself as to where she was, the little two-person dormitory room in the city being so different from the simple farmhouse where she had grown up. She still was not used to the dorm room even after two years. She turned over and listened. The room was dark with the sparse bluish light of early dawn coming in from outside.

In the night gloom, Miriam heard it again, "Miriam?" She barely recognized the hoarse, breathy voice.

"Leyla?" Miriam called.

"Miriam, I . . . I need help." Leyla's raspy voice was almost too soft to hear.

"What?" Miriam asked.

"I need help . . . I . . . I am . . . ." She coughed with a deep, raspy rattle.

Miriam kicked back her covers and swung her feet to the floor. She reached to the little study desk between the two beds and flicked on the desk lamp.

Leyla jerked in her bed and covered her eyes from the light, and then she coughed again, deep in her lungs. Miriam stood and quickly turned the green shade of the desk lamp towards the window. She moved to stand near Leyla's bed.

One of Leyla's hands limply tried to move her long black hair from her eyes. Miriam reached to Leyla to help and to straighten the pillow beneath her head, and she felt Leyla's nightgown on her shoulder was moist with sweat. Leyla tried to sit up but flopped back on the pillow.

Miriam could now see Leyla's face and was shocked by what she saw. Leyla was a pretty girl with a light olive complexion and almond eyes. But now, Leyla's face was pale and drawn, her eyes puffy slits and her full, once rosy, lips nearly gray. Miriam could see Leyla's hair matted to her forehead, wet with sweat. A little dried blood on her upper lip showed there had been a nosebleed earlier.

Miriam reached to see if Leyla had a temperature, touching her brow with the back of her hand. Despite the layer of sweat, the girl's forehead was feverish, very much so.

"Ya, Allah, Leyla. What's wrong?" was all Miriam could say.

Leyla gulped a breath and said, "Everything hurts . . . my bones hurt. I can't breathe."

"What is it? What's wrong with you? You were fine last night."

Leyla was rocked with a raspy cough. When she caught her breath, she said, "I'm afraid . . . I'm afraid . . . those little girls. I think I've got it. I talked with their mother."

"That was two days ago. You mean, you think you . . . ?"

Leyla coughed again, then, "Yes, . . . I think I have that flu."

Leyla collapsed into another round of rattling coughs. A thought flickered in Miriam's mind of whether she might get this flu, too. But it was too late for that, though. Miriam sat on the edge of the bed and put her arm around her friend's shoulder for a moment, then she stood and put on her robe to find the dormitory matron and get help for Leyla.

—

Chapter 2

Dakouten Zheng
Baodi District, North-Eastern China
10:00 AM Local Time February 28ᵗʰ

Quan Li parked the Lexus SUV by the huge, pre-fab steel swine rearing building. The door of the metallic red luxury vehicle had a logo for the Greater Zheng Collective on the door. Still, the vehicle was, for all intents and purposes, Quan Li's personal vehicle. As one of the original stockholders in the joint-stock company that had replaced the original collective farm for Zheng Township in the 1980s, Quan Li was a board member and senior manager for what had, over the decades, become a significant agricultural products company in north China. Their cattle, pig, and poultry operations, coupled with the field crop commodities business they had developed, made the corporation a major food producer.

The original main asset of the company had been the land they worked, and in modern China it was forbidden for rural farmers to sell their land. Thus, the stockholders of the Greater Zheng Collective had what amounted to a permanent, inheritable interest in the land and the collective farm that sprang from it. Curiously, the nominally communist laws meant to protect rural farmers from the exploitation of the wealthy coupled with newer laws to allow expansion of business in the commercial world had developed into a land-owning aristocracy, not unlike the primogeniture of medieval Europe.

Having inherited the founding owner shares of both of his parents to add to his own and his wife's, Li could easily have taken it easy and lived off the dividend checks sent by the Greater Zheng business office in Tianjin. But, he enjoyed the work he had done for a lifetime. With the expansion of business operations in recent years, his duties as Director of Animal Husbandry of Greater Zheng Collective brought with it a significant salary as a corporate officer, and a very nice company car and comfortable manager's quarters.

The local managers of both the swine rearing and poultry operations were waiting for him as he beeped the electronic key of the Lexus to locked. They were both the young, university-trained junior managers that Li loathed. Although they showed Li the respect due to an owner and board member of the corporation, they always assumed the old farmer who had worked his way up through the old collective system was uninformed in the ways of modern business. They were slightly condescending when they discussed things with him.

Both young managers nodded in respect, and the poultry manager pointed his arm, "It's easier to see around back behind the buildings."

The three men walked quickly around the building. Quan Li, with his quick pace, made sure that his age did not show to these younger men.

"You can see it from up on the levee," the poultry manager said.

Quan Li and his employees climbed the sloping rock wall to the top of the levee protecting the feed yard from the Chaobaixin River as it flowed south to the Yellow Sea. The footing was slippery as there were a few remaining spots of unmelted snow on the north-facing slope. It had been an unusually warm winter and, in late February there was little snow left.

They moved down the levee, where they had a view of the back of the long swine rearing building. Behind the swine building, there was a network of chain link fenced pens where the sows and the boars were put to mate. The piglets were born and reared inside the building and then shipped to the feed yards for growth and fattening before slaughter. The swine rearing building was built alongside the levee and immediately upriver beyond the swine building there was a poultry building where a similar mating operation went on for the breeding stock of thousands of chickens, ducks, and geese. The only difference was that the poultry was hatched in automated incubator rooms rather than the indoor nursery pens like the pigs.

As they topped the levee and headed toward the poultry building, Quan Li could hear the early morning traffic on the highway between Baodi and Tianjin across the river. Being on the levee and hearing the traffic into the city reminded Li of the time decades before when, as a young man, he had rebelled against the backbreaking work on the collective farm, building levies and farm roads. He had tried to make it in the big city, seeking a job in Tianjin. Fortunately, he had come back home when the unfriendly city life had become apparent to him and had never left the life in the countryside again. It was ironic that the choice of staying on the farm had made him a corporate manager, where the job in the city might have made him a faceless city worker.

The poultry manager pointed. "There. Perhaps over a dozen in all. Both wild and our ducks."

He was pointing at dead duck carcasses on the edge of a narrow pond. Between the back fences of the swine and poultry yards and the levee, there was a meter or two of open space. The area between the fill dirt that was added for the level ground of the animal pens and the slope of the levee was slightly depressed. The accumulated piles of pig and poultry droppings that piled up behind the pen fences made a low berm that kept the water from the melting snow on the levee slope from draining away. The result was an elongated pond a meter or so wide running most of the way behind the swine rearing building and partway behind the poultry building. Clumps of wild grass and weeds grew at the edge of the pond. The bodies of the dozen or so ducks were just inside the poultry pen fence and floating or laying on the dung piles and weeds beside the pond.

As the manager had said, Quan Li could see both the bodies of a couple of white-feathered ducks they bred for slaughter just inside the pen fences and several gray/brown bodies of wild ducks. He started down the slope to see the dead ducks up close. The managers followed him. As they slid down rough cobble of the slope, they scared one remaining wild duck hiding in the weeds beside the long pond. The wild duck with a prominent pintail flew up over the levee and out across the river to the northeast.

"And you didn't notice the dead ducks inside the pens before now?" Quan Li asked.

"That's how we found them at dawn this morning. A worker noticed a sick duck and went inside the pen to get her. He saw the others by the fence and called me." The poultry manager seemed nervous. "It seems to have been just in the last day. One worker says he was in the back of the pen the afternoon before last, and he saw nothing."

"Any other sick ducks? Or chickens? Geese?" Quan Li asked.

"We haven't had the chickens outside. Too cold this month. They don't mate well if it's cold. We kept them inside. Besides, we are just now rotating to a new breeding stock of roosters to maintain the genetic lines. And the geese are just now starting the mating season, so they are inside too."

Quan Li was amused at the university graduate changing roosters to ensure robust DNA pairing in the breeding flock. The same Chinese roosters had been breeding the same Chinese chickens for thousands of years without university graduates trying to choose their genetics for them.

Quan Li scowled, "But, inside the building, you have just one heating system, one airflow. If the ducks are sick from being outside with the wild ducks and they go inside at night, it doesn't matter if the chickens don't go outside."

Neither young manager had an answer.

They had reached the narrow pond. Avoiding the mud, Quan Li turned a gray carcass over with his toe. The long black tail of the wild duck flicked against his pant leg.

The poultry manager shrugged nervously. "What should we do?" The swine manager nodded agreement with the question.

Quan Li recognized that the deference shown by the young managers was not respect, but an attempt to pass the responsibility for any decision up to him. He thought of asking them what they thought they should do to turn the tables back on them, but instead, he just gave his advice, "Well, for now, unless you see illness, assume that the pigs are not a problem. Nothing in the government instructions on avian flu talks about the danger to pigs from dead birds.

"This could cost us dearly if we don't handle it right. We need to minimize the loss of revenue from culled birds. You have several thousand birds here, besides the ducks, we can little afford to lose. And, most importantly, you need to keep this quiet. Word leaking out could ruin our company's reputation. But to meet the letter of the law, take two of the dead ducks, the wild ones, not our farm ducks, and send them to the lab for tests. Then you need to clear out the breeding flock of ducks here. Truck all of them away from here to kill; we can't risk culling the flock here, both for appearances and maybe further contaminating the breeding rooms. Involve as few workers as you can, keep this quiet. Act like you're just rotating the breeding stock when you truck them out of here as you did with the roosters. Disinfect the building where the ducks are with steam hoses and clean the slaughter area, too. The collective has several steam pressure units we use to clean the dairy areas twice a month. I will have the dairy chief send those units over here. Just act like you're trying to be extra careful in the cleanup, don't explain why to anyone, tell them you're carrying out my instructions, if necessary. Bring in new stock from the Xianghe plant to replenish your breeders. If anyone asks, even within the company, say you're merely rotating breeding stock. If any chickens or geese get sick, do the same for them. Understand?" Quan Li stared at the poultry manager, who nodded his head.

Quan Li turned to the swine manager, "And you, since he will be busy with the ducks, I want you to fix this mess." Quan Li indicated the dead ducks, mud, and water at his feet. "First, bury these dead carcasses, except for the wild ones you send to test according to the law. Then get a sump pump, the kind we use in the rice fields. Pump this water up over the levee to the river. Don't drain the contaminated water onto our land or let any more of our animals contact it. Then, once this is dry, have a work crew dig a ditch down around your building, with a drainpipe, the black plastic ones with the holes to allow seepage, under your parking lot out to the field beyond. And then, fill this whole area behind both buildings in with gravel, not soil. Dirt will just turn to mud again. You should have been watching the condition of your area and not let a mess like this develop."

The swine manager nodded his understanding. Quan Li started to turn, but looked at the two managers and said, "It's your responsibility to make sure the company is damaged as little as possible by this, both monetarily and in reputation. Keep it as quiet as possible. Report directly to me if there are problems and when your efforts are complete. If there are any complaints or questions from our company staff or any official contacts, refer them to me. Any questions?"

The two men thought a moment and shook their heads, bowing briskly. Quan Li turned without further word and walked along the lower edge of the levee and over to his Lexus.

Quan Li realized that in all of his instructions, he had not told the managers how to dispose of the slaughtered carcasses after they were trucked away. But, he assumed culling and burying an infected flock was obvious. Certainly, they could handle that themselves.

Before getting in the car for the trip back to Baodi, Quan Li kicked his muddy shoes against the SUV's tire and flicked the mud from where the dead, wild duck's tail had smudged his pant leg with his hand.

—

Chapter 3

Abbassia Fever Hospital
Cairo, Egypt
11:30 AM Local Time February 28th

A half dozen Cairo police officers in their finest white cotton formal uniforms with black bandoleers and red epaulets fanned out on the broad sidewalk in front of the Abbassia Hospital. When a Mercedes limousine with a motorcycle escort came into view, they quickly blocked off the sidewalk as the car pulled up to the curb. A dignitary in a dark gray suit exited the car and was met by a cortege of two men in similar suits, plus a dark-skinned doctor in a white lab coat and a U.S. Navy captain in dress blue uniform. After brief introductions and handshakes, the dignitary was rushed inside.

Inside the hospital, the doctor in the lab coat, Doctor Mahmud Ghariid, pointed to a side hallway saying, in Arabic, "Your Excellency, the new infectious ward is in the next building on the second floor of the Research Unit."

As they walked through the covered passageway, the dignitary turned to the U.S. Navy officer and, in perfect English, said, "Captain Rogers, did you know that when I was an intern, I spent some time at your facility?"

The captain smiled, "Yes, Your Excellency. We are quite aware of that. I assure you the name of the Egyptian Minister of Health and Population is prominently featured on our distinguished alumni list. And your leadership in the coronavirus crisis made the staff of the U.S. Navy Medical Research Unit proud."

"What's the staffing of the facility now? Just your side, not the main hospital." asked the Minister.

"We have 141 Egyptian staff and 27 Americans, plus perhaps another dozen from Europe and WHO," answered the American officer as they entered the elevator.

"That's quite a change from when I interned here. That was back a decade or so after Sadat reinstated the center's charter and asked your country to restore your program in Egypt after Nasser died. Your American naval research facility has quite a storied history in Cairo and is an appreciated part of our health team here."

On the next floor, Doctor Ghariid moved ahead of the visitors and gave directions, again in Arabic. "If you will come this way." He hurried ahead of the minister, pointing as he went. "The infectious containment unit has three entrances, one for the patients' visitors and public observers, one for staff observation and one to enter the actual hot zone, that is, the quarantine area. We will use the staff observation area."

They passed down a long hallway, the hallway had the smell of being newly remodeled, and was freshly wallpapered in pale green. As they passed a doorway with the 'Visitors' sign, two photographers with press passes on neck chains standing there took quick pictures of the Minister's party as it passed. Through windows in the visitors' area, the Minister could see several people inside huddled along windows on the far side of the room, looking into another area beyond. A police guard who was stationed just beyond the visitors' doorway went to attention as the government minister passed. The guard kept the press from following down the hallway.

The Egyptian doctor directed them into a second door. There was a distinct sucking thump and rush of air as they passed into the next room. Ghariid explained, "The entire quarantine area is operated with a separate atmospheric pressure. That is, about the equivalent of an altitude of a thousand feet higher than Cairo, a lower atmospheric pressure, but with added oxygen for therapeutic reasons and the observation rooms have slightly higher air pressure than the interior hot zone or the outside air, just to be certain there is no airborne contamination between the adjoining rooms. The airflow is carefully monitored, and the observation rooms are quite safe. The actual quarantine area has a double airlock system for entrance, and the air system output is HEPA filtered and electrostatically disinfected. The entire facility, like the main NAMRU viral laboratory, is a Biosafety Level III containment facility, one of only three in Egypt. We handle the critical patients who are of scientific or other special interest here before transferring them to Abbassia Fever Hospital next door, when, or if, they are no longer critical, and we have satisfied our laboratory research." The doctor's explanation continued in Arabic, with jargon words like 'hot zone' and 'Biosafety Level' given in English.

Inside the observation area, the Minister and one of his assistants were ushered forward to the observation windows, and the others stood behind them. The observation area had glass windows on three walls, one windowed wall with curtains partially drawn facing the visitors' area, one wall facing a patient treatment area directly in front, and the third wall of windows whose view was blocked by sliding hospital ward curtains. Doctor Ghariid continued his explanation, "As you may know, we have five patients in two separate ICU rooms. And, currently, three of them have visitors." He indicated the people in the visitors' area who were crowded against the observation windows watching the patient area closely.

"Why are some visitors in hospital jumpsuits?" asked the Minister's assistant.

"They are the family members from the village. After we checked them for infection by throat and blood cultures, we had to decontaminate them, including their clothes. We have their own clothes disinfected and ready for them when they are ready to leave. Also, we continue to give family members and others with previous direct patient contact daily cultures to make sure they do not develop a latent infection. They were in full quarantine for the first three days, and they are staying in family quarters in a nearby building. We have an area that was built for just this purpose. We tried to get the nurses' parents from Banha also. We have one set of parents, as the roadblocks and quarantine prevented the second nurse's family from coming here."

The minister went closer to the window, where he could see several staff members, with five hospital beds in use with a few others empty, intravenous fluid bags on poles, ventilators, and what seemed to be an abundance of high tech medical equipment. The staff inside the windowed room wore full baby blue Tyvek protective gowns, hoods and face masks with ventilator cylinders on each cheek.

". . . and the patients?" the Minister asked.

Doctor Ghariid came to the window and pointed as he answered the minister's inquiry. "We, of course, have the two girls, ages 4 and 12, they're cousins from the village of Shunufa, near Minuf, south of Shebeen al Kom. They were given a young rooster chick as a pet by their father." The doctor motioned toward one of the men in the visitors' room. "They tried to play doctor and nurse with the little rooster when he got sick, and they did not think to tell the adults it was sick until too late. And we have the mother of one of the girls. We don't have any specific word on her contact with the poultry. Still, she may be a direct contact infectee as several birds in the village have tested positive to the H5N1 virus, besides the girls' rooster. We have not been able to get much information from her directly as she was quite sick, delirious, but is on the road to recovery now. We have questioned the female patient's husband, and her brother and sister-in-law," he pointed to the visitors again, "but they can't confirm she had any avian contact. We are assuming she did. And the other three parents are not infected."

"And the fourth and fifth patients?" asked the Minister.

"Yes, Your Excellency, that's the problem and why the Ministry was given special notice of this case." The doctor moved down the row of windows to the last bed as he spoke. "When the girls got sick they were taken by rural transit bus from Shunufa to the public health clinic run by the medical and nursing schools at Minufiya University in Shebeen al Kom. The village is only a few kilometers outside of the city of Minuf, but the free clinic the farmers go to is at the University. There, at the clinic, they followed all established protocols, took throat cultures, and forwarded them to the MOHP laboratory in Cairo. The patients were quarantined immediately, and the parents interviewed.

"However, the mother was not yet sick herself, or at least not showing signs of illness. It wasn't until the morning after the girls came in that the mother took ill. And, apparently, the nurse who took their medical history from the parents was infected by the mother during the viral incubation period prior to the onset of symptoms."

The minister cut in, "You're certain this nurse had no direct contact?" He asked his question in English.

"No, not with any chickens or fowl. She is a recent nursing graduate, doing a nursing residency at the clinic. She lived in the nurses' dormitory in the city. No zoonotic contact whatsoever. We interviewed her parents by phone, and they say she has not been home to Banha since Eid. And she had no direct contact with the sick girls. She only interviewed the mother before the onset of the mother's symptoms. And the nurse didn't take ill for another two days."

"You're reasonably certain of these facts?"

"Yes, Your Excellency. It appears we have the first confirmed case of human to human transmission of this avian flu."

"You mean the first in Egypt?"

"Well, there was one poorly documented case in Indonesia where it's suspected that the H5N1 avian flu virus mutated to infect a rural family group without direct animal contact and there were some suspicions of human transmission in China being covered up, but this is the first documented instance that someone totally unassociated with the agrarian contamination has become infected with H5N1 anywhere in the world. But yes, it is the first time in Egypt and the first time in at least two years worldwide that a human is known to have gotten any strain of novel avian flu from another human."

"And what's the current status of the patients?" The minister asked, again in English, observing a rush of activity inside the patient care arena before him.

"One girl is doing quite well. The younger girl. She is responding to antiviral medication. The virus appears to be semi-resistant to the standard antiviral medication, oseltamivir phosphate, that is, Tamiflu, but we are administering zanamivir, tradename Relenza, to the older girl and the three women. The older girl is very sick, and we can't get her to breathe in the zanamivir powder, which is administered as a powder inhaled into the lungs. So, the twelve-year-old is quite ill, on a ventilator, as you can see. The mother is well on the way to recovery since she was already at the hospital when she fell ill. As I said, the younger girl is stable; she is taking the antiviral therapy reasonably well. "

"And the nurse?" the minister asked, watching the flurry of activity around the nurse's bed they faced through the window.

"It's actually two nurses, the first one and her roommate at the nursing school. That's the problem." Ghariid shook his head. "The first nurse apparently fell ill overnight in her dormitory room, and by the time she got to treatment, she was quite bad off. The second nurse got sick shortly thereafter, with only contact with the first sick nurse. Rapid onset, even for H5N1. The first nurse initially responded to the antiviral treatment. But she developed a severe problem with fluid in the lungs, and she is on full respirator."

"Viral Pneumonia?" asked the minister.

Ghariid shook his head, "In truth, no. No sign of *Streptococcus pneumoniae* or the related pneumonic infections, just the H5N1. She may be exhibiting the same response noted in the Great Influenza of 1918 when otherwise healthy young adults were hit hardest by the flu virus, and their strong, healthy immune systems reacted catastrophically to the flu infection, and that powerful immune reaction caused many deaths. Here we have two young, healthy nurses who came down with the symptoms literally overnight and one is in danger of dying and a pre-teen girl in trouble while the older woman and the younger child are recovering. The records from the Spanish Flu of 1918 are quite clear that the young adults, particularly the soldiers, were hardest hit by that pandemic."

Ghariid walked to the intercom call box on the wall below the window and pushed the button. "Doctor Zarabby, what's the first nurse's status?"

One of the masked figures by the patient's bed looked up at them and reached for the equipment panel above the bed, flicking an intercom switch. "Her blood oxygen bottomed out, respiration is failing. We are trying to intubate her lungs to restore respiration and drain fluid. We have not been successful in getting full respiration restored."

As they watched the medical team work, the minister thought of another question. "So what other action have you taken? With the outbreak?"

One of the men in business suits who had met the minister at the hospital door now stepped forward. "The entire village has been decontaminated. Every fowl in that village and two nearby farming villages have been culled. All of the villagers have been tested for infection and moved to a quarantine area, as have many of the people on the bus the family took to Shebeen al Kom and everybody in the clinic and nurses dormitory has been tested. However, that bus passed through Minuf City on the way to Shebeen al Kom, and people got off. Everybody with direct known contact was quarantined for three days while being cultured daily. We have no sign of further spread, but the girls in the dormitory are still in the quarantine period. But, as you heard, the other nurse we already brought here is sick, too." He pointed to one of the occupied beds. "And she just had contact with the other nurse, no contact with the patients from the village."

"Let's hope you have stopped it." The minister shook his head.

Through the window, they saw Doctor Zarabby look at his watch, as he motioned the nurse's hand away from the patient. They could not hear what Zarabby said to her, but his act of disconnecting the ventilator tube and pulling the sheet up over the young women's face said enough. To the left, in the visitors' gallery, they saw an older couple grasp each other in a solemn embrace. Their daughter Leyla, one of the stricken nurses, was dead.

The Minister of Health and Population of the Arab Republic of Egypt turned from the window to the group assembled behind him. "Well, I've seen more than enough. Do whatever is necessary. Whatever resources the Ministry and our government have are available to fight this." The minister turned to leave but thought of one further question. He pointed to the third wall of windows, the view shielded behind the hanging curtains. "What's behind there?"

Captain Rogers answered this time, in passable Arabic, "That's our Level III surgical arena, that's where we do any necessary surgery on infectious patients. And . . . ," the captain paused, "that's where we do the autopsies."

———

Chapter 4

Pinnacle Ballroom
DoubleTree Hotel
Silver Spring, Maryland
8:45 AM EST March 3ʳᵈ

Most observers would naturally assume the tall woman in the blue/black military uniform was a U.S. Navy officer. However, a sharp-eyed observer might notice that the white-topped uniform hat she wore did not have the crossed gold anchors of the U.S. Navy, instead, one of the anchors was replaced by a caduceus, the ancient snake and pole symbol of the healing arts. The sleeve insignia above the three gold braids on each of her dark blue sleeves was not the Navy line officers' gold star nor any of the other badges of the branches of assignment for a U.S. Naval officer. The dark, sandy blonde page boy haircut of the woman was military regulation, ending just above the bottom edge of her uniform collar, and her stature was trim, bordering on lanky and quite tall, her posture erect, somewhat noble in bearing. Her face was somewhere between handsome and pretty, even features with little make-up. As she exited the security checkpoint at the entrance, she took the black bag she carried, obviously a laptop, in the one hand, and placed her heavy overcoat on her other arm with the black and white uniform hat in that hand. The epaulets on the overcoat had the same three gold stripes and curious gold military branch insignia.

The clerk at the conference registration table did address the woman as "Commander," however. The conference nametag she was handed read "CDR Karen A. Llewellyn-Craig, MD, DSc," on one line and on the next line "CDC, NCIRD."

———

Karen smiled at the name tag, both as to the myriad of acronyms it presented and at the use of her hyphenated married name. While the use of her married name was technically correct, she made a mental note to get NCIRD, the National Center for Immunization and Respiratory Disease to change their staff listing to just use her pre-marriage surname alone. She had not used her married name for the last year, having chosen the hyphenated name in the first years of her marriage, before the thought of being identified by her estranged husband's last name had somewhat soured. She pinned the name tag just below her standard black uniform name tag on her right breast pocket, which simply read "LLEWELLYN."

As a commissioned officer in the U.S. Public Health Service, she wore a uniform identical to a female U.S. Navy officer, except for the Public Health Service branch insignia and the gold cross above her twin rows of ribbon above her left breast pocket; the cross that indicated her status as a senior physician.

Karen Llewellyn momentarily sat down her laptop case as she put her uniform hat and overcoat on the racks by the conference room door that had been set up for the conference attendees to store their cold-weather gear. Winter weather in Washington, DC caused Karen to acknowledge the one item of the military uniform she appreciated, the officers' bridge coat, the warm wool overcoat, similar to an enlisted sailor's peacoat, but a full three-quarter length with ornate gold buttons and epaulets. She rarely had cause to wear a bridge coat back home in Atlanta, but her frequent trips to Washington and New England in winter made her appreciate the naval officers' standard cold weather apparel

She had a tinge of dread for another interminable conference, even one as important as this one. The incredible bureaucracy of the Centers for Disease Control (CDC) in Atlanta, of which NCIRD was a branch, was mirrored by an even denser bureaucratic morass at its parent organization, the U.S. Department of Health and Human Services (HHS) in Washington, DC. But the committee meeting she faced today presented not only her agency coworkers but the vaccine crew from another HHS agency, the Food and Drug Administration (FDA), staffers from a couple other federal agencies, and the invited observers from the World Health Organization (WHO), among others. The Vaccine and Related Biological Products Advisory Committee (VRBPAC) meetings each year were the culmination of months of study and research into what strains of influenza and coronavirus would be included in the batch of vaccine for the forthcoming season. There was a corresponding meeting in the Australian capital of Canberra in late August to prepare for the different timed viral season in the southern hemisphere,

Karen kept her laptop with her as she entered the room for the meeting. Her life's work was on the laptop's hard drive, and it would not leave her side. She had an automatic backup of its data to the cloud. Her specialty was precisely the technical focus of this meeting, the study of strains of influenza and coronavirus, and the ways the viruses changed their genetic make-up through what scientists called genetic shift and drift.

Karen saw Philip Reynes, her boss, the Director of NCIRD standing with other senior attendees, the actual VRBPAC committee members, on the rostrum area in front. Karen also saw Nancy Cox from CDC on the rostrum, where both the guests of honor and the voting members of the Committee always sat. Dr. Cox was CDC's pre-eminent epidemiologist and one of Reynes' chief assistants. Nancy was on the agenda to present the world surveillance and viral strain characterization report, the heart of the information they needed. Karen was intimately familiar with her work and was particularly interested in Cox's work, comparing the spreading potential of H1N1, H5N1, the several H9 viruses, and H7N9, Karen's current focus of study. Of course, after the COVID19 disaster, coronaviruses had been added to the traditional concern for influenza.

Karen took a seat halfway down from the center aisle, a few seats in. As she sat her things down, she acknowledged a wave from Reynes. He had easily picked out Karen's uniform in the crowd of tweed-jacketed scientists and doctors.

Besides those somewhat scruffily dressed scientists, Karen could see a cortège of men and women in expensive-looking gray pinstripe and black business suits all sitting together in the far left section of the room. Karen recognized them to be the executives from GlaxoSmithKline, HeptImun, Novavax, Medicago, and the other corporate entities who played a significant role in the annual flu vaccine production process. Once this VRBPAC committee made its decision on the precise mix of this year's recommended flu and coronavirus vaccines, these corporate entities would be sharing the billions of dollars and euros in income from both government contracts and commercial sales of the produced vaccine.

Karen checked the time, and there was still ten minutes before the agenda start time, so she decided to join the socializing going on in the room and make contact with the HeptImun corporate representative. She would soon be working closely with them in her forthcoming assignment.

As Karen approached a group of corporate types, Jared Bentley, a HeptImun vice-president, noticed her approach and split from the other group to turn toward her. She had met Jared at a planning meeting for the new vaccine plant program in Connecticut the previous November.

Jared Bentley was slightly taller than Karen, mid-30s and had handsome features, curly close-cropped black hair and complexion that hinted at partial African heritage. Jared's wardrobe today clearly announced he was 'corporate' not 'academic.' He spoke with a distinctive Boston accent. "Commander Llewellyn, I was hoping our paths would cross. You all ready to head to California?"

"Not quite yet. Coupla weeks."

"I got to go visit in February. The construction was done in January, and the Army Corps people who managed the construction contract asked us contractor types to go on the final acceptance tour with them. Nice place, and big, really big—three different campuses. Makes our main corporate plant in Connecticut seem ancient and tiny. They should be in the equipment move in and test stage. Probably ready to do trial runs in early April."

Karen smiled, "Well, I'll be there by then. I understand the Army contracting team is in place."

"Good, I'm sure we corporate types will be back out for a look-see when it's operational." Jared looked back over his shoulder at someone, "If you've got a minute, can I introduce you to someone?"

"Sure."

Jared turned and walked toward a woman standing near the corporate people, but standing apart from them a bit. Jared said something to the woman, and she smiled and nodded her head. Jared was guiding the woman over toward Karen. The woman was East Asian and wore a black business suit, conservative in design, but obviously fine silk. As Jared and the woman got closer to Karen, she saw the woman had her coal black hair perfectly coiffed in a long page boy cut, and her make-up and accessories spoke of cosmopolitan sophistication.

Jared said, "Commander Karen Llewellyn, may I introduce you to Dr. Zhao Xiang. Dr. Zhao is the Director of the Chinese vaccine production program, and as of late last year, one of our customers. Dr. Zhao, Dr. Llewellyn will be the commanding officer of the new vaccine plant we are setting up and running in California."

The two women shook hands. Karen looked at the woman's name tag, which had "Joan" in quotation marks after "Zhao Xiang, Ph.D." And, the bottom line read "Ministry of Health, SFDA, PRC."

Zhao saw Karen looking at the nametag and, in perfect British accented English, said, "In the West, I still use 'Joan' as it's a nickname that was conveyed by my colleagues at the King's College who struggled with Xiang. My father was a diplomat in London."

"Nice to meet you, Dr. Zhao," Karen said.

"Joan will be fine, if I may, Karen?" Zhao said.

Karen nodded, but before she could say anything, Jared interrupted with, "I thought it would be a good idea to get you two together as both of you will be in charge of a vaccine plant designed by our company. Well, actually, Dr. Zhao will have four."

Karen looked at Jared with surprise, "Oh really, four plants. I had not heard of that. I had not heard about any of these plants in China."

Jared started to speak, but now Joan Zhao cut him off, "Yes, our State Food and Drug Administration, a branch of the Ministry of Health, after seeing the production test results of the plant-based viral particle vaccines decided that we need to augment our existing cell-based and albumen culture vaccine programs. We went to the Canadian and U.S. companies that developed the technique, and they referred us to the three companies who were using their technology for the U.S. government, for your new government-owned plants. We were able to reach an accord with HeptImun and your State Department, plus the Canadians, to get four new plants in our country."

Karen looked at Jared, "Curious, I had heard nothing about this."

Jared replied, "Oh, yes, we got approval from HHS to use the same design concept we used for your plant and then we had to get the Canadians, both government and Medicago/Mitsubishi, to agree, since the license the U.S. got to the technology from their grant money that developed it was only a license for domestic U.S. production. HeptImun has been developing all four Chinese plants, plus the U.S. plants, in unison. In fact, the multiple plants have significantly reduced the cost to develop and build, for both China and the U.S."

Zhao now added, "Commander Llewellyn, ah . . . Karen, I'm glad to meet you. If possible, while we are here at the conference, I would very much like to have the opportunity to talk with you. We seem to have some common ground."

"Yes, of course. I would love to." Karen said as she accepted Zhao's business card. "I don't have my card on me. I'll get one to you later."

Jared directed his last comment to Karen, "And I'm sure we'll have time to talk also."

The three all smiled and proceeded to their seats.

Karen was not the only person in uniform, but one of only two women. She noticed Colonel Hal Kessler, an Army doctor who ran the viral disease branch at Fort Detrick's U.S. Army Medical Research Institute of Infectious Diseases (USAMRIID) laboratories. Karen and her husband, a doctor now in the Army Reserves, had once had dinner with this colonel, back in the days when she and her now estranged husband were a couple.

There were four other PHS officers like Karen, two of her contemporaries in other CDC departments, and two with the FDA. Another uniformed attendee was a Canadian Defense Forces officer she knew to be their chief of medical corps. The rest of the attendees were overwhelmingly male and past middle age. Karen knew by sight many of the attendees from years past, the scientists, American and foreign. But this year there were many new faces, more than usual.

Kessler waved and came over to her, sitting his computer and briefcase down at the seat on the aisle next to her. Kessler muttered, "I'll be right back," before heading over to greet some more of the conferees.

Hal Kessler finally came back and sat beside Karen while she was checking her emails. "How are you doing, Karen. I haven't seen you in a while. I missed last year's meeting here. I had to get the Afghanistan punch on my career ticket." He smiled and offered her his hand. "I see you're still a commander; the rumor mill has it you got a promotion to full bird." Hal used the Army slang for her promotion to O-6 or captain in the Public Health Service.

Karen smiled and shook his hand, "I was due for my captaincy later this year or next anyway and the powers that be decided to frock me for the new position. I put on the new rank later this month when I head for California. I guess PHS decided I needed the rank to keep you Army types in your place."

"Well, you deserve it. I was glad to hear that someone like you was being put in charge of one of the new vaccine plants. Exciting stuff."

Karen smiled again and said, "On the subject of vaccines, have you heard what came out of the WHO meeting two weeks ago?"

Hal shook his head, "Nothing to inspire confidence. Lots of divergent ideas and many moderately uninformed requests to cover the avian flu strains that are in various countries' poultry flocks. As though we should take a shot in the dark against an avian flu strain that has only appeared in animals instead of going after real human strains highlighted in last years' field results. The lack of sophistication in many WHO member representatives is astonishing."

Karen raised her eyebrows, "Well, we 'experts' guessed so badly on the Perth H3N2 strain this year that it wasn't far off from a shot in the dark. Not to mention how long it took us to respond to COVID19."

Hal smiled faintly and nodded. Karen was grateful that Hal had been diplomatic and not asked her about her estranged husband, Marty. Since she had first met Hal when she was coupled with Marty, but he had not mentioned him, it was clear Hal was avoiding the subject.

People were starting to take their seats, and the group on the rostrum seemed to be near complete. There was a new face on the rostrum, a man who Karen recognized from his photo as the new assistant secretary of Health and Human Services in charge of Planning and Emergency Preparedness, Stephen Royce. Along with Dr. Reynes, Karen and a few others from NCIRD were scheduled to brief Royce on their Center's mission before they left DC. This assistant secretary was not in direct authority over CDC, but he was nevertheless important. The ink on the presidential appointment of this new assistant secretary was barely dry, and everyone felt the need to brief him on their particular position, function, and *raison d'etre*. Royce probably needed little actual briefing, as Karen had read his biography, which indicated he was a retired Air Force Flight Surgeon, a colonel. Dr. Reynes had taken the opportunity of the trip to DC to do his briefing for the new political appointee. For some reason, he had elevated Karen to the level of attending the briefing. Dr. Reynes and Nancy Cox were the ones usually involved in political and public information briefings on matters involving pandemic preparedness and vaccination, not Karen. Formal contact with a number two person in HHS was pretty much above Karen's pay grade. Karen was intrigued to find out why she had been invited.

On the rostrum, the officials sat down, signaling the start of the meeting. Karen stifled a yawn and opened her laptop to take notes.

———

Chapter 5

U.S. Navy Research Unit
Cairo, Egypt
4:15 PM Local Time March 3rd

Return-path: <m.ghariid@namru.us.navy.mil>
Received: from mxoutps1.us.navy.mil ([10.24.21.211]) by us.navy.mil (DKO MTA-mail21-A)
From: "Ghariid, Mahmud, Med Dir NAMRU3, ES-2" <m.ghariid@namru.us.navy.mil>
To: "Rogers, Jonathan Jr CAPT USN NAMRU3" jonathan.rogers@namru.us.navy.mil
Subject: Bad News UNCLASSIFIED
Captain Rogers:
I couldn't reach you by phone. You must be out of cell range. I want to make sure you get word that the dormitory roommate of the nurse from Minufiya has been confirmed positive for H5N1. We have reconfirmed she had no contact with the flu patients, just the other nurse. She is very sick, but not as much so as the first nurse. Word is coming in about several other tentative cases, both at the clinic and in the farm town population in quarantine.

That confirms if there were any doubt, the human to human transmission. MOHP is considering quarantining the entire university, which would be quite a task, several thousand students in the middle of Shebeen al Kom, a major city. It's also quite a political issue, as Shebeen is the prime minister's hometown.

Please contact me ASAP. This needs to be reported in U.S. channels, and probably WHO. We cannot rely on Egyptian MOHP entirely to get the necessary word out.
Mahmud,
Mahmud Ghariid, MD
Medical Director, NAMRU 3
Cairo, Egypt

———

Poultry Processing Plant #2
Baodi, China
6:40 PM Local Time March 3rd

Yunan Qiuyue was ready for her workday to end. She was utterly exhausted. For some reason, the managers had scheduled more trucks of incoming birds than usual, and then they told the workers they had to finish all of them so they could steam clean the killing floors and do maintenance on the conveyor belts. This was odd in the middle of the workweek. Usually, if they did not kill an entire incoming shipment, they could just leave them in crates for the next day. But they were told to finish this whole load tonight, and many of these ducks had come in not in crates, but in bags and sometimes just loaded in the back of the big enclosed trucks of the Greater Zheng Collective. It was a strange way to handle poultry. The method of shipping the ducks had been hard on the ducks, for the workers had seen many of them were injured when unloaded, some could barely walk. A few were dead.

At age twenty-four, Qiuyue had worked in the poultry plant in Baodi for six years. She had been promoted up from the defeathering room to her present job. Some people might not think her job was a promotion, but Qiuyue was used to it, it paid well, and it was easy, stress-free, and required no strength or endurance, just a strong stomach. Usually no endurance, that is.

Her job was to take the defeathered poultry carcasses on the conveyor belt, open the already slit belly of the bird, and with her gloved hands, pull the guts from the bird. Then, Qiuyue and her coworkers in the giblet room would deftly pull and snip the heart, liver, and gizzard from the rest of the entrails and put them in the plastic tray. The occasional egg was also put aside, today's shipment had far more eggs than usual for reasons unknown to Qiuyue. The remaining entrails went in a chute to go to the rendering plant.

The heart, liver, and gizzard were boxed and processed separately from the whole chicken or duck. There was a market for these edible giblets in China. If they were working with ducks or geese on the killing floor, the women in Qiuyue's section had the additional duty of separating the liver from the heart and gizzard and carefully washing the livers for placement in sealed plastic bags. They were extra careful with the livers. They had been told the buyers of the ducks' livers were very picky, requiring fresh, undamaged, and preferably fat and plump livers. The Europeans supposedly thought of duck livers as a delicacy. Qiuyue knew little of that and had never eaten a duck liver, but she knew that the extra time it took to handle the duck livers in a shipment as big as today's duck kill was tiring. Today, Qiuyue had drawn the duty of washing and bagging the duck livers, and she had been busy beyond the usual eight hours. Qiuyue ended her extended shift tired and ready to go home to the workers' dormitory her employer provided.

———

The poultry manager for the Greater Zheng Collective had listened with great care to the instructions given by Director Quan Li. The director had said they couldn't risk culling the flock at the breeding farm, but he had carefully told them to kill the birds at the slaughterhouse and had never said to dispose of the dead birds. The poultry manager understood what he assumed was the unstated instructions from the director to kill the ducks, clean the breeding pens and killing floor and, ship the product out, as usual, to avoid losing any revenue. The poultry manager was a degreed food processing engineer, eager to make his place in the huge Greater Zheng organization. He did not want to be the cause of any decrease in revenues or shipments.

Understanding that the ducks had the potential of contamination, the poultry manager made sure the entire load of ducks they processed today would go directly to the cannery where the ducks would be quick-cooked in superheated steam and stuffed into cans for the whole duck canned product that was a big seller for Greater Zheng. There would be no fresh duck shipped out from this shipment. The poultry manager prided himself in making sure the possibly contaminated ducks were processed in a way that would ensure full use of the resource and protect from contamination by not shipping fresh duck.

Unfortunately, the poultry manager's food processing knowledge came mostly from lectures at the Tianjin Polytechnic University and not from practical experience in the processing industry. He did not fully appreciate that the danger of contamination was not just to other live poultry and people who might eat poorly cooked meat, but to the humans who processed the slaughtered ducks. And in his attempt to make sure the whole ducks were fully cooked and thus decontaminated, the poultry manager had failed to account for the by-products of a duck kill. He had failed to account for the people like Qiuyue, who spent eight hours inhaling the microscopic fluid spatters from a thousand dead ducks. He had failed to account for the raw duck livers that were shipped in their sealed plastic bags to the French restaurants in Beijing and Shanghai and food exporters for preparation of *foie gras*, the expensive delicacy that relied on the fat of duck and goose livers for its essence.

And, the poultry manager failed to account for one non-food product derived from the poultry slaughterhouse, the product Qiuyue had worked on in her first years at the plant. The first step in the slaughterhouse was to carefully pull the soft down feathers off the duck's bellies and underwing areas to stuff in bags for shipment to garment factories to make down pillows, parkas, and comforters, which the Chinese shipped worldwide. Then with the down removed, the automated defeathering machines took over as the remaining feathers were used in manufacturing, too. Of course, there were international standards for fumigation and sterilization of down and feather products, but Chinese quality control was notorious for its haphazardness, as the poultry manager had proven.

—

Chapter 6

U.S. Navy Research Unit
Cairo, Egypt
17:03 GMT March 3rd

UNCLASSIFIED
******.*.*.*** ***.
ARLINGTON ANNEX MESSAGE CENTER
ELEC MSG FRWD VIA EMAIL GRP PUBHLTH 41 *****
IMMEDIATE / FLASH PRIORITY**   ZYUW RUHGSGG8569
3501703
    o 03l7O3Z MAR
    FM   CMDR NAMRU 3//C1// (CAIRO)
    TO   COMUSNAVCENT
      USN BUMED
    INFO NMCC WASHINGTON DC//POC/APP/LPO//
      USCINCCENT//CCJ3//
      CINCLANTFLT NORFOLK VA
      CINCPACFLT PEARL HARBOR HI
      COMUSMARCENT//G3//
      SURG GEN HHS WASH DC
      DEPT STATE WASH DC
      AIG 01 – PINNACLE
      AIG 41 – PUB HLTH
      Declassified/ d by 1 @ //NO3000//CMD
    SECTION 01 OF 01
    SUBJ: OPREP 3 PINNACLE NR 01 AVIAN INFLUENZA
    REF/A/DOC/NVCCO 3010.2E/-//
    RMKS/
    1. CMDR U.S. NAV MED RESEARCH UNIT THREE CAIRO
       CONFIRMS MULTIPLE AND SUSTAINED HUMAN TO
       HUMAN TRANSMISSION OF NOVEL AVIAN INFLUENZA
       STRAIN (A/CHICKEN/MINUFIYA/EGYPT/AB-K8/(H5N1)).
    2. U.S. PERSONNEL HAVE CONFIRMED STRAIN TYPING
       AND NON-ZOONOTIC TRANSMISSION OF STRAIN TO
       HUMAN SUBJECTS. REPEAT - NON-ZOONOTIC.
    3. PREVIOUS CASES OF HUMAN INFECTION BY THIS
       STRAIN OF AVIAN FLU HAVE BEEN TRANSMITTED

FROM ANIMALS TO HUMANS, NOT HUMAN TO HUMAN. MORTALITY RATE FOR PREVIOUS CASES WAS AS HIGH AS THIRTY PERCENT (30%) DEPENDING ON CONTACT PARAMETERS.

4. TRANSMISSION OF THIS STRAIN TO THE GENERAL EGYPTIAN POPULACE OR SPREAD INTERNATIONALLY WOULD BE A MATTER OF THE GRAVEST CONSEQUENCE.
5. NINE (9) CONFIRMED CIVILIAN INFECTEES, EGYPTIAN NATIONALS. MULTIPLE NON-LAB CONFIRMED POSS INFECTEES. TWO (2) FATAL, FOUR CRITICAL/SERIOUS.
6. EGYPT MINISTRY OF HEALTH & POPULATION (MOHP) INTENDS QUARANTINE MINUFIYA METROPOLITAN DISTRICT, EGYPTIAN ARMY PARTIALLY MOBILIZING.
7. MOHP REQUESTS USA AND UN/WHO ASSISTANCE IN MASS INOCULATION. H5N1 VACCINE UNAVAIL IN COUNTRY AND NAMRU3 IS UNAWARE OF ANY VACCINE ASSETS ELSEWHERE. ANTI-VIRAL MEDS IN CRITICALLY SHORT SUPPLY.
8. CMDR NAMRU3 RECOMMENDS LEVEL ONE RESPONSE BY U.S. ASSETS. INCIDENT IS OF CRITICAL INTERNATIONAL SIGNIFICANCE.

MORE TO FOLLOW.

 NMCC WASH DC   ADV   44

COG POC(L)   (U,F)

INFO OS(l) CCT(3) C412(2) AVN(8) CC(3) IG(l) INT(2)

I -L (4) MED (13) DCS PP-0 (1) PL (1) RP (1) CtiC (1) MH (1)

OLA-PA(l) SO-LiC(l) MI(l) NAHD(L) LRCC(5) PO(l)

POR(L) TFK CK(l) AMRD(L)

———

Pinnacle Ballroom
Double Tree Hotel
Silver Spring, Maryland
11:30 AM EST March 3rd

Karen Llewellyn recognized the duality of her view of the VRBPAC vaccine strain selection meeting. She was personally intrigued by the importance of the subject matter; it was, after all, her life's work. But, she was, at the same time, slightly bored by the fact that nothing new was said, nothing groundbreaking even hinted at during the whole morning meeting, so far.

The first part of the meeting went as expected. Stephen Royce, the newly appointed assistant secretary of Health and Human Services, gave a short, not-quite inspiring welcome speech, before thanking everybody for their attendance and leaving the conference to the experts. A senior doctor from CDC reviewed the winding down of the previous year's H1N1 outbreak, the remaining impact of the coronavirus pandemic, and possible follow-on waves of the separate viruses, recent influenza, and coronavirus surveillance data in the U.S and vaccine effectiveness for the current year was discussed. Then, Dr. Cox did her review worldwide surveillance and strain characterization. Then two specialists from the Department of Defense did a review of vaccine coverage and effectiveness, and a sequence analysis of virus isolates, all very technical, but routine. This was followed by more discussion of the serological responses to current vaccines, other technical reports on candidate strains, and adjuvant reagents. The only new concept was the proposal to add the most recently circulating strain of coronavirus as one of the four strains included in the proposed quadrivalent vaccine for next year. Always before the four strains had been the most worrisome four strains of influenza and after the COVID19 crisis and the interminable wait for a corona vaccine, the coronavirus had been vaccinated separately.

Commander Llewellyn's interest perked up for the presentation by the vaccine manufacturers' presentation. The industry was in a major push to ramp up capabilities with live-attenuated vaccines and innovative plant-based and cell-based vaccine methods, making response quicker than using traditional inactivated viruses to produce vaccines. It was all an outgrowth of the coronavirus chaos. She was set to take over the government liaison duties at the newest vaccine facility, a government-owned contractor operated vaccine manufacturing facility in Thousand Oaks, California, in a few weeks. So, the presentation by the industry representative tweaked her curiosity.

A corporate vice-president for Novartis, the operator of a recently expanded live attenuated vaccine plant in North Carolina, was concluding his presentation on the state of the industry when Karen Llewellyn saw an email message window pop up on her laptop screen. Several dozen email alerts had come up and disappeared throughout the morning. However, she had not bothered to read them during the conference, but this message was a flash priority message from a Navy research facility in Egypt about the avian flu. She clicked the window and started reading the message.

As Karen read the message, there was a flush of whispered conversation throughout the auditorium as other attendees who also had their portable computers and cell phones got word of the Navy alert message. Within a few seconds, the murmur of conversation was so loud the Novartis VP stopped his talk and asked, "Excuse me, did I say something? Would someone mind filling me in on the buzz?"

Hal Kessler, who had been reading his own laptop, stood up and moved to the microphone in the aisle set up for comments from the audience. He announced, "Those of us with electronic messaging just received a Flash Message from the U.S. Navy research hospital in Cairo, Egypt confirming an outbreak of human to human transmission of H5N1 with nine confirmed infectees and two deaths. Quarantine of a major Egyptian city is underway."

The entire auditorium now broke out in conversation. The speaker looked to the Chair, the FDA Director of the Division of Viral Products, who keyed his microphone, which he thumped with a pen to get everyone's attention, "It seems that real-world events may have taken added precedence. If our speaker agrees, let's take our lunch break early, after which we can conclude this section and discuss the news."

Those who did not have access to the email gathered around the computers of those who did. Karen Llewellyn found a half dozen people crowding in towards her laptop. She tilted the screen and adjusted the window's zoom to allow people in the row above and behind her to read easier, and she re-read it again herself. The world had just changed, and the outcome of the otherwise dull committee meeting was no longer a known quantity.

———

Montauban Restaurant
Colesville Road
Silver Spring, Maryland
7:05 PM EST March 3rd

Jared Bentley and Joan Zhao were seated in one of the brocade Louis XV settees on either side of the maître d'hôtel's podium. Both of them had changed clothes after the conference session had ended, so Karen Llewellyn was glad she had changed also. Her long-sleeved, red, crepe dress was perfect for the occasion.

Jared and Joan stood up when they saw Karen, and the three were able to shake hands before the maître d' announced, "If this is your third party, I can seat you."

Karen gave her coat to the hat check table attendant, and they all followed the hostess. The restaurant was elegantly furnished with décor that seemed a bit too eager to announce that the place was an expensive French restaurant;

lots of faux Louis XV, floral wallpaper, and bare-bulb crystal chandeliers. The three were seated on a raised area opposite the windows that gave them a good view of the entire floor.

"I hope French is a good choice. In truth, I was here the night before last. We corporate types had a pre-meeting, and the guy from Sanofi reserved this place. I guess the French should know good French food." Jared smiled.

"I love French food; we have several good spots in Beijing now," replied Joan.

"Fine with me, too," Karen said. She then added with a quasi-humorous lilt to her voice, "I hope I didn't just hear that representatives of the world's biggest pharmaceutical companies met in a private meeting to discuss their joint plans for this year's vaccines. I think there are anti-trust laws to prevent such a meeting."

Jared gave a blank look for a second, then smiled and answered, "Very observant, Captain Llewellyn, that's why we invited Marsha Keating from FDA to that dinner. Marsha brought her HHS deputy secretary boss with her, and they acted as our 'chaperones.' Not a single monopolistic practice nor anti-trust violation was discussed."

"Mm-hmm," Karen said, smiling again. "And you're a couple of weeks premature in dubbing me 'Captain.' Please call me Karen."

Joan Zhao looked back and forth between Jared and Karen as though she were not sure whether the anti-trust talk was joking or serious.

The waiter brought menus and wine lists, announcing the daily specials. As they perused the menus, Karen was able to scan the restaurant. The clientele was what you would expect for an expensive restaurant a mile or so north of Embassy Row in DC, a very well-dressed crowd with most tables having one or two couples at each table. As she watched, she saw a couple of men escorted in by the waitress. The men, who had been waiting in the lobby when Karen came in, with short haircuts and plain, ill-fitting suits that did not match the expensive couture of most of Montaubon's clientele. One man was in his early-30's and the other quite a bit older. As the hostess took them to a table by the window on the far side of the room, Karen saw the older man scanning the room, and Karen thought she saw him hold his glance directly at her. When the hostess laid the menus on the table, the one who had been looking around the room touched the hostess' arm and pointed to the raised level on the other side of the room. The hostess tried to say 'no,' but the man seemed to insist. The hostess went back to check with the maître d', leaving the two men standing alone in the middle of the restaurant. When the hostess came back, she shrugged and motioned for them to follow her. She gave them a table on the same level as Karen, a few tables away. Karen dismissed the matter as the man wanting a good view.

"Are we ready to order?" their waiter asked. He had walked up while Karen was watching the restaurant floor, and he was looking at Karen.

"Uh, no, I was not paying attention. Joan, you go ahead and order. I need a minute." Karen motioned to Joan. Karen quickly ran through the menu's choices.

They eventually finished ordering. After hearing the women's choices, Jared added a bottle of Loire Chardonnay to the order.

"Well, Karen, I must say you clean up quite nicely, out of uniform. This is the first time I have seen you in anything but dress blues," Jared said. And then, realizing he needed to spread the compliment to both of the women at the table, he added, "And Dr. Zhao, you look marvelous, too. More fashionable than the outfits I've seen from the Chinese at the contract negotiation meetings."

"Well, Mister Bentley, the days of Mao jackets for the Chinese leadership have pretty much passed." Joan Zhao emphasized the 'Mister' to point out the Jared had called Karen by her first name, but Joan by her formal title.

"Yes, Joan, indeed, times have changed," Jared said, accepting the minor comeuppance.

Joan turned to Karen, "Speaking of uniforms, Karen, I only know the most basic information about your U.S. Public Health Service. I have met several PHS officers, but they seem to be here and there in your government agencies. One woman whom they called by the title admiral was an assistant department secretary who gave her approval of our getting the vaccine plant technology. Still, the people below her in the office were not PHS Can you explain this? And why Navy uniforms and ranks?"

Karen nodded, "Yes, I suppose there is a lot that's not intuitive to our little club. The Public Health Service started out in the 1800s, as a professional cadre of medical staff to provide medical care to American seamen through a number of hospitals built in our port cities for just that purpose. After our American Civil War, the head of that maritime hospital program decided to organize it along military lines and picked a uniform similar to the Navy's because of the connection with the Navy and the maritime service. In 1889, Congress followed up and officially made the Marine Hospital Service a formal uniformed federal service. Over the years, additional medical duties like handling quarantine, leprosy treatment, and infectious disease control were added to the duties, and the name became U.S. Public Health Service. In the great flu pandemic of 1918, the Public Health Service became a great tool to organize local governments into an effective force for fighting the influenza disaster. In World War II, the Public Health Service expanded greatly to handle things like refugee and prisoner of war health issues, as well as the great number of casualties in the merchant marine from the war."

Karen paused as the wine, water, bread, and hors d'oeuvres arrived, then she continued, "With the decrease in the number of ships operated by the U.S. Merchant Marine service, the PHS hospitals were finally closed in the early 1980s. The PHS professionals became a cadre of trained medical professionals supporting certain government programs like Ebola and pandemic response, federal prison health clinics, and the general duties of the Health and Human Services Department and other departments. Then, in 2005, our country was hit by a trio of massive hurricanes, and the PHS officers were pulled out of their normal duties, and 2400 of us were deployed to the Gulf Coast region to augment the existing medical services there. They discovered that it was nice to have thousands of doctors, nurses, and public health pros they could pull out of their civilian niches at a moment's notice and send to a disaster scene. I was only a couple of years into my PHS service when that happened. One day, I was a young MD doing virus research in a Washington, DC office, and the next, I was in my field uniform in a tent in Southern Louisiana doing emergency triage on people pulled out of the ruins of a major city flattened by the hurricane. Then, with the coronavirus pandemic, the American people got used to seeing uniformed PHS officers standing next to the president for pandemic briefings, and PHS became better known.

"So, yes, you will find PHS officers in various positions in the U.S. government. And, if a PHS officer has finished their current assignment term and they see a health or medical position open in the U.S. government, they can ask to be assigned to that position just like a regular civil service employee. And . . . ," Karen pointed both hands to herself "when the government starts a new program for vaccine production, they can follow the military's long-standing contracting template of a government-owned plant that the Army usually assigns an Army officer to command, and they have people like me who already have a military uniform to step in and do the commanding."

Joan Zhao nodded, "Interesting; I had no idea of any of that."

"Can I get you to do that again sometime with a video camera rolling? It would be a great background for our company video explaining HeptImun's new vaccine plant," Jared said.

Karen gave a playful frown and said, "First, it's not your new vaccine plant, it's Uncle Sam's new plant. And, no, I don't think doing corporate PR videos is in my job description."

Jared gave her a thumbs-up signal and said, "Roger that, I understand; change the project title to Department of Defense Pharmaceutical Plant Public Information Video and ask Commander Llewellyn again."

Karen did not answer that and turned to eating her crab cake hors d'oeuvre.

With the arrival of the first of their entrees, the conversation turned to how Joan's trip had been. She filled them both in on the WHO meeting in Geneva two weeks before, which she had also attended, as China's medical representative. She added the news that her father would soon be moving from London to Geneva as China's ambassador to WHO and other United Nations organizations in Geneva.

Joan put her fork down as she spoke, "Of course, the news from Cairo changes the entire discussion we had in Geneva. I guess that after we see the outcome of this meeting here in Washington, they will talk about whether they really should have another WHO vaccine strain selection meeting or just rubber-stamp whatever is done here. You Americans have to realize there is an undercurrent of . . . what should you call it, nationalism, or maybe the last dregs of anti-colonialism, amongst the WHO representatives that don't like feeling that the big western countries are stuffing a decision down their throats. And please understand that I say that as a fellow professional, not as a Chinese official."

"Yes, I heard exactly that from Hal Kessler. He was in Geneva, too."

"He's the Army officer, right?" Joan asked.

Karen nodded.

They ate in silence for a short while before Joan said, "You know, I was very interested to learn that the U.S. had decided to create this new generation of vaccine production plants as government-owned. If you stand back and look at our countries' approaches, China and America are doing this almost the same way and with the exact same equipment from HeptImun and Medicago. Both with the government controlling the means of production and calling on corporate expertise for the 'business' end of things."

Karen smiled, "Please don't say that too loud. If Congress heard that the new vaccine plants were being run the same way as Communist China does it, they might reconsider, and Jared would lose a customer."

Now, Jared chimed in, "But as I understand it, this process is the same way as the Army has been handling critical defense production for decades."

Karen replied, "I wasn't involved at that level, but I understand they had to work hard to sell the concept of government ownership to Congress. And then your corporate overlords had to hear that the companies' profit margin was built into the equation. And, we had to promise all of the Big Five pharm companies that they each would get their share of the action."

Jared nodded but said, "No comment."

"And," Joan continued, "I understand that the analogy between the two countries goes deeper. Your bureaucracy is almost a perfect match for ours. You have the FDA and CDC in the Health and Human Services Department both trying to steer the vaccine program, with Defense playing its national defense card and a dozen other agencies all having their say, in finance, emergency preparedness, etc. We have the Ministry of Health in general control, but various branches with different issues they care about in this field. The Ministry of Public Security and the Ministry of Defense both have their fingers in the 'national defense and preparedness" issues. We have the funding for everything in other agencies, Ministry of Finance for program funding, but the National Development Research Center for funding things like the infrastructure, i.e., the vaccine plant itself. It sounds like governments run the same no matter what political label you put on them."

Karen said, "But, as I understand it, a major difference is how China's provincial and local governments function as local arms of the national government. Whereas in America, our state and local governments are autonomous and look to the national government for some funding and technical advice but are self-directing as to the specific actions in a public health emergency. Except, of course, that technical vaccine decisions are almost exclusively a federal prerogative." As Karen spoke, Joan nodded.

The Chinese scientist waited a minute before answering, "I was talking about government vaccine programs, and you moved the subject to 'public health emergency' and inserted provincial and local governments. Perhaps you're looking for comments on how SARS was handled and the mess they made in Wuhan with the coronavirus?"

Karen blinked and said, "Oh, no, I had no intention of moving to a touchy subject if that's what it is. It's just that all of our decisions as to vaccines are meant to ward off the possibility of a true public health emergency. I apologize if my comment seemed that I was alluding to any specific, ah, issue, or events."

Joan shook her head, "No apology needed. I was still in school in Europe when the SARS epidemic happened, so I do not have any 'skin in that game,' as I think is the popular term for that. And, I was not in the loop, so to speak, regarding Wuhan. And, the places where China went wrong have been thoroughly analyzed, ad infinitum. It was a problem with how the provincial government handled things that made SARS and the Wuhan coronavirus bigger than they should have been. Coronavirus got totally out of hand worldwide, killing thousands. You can't have the national and provincial disease response teams analyzing the status of the epidemic and then sending a 'top secret' report to a provincial government which didn't happen to have any leaders available who could read a 'top secret' document as happened with SARS. That's a guaranteed catastrophe. And there were other mistakes we all are probably aware of in the early days of the coronavirus pandemic. If you have an accident at a laboratory, it's moronic to punish the local doctor who tries to put out the warning. It's quite true that the powers that be wanted to punish some health professionals who tried to spread a warning about coronavirus."

Karen was going to let the subject drop, but Jared now chimed in with a follow-up question, "America had its own problems with secrecy and lack of transparency when the coronavirus hit us. But, do you think the Chinese system has solved that secrecy problem?"

Joan Zhao thought for a long time and then answered, obviously choosing her words carefully, "Please do not quote me beyond this table, but the answer is complex. The Ministry of Health, my employer, has policies in place to prevent the specific internal secrecy problem the SARS and coronavirus cases highlighted. But, since the provincial officials are part of the same hierarchy reaching up into the national level and we have no fewer than four major ministries, Health, Public Security, Defense and Agriculture that all have key responsibilities in epidemic response, there could still be problems. The missteps in Wuhan in the first days of coronavirus were retold around the world. Also, in a few cases, the Ministry of Agriculture hierarchy has been slow to act in culling commercial animals in response to the zoonotic avian flu infestations, and the Ministry of Agriculture experts have failed at providing directions to farmers that are based on proper epidemiological science. The Agriculture bureaucracy has different points of emphasis than Health officials. Then, once you get into a crisis mode, there are both police functions and military functions that must be called on to respond, besides the healthcare issues. There is a question of who is in charge. Provincial-level officials have been shown to avoid reports of problems that would raise doubts that their areas of responsibility are well-managed. And, I fear that we Chinese have learned a lot from the United States in terms of political leaders becoming adept at producing misinformation that tries to make one thing appear as another. In a country with 1.4 billion people, how many infected people does it take before a minor, inconsequential outbreak becomes a reportable incident or a crisis?"

Both Jared and Karen now realized there was no response to that rhetorical question. Karen changed the topic of conversation to a discussion of the latest news from Egypt and how everyone thought it would change the vaccine strain mix decision that the conference would be discussing again in the morning.

———

Chapter 7

Dongbei—Northeastern China
Early March

The young drake flew northward across the Dongbei region. He flew alone. The last of his duck siblings had died in the pond at Dakouten Zheng. He had not seen his parents since the flock left their winter home in Viet Nam. The drake was not healthy. He had grown fat and strong eating insects, leeches, and larvae in the swamps on the Mekong River Delta. But now, his strength waned.

Like most Northern Pintail ducks, this drake was driven by the instinct of his species to fly north for the mating season in the faraway Arctic where he had been born. His parents had met and mated in the mosquito and fly-infested wetlands that appeared when the tundra melted in spring and summer in the Arctic. After the first summer season in the Arctic, they had flown south with his sibling brood of six ducklings to the subtropics of Southeast Asia. Now, almost a year later, as a young adult, the drake followed ancient instincts to fly north to start the cycle anew.

The air above Dongbei was still cold as he flew north. The cold and the aching sickness in his body and wings made the drake miserable, but his instinct prevailed and urged him northward. The conflicting signals of the changing climate caused the Pintail Ducks to leave the subtropics before the usual time, and the drake found himself traveling north in much colder weather than their northward migration would typically face.

The drake was a member of a somewhat unique species. The humans who studied bird species recognized that the Northern Pintail duck had a range covering most of the northern half of the planet. Pintails defied genetic specialization theories in their sheer wanderlust. Their travels were so widespread that they had never separated enough to break into different species geographically, as many animal and bird species did. With their seasonal flight patterns from tropics to the Arctic and multiple habitats in between, Pintail ducks had been tracked through ornithologists' leg tags from Japan to Mississippi, or as in the case of the drake, from his winter home in Viet Nam, across China, to the wetlands of southwestern Alaska he now struggled towards. From their Arctic mating areas, flocks of Pintails would return south in the summer and autumn to California, the Caribbean, Sub-Saharan Africa, the Nile Valley, the Deccan Plateau, or the drake's childhood home in South East Asia. Their instinct drove them, when the weather warmed sufficiently down south, to fly northward to common grounds of their birth in the spring and summer. But that same instinct let them choose whatever southern wintering ground the flock which the individual ducks joined in the Arctic chose, most scientists suspected the males simply followed the female on her route back south. Biologically, this seemed to work for the Pintail ducks, it kept the species worldwide of a common genetic heritage and let them adapt to a wide range of possible habitats. It also meant that any illness the species picked up anywhere in the world could go with them anywhere.

The drake knew nothing of this, save for the part his instinct played in pushing him north. His aching wings made him often stop as he pushed north, feeding wherever he could in riverbank, canal, or farmyard pond across China, Dongbei, and the Russian Far East. Eventually, the solitary drake joined a flock of Pintails from Japan on the coast somewhere north of Vladivostok. The Japanese ducks were stronger than he was due to his illness but were not so large as he to start with, his juvenile months in the river delta had been good to him. In the new flock, he recognized the shiny black and white head and neck and the pointed black tails that gave his species their name on the males who would be his rivals. And he was attracted to the mottled brown camouflage coloration on the numerous young females who flew with this Japanese Pintail flock. Even in his illness, he managed to keep up with this flock, feeding with them when they landed to rest. Finally, after many weeks of flying, they crossed the Bering Sea and circled toward the swamps and wetlands south of Nome, Alaska. Their instinct told the Pintails that the marsh flies and mosquitoes were waiting for them by the billions in the tundra thawing in the Spring sun and warm southern winds. Luckily, the signal sent by the warming climate that caused the drake to start the northerly migration early also caused the annual melting of the tundra to occur on time for the Pintail assembly, a full month early.

With a few tasty meals of Alaskan larvae in his belly, the drake felt better. The worst of his sickness passed. The drake set about to find a mate. His instincts told him to avoid several of the females in the Japanese flock who now seemed to be sick like he had been.

A few of the Japanese ducks had not made it across the Bering Sea, but like him, most wild ducks could survive a bout of influenza. Most wild ducks had influenza virus within them, several influenza strains were endemic to the species, and ducks rarely got sick from it, carrying it with them wherever they went. These strains included the older flu strains that had long since passed to humans, pigs, and a dozen other species, causing human pandemics, as well as the new strains that had been spreading throughout poultry flocks worldwide and scaring the human epidemiologists. The avian flu strain that was currently spreading to domestic flocks worldwide killed many types of poultry by the millions, but it was usually relatively mild to Pintails. But, the strain of influenza the drake had picked up on his trek north through China was not the endemic avian flu the humans called H5N1, it was H7N9 and worse than the earlier strains, even sickening a few of the Pintails, killing some.

Eventually, the drake found a suitable female Pintail in the Alaskan swamps. She happened to be from a flock that had traveled northward up the Pacific Flyway along the west coast of North America. After a brief Pintail courtship which consisted mainly of the drake showing off his neck and tail feathers and the female preening him to show her interest, the drake established himself in his mate's American flock, leaving the Japanese pintail flock, now somewhat decimated by the disease he had passed on to them. Some of his mate's flock became sick, but they survived better than the Asian ducks had. As the drake's mate incubated the clutch of eggs in the nest in a grass clump, the drake carefully brought her grubs, insects, and seeds he collected, regurgitating a food pile for her to eat as she lovingly warmed their eggs. The drake eventually lost interest as the nesting and then hatching continued, as was the nature of male Pintails. Still, he and the other drakes stayed around the nesting area, and all would fly south together when the ducklings were ready to migrate south. The female did not get as sick from the flu strain as the drake had, perhaps having a different immunity than the drake, or perhaps the strain itself was changing genetically, as was the nature of the influenza virus.

Most of the newly hatched ducklings survived, despite the parents' manner of feeding the ducklings by regurgitation and the fact that they had been hatched far earlier this spring than was the norm. The southern home of the drake's mate on the shores of the Lower Colorado River of California would not be as fertile as his former home along the Mekong River, but it would probably be where the drake and his new family and flock would head, as would the new avian flu virus the flock carried in their blood, spittle, and droppings.

—

Chapter 8

Los Angeles County Sheriff's Station
Lost Hills/Calabasas, California
7:30 AM PST March 7th

Deputy Sheriff II Matt Relford sat and listened to the morning briefing the sergeant gave to the oncoming shift of deputies sitting in the squad ready room. The station served as the police station for not only the unincorporated county lands but also for Calabasas, Agoura Hills, Malibu, and several small cities in this wealthy suburban area on the far north-west corner of Los Angeles County. The cities found it cheaper to contract for city police services with the county sheriff, who had jurisdiction over the neighboring unincorporated areas than to pay for their own police department. Matt Relford listened somewhat absentmindedly as Sergeant Rick Gonçalvez read through dozens of status updates and handed out several warrants to the two-person teams who made the parole violation arrests and picked up wanted suspects and felons. As a fairly senior patrol deputy whose primary duty was to do a one-person patrol in the area between Calabasas and Malibu, Matt rarely had anything come his way in the pre-shift briefings. And anything he needed to know was on the photocopied BOLO sheets the duty sergeant always handed out before reading through them to let people know of any "Be On the Look Out" cases they should watch out for on patrol. So, he was surprised when he heard his name called out as the sergeant gave out individual duties for the day.

"And Relford," Gonçalvez looked over to make sure Matt was looking at him. "Civil Division out of Chatsworth is coming in with an eviction in the 28 thousand 900 Block of Malibu Rancho Road at 10 o'clock. The owner is trying to evict ten to twelve people living in a trailer home, and he warned Civil to expect trouble. Civil wants backup from Patrol, and that's you. If things get out of hand, contact Guthrie in Lima 201 or me, and we will back you up. Have fun with that one."

Matt Relford rolled his eyes at the "have fun" comment. Second only to domestic disturbance calls, civil evictions were thankless tasks that often turned messy. Quite often, the evictee thought they had a legitimate gripe with the property owner who was trying to kick them out of their home. Then, the evictee took things out on the deputies whose duty it was to serve the court orders and, if necessary, physically remove the tenant from the property. The Sheriff's Civil Process division attached to Court

Services carried out the main duties, but in cases like this, they often needed additional strong-arm backup to complete their unwelcome duties.

The sergeant finished up this tasking of Relford with, "Meet the Court Services van at the scene at quarter to ten. That's 289 hundred block Malibu Rancho Road. That's just west of Lake Vista Drive."

Matt nodded, semi-annoyed that Gonçalvez had thought he needed to give him directions to an address in the heart of Matt's normal patrol area. But, it was better to make sure than to make a silly mistake. He just nodded to Sergeant Gonçalvez.

The briefing ended shortly after that, and Matt Relford went to check on his vehicle for the day. The duty list showed him in his usual Lima 211 this morning. Good. Matt liked the roomy, new Explorer patrol vehicles. They were the norm for the patrols in the rough, hilly area between Calabasas and Malibu.

——

The Court Services van showed up right on time. The target property was a large mobile home with a slide-out section sitting with a couple derelict RVs and some junk cars in a cluster of trees just out of sight of the main road into Malibu Lake. The Court Services/Civil Process team consisted of one uniformed deputy, Dan O'Meara, and one female civilian legal services "technician," Clara Quinonez, who handled the paperwork and often served as a translator for the frequent Spanish-speaking subjects. Matt could not remember ever having met O'Meara, which was not surprising given that nearly ten thousand sworn deputies worked for the LA Sheriff in a county as big or bigger than several U.S. states. Matt guessed that O'Meara was using the assignment with Court Services as a laid-back swan song assignment prior to retirement. Working as a court bailiff or civil process server was usually far easier than typical patrol, jail custody, or other law enforcement duties that sheriff deputies could be assigned to. Evictions like today were the exception.

A well-dressed woman carrying a clipboard was leaning against a Mercedes sedan parked just off Lake Vista Drive. She seemed to be waiting for the Sheriff's crew. Matt waited while Deputy O'Meara went over to the Mercedes to make contact. There was a medium-sized stake truck with two contract laborers from a moving company that pulled up behind the van. The movers were there in case it became necessary, as it usually did, to clear out personal property along with the evicted people. Court Services would send a bill for the moving men and Matt's time to the court for collection from the property owner when they returned the eviction paperwork.

Matt had driven by this semi-squalid area many times, but with no complaints, there was no reason to hassle anyone. There were several areas in the Hills between Malibu and Calabasas where atypical hovels conflicted with the usual ritzy real property of the area. Usually, they were a bit farther off the beaten track than this dumpy place just off the main road. The lack of housing for the average working person was a universal problem in suburban LA, and the Calabasas area was worse than most areas. Anyone who could not afford the million-dollar-plus prices on the single-family homes that were the norm for the area was lucky to get one of the few nice apartments newly built up near the 101 freeway. If you could not find one of the scarce apartments and you worked in Calabasas or Agoura, you usually had to drive up the 101 freeway from the cheaper San Fernando Valley, as Matt did. The landowner had probably watched the population of the rented trailer creep up as more people were stuffed in to share expenses. Either that or someone had complained, and County Planning had lowered the boom on a residence that Matt could not imagine being legally permitted in this area.

There were four older cars parked near the trailer, besides the obvious junkers. There was also an old Porta-Potty, a small shed, and ramshackle cage enclosure that had a dozen or so chickens in it near the trailer. A single wire ran to the trailer from a nearby power pole, but Matt doubted there was any sewer or water connection for the trailer, hence the outdoor toilet. Matt waited a few yards back while the other two went up to the door. Malt saw that the technician had a Sheriff logo shoulder bag of the same type as CSI crews used for their equipment. He knew from experience that the bag had things like bolt cutters, chain locks, and similar equipment needed to carry out an eviction. Matt noted that there were two children's bicycles leaning against the trailer. The woman in the Mercedes now stood behind where Matt parked his Explorer and waited nervously, taking cellphone pictures.

Deputy O'Meara climbed the cinder block steps and pushed the rusty doorbell. But not hearing any ring, he also knocked twice on the door. After a moment, someone said something from inside, and the civilian technician stepped toward the door and spoke in Spanish. Matt had attended the Department's perfunctory Spanish for the Workplace training, but all he understood was "*el departamento del sheriff*" and the command to "*abre la puerta*" or "open the door."

After a long wait, the door opened slightly. O'Meara quickly moved the toe of his steel-toed uniform shoe over the door's threshold and put one hand on the door while passing a stack of court documents through the opening. He then started reading from a plasticized card, explaining the purpose of the visit, the eviction, in English. When he seemed to feel the movement of the door, he interrupted reading with another command of "*Abre la puerta!*" A woman's voice said something unintelligible in Spanish, or possibly Oaxacan.

The technician stepped closer and chimed in with "*Alguien habla inglés?*" That seemed to cause the person at the door to move away as the deputy took the opportunity to push the door fully open.

Matt could hear that a man who spoke broken English had come to the door, and O'Meara renewed his explanation of the eviction. From his spot down the stairway, Matt could hear little of what the man inside said, but the gist of the conversation could be gleaned by the Deputy's responses. "You can go talk to an *abogado* if you want, but that will not stop the eviction today. You should have talked to the attorney last month when you were served with the court papers . . . . No, there is no extra few days available, you're out of here today . . . . I'm sorry, everyone has to leave immediately. You can take any property with you if you want. If you don't cooperate, we have a crew that will move the property out to the roadside, or if you sign a paper promising to pay the storage bill, they will put your stuff in storage for up to 30 days."

Matt listened as this discussion continued. Eventually, O'Meara and the technician went inside the trailer, and Matt walked the rest of the way up and stood on the upper steps.

Matt looked in the open door. He could see little inside the darkened mobile home. The two Sheriff personnel were talking to several people inside, and O'Meara seemed to be moving about. Matt stepped closer to hear what was going on.

Three people in their 20s, a man and two women came out. All of them had dark skin, broad facial features, and the stout stature of southern Mexico. Each was holding a small suitcase or box of belongings and had an armload of clothes. Matt saw that both women had waitress uniforms on with nametags from the Middle Eastern restaurant in Agoura Hills. The young man wore some kind of utility jumpsuit. They seemed to be roomers clearing out before the rest of the people inside. He watched as the three quickly walked to an old Toyota Corolla and left.

After a few moments, Clara, the legal technician, stepped out of the door. Matt saw that she was wearing a blue N95 mask over her mouth and nose. She said, "We've got a problem, you should go in. I need to talk to the real estate lady. Wear this!" She handed Matt another N95 mask and a pair of rubber gloves she took from her shoulder bag.

An N95 mask and the gloves were standard issue equipment. Matt had a supply of them in his patrol duty bag in the back of the Explorer. You used them to protect from dust and bacterial/viral contamination. The last time Matt had worn them had been when he was called to the scene of a particularly gruesome crime, using the N95 to prevent blood born contamination from the blood spatters. Matt had no idea what to expect as he donned the mask and gloves and stepped into the darkened mobile home. He unlatched his holster strap.

As his eyes adjusted to the light, Matt saw that O'Meara had a mask on too and was talking to a portly middle-aged Hispanic man to the rear of a living room. Several people sat or stood around the room, both adults and children.

Matt walked over to the deputy and made a 'what's up' gesture with his hands.

O'Meara turned his head to Matt, "Besides the three who already left, we have six more still here. They are slowly getting the message that they have no choice but to leave. However, a bunch of them are sick. Really sick. The guy over there in the corner on the futon. Three of them in the bedroom, an older woman, and two kids are supposedly really bad. Non-ambulatory.

"Clara is checking with the Owner's Rep to see if we can get the owner's OK to let them stay. Because without agreement by the property owner, I have no discretion not to enforce the eviction. Court order stands."

"I'm gonna try to get these others moving out. I wanted you to deal with the three in the bedroom. This is Raul, the main tenant. The old woman in the bedroom is his mother, and the two sick kids are his niece and nephew. Their parents, his brother, and sister-in-law are out working right now at a restaurant in Agoura."

The deputy turned to the Hispanic man and said, "Mr. Morelos, this is Deputy Relford. He is going to look at your mother and the children."

Before Matt could move to the bedroom, the legal technician, Clare, came back in and said, "Real estate agent says 'no.' They have been cited for a building code violations, spent hundreds of dollars and several months to get the eviction order. The owner won't give any extra time. If we don't get them out today, they need to start the process over. So, out they go."

"I figured as much." O'Meara said, turning to Morelos. "You're going to have to get out. Today--this morning. As I said, you can move your stuff out yourself, or we can get the moving crew to take your stuff to storage, and you agree to pay the storage fee."

Matt did not listen to any more of the eviction discussion, and he turned past the tiny kitchen to the rear hallway. There were three doors, a bathroom that seemed to be full of plastic jugs of water, a tiny, empty dark bedroom, and a closed door. Matt knocked, waited, and opened the closed door.

The room was hot, stuffy, and had an overwhelming stench of human sweat. Dark curtains were pulled shut. Matt felt for a switch and then turned on the room light. There were two mattresses on the floor, one of them a single and one a double bed size lying in opposite corners of the small room. No beds or regular furniture, just mattresses. The other corner had a pile of cardboard boxes, full of clothes, and miscellaneous junk. Another single mattress was on end up against the wall.

The two people lying on the larger mattress reacted to the light going on. Matt could see that they were an old, white-haired woman with a toddler cradled in one of her arms. As Matt kneeled next to that mattress, the old woman let loose with a lengthy, deep cough. The sound from her lungs was thick and raspy. She had lots of phlegm in her throat.

Matt asked the old woman, "*Como estas?*"

The woman tried to mouth some words but broke into a cough again.

Matt touched the cheek of the toddler. The cheek was hot, feverish. The little boy was wide-eyed, staring straight up but did not look toward Matt when he touched him. The little boy did not make a sound except for his short, panting breaths.

Matt moved to the other mattress, where he pulled the blanket back a bit to show a young girl, probably age ten or eleven. The girl's pink pajamas were wet from sweating, as was her shiny black hair. The girl's eyes were closed, and she was breathing heavily through her wide open mouth. The breaths were noisy. Matt tried to rouse her by gently shaking her shoulder. There was no reaction. A check of her skin temperature was the same as the toddler. Both had a high fever.

Matt stood and thought over the situation. If they had no choice other than evicting the tenants, he certainly couldn't put these three very sick people out on the streets. He considered all three of them in life-threatening condition. And he had not even checked on the person in the corner of the living room.

Matt reached for his shoulder microphone and keyed it. "Dispatch, Lima 2-1-1, Over."

The answer came back, 'Lima 2-1-1, Lost Hills Dispatch, over."

"My 10-20 is the 28 thousand nine hundred block Malibu Rancho Drive. I need Paramedics Code Three and at least two ambulances. Multiple parties need transport to the hospital. Over."

There was a short wait and then, "Lima 2-1-1, What's the condition of the patients needing transport? Over."

"At least three parties are 10-45 Charlie, others unknown. One Hispanic female age sixty-plus with high fever and extremely labored breathing. Non-ambulatory. One male, age two, high fever, semi-conscious. Female age ten, high fever, labored breathing, comatose. At least one other also sick. Besides the paramedics, you should do a referral call to County Public Health. This meets the Public Health notification specs. We have a family in a nonconforming dwelling with a very serious disease, maybe influenza or pneumonia. This is a civil eviction call, and they are going to be out on the street shortly. Several of them are in critical condition, even aside from the eviction situation. Over."

After a short pause, he heard, "Roger, Lima 2-1-1, we are dispatching paramedics, they are only five minutes out, and one ambulance and calling Public Health in Reseda. We'll let the paramedic decide how many more ambulances they need. Dispatch out."

After a moment, Matt heard Sergeant Gonçalvez on the radio, "Lima 2-1-1, this is Lima 2 Hundred. If this is a medical emergency, why don't they cancel the civil process, over?"

"Lima 2 Hundred, Lima 2-1-1, not my call. Court Services says they have no leeway but to finish the eviction. The property owner wants them out, and they have a court order for today. This scene is pretty bad. I could use back-up. Over."

"Lima 2-1-1, On my way. Dispatch, notify the Watch Commander of this situation, Lima 2 Hundred, out."

Matt Relford left the bedroom to check on the sick person in the corner of the living room. This morning's call was one for the books. The morning sun on the metal roof and the number of people in the cramped quarters made it miserable in the trailer. Matt felt a drop of sweat roll off his forehead and down his nose under the N95 mask.

———

Chapter 9

Headquarters
U.S. Department of Health and Human Services
200 Independence Avenue SW
Washington, DC
2:40 PM EST March 7th

Karen Llewellyn had followed Phil Reynes' advice and switched from the hotel in Silver Spring, Maryland, to the Marriott Residence Inn just south of the National Mall near Capitol Hill last evening. The VRBPAC meeting had ended its extended schedule late yesterday afternoon. Its primary duty of determining the viral strain mix for the forthcoming year's vaccine had been thrown into turmoil by the news of the H5N1 human-to-human spread in Egypt. The NCIRD team from Atlanta had stayed over an extra day and had managed to move their appointment with the HHS assistant secretary to this afternoon. The downtown Marriott was a much handier place to stay for today's meeting.

The Health and Human Services building was strategically located diagonally across from the Capitol Building itself. Karen went by two of the office buildings used by members of Congress as she walked the two and a half blocks north from the hotel to the HHS headquarters. Phil and the other NCIRD people had some meetings at the Washington CDC office after lunch, and Karen was not part of that. The Washington offices for the Centers for Disease Control were adjacent to and just to the west of the Marriott. That CDC building was where Karen had first worked after grad school and before her move to CDC Atlanta. It was also where she had met Marty Craig, who had been serving as medical liaison for the Army medical staff at USAMRIID to CDC. They had married and moved to Atlanta together. That building and these environs had many memories for Karen, conflicting memories.

The security guard in the HHS lobby accepted Karen's identification card with barely a glance, as she was both in uniform and, technically, an HHS employee. Another guard was standing by the elevator that was simply labeled "Executive Offices." After a quick inquiry, that guard pushed a button, and Karen entered the elevator. There was a hinged plexiglass cover over all of the elevator buttons except for the ones for the lobby and the sixth floor.

The elevator opened onto an expansive reception area, walls paneled with reddish fruit-wood and with thick federal blue carpet. There were several chairs and couches clustered in groups near the four arched exits from the reception area. Three women sat behind a counter, two of them wore telephone headsets.

A large brushed metal oval with the stylized HHS seal was on the wall behind them. Karen had always thought the logo, a modernist graphic of a human face morphing into an eagle, was engaging, but with nebulous meaning. One of the young women at the counter directed Karen to wait on one of the couches. Karen was the first of their group to arrive.

As she waited, Karen saw a constant stream of visitors pass through the elegant waiting room. Before coming here today, Karen had Googled the org chart for HHS. Besides the Secretary himself, there were no less than six assistant secretaries who managed the vast federal Department, along with various chiefs of staff and super-grade executives. She assumed that most of those assistant secretaries would be co-located here in the secretarial offices. An office near the seat of power was crucial in such bureaucracies.

—

Phil Reynes and Nancy Cox arrived in the reception area accompanied by no less than Dr. Marta Le Salles, Reynes boss, who was the director of the Centers for Disease Control and Prevention.

The receptionist had them wait while she called someone, and shortly after that, a secretary came out and escorted them to a spacious conference room. One wall of the conference room had windows with a full view of the U.S. Capitol just beyond the glass dome of the U.S. Botanic Gardens below them. From quips of conversation Karen heard while they waited, she concluded that Le Salles, Reynes, and Cox had held a pre-meeting in preparation for this briefing. Nothing she heard gave Karen any idea of what her part in this meeting was to be. She was a bit perplexed that she seemed to be out of the loop. Karen realized, however, that what that meant was a vote of confidence by Phil Reynes that he had faith in Karen's ability to "tap dance" in a meeting with top brass.

Stephen Royce, the Health and Human Services assistant secretary for Planning and Emergency Preparedness, came in. He was accompanied by another older man. Both were probably prior military from both demeanor and buzz-cut hairstyles. Royce introduced the other man as his chief of staff.

After introducing herself, Dr. Le Salles introduced her group. "This is Dr. Philip Reynes, director of the National Center for Immunization and Infectious Disease. Dr. Nancy Cox, our pre-eminent epidemiologist in the Office of Infectious Diseases. And Doctor, err . . . , Commander, Karen Llewellyn-Craig, who is an expert in viral gene typing and slated to become the commander of one of the new government-owned, contractor-operated vaccine manufacturing facilities in a few weeks."

After handshakes all around, Royce sat at the end of the large table and motioned for everyone else to be seated. It happened that Le Salles, Reynes, and Cox were seated on one side of the table, and Karen found herself sitting next to Royce's Chief of Staff on the other side.

Royce spoke first, "So, what's the topic of our talk today. I'm still a bit new here, but I checked the departmental organization chart and CDC, and your whole operation seems to be under the Assistant Secretary for Health, not in my bailiwick."

"Yes, Colonel Royce, that's true," Le Salles responded, "But, within your bailiwick of 'Preparedness' is a function and a brand new operating arm that's of great importance to CDC and the entire epidemiological response effort of the Department. We want to talk about that new operation."

Karen looked over at Dr. Le Salles as she called the assistant secretary by his retired military title. Karen knew that you only spoke to the actual Secretary using the "Secretary" title. You did not call an assistant secretary, "Mr. Assistant Secretary." The same for undersecretaries and the various deputy secretary titles. But, it seemed odd to call the civilian executive by his retired military rank. However, nobody else seemed to react.

Dr. Le Salles continued, "For decades there has been a conflict or a disconnect between the needs of the federal government to respond to an epidemic as a national emergency and the need to contract with commercial entities to get the vaccines needed to respond to critical emergencies. The government agencies involved, primarily HHS, but also Defense and emergency response authorities like Homeland Security, rankled at the necessity to go hat in hand, or checkbook in hand, to a limited number of corporations who had control of international pharmaceutical production. The chaos of the coronavirus fiasco and the vaccine testing and production problems firmly reinforced that conflict.

"The problem came to the fore several years ago when a new strain of influenza appeared in the Third World after the strain typing for that year's vaccine mix had been determined. The Pentagon deemed it essential that they get a sufficient quantity of vaccine to protect the U.S. operating forces from the unique, emergent flu strain. But, when they went to the corporations with the capabilities to produce the vaccines, they hit a brick wall. Nobody wanted to change lanes and produce what the Pentagon wanted. It interfered with their financial commitment and vaccine market plans. It was not cost-effective for them. None of the contracts in place to produce vaccines was set up to react to the new needs of the government in a unique foreign situation that only the Pentagon cared much about. In particular, one key producer, which was a subsidiary of a German corporation, told the Pentagon to go fly a kite, for all intents and purposes. HHS totally agreed with the Pentagon, but we were unable to do anything other than producing a limited quantity of vaccine under a test and evaluation contract we had."

Dr. Le Salles paused and then continued, "The vaccine production contracts for subsequent years were modified to prevent the occurrence of the blanket refusal by the corporations to do emergency change orders, but the corporations attached a huge cost to any changes that would occur. Both HHS and Defense thought it was patently ridiculous for these companies to be developing new virological tests and vaccine production methodologies using government grants and then refusing to use those breakthroughs for the government's emergency use. We particularly did not like foreign corporations having veto power, by contract, over our national emergency decisions.

Dr. Le Salles turned to Phil, "Dr. Reynes, you can continue from here. You were directly involved."

Phil faced Royce and started, "With that background and the chaos of how the coronavirus crisis hit us, the best minds in both HHS and the Pentagon got together to come up with a better way to produce vaccines needed for our nation's critical needs. And, at some point, the issue of how the Pentagon produced other critical national defense supplies came up. That is, for a hundred years or more, the military has produced military munitions in government factories, both the old Arsenals and in the Government-Owned Contractor-Operated facilities, nicknamed GOCOs, that were born in World War II.

"Today, the vast majority of the bombs, shells, rockets, explosives, and bullets needed by the U.S. military, all services, are produced in a string of what they call Army Ammunition Plants organized under a Joint Munitions Command headquartered by the Army at Rock Island Arsenal, Illinois. Those GOCO plants are run by the military, and then a corporation is hired to do with the munitions factory exactly what the government wants. A corporate manager is running the business operation, but he is directly answerable to a military commander. If the Air Force needs more Mark 84 bombs, the plant commander tells the manager to make more Mark 84 bombs, and it happens. The corporation gets a percentile profit from its operation, but the production facility is run according to government needs and dictates.

"When we got to thinking about this, it started to make some sense. The U.S. Government has patent rights or usage licenses to many of the vaccine production methods our government grants have funded. Such a GOCO operation would appease several of the vaccine production concerns of the corporations, like product liability, profit margins, hidden costs, etc. With the possibility of a catastrophic pandemic, like coronavirus, always looming on the horizon for us, it seemed to make sense to have a massive government-controlled vaccine production arm that was not controlled by the corporations.

"Of course, there were two major obstacles. First, the powerful corporations were livid about losing a very lucrative and near-monopolistic power they had over vaccine productions. And second, with both HHS and Defense interested in the outcome, it was not at all clear who should run such an operation. It was heart and soul within the HHS bailiwick of national health. But, then, pandemic response, possible germ warfare defense, and vaccinating a military force was also a critical national defense issue, and the Pentagon had the experts on how to run a GOCO operation. In the end, there was a hybrid plan, which the Pentagon sold to the hawks in Congress, for HHS to take the lead on the medical and scientific matters and the related public policy issues and the Pentagon, through the U.S. Army at Fort Detrick, Maryland to handle the contracting and operations of the plants. Five such GOCO vaccine production facilities are approved by Congress. Three for this fiscal year and two more for next. Research Triangle, North Carolina, Schaumberg, Illinois, and Thousand Oaks, California open in a few weeks and Natick, Massachusetts and Everett, Washington, next fiscal year. All five will be capable of producing vaccines using both the new cell-based and plant-based methods, as well as the old attenuated virus vaccines. Truly state of the art."

The assistant secretary was nodding throughout Reynes' presentation.

Dr. Reynes gave a wry smile and said, "And, there just happens to be five major vaccine production companies in the US, and each one will be contracted to run one of the plants. Corporate greed problems solved.

"The entire scheme of locating, constructing, and operating these new GOCO vaccine plants was the product of intense negotiation between HHS and Defense, not to mention the congressional powers that be. Funding comes through both the HHS and Defense budgets, but with the majority coming through Defense since national defense is an easier sell to Congress in most years. With an Army command being in overall operational charge of the plants, we dug our heels in and said it was still a public health concern and the military acquiesced and let commissioned Public Health Service officers be in command of the plants, just like Army officers are in charge of GOCO plants building bombs for the Air Force. Which leads us to Doctor Llewellyn here, who will be the commander of the plant in California."

The assistant secretary interrupted with a comment, "A plant like that, that's a huge operation, hundreds of millions in investment. That's quite an assignment for an O-5."

Karen realized she probably should not speak up, but she could not help herself, because she had a gut feeling there was a bit of sexism in Royce's comment, as well, since she was a female O-5. "I'm being frocked as an O-6 upon assuming command. And, the officer who ran the entire massive Manhattan

Project, building the atomic bomb in World War II, was just an O-6 when that project started."

Karen saw a small smile from Dr. Le Salles, but before she or anyone could speak, Royce nodded and continued, "And let me guess at my part in this story. With an Army general and, I assume, an Army assistant secretary in operational charge of these plants, I'm guessing that HHS public policy control for medical and scientific matters would be placed in the hands of a certain retired Air Force O-6, who is now an assistant secretary of HHS for Preparedness. Am I correct?"

Le Salles and Reynes both nodded.

It was now Royce's turn to smile. "OK, I get the gist of this. So, tell me, what are your specific concerns as we head into this new venture? How do you think I can help make sure HHS's interests or concerns are protected."

Dr. Le Salles opened a file folder and took out a handout, copies of which she handed around the table.

—

Green Lotus Housing Complex
Baodi City, China
8:30 AM Local Time March 8th

Inspector 2nd Class Xi Zemin and the housing manager watched as the ambulance crew spread the gray vinyl body bag on the stretcher. They pulled down the blanket on the nearby bed, and, for modesty's sake, they tucked in the red velour robe that Yunan Qiuyue had been clutching when she died. One of the attendants scribbled something on a manila tag and tied the tag to Qiuyue's big toe. Her body was moved to the stretcher, and the zipper of the bag pulled up over her head. Before they pushed the stretcher out of the room, the ambulance crew chief walked up to Xi Zemin and, with a wordless bow, handed him the dead woman's identity book and a pink face mask. The mask was his recommendation to his fellow civil servant. They rolled the stretcher gurney out.

The room they were in was a sizable dormitory-style sleeping quarters with twelve beds, lockers, and a common area at the far end. Besides the deceased woman, two other beds were occupied, even though it was a workday for the factory workers who were housed in this dormitory. This multi-story housing complex had dozens of similar open bay rooms for single, low-level workers. Such accommodations were the norm for workers in Baodi and similar Chinese cities. Families and more senior workers had other residence options.

The team of paramedics who had called the police and ambulance was still working with the two young women in beds at the other end of the room. Like the ambulance crew, the medics wore pink face masks. Xi was questioning the female housing manager and writing down her answers.

"How long was this woman sick?" Xi asked, thumbing through the dead woman's identity booklet.

"I have no idea. It's not my job to keep track of such things. I'm the building manager, not their mother, but perhaps two days, the plant these women work in was closed yesterday," huffed the woman with officious gruffness. "The residents told me this morning when this one did not get up, and I came in and found her, and those other two were sick."

"Her papers say this woman works at the poultry plant. What about those two?"

"All of the residents work for Greater Zheng Collective, either the meat processing plants or the food factories. Most in this room work on the poultry floor. The company owns this housing complex."

"Fine, you will gather up her personal belongings, they should go to her family." Xi turned to go and talk to the other two women in their beds before turning back to the manager. "And, you should wait until the Baodi District Health Authority clears this up. It is standard procedure for us to report such deaths and illnesses to them to get to the bottom of things. They should be here within the hour and will need to speak to you and those two down there, provided the medics do not send them to the hospital. It will be the Health Authority who decides if an autopsy is needed or if this disease requires some kind of quarantine and clean-up."

At the word 'quarantine,' the manager rolled her eyes and muttered a cuss-word. Xi frowned at this.

Xi clipped the identity book to his clipboard and added, "I will be back also after I talk to her employers and co-workers at the plant. I will try to be here to brief the Health Authority team."

He put his mask on and went down to talk to the medics and their patients.

———

Chapter 10

Beaumont Family Ranch
Santa Ynez Valley
Santa Barbara County, California
3:30 PM PDT March 11th

"Kids, go feed your animals now. Dad will be home at five to take us to Buellton. You have to have your chores and homework done by then." Inga Beaumont shouted from the kitchen. There was the barest hint of a Scandinavian accent in her voice. She waited through a moment of silence and then shouted, "Did you hear me?"

The reply, "I'll get it in a minute, Mom. I need to sign off this Admissions Office website first," came down the stairs from Heather, her teenage daughter.

Then Inga heard, "Yeah, yeah." from Mark, her slightly younger son.

Shortly after that, Inga heard the screen door bang once and then again. The kids were headed to the barn.

Although the sign out by the highway said Beaumont Family Ranch and the hundred-plus acres qualified as a ranch, the Beaumonts were hardly ranchers. The main family home was more of a sprawling mansion than a ranch house, at least by any standards other than Santa Barbara County. Derek Beaumont was a semi-retired hedge fund manager, and Inga was his quintessence of a trophy wife, and neither wanted anything to do with ranching other than the status of owning a ranch. The bulk of the land was leased to a real rancher who used half of it for cattle and the rest for a recently planted vineyard operation. However, the Beaumont children did have a modicum of ranching, or at least farming, in their daily routine, hence their chores.

A large well-kept, modern barn, painted vanilla yellow to match the house, sat across a wide courtyard from the house and overlooked the large pond and pasture area beyond. The beautiful pond and luxuriant pasture could be seen from the State Highway, as could the Art-Deco "Beaumont" logo on one end of the barn.

The barn and pasture's primary occupants were three seldom-ridden quarter horses that Derek Beaumont had once felt were necessary to the façade of "ranch owner" but which were now cared for by an equine care contractor from Los Olivos, but which still needed daily feeding by the Beaumont kids. The other occupants of the barn were the objects of the Beaumont teenager's current chores, a young pig, and a pair of geese.

Both the geese and the pig were the result of the influence of a popular teacher at their high school. In her freshman year there, Heather had confided in the teacher that she was thinking about setting a goal for herself of being a veterinary doctor. The teacher, Miss Carnes, also happened to be the faculty sponsor of the Future Farmers of America (FFA) club at the school. She had convinced Heather to learn about animal husbandry by caring for one of the many farm animals that were eligible to enter the annual competitions at the Santa Barbara County Fair held each July, a highlight of the FFA members' year. Heather had finally settled on getting a goose, a decision based mainly on the fabled goose from the fairy tale. Heather convinced her BFF and fellow animal lover, Chelsea, to join her in the venture. Derek Beaumont's credit card had paid for a clutch of six Chinese Goose eggs sent via FedEx from Bakersfield. After incubation in Miss Carnes' classroom incubator, the six eggs produced a goose and a gander each for Chelsea and Heather, and the two hatching failures resulted in a couple of goose embryos that the Ag Biology class dissected.

Heather's pure white geese with their signature knobby forehead were impressive enough that her gander won Best in Show for the young gander class at the Fair in July after her freshman year. However, by Heather's sophomore year, she had turned her attention from veterinary interests to boys, the social issues of high school, and the closely collateral subject of cheerleading. But she had developed an attachment to her goose pair, and she kept good care of them. But, with this now being her senior year, she wondered what would happen to her geese when she and then Mark went to college, for the average Chinese Goose has a lifespan of 20-odd years, and Heather could not imagine Inga Beaumont goose tending.

Mark's pig had come about much the same way. He was two years younger than his sister and had been impressed by his sibling winning the trophy at the fair. After talking to Miss Carnes when he got to high school, he made plans to start raising a pig at the start of his sophomore year as it seemed that a pig who would reach the "market swine" class in about 25 weeks would be a good subject for this, his first animal husbandry class project. He could start in the fall and be done with the pig when he sold him at the market swine auction at the Fair in late July. Mark was not interested in a 20-year commitment to an animal, and the financial genes he inherited from his father liked the idea that he got paid to raise it and auction it off at the conclusion of the county fair.

Derek Beaumont did not appreciate why his son wanted to raise a pig, but he had paid a handyman to convert one of the small horse corrals and adjacent barn stalls into the pigsty. When the baby pig arrived, it turned out the geese enjoyed the company of the piglet, and they all lived together. The handyman was hired to come back and make a goose crib that allowed the goose to lay her eggs without the pig eating them. Collecting the fifty to sixty eggs that the goose laid in winter and spring was an additional duty for the Beaumont kids.

Both of their parents were tall and light-haired, and neither Heather nor Mark had strayed from the Beaumont physical standard. They wore nearly matching orange and black hoodies and jeans on this chilly and windy March day. Orange and black were the team colors of the Santa Ynez High School Pirates. Mark threw some hay over the fence for the horses and made sure they and the pig had full troughs of the commercial horse pellets and the crumbly pig feed that was delivered bi-weekly to the Beaumont Ranch from the feed store in Santa Ynez.

Heather climbed two rungs up the gate to the pasture and waved her arms. Her geese obediently ran squawking up from the large pond where they spent their day swimming. Both goose and gander shuffled around her feet, clucking, clearly happy to see their human. Heather stroked their sleek, white necks and backs. Heather made sure there was poultry mash in the goose crib food tray, fresh water in the pan, and she put fresh hay in the nest area. She grabbed the large goose egg she found there and headed back to the house with Mark. Their father had promised to be home from his investment firm's sub-office in the city of Santa Barbara in time to take them to the newly released sci-fi movie at the theatre over in Buellton.

———

The Conclave Apartments
Warner Center
Woodland Hills, California
7:15 PM PDT March 11th

Matt Relford closed the door behind him and flipped the deadbolt closed. He dropped his duty bag, gun belt, and shoulder radio in their usual place by the television cabinet.

Matt's live-in partner Marjorie was at work in the kitchen. She had her hands full, cutting salad on the chopping board. He went into the kitchen and hugged her from behind, squeezing in the usual strategic location, and kissed the back of her head. Her curly golden hair had its usual wonderful smell. She was great. Matt wanted her to be more than just a live-in girlfriend. He considered her his fiancé, but she was not quite ready for that, having gone through a bad marriage break-up before she met Matt. She had agreed to move into Matt's apartment but was still getting used to committing further. The fact that she was about ten years younger than Matt seemed to be part of that. Matt was hopeful, though.

"Don't go to too much work on food. I'm more tired than I'm hungry," Matt said as he pulled out the stool at the breakfast bar and sat heavily.

"You still need to eat something. I've got the salad made, and we still have the pizza to warm up from yesterday. Why so tired?"

"Not really sure. It was just a normal day. Nothing special. But I kinda feel like hell. I have all day. Headache and kinda got the chills."

"I hope you didn't get that crap from those people you evicted. I remember how the coronavirus was. That was bad." Marjorie, like Matt, was still in her work uniform. She was an airline ticket agent at the Burbank airport.

"That wasn't coronavirus the other day. We got the report from County Health that those people had some flu like they're having over in the Middle East."

Marjorie looked over to him and frowned, "Oh, Matt, I hope you don't get it. I hate your job. How can you stand that?"

"I've had my flu shot. Besides, you probably have to meet a lot more people every day that can get you sick than I do."

"Yes, but I don't have to touch them and go into their bedrooms. All I have to do is smile and stamp their ticket."

"And inspect their ID and grab their germy luggage," Matt countered.

Marjorie just frowned at him.

They ate the salad and warmed-up pizza in near silence. Matt refused Marjorie's offer of a glass of wine. Matt coughed once during the meal.

Matt said, "I think I'm going to just take a Tylenol and hit the sack. Maybe turn on the electric blanket to warm up."

Marjorie looked at him and smiled, "Forget the electric blanket. I'll be in after I clean up the dishes. I'll spoon with you. I'm better than any electric blanket."

Matt did not disagree.

———

Red Sunrise Apartment House
East Ring Road
Baodi City, China
10:15 AM Local Time March 11th

Inspector Xi Zemin smiled at the two women of the Baodi District Health Authority who were waiting for him in front of the apartment block. Then he realized they could not see his smile under the mask that had become standard practice to wear recently. An ambulance was parked nearby, but no sign of the attendants. This was the fourth time in as many days that his path had crossed the Health Authority team, and Zemin was developing an attraction to the younger woman, Yang Xinru. She was quite pretty and well-educated. And, the older woman had, with obvious intent, mentioned that Xinru was single and unattached. Zemin was thinking about how to ask her out.

He greeted them both and then added, "Another one of these cases, right. Same as before? What is this, five?"

The older woman nodded her head and said, "Yes, five dead and twelve sick."

"Fortunately, I only have to count the dead, not the sick."

Xinru now spoke, "Do you include the ones who die in the hospital?"

Zemin shook his head, "Not a police problem. If they die in the hospital, that's a medical matter. The police only investigate the deaths outside, the ones classed as suspicious deaths."

As they walked into the building, the older woman commented, "We have to count the ones in the hospital, too. If you add the hospital, our dead number is seven. And there are many more sick in the hospital. But, these really are not suspicious anymore. It's fairly clear that they are influenza deaths."

"But, so many, so quickly. That's unusual. No?" Zemin asked.

"Unusual, yes, but not unprecedented. The coronavirus was like this, at first, but then . . . you know. Our district manager says these animal-caused infections happen from time to time." She entered the building through the door Zemin held open for the two of them.

"Animal caused? The banker who died at the hotel was never near any animals since he came from Beijing. His assistant said so."

Yang Xinru shook her head and said, "Our district manager says that they know the type of influenza this is. They know from blood tests. It's called H7N9, and it can only be passed from animals to people by contact or contamination by animals, not person to person. So, there must be something we missed with the banker."

"Maybe they are mistaken about the way it is passed."

"Our district manager says that's impossible. It's very solid science." Xinru spoke with coquettish confidence. Zemin liked her.

They climbed the stairs and found the ambulance stretcher bearer leaning lazily on the hallway wall. An apartment door was open. As Zemin and the women reached the doorway, the paramedic came out. He looked at Zemin and shook his head; there was nothing for the medic to do for whomever was in the apartment.

—

Chapter 11

Cedars-Sinai Hospital
Center for Infectious Disease
Los Angeles, California
7:45 AM PDT, March 13th

Deputy Matt Relford awoke with a start at the loud, sucking 'thwuck!' sound. The sound was produced by the inner door of the hospital room being opened by a nurse. They had explained the operation of the negative atmosphere hospital room when he had arrived here. But, Matt had not been in a condition to fully understand the airlock explanation then. It was only as he lay awake earlier this morning that Matt was starting to appreciate the situation. The room he was in had a double door airlock to go in and out, curtained windows on the hallway wall to observe inside, and the corner of the room had a glass-windowed cubicle facing his bed so visitors could visit the patient without coming into the room. That little visitor's cubicle had a speaker to talk, just like a County Jail visiting room.

Marjorie had driven Matt to the ER at Valley Presbyterian in Van Nuys when the fever and shakes had hit him in the middle of the night. After finding out Matt was involved in the Agoura Hills flu case, the decision was made to transfer him by ambulance to Cedars-Sinai, which had a better set-up for dealing with dangerous viral infections. Cedars-Sinai had even kept Marjorie in a hospital room as a quarantine measure, although by that time, Matt was pretty much out of it and not paying attention to such details.

The nurse who came in now was clothed as all his caregivers were with an oversized, light blue jumpsuit that reminded Matt of a child's footed pajamas. Her head was covered with a fully enclosed light blue cap, and she had both a face mask over her mouth and nose and a clear, full face shield similar to what a welder might wear. He had watched through the window as previous nurses and doctors who left his room had, in the space between the two airlock doors, quickly put the jumpsuit and mask outfit into a trash bag labeled with a red and black bio-hazard emblem. They then scrubbed their hands, face, and arms down with a canister of sanitary wipes, which were then also dropped in the bio-hazard bag before they left through the second airlock door. Clothing for staff coming into an enclosed sanitary room seemed to be a very wasteful process; lots of discards. Matt remembered the horror stories about shortages with coronavirus. Things seemed to be better now.

The nurse's voice sounded cheerful, but Matt could not see her smile as she said, "Are you feeling a bit better this morning?"

"Yeah, quite a bit." Matt's voice was a bit gravelly. The oxygen mask over his face made it hard to talk.

"But, not good enough to eat any of your breakfast, huh?" she asked, indicating the food tray on the tray stand, which she pushed back from Matt.

"Uh, I'll probably be able to eat some of that, but when I got it, I just sort of sat for a minute and fell asleep again."

"Yeah, you can use the sleep, you had quite a time of it the night before last. We are actually quite happy you have snapped out of it as well as you have. But, you should be warned that the flu sometimes comes in waves. You could slip back into the fever and breathing problems. And, if they occur, those second waves are often worse than the first."

"Great, something to look forward to."

The nurse set a plastic medical supply tray on the bed, and said, "For now I need to get your vitals, get another blood sample. And when I'm done, I understand you have some visitors."

"Marjorie?"

"Is that your lady friend? No, I understand she is still in a quarantine room. That runs five days for people with close contact with influenza. If she tests clean, she'll get out of there in a couple of days. No, your visitors are official visitors. Some people have questions for you. They came yesterday, but you were too out of it to talk."

Matt cleared his throat and said, "Speaking of visitors. Do you have any news on the others . . . you know the people in the trailer or the other sheriffs?"

Matt saw the perceptible drop in the nurse's shoulders as she heard his question.

"You sure you don't want to just concentrate on getting yourself better? Worrying about them isn't going to help you."

"Are you kidding? I need to know," Matt punctuated this with several coughs.

"Yes, I suppose. We just don't like to give that info to patients who are still . . . well, you know." The nurse stopped and then wiggled the purple Relenza inhaling disk at Matt and said, "Tell you what, let's finish this up; then, I will catch you up with what I know. OK?"

Matt nodded and tried to clear his throat of phlegm. He reached for a tissue and lifted the oxygen mask to spit into the tissue and left the mask up on his nose, waiting for the nurse. The nurse set up the inhalation disk for the inhaled medicine and handed it to Matt. As he had several times before, he breathed in deeply, feeling the micro-powder go down into his lungs. He tried to stifle the urge to cough, as they had told him.

"Does that stuff really work?" he asked, handing the inhaler disk back to the nurse.

"That's what they say. The Relenza is a wonder drug. Helps your body fight the flu germs." When she was done with the thermometer and blood draw, the nurse put the inhalant disk back in the tray, set the supply tray back and said, "OK, here it is. We got half the new flu patients here at Cedars-Sinai, the others went to UCLA. The first ones, the kids and the family that came in several days ago went to UCLA after West Hills Hospital punted them as hazardous infectious. I hear a little boy, and one adult male survived, at least so far, but a young girl and an old woman died. Some others of that family are at UCLA, too, as patients, and I have no news on them.

"Of the ones here . . . we have several in quarantine rooms, like your girlfriend and the people from your sheriff's station. We have two other patients like you. And . . . we lost two . . . the young lady from Public Health and the other deputy died yesterday."

"Sergeant Gonçalvez?" asked Matt, jerking up in bed.

"Uh, no, that's not his name. I think Gonçalvez is one of our quarantine 'guests.' The deputy who died was the older guy . . . O'Meara."

The nurse finished her tasks with Matt, and she moved the tray table with his breakfast on it back within his reach. She was in the airlock shedding her gown and mask when Matt saw movement in the window frame of the visitor cubicle.

Matt saw two people were inside the cubicle. A young woman in a red windbreaker with a Los Angeles County seal on the front and an older man in a dark business suit. The woman clicked the speaker button beside the cubicle window. The man flashed a badge wallet that was impossible for Matt to read from inside the hospital room.

"Officer Relford, I'm Kaitlin Jenkins from the Los Angeles County Health Department. This is Inspector James Maitland with the U.S. Department of Health and Human Services. We need to ask you some questions. We hope now is a good time." The woman's voice came from a speaker below the window.

"Deputy." said Matt.

"Pardon?" asked the woman.

"My title is deputy, not officer." Matt punctuated this with a cough.

"Of course, Deputy Relford. I see you have your breakfast there. Can we talk to you while you eat?"

"Sure, go ahead." Matt pulled the oxygen mask down below his chin to eat.

The man now spoke through the speaker, with the woman moving to the side a bit. "We are trying to put together all the facts about the influenza transmission that resulted in your hospitalization. Our job is to track disease contacts. We spoke with the paramedics and Sergeant Gonçalvez, but they arrived after initial contact, and we need to know what happened earlier. The other deputy passed away yesterday," he paused, "I trust you knew that."

Matt nodded, and the man continued, ". . . and the female sheriff's employee is still very sick. The residents of the trailer are either deceased or very sick, and we suspect the one person, an adult male, we spoke to is not being truthful due to immigration concerns."

"Yeah, he is probably sure you're *La Migra*. That's a common problem."

"Understood. We were able to talk to the lady from the real estate company, too. But she is also sick, but not very. Apparently, she and her assistants spent that afternoon cleaning out the trailer and getting rid of the chickens and the dog at the shelter."

"I didn't see any dog there," Matt said.

"Yes, she said she found it under the trailer later on. It was sick too."

"Dogs can get this flu?"

Now the young woman spoke up. "With this type of flu, H5N1, there is some history of it infecting canines. In one recorded case, a dog in Thailand ate a sick duck's entrails and was infected, which may have been the case here, with the chickens. This dog from the trailer died, too; they do not have any natural immunity to the flu."

The man seemed annoyed at the woman's interruption and asked Matt, "Could you give us a play by play like you would in a police incident report on everything you saw at the scene? And we will be recording."

"Sure," Matt said, before finishing off his orange juice. The juice made him cough again. He waited a moment before starting. Through the viewing window Matt saw the man put a small digital recorder up next to the speaker box.

Matt started, "Well, you have the basic picture. Deputy O'Meara and the legal technician, Clare Something, went up to the door. I stood back a ways. O'Meara knocked, and somebody answered inside. O'Meara was explaining about the eviction at the door and finally got somebody who spoke English. Then he finally went inside, and before I could step up to the door, the first three people from inside came out, got in a car and left."

"Whoa, whoa, hold it!" Maitland blurted out.

The eyes of the young woman went wide open at this.

The agent's voice was excited when he asked, "There were three people in the trailer who left the scene? We've never heard anything about that."

"Yes. Three people, two women, one male, all Hispanic, in their 20's. They came out when O'Meara went inside to explain the eviction to the occupants. They came out with their clothes stacked on their arms and their stuff in boxes, clearing outta Dodge."

Matt heard the HHS agent mutter 'Shit' under his breath before he continued his questioning, "Didn't you get their names or . . . something?"

Matt shook his head, "No, no reason to get their names, this was a civil eviction, not a criminal incident. No reason to ask their names. We just wanted them outta there, whatever their names were."

Maitland took a deep breath and continued, "Okay, what can you tell us about them?"

"20's-ish, dark-skinned Hispanic, all three of them, maybe related, they looked alike, stocky south Mexican, you know, Oaxacan, especially the women. Oh yeah, looked like they were ready for work. The guy was in a maintenance type uniform, you know, janitorial. And both women were in waitress uniforms. Nametags from the Middle Eastern restaurant in Agoura Hills, you know 'Kasbah Kebab' or something like that."

Both of the investigators quickly looked at each other, shaking their heads.

Matt coughed and continued, "And all three left the scene in an old, maybe late 90's, Toyota, a Corolla. Dark gray or silver, with a bondo-ed left front fender as I recall. And . . . you know . . . if you can get them to pull the dashcam video from my patrol unit, they parked by the trailer, and I parked facing in. I bet you can get their license plate off my dashcam and maybe visual ID."

The talking had gotten to Matt, and he now broke into a deep, rasping cough.

From behind the two in the visitor's booth, the nurse appeared and said, "Can you take a break for now. My patient is still quite sick, and he needs to rest. And he needs to finish his breakfast in peace. You can come back later today if you need to."

The two investigators left. They had plenty to do to start tracking the three missing, probable H5N1 avian flu infectees who were at large in Los Angeles.

—

Chapter 12

Tianjin, China
March 16th

郑集体
Greater Zheng Collective
Emperor Place,

99 Nanjing Rd,

Heping Qu, Tianjin Shi,

China

March 16th

PRESS RELEASE

It is with great respect and sadness that the Board of Directors of the Greater Zheng Collective and the Zheng Foods Consortium announce the passing of our Honorable Board Member and Director of Animal Husbandry Quan Li.

Director Quan passed away after a short illness earlier this month in Baodi City, China. He is survived by three adult children. His eldest son, Quan Jinping, will assume Quan Li's seat on our Board of Directors. Director Quan Li's loving wife, Quan Yu, also passed away this month.

Director Quan Li was a dedicated employee of the Greater Zheng Collective for over forty years. His sage advice and firm management style will be sorely missed by all of our associates.

A memorial service will be held at a later date.

———

Chaldean Apartments
Panorama City, California
6:30 AM PDT March 16th

The cellphone rang incessantly. The caller was not giving up. Gloria Morelos grabbed it from the nightstand and answered.

"Glori, that you?" Lena, her friend from work, asked.

"Yeah, wassup, it's early."

"Well, I hadn't heard from you for a few days, and I wanted to warn you not to come into work if you were planning on it."

"Huh, why? What's goin' on?"

"Well, I got called in here this morning, and they've got a crew of police-types interviewing everybody. Apparently, they've closed us down. Oh, and all of the cops are wearing face masks. I haven't talked to them yet, but we're worried it's some kind of *Migra* raid. They asked Mrs. Saidi for all the employees' papers. I'll let you know what I find out.

"Gosh!"

"Where are you anyway? What happened to you?"

"Well, Guillermo's uncle got evicted from the trailer. So, we cleared out and did'n' go into work. Yermo finally shelled out for an apartment closer to his work at Universal City. Alissa chipped in. It's a nice place, sort of, with two bedrooms. One for Yermo and me and one for Alissa. It's too far from Agoura for Alissa and me to work at Kasbah anymore, even if *La Migra* weren't there. Alissa and I will go looking for work here as soon as she feels better. Yermo says there are lots of help wanted signs where he works at Universal City."

"Alissa sick?"

"Yeah, I think she has that same shit that Yermo's grandma and his little sister and brother had. I hope I don't get it.

"How are they anyway? You said the family was evicted."

"I have no idea. Nobody is answering their cell phones. And I don't know where they all went. Weird."

"Yeah, Mr. Saidi isn't here this morning, just Mrs. Saidi. I heard he was in the hospital. No idea why. Well, I hope it all turns out, OK."

"Yeah, and hey, don't tell anybody at work where we are. We don't need nobody coming to get us. We prob'ly have to get a new ID, though, since Mrs. Saidi prob'ly is giving the cops our old information. We'll need to go see that *Notario* in Sherman Oaks, who sells the work papers."

"Of course, I wouldn't tell anybody. But, be careful with who calls you. Didn't Mrs. Saidi have your cell phone number."

"Yeah, she did. I'll be careful, you take care, too."

"Bye."

———

Chapter 13

Office of the Grand Mufti
Dar Al Ifta, Al-Azhar University Complex
Cairo, Egypt
March 18ᵗʰ

Translated from the Arabic

Fatwa of the Grand Mufti of Egypt

In the name of Allah, the Most Gracious, the Most Merciful:

After deliberation with the Council of Senior Scholars and upon consultation with the Government of the Arab Republic of Egypt, the Grand Mufti of Egypt hereby issues the following Edict and Fatwa:

Whereas scholars have interpreted the word of God to direct the faithful to disdain the practice of cremation of the dead and to act with the utmost respect in assuring the cleanliness and honor of the bodies of the dead, it has been determined that the Holy Koran does not tell us directly of God's commandment as to cremation and the hadith which we honor telling us to avoid cremation and to act to cleanse, shroud and act honorably to the bodies of the dead is based upon the faithful interpretations of past scholars. This hadith should be followed as a direction as from God, in all but the most trying circumstances. It is hereby decreed that the current infestation of disease in which our nation finds itself is an occasion for the faithful to act in the best interests of our children, our families, and our nation and that this period of disease shall require a temporary exception to the hadith regarding the burial of the dead, forbidding cremation and requiring certain acts of ablution for the bodies of our dead.

It is therefore decreed as Fatwa, that:

- Until annulment of this Fatwa, the practice of cremation shall be allowed, and in most cases required, for the bodies of all persons whose death resulted from the pestilence.
- Until annulment of this Fatwa, the practice of ablution and shrouding by hand of the bodies of the dead is not required and should be avoided. Touching the body of a victim of the pestilence is to be avoided, if at all possible, without sanitary protection.
- Handling of bodies of the dead from this pestilence shall be accomplished with the display of utmost dignity to the dead,

and the act of cremation shall be conducted with the utmost solemnity and prayer.

- Cremation of human beings should be separate from the cremation of any animal or burning of any refuse.
- The ashes of the cremated dead shall be handled and protected in the same manner as would the burial of bodies in times past.
- If facilities and supplies are not available for the prompt and dignified cremation of the dead, the burial of the dead from this pestilence without shrouding or ablution and the burial of multiple dead in a single burial site shall be allowed.
- Cremation or burial of the dead shall be accomplished in the promptest manner possible. It is a hadith that burial of the dead is a communal duty for the faithful, including the cremation or burial of dead strangers or foreigners.

This Fatwa acknowledges and retroactively approves the fatwas and emergency orders on this subject previously issued by the learned brethren and other authorities in Minufiya, Sharqiya, and Al-Qalubiya Governorates, and other locales as may be the case.

So prescribed and ordered in the name of Allah, may He be pleased,
by the Grand Mufti of Egypt,
and attested and agreed by the Council of Senior Scholars.

—

Corner of Lankershim Boulevard and Moorpark Street
Toluca Lake area of Los Angeles. California
6:30 AM PDT March 18ᵗʰ

The two LAPD officers were parked near the intersection on Lankershim, watching the traffic get worse as morning rush hour worsened. As the southbound traffic on Lankershim stopped for the light, the rookie in the passenger's seat slapped the arm of the sergeant driving and pointed with his other hand to one of the stopped cars.

The rookie announced, "Silver Toyota, fender damage, license FOUR GEORGE-EDWARD-NORA . . . they're on the BOLO list."

The sergeant squinted at the car and then confirmed, "I'll be damned, you're right."

The sergeant set his coffee cup in the holder, turned on the lights, and pulled toward the traffic lane, squeezing in, motioning out the window to the driver next to him to back off. The cop in the passenger seat called their pursuit status into dispatch; then, he looked the BOLO up on the computer screen.

After he found the details of the wanted bulletin on the car, the rookie cop said, "That's strange, they are not considered dangerous, but may flee, and when we arrest we are supposed to wear N-95s and gloves and wait at the scene for the arrestees to be picked up by County Health. Do not transport, it says. Vehicle to be sealed with evidence scene tape and towed without inspection."

"That's an odd duck," the sergeant said as he pulled into traffic.

The other cars cleared out from in front of the police cruiser, and after a short chirp of the siren, the silver Toyota pulled over. The cops put on their N-95 masks and gloves. The rookie took a cover stance, feet wide apart, gloved hand on the unlatched holster, on the sidewalk facing the Toyota. The sergeant approached the vehicle and ordered the driver to come out, hands first, and stand by the trunk.

As he was ordered, Guillermo 'Yermo' Morelos, wearing his maintenance jumpsuit from the movie theatre complex at Universal City, got out and put his hands on the trunk. He shook his head at his misfortune. Right after the sergeant handcuffed him, Yermo gave a vicious sneeze, followed immediately by another sneeze. With his hands cuffed behind his back, Yermo had to awkwardly try to wipe his runny nose on the shoulder of his uniform. The cops called in to Dispatch and sat Yermo on the low brick wall next to the sidewalk, waiting for the van from the Los Angeles County Health Department to come to pick him up. Yermo cleared his throat and spat a large wad of phlegm toward the gutter near the squad car.

—

Chapter 14

Centers for Disease Control
Atlanta, Georgia
2:15 PM EDT March 19ᵗʰ

Karen Llewellyn saw the red flag next to the message in her email directory. She had been waiting for the update. Typically, she would have been directly involved in its preparation, but her upcoming assignment out in California had changed her level of involvement in this basic information task at CDC. She clicked the email attachment open:

Centers for Disease Control
Status Report
on
Human Seasonal and Emergent Influenza Activity

Volume 24, Number 12—March 19th

Synopsis

Seasonal -

With the flu season nearly over, the seasonal outbreak of established influenza strains in the continental United States were within expected historical norms. Both trivalent and quadrivalent vaccine formulations for the current season were within acceptable effectiveness ranges except for strain A/Perth/16/2009 (H3N2), which achieved only 30% effectiveness for the general adult population due to apparent genetic drift in the extant strain, post sample. Both of the B-type strain choices and the A/duck/Alberta/35/76(H1N1) were satisfactorily effective. The ineffectiveness of the H3N2 vaccine component in this year's distribution of vaccine has resulted in a high level of infection, especially in the North Central U.S. and Canadian Maritime provinces. European authorities report similar epidemiologic history for the current year. Fortunately, the morbidity level of this H3N2 strain is lower than normal for seasonal flu.

Emergent Strains -

The widely reported outbreak of A/Minufiya/21/04(H5N1) in several Egyptian metropolitan areas follows laboratory confirmation that the previously zoonotic-only strain has likely achieved human-to-human transmission. A major quarantine effort is expected, and research into a possible vaccine response

"I had wondered how you and Marty were doing."

"Well, he says he is no longer with the nurse at the center of our split, but . . . you know . . . some things do not heal so easily."

Phil nodded and quickly changed the topic, "You mentioned 'LA.' The new plant is, I thought, Thousand Oaks. Is that right in LA?"

"Well, yes, it's in Thousand Oaks. That's a suburb west of LA. Different county. But I've gotten in the habit of calling it LA since nobody here knows what a Thousand Oaks is." Karen paused and then continued, "That brings up why I came to talk to you."

Phil took off his glasses and turned fully in his chair toward Karen, "Yes?"

"I've been out of the loop on most of the goings-on since we got back from DC, with my upcoming transfer and all. And I've not had time to contemplate the new H5N1 issue out in LA, with the backyard chickens infecting what? Nine, ten people? I just read today's human activity summary and realized that the issue of the genetic variation between the Egyptian and the California H5N1 strains could very possibly be the most important viral strain identification work in history. You know, Phil, I've literally spent the majority of my adult life learning about the genetic drift of hemagglutinin and neuraminidase and how to track and identify the key factors. Now, when CDC is faced with the question of a possible pandemic riding on the HA and RA typing differences between the Egyptian and this California strain, here I am, off to play factory manager. I . . . ."

Phil held up a finger, urging Karen to stop.

Phil continued, "You should know that I had almost this exact conversation with George Riggs before he left for the Schaumberg, Illinois plant yesterday. Both you and he, and probably Loretta Haynes too, seem to think that when Marta Le Salles and I fought with the Army about who to put in charge of these new GOCO vaccine plants and we choose three of our best PHS virology scientists, that we were somehow sending you down to the farm team, out of the Big Leagues here at CDC. In reality, we chose you three because we view the opportunity to have a vaccine production facility that can react to emergent virus dangers in a fraction of the traditional time as being so important we wanted our best people in charge.

"Marta and I happened to meet up with the Army general in charge of their side, General Harding, who was of a like mind to us about the importance of having the best people at the helm of these new vaccine plants. We were all in agreement that each plant needs to have in-house capability of reacting to the emergency needs of the nation. Coronavirus kicked our asses on reaction time. And we agreed that the plant commander had to be fully conversant with how to deal with any change in circumstances that might be needed, both scientifically and operationally. And, since we were, in effect, planning on reacting to a potential state of emergency, we wanted the plant commander to have a state of the art laboratory and emergency response capability and the knowledge to use it right."

Karen nodded, "I'm supposed to go to Fort Detrick to talk to General Harding as part of my briefing on my way out to California. I know many of the Army people at USAMRIID, but not Harding, I guess he is the head of their Medical Research and Development Command, the next level up the Army's chain."

"Good, I think you will be impressed with General Harding's ah . . . attitude."

"Gung Ho, huh?"

"Somewhat, but in a good way. I understand he got to where he is by being one of the best combat trauma surgeons in Iraq and then Afghanistan. And then, he led our Ebola response in Liberia in 2014. So, he knows his epidemiology, too."

"So, I should be quiet and give the new job a chance, huh?"

"I cannot think of anybody else on earth I would want to be in charge of a facility like that when we get a unique, bad boy virus we need to deal with.

———

Briarcliff Road NE
Atlanta, Georgia
6:26 PM EDT March 19th

Karen heard the knock and started to turn from the packing work she was doing when she heard the deadbolt open. She figured that Marty had decided to let himself into the condo.

Martin Craig, MD, was still in his white lab coat. He had a habit of wearing it home after work. But, he had a blue shirt and tie on underneath it, so he must have been coming from office hours at the clinic and not directly from the ER. He still looked pretty much the same as he had when Karen had met him; tall, handsome, broad-shouldered, curly black hair in a short cut.

As Karen faced Marty, there was an awkward moment where neither of them knew what to do. Hug? Kiss on the cheek? How do you greet a former intimate partner who you had not seen for what . . . ? Several months?

Karen finally broke the awkward delay by moving toward the kitchen and offering, "You eat yet? I bought enough Orange Chicken to share."

"What? Yeah, that would be good." Marty started toward the kitchen but stopped by the sofa where Karen had several garment bags laying. He fingered the sleeve of the dress uniform on top and said, "Ah, four stripes, you finally outrank me."

Karen looked at him and said, "I wish I were better at snappy rejoinders, because I'm sure there is a good comeback line I could use with that comment."

"Nah, you've never been very good at being a smart ass."

"I guess I'll take that as a compliment." She handed him a plate of the orange chicken and chow mein noodles along with a bottle of water.

"On the subject of compliments, you look nice. New hairstyle?" he asked.

Karen waited a moment and answered, "I've got to go to Detrick on the day after tomorrow, and I thought the general would like a good military look."

"Yeah, you mentioned this new assignment was under an Army Medical Command. Major General Tom Harding? Is that who you're meeting?"

"You know him?"

"He did a welcome visit to our response team training at Reserve summer camp at Detrick last June."

"Anything I should know about him?"

"Not that I know of. He mentioned he had run the Ebola field hospital in Monrovia, Liberia. So, he knows epidemiology, which I guess is good for you."

Karen nodded. She leaned back against the serving counter between the kitchen and dining room.

Marty pulled out a chair from the dining room table and sat. "So, tell me more about the new gig of yours. You didn't say much on the phone, and I didn't find too much when I Googled it."

"Well, HHS and the military put their heads together to solve the old problem of how to manage vaccine manufacture and distribution, plus balance the emergency needs of the government with the business of manufacturing vaccines. They're setting up three new plants, two more next fiscal year, that use the newest vaccine techniques, both cell, and plant-based, the 'virus-like particles' processes and with a real 'surge' capability for emergencies. They're using an old Army contracting technique to build a vaccine plant at government expense and hire a corporate contractor to run it. It's called GOCO, government-owned, contractor-operated. Same as they still use to make ammunition and used to use for chemical weapons and nukes. There is a military commander in overall charge, and the pharmaceutical company operates the plant."

"And you're the 'military' commander? Under an Army general?"

Karen thought she heard some sarcasm in Marty's question. Hence her response was, "Yeah, you gotta problem with that?"

"No, I guess not. It's just that you PHS types, besides the uniform and the rank, have never been much of a military-unit-oriented bunch."

Karen gave a slight frown, "Well, my job is apparently the result of a grand compromise on how to get the civilians in HHS to agree to let vaccine funding from the general health budget get sent to an Army command to spend.

Anyway, the plant is civilian, there is just a small military staff that coordinates with the corporate managers. And I'll have a government employee executive to help me manage the show."

"But, this isn't replacing all the old vaccine production, is it?"

"No, no. This is just for the direct government-financed stuff. What they use to stockpile and give to the military and to fill in when the commercial sources failed. And for foreign aid, too. This will give the government control over hundreds of millions of doses, without having to worry about the corporations balking like they did when they didn't want to switch the strain mix mid-year to react to that Iraq problem."

"So, how long is this? How long you gonna be out there."

Karen shrugged, "It's a standard personnel assignment. Unless I blow it. What, two-three years?"

Marty frowned. "You know, that. . . ," he paused. "I had mentioned I wanted to talk about us maybe getting back together and you didn't, ah, seem to object to that idea. You being out in California kinda puts the crimp on any *rapprochement*."

Karen stared at Marty for a long time. "I understand, but . . . you know I'm not saying no to that. I've thought about it too. But, you know, there was a whole lotta hurt . . . that you caused. And, I thought about that when they asked me to go. But, this is really important, and it's a real gem for my career." She paused again. "This really is not a good time for this. I need to get my shit together and move to the other side of the country. If there is any hope for us, our marriage, it is going to have to come from what we do going forward. If we are going to work together . . . if we can . . . It will all work out."

Marty stared at her, then nodded. "Then, you wouldn't mind if I came out to see you there?"

"Yeah, maybe when I get settled. We'll see. Call me, and we'll talk. For now, let's get this organized if you're moving in here."

"Except for my clothes and stuff, I never really moved out."

Karen nodded and smiled, "Yeah, sorting out your junk from mine has been a nightmare."

———

Chapter 15

Hôpital Tenon
Salle d'Urgence
4 Rue de la Chine
Paris, France
7:30 AM Local Time March 20ᵗʰ

The taxi pulled through as the guard lifted the security gate to the drive-through Emergency Room entrance on the back corner of the hospital, off of Rue Pelleport. Maximilien Tauty had to help Marguerite to exit the taxi in front of the emergency room.

Marguerite Tauty had been out of sorts the previous day. It was unlike her. Max had always called her his "farm girl from Brittany" for her resolute character and physical strength, plus her girl-next-door beauty. Now she could barely stand. An alert orderly rolled a wheelchair out of the automatic doors toward them. Marguerite sat heavily in the wheelchair, her purse falling off her lap as she did.

The middle-aged woman now lay with her eyes closed on the gurney. While Max held Marguerite's hand, the emergency room nurse checked her temperature, listened to her lungs, and clipped on her index finger the little finger clamp that checked her blood oxygen level. When she saw the initial oxygen reading, the nurse quickly turned Marguerite's hands over to look at the palms, which had a blueish cast. The nurse pulled an oxygen mask from the wall above the gurney and put it over Marguerite's face. She was dangerously cyanotic, low blood oxygen. The nurse went quickly to get the duty physician.

It only took the physician a few moments with Marguerite before he checked with the ER desk and told the orderly to roll her gurney from the screened-off station in the multi-bed triage area to an enclosed private room at the far end of the emergency room. When the physician and nurse came into the private room, Max noted they were now wearing face masks.

The physician asked Max a series of questions, including whether Marguerite was allergic to penicillin or any other drugs. Hearing that she was not, the physician had the nurse give her an injection, a strong antibiotic to ward off bacterial pneumonia.

While the nurse was drawing several vials of blood, the doctor asked Max several more questions.

"Has she been outside of France recently?" the doctor asked.

Max furrowed his brow, "Why, yes. We recently returned from four weeks in China. You see, I write books on travel and cuisine. I . . . "

The doctor cut off Max's explanation and asked, "Did she have any contact with animals, alive or dead, in China?"

"We walked through the markets. There are animals in the live markets in China. She picked her own lobster out of the tank in Tianjin. Wonderful seafood in Tianjin, you know. It's right on the sea there."

"Not lobster. How about poultry . . . swine?"

"But, of course, the markets have chickens and ducks hanging by their feet for you to choose from. And little pigs in these wooden cages." Max frowned, "Why do you ask?"

The doctor did not answer the question. Instead, he gave instructions to the nurse for a different small drug pouch to be attached to the intravenous drip. The pouch contained Tamiflu, the anti-viral drug of choice, to fight influenza.

Telling Max that he would be back in a moment, the doctor went out to the desk and made a call up to the Hôpital Tenon Infectious Disease center several floors above. They had a new patient.

———

Emergency Situation Office
Epidemiological Branch
Sante Publique France
Paris, France
9:10 AM Local Time March 20th

Inspector Michel Dormer was one of the more senior staff members of the Epidemiological Branch of the French Public Health Agency, *Sante Publique France*. He was a veteran of the dark months of the coronavirus pandemic, unlike the many young, French civil servants he now worked with. His office had been greatly expanded after coronavirus. He admired the fervent enthusiasm of these new staff members. Michel Dormer was reporting on the work of the teams of contact tracers and health inspectors to a meeting of the agency's leadership who were trying to form a coherent response to the avian flu epidemic raging in Egypt and southeastern Europe. Did France need to take drastic measures to prevent the spread of avian flu? Michel Dormer had already made up his mind and needed to convince his managers, the minister, and the other politicians.

Dormer carefully narrated his PowerPoint presentation. He had started with a slide showing the history of infection and deaths from the H5N1 animal-borne influenza virus and its close cousins. He had a slide showing the spread of the virus within Egypt from late February through today. He had a map of the other countries with initial outbreaks of the H5N1 avian flu. The next slide was a graphic showing the connections between Egypt and those countries. He had a slide showing the list of aircraft entering France from Egypt in the two weeks since the news of the avian flu in Egypt had been made public. He had a slide showing the numbers of contacts traced by his office's staff of the passengers of those aircraft from Egypt, and the numbers who had become sick in France. Dormer's final slide was a compound line-graph of the numbers of infected in France with red color for the sick Egyptian passengers and yellow color for the number of French citizens who could be expected to get sick of avian flu if nothing was done to stop the flow of sickness from Egypt to France. The yellow slope soon shot off the top of the chart.

Inspector Michel Dormer ended his presentation with, "We are rapidly approaching a point where nothing we can do will prevent an avian flu epidemic in France. We need to cut off transport from Egypt, and possibly Turkey and the Balkan region. We probably need to invoke the lessons learned from coronavirus to stem the flow of this new pestilence."

———

Health Advisory Brochure for Air Travelers
Published by
Sante Publique France (French Public Health)

AVIAN INFLUENZA

You are traveling to an area affected by type A avian influenza (or bird flu). This illness affects poultry primarily. Cases of transmission to humans have been confirmed.

To date, contamination occurred through direct contact with sick animals. In humans, the illness is a flu-like syndrome, with a fever above 100.4 °F (38°C), sore throat, muscle and joint pain and difficulties in breathing (shortness of breath, cough).

The virus is transmitted essentially by air (respiratory airways) or through direct contact notably with fecal matter and respiratory secretions of sick animals, or indirectly through exposure to contaminated objects (via the hands). Closed spaces favor the transmission of the virus.

During your stay, avoid all contact with poultry, both dead and alive: for instance, do not visit industrial breeding or poultry farms or bird and poultry markets.

Recommendations regarding basic hygiene when traveling in developing countries are more than ever encouraged in particular:

• Wash your hands regularly with soap and water or a special disinfecting solution.

• Eat only well-cooked food and bottled drinks.

You are traveling from an area affected by type A avian influenza (or bird flu).

If during your stay in one of these countries, you have been in contact with flu-affected people or with poultry alive or dead (uncooked) AND if you develop signs of flu-like illness within ten days after your arrival, immediately seek medical aid by dialing 15 from anywhere in France.

Remember to mention that you are returning from an avian influenza-affected country. If the above symptoms appear during the flight back, report immediately to the cabin crew: appropriate medical care will be organized upon arrival.

———

Centers for Disease Control
Information Webpage
Updated March 21ˢᵗ

Novel Avian Flu (H7N9 & H9N2) in China

What is the current situation?

As of February 28th, Chinese health authorities have confirmed 512 new human cases of Avian Influenza A (H7N9) to the World Health Organization since September 2016, as well as 46 cases of avian influenza (H9N2) in recent months amongst workers in animal processing factories. Most of these patients reported exposure to live poultry or poultry markets. A few cases of H7N9 & H9N2 have been reported outside of mainland China, most recently in France (H7N9), but most of these infections have occurred among people who had traveled to mainland China before becoming ill. CDC advises people traveling to China to avoid contact with poultry (including poultry markets and farms), birds, and their droppings and to avoid eating undercooked poultry. Infected birds that appear healthy may still be able to transmit this virus to humans. There are no recommendations against travel to China.

What are Novel Avian Influenza Strains A (H7N9/H9N2)?

Avian Influenza A (H7N9) and Avian Influenza A (H9N2) are viruses found in birds that do not normally infect humans. However, in the spring of 2013, the first human cases of H7N9 virus infection were reported in China. Since then, 924 laboratory-confirmed cases of human infection with H7N9 virus have been reported, with about one-third of cases resulting in death. Most of these infections have been associated with exposure to infected poultry or contaminated environments (such as poultry markets) in China. In rare cases, limited, non-sustained person-to-person spread of H7N9 virus likely occurred, but there is no evidence of sustained human-to-human infection. Early symptoms are similar to those of other respiratory viruses, including seasonal flu and may include fever, cough, sore throat, muscle aches and fatigue, loss of appetite, and runny or stuffy nose. However, infection with this virus often causes severe respiratory illness and, in some cases, death (see http://www.CDC.gov/flu/avianflu/h7n9-virus.htm). Risk factors for severe and fatal outcomes include older age and having certain chronic medical conditions.

Initially infecting poultry, Avian Influenza A(H7N9) viruses have been sporadically identified in pigs and humans, which suggests that some of these viruses have adapted to bind mammalian host receptors or have acquired mutations that increase mammalian receptor specificity. Human infection with Avian Influenza A(H7N9) virus was initially identified in Hong Kong and China in 1999; in 2011, infection with this subtype was reported for a patient in Bangladesh. Detection of these viruses in humans outside of China highlights the necessity and urgency for comprehensive surveillance because of the viruses' expanding host range. The recent upturn in H7N9 cases in northern China highlights the danger the possible mutation of this strain presents as the genetic typing of recent H7N9 cultures show a pronounced shift from earlier Hong Kong and Myanmar strains.

What can travelers do to protect themselves?

There is no vaccine available to prevent H7N9 and H7N9 virus infection. To protect yourself when visiting China, take the following steps:

- Do not touch birds.
- Repeat, don't touch birds, whether they are alive or dead.
- Avoid live bird or poultry markets, including where birds are slaughtered (wet markets).
- Avoid places that might be contaminated with bird feces.
- Eat food that is fully cooked.
- Eat meat and poultry that is fully cooked (not pink) and served hot.
- Eat hard-cooked eggs (not runny).
- As a general precaution, don't eat or drink dishes that include blood from any animal.
- As a general precaution, don't eat food from street vendors.
- Practice hygiene and cleanliness.
- Wash your hands often.

- If soap and water aren't available, clean your hands with hand sanitizer containing at least 60% alcohol.

- Don't touch your eyes, nose, or mouth. If you need to touch your face, make sure your hands are clean.

- Cover your mouth and nose with a tissue or your sleeve (not your hands) when coughing or sneezing.

- Try to avoid close contact, such as kissing, hugging, or sharing eating utensils or cups with people who are sick.

- If you feel sick after visiting China:

- Talk to your doctor or nurse if you feel seriously ill, especially if you have a fever, cough, or shortness of breath.

- Tell your health care provider about your travel to China.

- For more information about medical care abroad, see Getting Health Care Abroad (https://www.CDC.gov/travel/page/getting-health-care-abroad)

- Avoid contact with other people while you are sick.

Clinician information

Clinicians should consider the possibility of avian influenza A (H7N9) or (H9N2) virus infection in people presenting with respiratory illness within 10 days of travel to China, particularly if the patient reports exposure to birds or poultry markets. Although most H7N9 and H9N2 cases have resulted in severe respiratory illness, the infection may cause mild illness in some people, including both adults and children. Guidance is available for clinicians who suspect avian influenza A (H7N9/H7N9) virus infection in a returned traveler from China. Clinicians should initiate infection control precautions (airborne, droplet, and contact), obtain appropriate specimens, and notify their local or state health department promptly. State health departments should notify CDC of suspected cases within 24 hours. Empiric treatment with influenza antiviral medications may be warranted while testing is pending.

Note that influenza diagnostic testing in patients with respiratory illness of unknown etiology may identify human cases of avian influenza A virus infection. Patients with H7N9 and H9N2 virus infection are expected to have a positive test result for influenza A virus via reverse-transcription polymerase chain reaction (RT-PCR testing), although most assays will not be able to determine the influenza virus subtype. The use of rapid influenza diagnostic tests is not recommended if H7N9 or H9N2 virus infection is suspected.

———

Chapter 16

U.S. Navy Medical Research Unit
Abbassia Fever Hospital
Cairo, Egypt
12:30 PM Local Time March 21ˢᵗ

The orderly disconnected the equipment wires from Miriam Mansoor's bed, and the nurse removed the intravenous tube from the needle in her arm, and then removed the needle itself. Miriam watched with a strange sense of joy as the orderly rolled the wheelchair over by the bed and helped her move to the wheelchair.

Miriam was being moved out of the crowded ICU. They had moved her here from the first ICU with the windows where she had first been treated. With that earlier move, they had said something then about moving her over to the hospital, which Miriam could not understand. Outside the door, in a small room, a female orderly rolled the wheelchair behind a folding screen, and she put a plastic bottle of sanitary wipes and a new hospital smock on a small table.

"We need to wipe you down, all of your skin area with the wet sanitary wipes, and your hair. Help me do it if you can." The orderly made a motion of moving her hands around her body. As they finished with the wipes, they went in a red trash canister. Then Miriam put on the new gown, and the orderly threw the old gown in the red canister, too. Miriam was given another wipe to do her hands again.

"Do you need a wheelchair, or can you walk?" the orderly asked.

"I can walk."

The orderly pointed toward another door. "The ward nurse will come in to check you out. You will be able to take a regular shower in the new ward."

The nurse in the next room was the first person in many days that Miriam had faced who was not wearing a full protective suit and face shield. But, she was still wearing a mask. Miriam was able to read the nurse's nametag, Nagwa. The protective suits never had nametags, and none of the medical staff had ever introduced themselves. Miriam had been cured of this sickness by strangers whose names she did not know.

"Our first ICU graduate," Nagwa announced, with a Cairo accent slightly different from the accent of the Delta. "Hopefully, you're the first of many. Let me get you to your new bed. Do you need a wheelchair, or can you walk?"

For a second time, Miriam said, "I think I can walk."

"Come." The nurse pulled the screen aside, and they walked out into the hall. Several people were walking to and fro down the hallway. All of them had masks on.

Miriam put her hand to her face. "Don't I need a mask?"

Nagwa laughed, "No, you're one of the very few people in Egypt who does not need a mask. You're an avian flu survivor. You're immune. Our angel who doesn't need a mask like us mere mortals." Once again Nagwa's city accent showed through with English words added to her Arabic

Miriam smiled at this thought. Then she thought of her friend Leyla and the smile disappeared. Miriam had been in the first ICU room when they had told her the first Minufiya nurse there, Leyla, had died.

The hallway they walked through was modern, far more sophisticated than anyplace she had ever been, even at the University in Minufiya. Through glass windows, she could see scores of patients being helped by medical crews, all in the protective gear. Some patients were on folding cots. It was crowded.

Nagwa took Miriam up an elevator and down another hallway. Here there was a large open hospital room with multiple beds and more cots placed between the regular beds, and most of the beds were full, all men. A nursing station had only one nurse.

They passed through a closed doorway with a sign saying, "Female – General Care." All of the thirty-plus beds in this room were occupied, by women and girls, and the nursing station, again only had one nurse.

Nagwa took Miriam to one of the two private rooms behind the nurses' station. "We'll put you in here for now. You'll probably be discharged when the physicians can get to you."

Miriam heard the sound of a television. Looking around, she saw that there was a television hanging from the ceiling. The room had a television. Miriam was amazed.

Before she left, Nagwa handed Miriam a large plastic bag. It contained Miriam's purse. The contents of the small leather purse, including her ID cards along with Miriam's earrings and her wristwatch, were all jumbled together in a smaller sealed bag.

"The things you came in with. They have been disinfected." Nagwa explained.

Miriam smiled, and Nagwa left.

There was a nice white terrycloth robe sitting on the table beside the bed. Miriam put it on and found the controller for the television underneath it.

Miriam realized she was feeling quite good, especially in comparison to recent weeks. Her memories of everything since that night in the dorm with Leyla were a jumble.

An orderly brought in a food tray. It was simple food; a small beef sausage, bread, broth, a nutty cookie, a water bottle, and a marvelous big orange. Miriam sat on the edge of the bed, eating and watching the television.

The television had two Cairo commercial stations, the Egyptian national public channel, and several international cable channels Miriam was not familiar with at all. The cable television they got in Minufiya, on the dormitory dayroom television, was rather limited.

The Cairo stations were just the usual translated soap operas, and the public TV channel was showing a show on history. Miriam found a cable news channel, in English, that was reporting on the epidemic. She could understand much of the report.

There was a knock on her door, and Miriam looked up and said, "Yes?"

A man in a white lab coat and mask came into the room. "My, my, you seem to be doing much better," he said in Arabic.

"Yes," Miriam nodded. "You're the director." It was a statement, not a question.

The man looked down at his lab coat, and seeing he had no name tag on; he asked, "And how would you know that?"

"When you came into the first ICU where I first was admitted, they all called you 'director.'"

"And you recognized me with this mask?"

Miriam blushed and smiled, "Yes, I remember your eyes. You have bushy eyebrows."

Dr. Ghariid seemed to smile, too, under the mask, "Yes, they are getting bushier and grayer with every passing year.

"My name is Mahmud Ghariid. And yes, I'm the 'director,' but of the American Medical Research Unit next door, that's where you came in first. This, where you are now," he motioned to the building around them, "is Abbassia Fever Hospital, next door. We work together, especially in times like these."

Miriam pointed to the television, "Yes, I've been watching. I had no idea it was so bad. They are burning the bodies!"

Ghariid nodded his head, "My best estimate is that it's worse than you see on television."

"It's really horrible. And were we first? From Minufiya?"

"You're the first we heard of. They sent you down here. The two little girls, their mother, and then you and the other nurse. Your friend . . . I . . ."

"Yes, they told me, and the other little girl."

Ghariid nodded and paused, "But, you're doing so well. They tell me you're being discharged today."

"Yes, I heard. But what will I do? How do I get back home?"

Ghariid shifted his stance and folded his arms in front of him. "That's what I'm here to talk to you about. Things are very bad up in Minufiya and the Delta area. You may have seen the videos. Shebeen, Banha, Tanta . . . it's chaos up there. I understand the staff tried to reach your family, but the phones are not working at the government offices near your home. You probably would not even be able to get back to Minufiya with the quarantine and roadblocks."

"So?"

"Well, the staff checked with the Ministry and your records indicate you have finished the two-year registered nurse program, you passed the exam and you were finishing your nursing residency at the clinic in Minufiya."

"Yes."

"In the current circumstances, medical staff are at a premium, and we could use another good nurse. Especially one who is immune to this influenza. I want to offer you a job," Ghariid said with a smile.

"At this hospital?"

"No, over at the U.S. Navy Medical Research Unit, next door. And we have living quarters for staff nearby."

Miriam blinked and paused. "I guess . . . yes, certainly, I would be honored. What would I be doing?"

"We have many exciting things going on—very important things. I'm sure you will be able to find something that intrigues you. It's very rewarding work at the Research Unit." Now Dr. Ghariid pointed to the American cable news Miriam was watching and switched to English, "Do you speak English?"

Miriam gave the waving flutter of her hand that indicated 'sort of.' She added, in halting English, "They taught enough English at nursing school for us to answer, ah . . . to read the medicine box instructions. And also . . . many videos for laboratory subjects in the second year were in English."

Ghariid switched back to Arabic, "Well, that's good, and I'm sure you will fit in. Most of our staff are Egyptian, only some of the senior scientists and a few Navy officers are American or European."

Now, Dr. Ghariid offered his hand to Miriam to shake, "Registered Nurse Miriam Mansoor, welcome to our team. I'll have our chief nurse gather up a nurse's uniform for you to wear when you're discharged. She will be over to see you later this afternoon. She can probably help you gather up the things you need to get your life set up here since you came here in the medical van with next to nothing."

Miriam smiled. Dr. Ghariid turned and left. Miriam sat on the bed. A commercial for a German beverage was showing on the television. Miriam picked up the plastic bag Nagwa had given her and started to move her few possessions back into her purse and put her earrings and wristwatch on. Life had delivered an odd turn to her.

Chapter 17

U.S. Army Medical Research and Development Command (USAMRDC)
Fort Detrick, Maryland
9:00 AM EDT March 21ˢᵗ

Karen Llewellyn remembered from years before, when Marty had to drive up from Washington, DC to meet with his USAMRIID superiors at Fort Detrick, how far away it was. It was a two-hour drive, or worse, from the city in normal traffic. But Karen had finished in Atlanta and was on her way to California, driving her Audi cross-country and stopping in Maryland as a lengthy side trip. She could have flown up from Atlanta, but she figured fitting Fort Detrick into the road trip was handier.

She had a mid-morning meeting with Major General Thomas Harding, and she had rented a hotel room in Frederick, Maryland the night before. The Travel Office at CDC had given her Department of Defense forms she would need to get reimbursed for her journey from the Army, her new employer. It was her first of many experiences with a new bureaucracy.

This morning was her first time wearing the dress uniform with four gold bands on the sleeves. The Uniformed Services ID card she had to flash at the gate showed her to be an O-6, a Public Health Service Captain, the equivalent of an Army Colonel, which elicited a crisp salute from the military policeman at the gate. Having spent most of her career at the CDC in Atlanta, Karen had mostly avoided the military protocol that the other uniformed services lived with, although the commissioned PHS officers proudly wore their uniform to distinguish themselves from the regular civilian employees.

Karen presented herself at the general's office and was shown a seating area where she could wait. While she was waiting, a female Army major in camouflage ACUs walked up and introduced herself, "Good morning Captain, I'm Major Sarah Morton, the general's adjutant. Any trouble on the trip up to Fort Detrick."

"No, everything went fine."

With pleasantries exchanged, the major started to leave when Karen asked, "Major, a question?"

"Yes ma'am."

"Yes, a bit of protocol. Public Health Service is not big on ceremony and certainly not Army protocol, but it's my understanding that since I'm a new commanding officer reporting to my commanding general, that I should salute the general and say that I'm reporting for duty even though we are inside and I'm not wearing my hat. Is that correct?"

The major smiled and said, "Captain, you are correct, and I suppose we normally would not expect a PHS officer to know that, nor worry about it. And, I guess it's a rarity for a PHS officer to be reporting for duty as an Army commander. But, yes, the general would probably appreciate the correct formality."

Karen smiled and thanked her for the advice.

The secretary finally told Karen the general was ready for her. The general sat behind his large oak desk. He was wearing his dress pink and greens uniform with a chest full of medals and various badges. Karen walked up between the two armchairs in front of the desk and saluted. "Captain Karen Lewellyn reporting for duty, Sir."

The general returned the salute crisply, with a hint of a smile. "Please have a seat, Captain."

When Karen sat down, the general added, "I suppose a formal reporting for duty is not common in your service. Aye, Captain?"

"No, Sir. The Public Health Service is not big on formality and has very few actual military command situations."

"I thought not. Your fellow vaccine plant commander, George Riggs, walked in here yesterday and came up to the desk, offering his hand to me to shake."

Karen smiled, "Well, sir, they send us up to the Commissioned Officer Training Program for a few weeks when we sign up to Public Health Service. But after that, there is little military protocol unless you're assigned to a regular military unit. My husband was, or is, an Army officer, so I knew enough to ask your adjutant to confirm the 'reporting for duty' procedure."

"Army, huh. Where is he stationed?"

"He is in the Reserves now, Medical Corps."

"Good, on the same team. Is he going with you out to California?"

Karen paused, "No, Sir. Not for now. He is an ER doc in Atlanta. His Reserve unit is a Response Team here at Detrick."

"Yes, well, once this new assignment is underway, I'm sure you two can make arrangements to get back under the same roof. With my deployments overseas, my wife and I have been separated, probably a third of our marriage."

Karen saw no need to fully explain the background on the Llewellyn-Craig couple's "separation" to the general.

The general now leaned back in his chair and cracked his knuckles. "Captain Llewellyn . . . can I call you Karen?"

Karen nodded, "Yes, sir," knowing that her calling the general "Tom" was not reciprocal.

"I don't have a whole lot for you today. And I need to be going soon, another damned trip to San Antonio, to talk to my boss and her staff officers. But, I did want to tell you how important I think your new assignment is. In fact, I could easily say that there is not a more important job on earth right now. I see the reports of the mess they have in Egypt. Bodies piling up in the streets. My job is to make sure the Army's medical research, development and materiel mission is on the right track, and I want you to know that whatever you need to do your job will be arranged.

"I'm not just blowing smoke with those words, Karen. You're supposed to be the best person we have to know how to make vaccines to keep our country from getting its ass kicked like Egypt. And I see Turkey is not much better according to this morning's CNN. I know you have the full support of your cohorts back in HHS, but I want you to know that if you need anything, supplies, personnel, or some red tape cut for you, that my command's full capabilities are here to help you out.

"I hope this government-owned contractor-operated system works for this task. When they suggested it, I actually went out to Rock Island, Illinois, and talked to my fellow general at the Joint Munitions Command who handles the GOCO's for ammunition and projectiles; they seem to like it. We'll see. If it doesn't work right, it's your duty to let us know before the problem becomes critical. If the system needs tweaking, you let us know, and my people will get things moving.

"You will be given a commanding officer's packet, like every other CO in this command. It has my personal phone numbers, email and the name and contact info for every key person in the command. If a problem is interfering with your mission, I want to know about it. Is that clear?"

"Yes, Sir."

The general picked up something from his desk and stood up to come around the desk towards Karen. She also stood up. He faced her and opened a small blue box in his hand. "Captain Karen Llewellyn, I've been authorized by the Surgeon General of the United States to deliver this to you. May you wear it with honor."

General Harding turned the box around for her to see and handed it to her. "I'll let you put this on your uniform. I'm not exactly sure where it goes."

The box contained a silver badge with a circular wreath and a silver star with the symbol of the Public Health Service in the middle. It was the Public Health Service Officer-in-Charge badge. It was now mostly worn by senior officers running top-level agencies or sub-Cabinet offices, but it had once, decades before, been worn by the officers in charge of Public Health Service field commands, like the old Public Health Service Hospitals. They were designating the Defense Pharmaceutical Plant commanders with this badge of respect. The act of awarding Karen and her two fellow commanding officers this honor belied the comments that had been made about the PHS not being in synch with military protocol.

General Harding now said, "I understand they are going to run you through the Acquisitions Office and the Defense Contracting Service people upstairs this afternoon to make sure you're clear on the contracting program of this GOCO operation, followed by an Ops Briefing. And then I understand Colonel Glenby over at USAMRIID wants to meet with you. Then, I guess you're off to the land of fruits and nuts to make us some vaccine. I'm going to make sure my staff schedules a visit to all three new defense pharmaceutical plants in a few weeks, once you new commanders get a chance to take charge. Good luck, Captain."

They shook hands, and the general ushered Karen to the door.

———

U.S. Army Medical Research and Development Command (USAMRDC)
Fort Detrick, Maryland
2:35 PM EDT March 21st

After lunch, the briefing for Karen from the USAMRDC Acquisitions staff and the Defense Contract Management Agency people had taken the better part of an hour and a half. Knowing that contracting matters were something new to the new plant commander, they had put together a PowerPoint presentation for Karen on the defense contracting system, regulations and the GOCO contract that would serve as the operating plan for her Defense Pharmaceutical Plant in Thousand Oaks.

They had explained that a former manager of one of the Army's GOCO ammunition plants had been transferred to the plant in California to act as her assistant. Lastly, they had given her contact information for the commanding officer of one of the existing Army GOCO operations at Radford Army Ammunition Plant in southwestern Virginia. They suggested that she stop by the Radford plant to see how one of the most important GOCO facilities in the country operates.

Karen emerged from the briefing room with a two-volume set of Defense Acquisition Regulations and a thick green three-ring binder containing the GOCO contract for the Thousand Oaks plant and all the essential design, capability and technical specifications the experts thought a commanding officer might need.

The Army 2nd lieutenant who had been assigned to be Karen's host/shadow for the briefings, was waiting when she came out of the contract briefing. He asked her, pointing to the big binder and regulations books, "Can I take those for you? We can have them sent to California if you like."

Karen thought for a moment and answered, "Maybe the binders of regulations, but I want to take the plant info binder with me. I might have a chance to read about the plant on the trip west."

The young officer smiled, "A little light reading to cure insomnia, huh?"

Karen smiled and asked, "What's next?"

"Colonel Morehouse says he has a short Ops briefing for you. Mostly info about our command and who is who. Then I need to get you over to see Colonel Glenby at USAMRIID by four. But first, there are a couple of other gentlemen who have asked to talk to you."

"Who's that?" Karen asked.

"I think it would be best if I let them explain. They're in the small conference room, over beyond Ops." The lieutenant took the two binders of regulations from Karen and led the way across the office.

As they approached the glass-windowed conference room, Karen could see two men in civilian suits sitting at the table. They looked vaguely familiar. By the time the lieutenant opened the door for her to go in to meet them, Karen remembered where she had seen the men. They stood when she entered the room.

The lieutenant closed the door behind her, and the two men gave her their first and last names and shook her hand, without explaining their purpose.

Before sitting down, Karen sat her book and papers on the table, crossed her arms, and faced the two men. After waiting a moment, "Before we continue with whatever you gentlemen need, can I offer you some advice?"

The younger man shrugged. The other said, "Yes, sure."

"When you go into a ritzy, reservations-only restaurant as a walk-in and they are kind enough to give you a table anyway, don't refuse the table the hostess offers you and demand something closer to the people you're tailing. You stand out like a sore thumb. OK?"

The older man smiled and asked, "We were that obvious?"

"Obvious enough that I remember seeing you three weeks later. You're D.I.A.?"

The man shook his head. "A little farther up the Potomac."

"CIA? And you were following me?"

"No, you were having dinner with a senior official of the People's Republic of China, Zhao Xiang. And her father is one of the top people in the P.R.C. Foreign Ministry."

Karen gave a slight frown and took a seat across the table from the men. "How can I help you?"

The older one continued to take the lead, "We are with the Agency's National Resources Division. We work within the United States to follow up on the travels of U.S. citizens overseas and foreign citizens traveling in the U.S. You met with Zhao Xiang for over two hours and apparently were with her for a day or two for the FDA conference. Would you mind answering our questions about those contacts?"

"I don't mind answering your questions. But if they are about the VRBPAC meeting and what we did there, the transcript will be posted on the HHS website, probably there already. And I really had no further contact with her after dinner. Nothing more than waving hello."

"What was discussed at dinner?"

"Well, multiple things, all centered around influenza and viral strains . . . and vaccines. That was the day we first got word about the avian flu outbreak in Egypt, and the news of that upset the apple cart for our vaccine meeting. We discussed the impact of the Egyptian H5N1 flu strain on our vaccine choices. We discussed the vaccine plant issues we have in common. And, oh, Joan talked about the . . ."

"Joan? Who's Joan?" the younger man asked.

Karen stared at him for a second and answered, "Zhao Xiang, 'Joan' is her anglicized nickname for her given name 'Xiang.' It's easier for westerners to pronounce."

The young man wrote that down as if it were critical information and said, "Please continue."

"So, Joan, Dr. Zhao, also talked about the SARS epidemic in China in 2002-2003 and coronavirus in 2020, and she mentioned what bureaucratic screw-up had been behind the spread of the disease, both times, and the deaths of so many people. She compared SARS to the coronavirus situation in 2020."

"Which was?"

"In 2003, the national and provincial officials with the best information on the epidemic had classified it, which prevented the people that needed to know the information from stopping the virus spreading until too late. In early 2020, they still had significant problems with local officials not taking charge and accepting responsibility. We all know now about the big mistake at the viral laboratory in Wuhan. And, they even had senior officials punishing people who tried to spread the warning about coronavirus."

The younger man jumped in again, "Did she disclose that classified Chinese information to you?"

Karen gave a short laugh and said, "Yes, she did, but it's no longer classified. There is a CDC whitepaper on the same subject that gives precisely the same information as she talked about."

The older man now asked, "Did Dr. Zhao seem frustrated or angry at the Chinese bureaucracy for having caused the deaths?"

Karen was amazed at the one-track mindset of these men and decided to answer accordingly, "No, not really; she acted like a competent medical professional who was frustrated at silly security professionals who tried to classify critical information when such secrecy was totally unnecessary and, in fact, counter-productive."

The older man understood the intent of Karen's words, but the young guy was oblivious of her zinger.

The younger man read from his notes and asked, "What were these 'common issues' about a vaccine plant you had with her."

"The third person at that dinner, Jared Bentley . . ."

"I was going to ask about him," the younger man interrupted.

Karen took a deep breath and continued, "Jared Bentley is an executive with HeptImun Corporation. They are the contractors running the new state-of-the-art vaccine plant I'm going to be commanding for the Army out in California," Karen patted the big green binder to indicate its connection to what she was saying. "And, HeptImun is also building four very similar plants for the Chinese, which Dr. Zhao is in charge of."

"HeptImun, that's an American company?"

"Yes, out of Connecticut."

"And does the U.S. government know about and approve of the Chinese getting a high-tech plant built by a U.S. company? Did they use American trade secrets in the plant?"

Karen struggled to not roll her eyes at how the young CIA spook tried to turn everything into something surreptitious. She answered, "My understanding is that the U.S. government was happy to give a secretarial level sign-off to the Chinese building program as it just happened to reduce the costs to design and develop the five plants America is building. And, to my knowledge, the most innovative technology in the new vaccine plants is from a Canadian company that is owned by a Japanese conglomerate, not an American company. If you get your copy of the transcript of our VRBPAC conference off the HHS website, you should look at the presentation about plant-based virus-like particles. It's amazing stuff. Or, you might ask that nice young lieutenant who brought me in here to see if there is an extra copy of this green binder. I'm sure you would find it enlightening."

Karen pushed her chair back and asked, "Will that be all gentlemen? I have a very busy schedule this afternoon."

The older CIA man took a business card out of his pocket and pushed it across the table at Karen, "No, Commander Llewellyn-Craig, that's about it, except we would ask that if you have further communications with Dr. Zhao that might be of interest to us, that you contact me."

"Rest assured; I will do that," Karen said. And then she held her sleeve up for the CIA man to see. "Four stripes, sir, that's a Captain, not a Commander. I got a promotion since you ran your National Agency Check on me. In a profession like yours, you need to notice little things like that. Good day."

Karen took the business card, and her stack of books and papers, got up and left without offering her hand to the men.

—

Chapter 18

Minuf City
Minufiya Governorate, Egypt
March 21st

Minuf is an ancient city. The city is near the west branch of the Nile in the fertile delta.

It has a long and storied history. Julius Caesar, Napolean, and Field Marshal Montgomery had each passed through Minuf on their conquests. Minuf was a proud example of both Muslims and Coptic Christians living in peace together, with both religions having important relics and edifices in the older quarters. Two centuries before, the foreign rulers, the Ottoman Turks, had built the new main road and then a railroad from Cairo to Alexandria. When the Ottoman road and railroad bypassed Minuf, the old city had lost its status as the capital of the governorate that was named after it. But, it had ancient buildings and historic sites galore. The southern quadrant, the ancient bazaar area with its narrow streets and marketplaces, was normally a bustling hive of activity.

The newer sections to the north and east were where the technical school, modern business district, and several hospitals were located. The Minufiya Governorate had been lucky enough to be the birthplace of not just one, but two leaders of the modern Egyptian nation, who had, over the years, bestowed on their birthplace more than its share of modern facilities and public improvements. If the Egyptian nation had a true heartland, it was the prosperous Delta farming regions like Minufiya, not the crowded slums of Cairo.

But today, the city of Minuf was abnormally quiet. There were crowds gathered, but they were somber and still, for the most part. They gathered around the three small hospitals in Minuf. These crowds had been noisy earlier, but once they learned that there was no help coming from the hospitals, a strange silence fell on the crowds. The hospitals had closed their doors when the dead and dying had filled their halls, and the limited antibiotic and antiviral supplies ran out. The crowds had parents carrying children in their arms, while other tiny children and their grandparents were lying silently on the roadway. Occasionally there was an outburst of a mother's anguished cry or the wail of an infant in distress.

The few remaining policemen and the Army soldiers who had driven up from Cairo in their dun-colored trucks still tried to keep a semblance of order. Copies of the Fatwa about dealing with the dead were handed out. They had declared the huge area of football fields south of the bazaar to be a staging area where the bodies of the dead could be brought out of the residences. The residents brought body after body to the playing field and reverently laid them, mostly shrouded, in row after row. Other bodies were simply carried to the street where the Army trucks picked them up. The first ones at the football fields were covered with tarps, but soon the tarps ran out, then it was clear the rows needed to be stacked.

———

Influenza had started in the farming villages to the south of Minuf. Then, the word spread that the Army had come and surrounded Minufiya University campus in the larger, nearby city of Shebeen al Kom, just to the north. The troops were an attempt to quarantine the university and the adjacent hospital. Other Army troops from the garrison in Cairo poured cans of fuel oil over the houses and buildings in the southern farming region, setting fire to several villages, killing all of the farm animals, burning the villages to the ground and trucking the residents to a tent city set up to the east of the city.

Rumors of the terrible fevers and choking coughs had spread throughout the two cities. Those who had means tried to escape Minuf and Shebeen al Kom to the south towards Cairo or north to Alexandria, but roadblocks of Army troops had blocked their way. More troops guarded the train stations at Birkaat and Quweisna, and the trains no longer stopped there on the runs from Cairo to Alexandria. Then the trains stopped running entirely.

What had earlier been rumors had become a reality, and the residents of Minuf's crowded bazaar area started falling sick in droves. Within a few more days, much of Minuf City was ill. Shortly after that, the entire Minufiya Governorate, with a population of over three million, was blockaded by a full division of the Egyptian Army. Soon, though, those soldiers were getting sick, too. Indeed, the few doctors available to treat the sick noted that the soldiers fell ill in proportionally higher numbers than the populace at large.

———

Office of the Police Commissioner
Baodi City, China
1:20 PM March 21ˢᵗ

Xi Zemin was at his desk reading through emails when the Baodi Police Commissioner's secretary came to his desk. "Inspector Xi, the commissioner wants to see you immediately. He has a 'guest.'"

The formality of the normally amiable secretary was a bit odd, as was her emphasis on the word 'guest." Xi buttoned his uniform jacket.

Zemin followed the woman to his supervisor's office, where she motioned him into the commissioner's office. Zemin walked into the office, and upon seeing another officer rising from a chair next to the commissioner's desk, he came to attention and said, "As ordered, sir."

The commissioner was sitting at his desk, and the other man was in a police uniform, but his shoulder boards had three pips and olive leaves on them, indicating he was one rank higher than the commissioner.

The commissioner spoke, "Inspector Xi, this is Superintendent Tong, from Tianjin. He would like to speak with you about one of your cases."

Zemin turned to face the man. The man was stocky, slightly graying, with an imposing demeanor and wore both the police command badge as well as a decoration for bravery. A police command badge for Tianjin would indicate this was the new provincial police commander. Zemin waited.

The commander spoke, "Inspector Xi, your work on the recent deaths from illness has come to our attention."

"Yes sir?"

"It seems that you reported on the multiple flu deaths recently here in Baodi. Your report was summarized in your district's weekly report and sent up to our office and then Beijing. It seems you reported fifteen deaths from apparent fever were investigated by you, and the matter turned over to the Ministry of Health for follow-up."

"Yes, sir." Xi Zemin was not sure where this was going. *Did they like his work on this?*

"But then, in your summary, you noted that several of the persons you investigated as deaths in public places had, in your opinion, never been in contact with animals and so could not have been infected with influenza by animal contact. You concluded that these several persons had obviously fallen ill and then died from human-to-human contact and not animal contact, as you had been told by representatives of the Ministry of Health."

"Yes sir."

"Well, Inspector Xi, it should come as no surprise to you that it was a matter of concern in Beijing when it was discovered that the Ministry of Public Security was disagreeing with the Ministry of Health on the cause of death for what is, in reality, almost fifty Chinese citizens if you count the ones who have died in the hospitals. This 'concern' was expressed by the minister himself to the Province of Tianjin. I've been asked to resolve this difference of opinion." The superintendent now paused.

Xi spoke, "Sir, would you like me to show you the evidence. It's quite clear?"

The superintendent shook his head. "No, I do not need to see your evidence. Although I will be collecting your evidence and any files and notes you may have. I've been instructed to extract the police force from this issue. Apparently, the prevailing scientific data is that this type of disease, they call it H7N9, is only transmissible via animal contact. We will be turning over your 'evidence' to the experts in this type of matter, and they will resolve any matters that need to be investigated.

"And, henceforth, the police will not investigate nor report on any death once it is determined that the cause of death was illness, fever, or any sort of disease." He looked at both Xi and his boss, the Baodi commissioner, when he gave this order. Both men said they understood.

The superintendent continued, "And, one more thing, the information regarding the manner of transmission of this disease and the disagreement over it, when it was being discussed in Beijing, was inadvertently brought to the attention of certain international groups. These groups have started their own inquiry into this matter, and it's not in China's best interest that they are involved. If there is any outside inquiry into this disease in Baodi, whether from official foreign agencies or the news media, those inquiries will be directed to the Health Ministry in Beijing. The Baodi Health Authority has been given similar instructions. And any outside persons coming to Baodi and inquiring into this matter will be reported to my office immediately. Is that clear?"

Both police officers again indicated their understanding.

Baodi's H7N9 influenza was to be officially and irrefutably deemed by the People's Republic of China's bureaucracy to be caused by contact with animals.

—

Chapter 19

Emirates Airlines Flight 1214
Airbus A380 Jumbo Jet
36,000 feet just south of Genoa, Italy
10:30 AM GMT March 21ˢᵗ

The 436 passengers on the flight from Dubai to Paris-Charles De Gaulle Airport with a stopover at Cairo International Airport had just been served their mid-day meal when they felt the Airbus make a wide, sweeping turn to the left. The observant passengers could see that the sun changed from starboard side windows to the port side.

Shortly after that, they heard the plane's public-address speakers click and announce something in Arabic. The non-Arabic speaking passengers saw the Arabic speaking passengers get upset as they listened.

After the lengthy Arabic announcement, a different voice came on the speaker. It announced in English, "Ladies and Gentlemen, the captain has asked me to announce that we have been informed that the French civil aviation authorities have directed that this aircraft is not permitted to land at Paris Charles De Gaulle airport. This is apparently at the direction of public health authorities as a result of the current health crisis in the Arab Republic of Egypt, where, as you know, several dozen passengers boarded our flight.

"We have just changed course to Lamezia Terme International Airport in Calabria, Italy, as directed by the authorities, where we expect to land there and refuel before our return to Cairo. No one will be allowed off the plane in Calabria; it's a refueling stop only.

"We understand that this information will be of great concern to many passengers, and we will try to get additional information as to what you can expect as soon as we can. The captain has turned on the fasten seat belts sign and requests all passengers to remain in their seats until we land. Please cooperate with the flight crew. They cannot answer your questions as they know nothing more than what we have announced."

A woman's voice now came on and gave the same announcement in French.

Most of the passengers ignored the announcement and peppered the flight crew with questions as the crew tried to collect the meal service trays.

———

Lamezia Terme International Airport
Calabria, Italy
12:45 PM GMT March 21ˢᵗ

The runway at the airport in Calabria was barely longer than the flight manual's required runway length needed for the huge Airbus jet, but it landed with some room to spare. After landing, the Emirates jumbo jet rolled past turnouts leading to the curiously brick-red colored, ultra-modern terminal building and proceeded west on the tarmac. The airport was mostly used for summertime visitors to the tourist destinations in sunny southern Italy. And, unlike most international airports, Lamezia Terme, in its location in the 'toe' of the Italian boot, was far from any major population area. Contrary to most international airports, this small airport used rolling, wheeled stairways to deplane from jets rather than the telescoping jetway tubes used by most modern airports. On this last day of winter, only one of the dozen or so passenger jet deplaning areas were in use and that one by a small regional jet. The lumbering Airbus seemed sorely out of place.

Instead of taxiing to the main terminal, the Airbus was hooked up to a tow tractor and headed to the far west end of the airport, which was occupied by a military airfield for the Italian Army's 2ⁿᵈ Air Regiment. There, the jet joined another Emirates jet and a smaller Alitalia jet already parked there, away from the military hangars and rows of combat helicopters.

As soon as the engines of the Emirates plane were shut down and the auxiliary power units engaged, several squads of troops in blue berets and olive drab jumpsuits surrounded the plane. They were armed with assault weapons. Similar squads were already in place around the other two planes. The pilot's warning that no one would be getting off in Calabria was being enforced by the men of Italy's elite airborne assault force, whose home turf the airliners were infringing upon this day.

Two large aircraft servicing trucks with their cargo pods elevated on hydraulic risers were next to the other planes, re-provisioning the jetliners. The workers on the service trucks wore face masks. Red and yellow striped tanker trucks were refueling the planes.

While they waited for their turn with the service vehicles, the flight crew of Flight 1214 moved through the Economy-Class cabin asking certain passengers to come with them to new seats in the Business-Class area, upstairs from the main cabin.

In the meantime, most of the Business-Class passengers who boarded in Dubai were moved forward on the upper deck to First-Class, while the Cairo boarding Business-Class passenger remained where they were. The cabin crew assisted the passengers in moving their carry-on luggage to their new seats.

Out of all the passengers moved around, only the First-Class Cairo passengers who now got bumped back to Business Class complained. Bribes in the form of passes for future First Class Emirates flights were handed out to the unhappy, demoted Cairo First-Class passengers. Many of these First-Class passengers had taken advantage of their top tier status and had multiple carry-on bags that needed to be moved.

One of these First-Class Cairo passengers was a tall black man in a dark suit with a distinctive athletic build, a head and shoulders taller than the average passenger. When asked to move to Business-Class, he flashed a black passport and some papers in a leather-bound folder. After viewing the proffered documents, the head flight attendant shook her head and still required the black man to move to Business-Class. The man pulled two over-size coal-black valises from the overhead. He refused the free pass she offered him and insisted that he carry the two valises and his carry-on bag himself.

When the flight crew was done, all of the passengers who boarded in Cairo were sitting together in Business-Class at the rear of the upper deck of the two-deck Airbus.

Eventually, the service trucks came over to Flight 1214 to transfer food and supplies to the Airbus. There was a bit of a problem because the catering company with the contract to supply food to airliners at Lamezia Terme Airport was not used to servicing the huge Airbus A380 and did not have the right-sized food carts for the Airbus galleys. An impromptu tray moving exercise was carried out by the food service workers, which for 450-odd passengers and crew took quite a lot of time.

During the wait, passengers whose cell phones had roaming capability in southern Italy called their family and friends and informed them of the news about their flight. Most found the cell phone connection bad. The big black man in Business-Class pulled an odd-looking phone from his bag. Passengers watching him assumed that he had an old brick-like cell phone from the '90s. But, the man's oddly-shaped phone seemed to work perfectly, and they heard him tell someone about the airline schedule change.

It seemed that the supply trucks had carried more than just the food and drinks. Shortly after the doors were closed following the resupply, the flight crew came through the cabin handing out mint green face masks, which the crew themselves also wore, and instructed the passengers to keep their masks on during the flight. Further, if the need for oxygen masks should occur, the oxygen mask should replace the green mask and would function as a face mask.

Emirate Airlines Flight 1214 had to wait for the other two airliners to leave the 2nd Air Division's tarmac and for a new Lufthansa airliner to roll up and park beside it before it could taxi out to the main runway. But there was no wait at the end of the runway; Flight 1214 was pre-cleared by air traffic control to take off.

After a very noisy, full power take-off, the huge Airbus veered right to a 120 degree heading en route back to Cairo.

—

Emirates Airlines Flight 1214
Airbus A380 Jumbo Jet
34,800 feet over Eastern Mediterranean
4:30 PM GMT, March 21ˢᵗ

The flight back across the Mediterranean was uneventful. The flight crew had to make an announcement explaining that the face masks that had been distributed could be flipped up temporarily to eat and drink the dinner that was being served, but the mask should be immediately put back on afterward.

The passengers who were following the flight path on the seatback computer video screens noticed as they approached and passed the Egyptian coast that the aircraft did not start descending to land in Cairo. Any curiosity about the failure to descend into Egyptian airspace was soon explained by another three-language announcement from the flight deck.

After the Arabic announcement caused a twitter of conversation amongst the Arabic speakers, the English-speaking passengers heard, "Ladies and Gentlemen, the interruption of our scheduled flight today was the result of the public health authorities of the Arab Republic of Egypt and world health agencies placing a full quarantine on all travel into or out of Egypt. Our departure from Cairo this morning was shortly before the quarantine was announced and led to our inability to land in France. At the request of the Egyptian government and in cooperation with both the United Arab Emirates and Saudi Arabian authorities, Emirate Airways is happy to announce that we believe we have made arrangements that will minimize the impacts of the quarantine on most of our passengers.

"While the disease outbreak and resulting quarantine might result in weeks of quarantine for those in Egypt, we have made arrangements for this flight to land at King Khalid airfield in Saudi Arabia. At King Khalid airfield, we believe the quarantine issue may be more effectively dealt with than on the ground inside Egypt, while still minimizing the health threat posed by persons leaving the quarantined area.

"So, we expect to be on the ground at King Khalid airfield at approximately 8:30 PM local time. We will give you additional information as we obtain it. The flight crew will be distributing another meal and beverage service shortly."

Another announcement by the woman speaking French followed.

The announcement made by the Emirates crew avoided two important pieces of information. First, it did not hint that a key reason behind the change in plans was the fact that several members of the royal houses of both Dubai and Saudi Arabia were passengers in the First-Class section of the plane. The Royals had objected to being dumped into the influenza quarantine quagmire that Egypt was becoming. Besides, the Egyptians did not need any more problems to deal with on the ground. And, second, the mention of their destination as being King Khalid airfield was misconstrued by most passengers as meaning they were going to the magnificent King Khalid International Airport in the Saudi capital, Riyadh. Instead, the Emirates pilot had received directions to land at the massive military complex built by the U.S. Army Corps of Engineers for the Saudi Arabian government, King Khalid Military City, in the remote northern desert of Saudi Arabia. Saudi Arabia had two airports named after King Khalid. The governments involved would not let even the wishes of a few Royals result in the inadvertent spread of the deadly influenza strain.

At King Khalid Military City, arrangements were already underway to process the Cairo passengers separately from the other passengers and deal with the situation as best they could. The military field hospital that had been largely mothballed after the second Gulf War was already being brought online. The Americans had given the Saudi Arabian National Guard a draft operations plan written by a consulting team at Northrup Grumman detailing just how to use these remote military medical facilities in the event of an epidemic.

—

Government Message/Email
From U.S. Military Attache
Embassy of the United States
Cairo, Egypt,
5:15 PM GMT March 21st

SECRET

******.*.*.*** ***.

STATE DEPT FWD TO SECDEF CHNLS
ELEC FRWD VIA EMAIL GRPS PUBHLTH 41 DIPL SEC 901
****

IMMEDIATE / **FLASH PRIORITY**   ZUQE ZEF4T 197853
o 211715Z MAR
FM   U.S. MIL ATTACHE CAIRO

TO   DEPT STATE WASH DC
USCINCCENT
U.S. MIL ATTACHE RIYADH

INFO NMCC WASHINGTON DC//POC/APP/LPO//
CINCLANTFLT NORFOLK VA
COMUSNAVCENT
CMDR NAMRU 3
CINCPACFLT
USN BUMED
COMUSMARCENT//G3//
SURG GEN HHS WASH DC
AIG 01 PINNACLE
AIG 41 – PUB HLTH
AIG 901 - DIPL SEC
    SECTION 01 OF 01
SUBJ: U.S. EMB CAIRO SITREP NR 01 TO NAMRU3 OPREP 3 PINNACLE NR 01 AVIAN INFLUENZA -- CONFIDENTIAL
    Date   Signed
REF/A/DOC/SECSTATE OPPLAN 24-1

1. U.S. DIPLOMATIC COURIER CARRYING CRITICAL BIOLOGIC SAMPLES FROM NAMRU3 CAIRO TO U.S. CDC WAS ABOARD A COMMERCIAL AIRLINER REROUTED FROM PARIS TO SAUDI ARABIA DUE TO EGYPTIAN QUARANTINE. NAMRU3 INFORMS THIS STATION THAT RCPT OF BIO SAMPLES BY U.S. CDC IS OF CRITICAL NATIONAL IMPORTANCE.

2. COURIER USMC MSGT JACK HAMILTON REPORTS EMIRATES FLIGHT 1214 IS NOW BOUND FOR SAUDI ARABIA KING KHALID MILITARY CITY AIRFIELD (KMC). OUR ATTEMPT TO CONFIRM WITH EGYPT GOVT UNSUCCESSFUL.

3. NAMRU3 INFORMS THIS STATION THAT BIO SAMPLES ARE 100+ BLOOD VIALS NEEDED TO RESPOND TO CURRENT EPIDEMIC THREAT IDENTIFIED IN ORIG OPREP 3. CONSIDERED OF CRITICAL NATL IMPORTANCE.

4. U.S. MILITARY ATTACHE AND U.S. AMBASSADOR CAIRO REQUEST IMMEDIATE ACTION BY U.S. EMBASSY RIYADH AND U.S. CENTRAL COMMAND ASSETS TO

> RETURN COURIER AND CRITICAL BIO CARGO TO
> UNITED STATES ASAP. COORDINATION WITH SAUDI
> GOVT REQUIRED.
> 5. COURIER IN CONTACT VIA SATPHONE. CONTACT
> THIS STATION FOR LIAISON.
> MORE TO FOLLOW.
> SECSTATE WASH DC
> COG POC(L)   (U,F)
> INFO OS(l) CCT(3) C412(2) AVN(8) CC(3) IG(l) INT(2)
> I -L (4) MED (13) DCS PP-0 (1) PL (1) RP (1) CtiC (1) MH (1)
> OLA-PA(l) SO-LiC(l) MI(l) NAHD(L) LRCC(5) PO(l)
> POR(L) TFK CK(l) AMRD(L)

—

King Khalid Military City
North Central Saudi Arabia
9:45 PM GMT March 21st

The flight line at King Khalid Military City Airport was already a beehive of activity when Emirates Flight 1214 arrived. Two of the large hangars built to house military combat aircraft were brightly lit, and dozens of buses and other vehicles were parked nearby. In one hangar, dozens of figures in white medical scrubs and face masks were waiting in groups at rows of tables on the floor of the hangar. The other hangar had rows of chairs and tables set up to process passengers through.

Squads of armed Saudi Arabian National Guardsmen stood on guard around a Saudia Airlines Boeing 787 Dreamliner parked near the hangar with two passenger loading ramps beside it. Small groups of passengers disembarked from the Saudia airliner and were escorted by the Guardsmen in surgical masks to the hangar with the medical team.

The pilot of Flight 1214 followed ground crew directions and parked on the flight line a considerable distance from the Saudia jet.

While they were taxiing, another set of three language announcements informed the passengers, "We have arrived at King Khalid City on Saudi Arabia. All passengers are requested to remain seated at this time and until told otherwise by cabin crew. We will be following the directions of the ground crew to disembark. Arrangements are being made to provide whatever assistance you may need and to answer your questions after you disembark. Again, all passengers are directed to remain seated at this time."

Do not stand or retrieve your carry-on bags until specifically directed by the cabin crew."

There was a buzz of conversation when the passengers familiar with Saudi Arabia realized they had not landed at the King Khalid International Airport in the capital city Riyadh, but at the remote military base in the far northern desert area of the country. Again, as in Italy, many passengers made cell phone calls or tried to, as normal roaming cell phone service did not seem to work out here in the middle of the far northern desert.

There was a short wait until two more stair units were rolled up next to Flight 1214, and the doors were opened. The announcement to remain seated was made again. Passengers watched as the teams of armed soldiers surrounded the flight, and several came up the stairs, forward and rear. The flight crew got their instructions from officers at both exits. The strange block-shaped phone of the huge black man in Business-Class gave off an odd warbling ring tone, and the man answered it. Unlike everyone else's, his phone worked.

After the Saudi officers talked to the flight crew, at the rear exit, a team of a Saudi officer, a Saudi sergeant and one man in a U.S. Air Force desert camouflage ABU uniform with the ever-present face masks boarded Flight 1214 and followed the flight attendant to the Business-Class section on the upper level. There, the Air Force officer started to shake hands with the black man but stopped pulling his hand back. The passenger took his two big cases out of the overhead. The Saudi sergeant offered to help him, but the man refused, instead just giving the Saudi sergeant his regular flight carry-on bag. The man refused to let anyone handle the two cases other than himself. They moved to the lower level and left the Airbus jumbo jet.

Passengers on the left side of Flight 1214 could watch as the passenger and the men accompanying him were approached by another group twenty meters from the plane. There were several U.S. military personnel in this group. The passenger was handed what looked like a jumpsuit that he put on over his suit.

As Master Sergeant Jack Hamilton donned the HazMat suit, the landing lights illuminated on a U.S. Air Force C-37A Gulfstream V passenger jet that had been parked near one of the hangars. The twin jet engines of the jet were already running. A young woman in a U.S. Air Force flight suit sprayed down the two black valises and Hamilton's carry-on with an olive drab aerosol can. The group turned and headed for the Gulfstream jet. Even now, Master Sergeant Hamilton refused assistance in carrying his charge, the two diplomatic courier cases. The Marine master sergeant was getting a ride on the C37A jet that normally was used by the general staff of the U.S. Central Command. A flight home from Qatar to MacDill Air Force Base in Florida had been diverted to pick up the diplomatic courier and the vials of blood collected from the victims of the H5N1 avian flu in Egypt. Master Sergeant Hamilton was quarantined in the private office in the back of the C37A, where the general usually flew.

Back onboard Flight 1214, the process of deplaning was underway. The passengers in Business-Class, who had come from Cairo, were sent to the hangar with the medical teams ready to take blood tests. The First-Class and Economy-Class passengers were loaded on buses headed for a three day stay in barracks buildings at King Khalid City. Some of the First-Class passengers were sent to Visiting Officer's Quarters at the base, but they, too, would stay for three days, after which they would have their blood drawn also. The Saudis would not let even the Royals avoid the quarantine rules.

A maintenance team flown in from Emirates Airlines headquarters in Dubai the next day gave Flight 1214 a thorough interior steam cleaning and sterilization before the big Airbus was returned to service, flying most its passengers back to Dubai after their three days in the desert. That is, all the passengers except for the fourteen from Cairo whose blood test indicated contact with or infection from the H5N1 virus. Those fourteen had an extended stay in Level One quarantine at the King Khalid Military City hospital.

———

Chapter 20

Cairo, Egypt,
3:30 PM Local Time March 22nd

Seashaidh 'Shaysee' O'Neil struggled in the stiff breeze to hold the hijab on her head and keep the earphone in her ear with one hand while holding the microphone and notecard in the other. In Egypt, the hijab was not worn by all women, but the network told Shaysee she should, both for the propriety when interviewing people who expected it and for the 'visual' effect of the American network's female reporter complying with the Islamic dress code, even in this comparatively fashion-conscious country. But despite the hijab and even in this report from the field, Shaysee was the epitome of the beautiful, stylish 'talking head' the cable news networks had become famous for over time. Shaysee was paying her dues as a field correspondent, hoping for the reward of a regular spot on the network from New York or Washington.

Her producer and the cameraman stood waiting for the cue from the network for a live shot for the network's early-morning news program back in the U.S. Behind the reporter, hundreds of people could be seen waiting in line as aid workers handed out packages and water bottles from large military trucks.

Finally, they heard the cue over the satellite link, and Shaysee nodded and looked at the camera, "Yes, Maria, we were caught off guard, like almost everyone else, when the Egyptian government closed off all air traffic into or out of Egypt due to this deadly influenza outbreak. We are told by sources that the action of the Egyptians to quarantine this entire country was not entirely voluntary on their part. Word is that several foreign governments had informed the Egyptians that flights from Egypt were not welcome to land, so the action by the Egyptians may have been a simple *fait accompli*.

"This was not our team's first exposure to the rigid quarantine rules imposed in Egypt. Several days ago, while trying to report at the location of the original outbreak in the farming lands to the north of Cairo, we found ourselves caught up in the original roadblocks that the Egyptian Army set up to try and contain the outbreak locally. I believe you have our video of that scene in Minufiya district."

Shaysee waited a few seconds to let the control room back in New York roll the earlier video and took the opportunity to flip her notecard, then she continued, "Of course, as we all know now, that initial attempt to stop the outbreak was unsuccessful, and influenza has spread virtually nationwide within Egypt. Scientists in Egypt and elsewhere are in agreement that the influenza strain is the infamous avian flu labeled H5N1 that has been spreading through poultry flocks around the world in recent years. Unfortunately, it has now mutated genetically. Whereas before it was only a disease of poultry and birds, wild and domestic, and humans only got this flu infection directly from the sick birds, the virus has now developed the ability to pass from one human to another, hence this epidemic.

"And now, there is confirmation that similar outbreaks among the human populations of Turkey and Bulgaria are taking hold, although they seem to be better controlled than the massive epidemic that has hit the nation of Egypt. It's unclear whether the outbreak in those countries was a result of a spread of the infection from Egypt or a new occurrence in those countries. Both Turkey and Bulgaria have reported the animal version of the H5N1 avian flu in the past.

"Egyptian authorities have been reluctant to announce an estimate of the number of sick nor the number of dead from this influenza epidemic. But, from our visits to the smaller cities and agricultural areas north of Cairo, we are sure the number of sick must be in the tens of thousands, if not hundreds of thousands. In the city of Banha, a short distance north of Cairo, we saw funeral pyres with hundreds of bodies being cremated. Yes, cremated, and in a Muslim country which follows the Islamic law forbidding the cremation of the dead. To help control the spread of the disease and deal with the great number of dead, the Grand Mufti, the highest Islamic official in Egypt, has directed that Muslims should cremate the dead from this epidemic despite the ancient religious law to the contrary. Such is the state of emergency in Egypt, where the epidemic has spread to the capital city, Cairo, with a population of ten million, one of the largest cities on Earth.

"Now, all anyone can do is wait and see if this influenza outbreak will abate, as the flu often does in late spring and summer. In normal years, flu season ends in spring, and everyone is praying for that to happen this time, as world authorities are racing to prepare sufficient vaccine to counter this specific type of flu strain. The formulation and production of a flu vaccine normally takes from six months up to a year. If this avian flu outbreak ends with the normal flu season, there is some hope of being prepared when it returns in the late summer and fall.

"This is Shaysee O'Neil reporting from a government medical aid station near Cairo, Egypt. Now, back to you in New York."

———

Chapter 21

Topanga-Victory Urgent Care Center
Los Angeles, California
8:30 PM PDT March 28th

Dr. Teresa Rohrbach shook her head at the metal rack that, in years past, held the medical record folders for the incoming patients and now just had an info slip to give her the account numbers to look up the records on her ubiquitous iPad tablet. She had just gotten rid of one of these damnable flu walk-ins, and two more were waiting for her at the counter. She assumed they were flu walk-ins; she had been seeing flu cases all evening; actually, they had been most of her patients for a couple of weeks. She signed off her initials and a brief synopsis on the slip from the last patient and handed it to Cyndi.

Cyndi, the LPN receptionist, reached for one of the new slips and handed it to Dr. Rohrbach, "See these folks first, Exam B, two sick kids, boy and girl, and their single dad, all with fever and the usual complaints. The boy's fever is almost 103."

"Jeez." Dr. Rohrbach wiggled the slip at Cyndi. "They all ready? Blood work and nasal swab done yet?"

"Yep. The test kit indicated Type A flu."

Dr. Rohrbach picked her iPad up from the counter and started to turn to the examination room, when she stopped and raised her eyebrows at her nurse/receptionist, "Cyndi, stop touching your face and pull your mask back up. You don't want to get this shit."

Cyndi nodded guiltily. Dr. Rohrbach waited a moment, thinking, and then pulled a sanitizing wipe from the plastic container on Cyndi's counter and wiped down her iPad.

As she turned to the exam room, Dr. Rohrbach added, "And get me two more blister packs of Tamiflu from storage, I'm almost out."

The examination results of the two children and their father were quite familiar to Teresa Rohrbach. High temperature, flushed face, nasal drainage, lung congestion, and complaints of body aches. The little girl was the worst, even though her brother had a higher fever. As Teresa touched the girl's chin to use the tongue depressor to look at her throat, she could feel the heat from the girl's skin through her nitrile glove.

Teresa looked the father in the eyes and said, "Both children are very sick. You need to keep checking whether they are having trouble breathing. If you find that they, or you, are having difficulty breathing or if they complain about pain in their chest, you need to get them to the Emergency Room."

"So, what have we got? Is it coronavirus or this 'New Flu? That's what they are calling this new stuff, right?" the father asked.

"Well, Mr. Petrie, you've all got the flu. The test kit we have here at this office can tell that you have Type A influenza. So, it could be the 'New Flu' strain, which is Type A. We'll get answers on the exact strain in a couple of days. All three of you had this year's flu shot, which should have covered you for the regular flu strains. But, it really does not matter. We need to respond the same, whether it's the new strain or the regular seasonal flu."

The man shook his head as he took his little daughter in his arms, "It's springtime. Isn't the flu season supposed to be a winter thing? Why've we all got this now? Even the coronavirus slowed a bit in the spring and summer."

"Yes, flu season usually maxes out in California in late February or early March. And, the limited time we have had to look at the novel coronavirus indicates the same, but not quite as much. But, you can have upper respiratory cases year-around. You've obviously heard this called the New Flu. The health department says this strain just started a few weeks ago out in Agoura Hills. We're just getting a late-season spurt from that."

"Is this the same stuff we see in all of them news reports from Egypt and Europe?"

"From the information they have sent us, this Agoura or New Flu may be slightly different from the Egyptian strain. At least we don't have people dying by the thousands as they do. Yet. This may not be exactly the same strain, so to not scare everyone, they are calling it New Flu. But, we are really getting a lot of people in, getting pretty close to epidemic for us. Your family is not alone; this is going through San Fernando Valley schools like wildfire."

"Yeah, when I picked them up from after-school care, they had a note from their school that they shouldn't come back to school until they are better. I'm not sure what I will do with them."

"Well, for now, you all need to stay home. You can't work either. Health Department has issued a home quarantining order for everybody with this flu. Stay home."

The man shook his head, "Yeah, I hear you, but if I don't work, the bills don't get paid."

Dr. Rohrbach had no good answer to that, so she said, "I'll be back in a minute with some Tamiflu for all of you. It's an antiviral treatment that may help fight the flu and make things a bit better for all of you. I'll be right back."

The young boy sneezed loudly. He put his face into his sleeve like they had been taught in school. The doctor handed him a tissue and left to get the Tamiflu.

———

Message/Email
Centers for Disease Control
March 28ᵗʰ

From: nancy.cox@epi.CDC.gov
To: philip.reynes@CDC.gov
        marta.le_salles@CDC.gov
        flu_updates@CDC.gov
        infogroup4@HHS.gov
        medrespgrp@us.army.mil
        wholiaison@dc.CDC.gov
        infogrp1419@DHS.gov
Subj: Initial H7N9 Avian Flu Outbreak Analysis and Projections
UNCLASSIFIED - NOT FOR PUBLIC RELEASE
Forward within USG as needed

1. This email will provide a general synopsis of the recent Avian
    Influenza H7N9 strains which resulted in human infection;
    A/21/836/003/ PARIS(H7N9), A/21/117/311/ BAODI(H7N9)
    and A/21/406/312/ BAODI(H7N9) compared with a detailed
    genetic analysis with earlier extant zoonotic H7N9 strains,
    to wit, A/Env/9306/2010/BANGLADESH(H7N9) and
    A/1999/436/910/HONGKONG(H7N9). At present, these H7N9
    infections are assumed to be zoonotic only with no documented
    human-to-human transmission, as per both the Chinese and
    French government reports.

2. First, it is necessary to explain the sources of the new strains.
    a. A/21/836/003/PARIS(H7N9) was cultured from a human
        infectee in Paris, France (female age 43), who had recently
        returned from a trip to China, including a visit to a city
        near Baodi, China and who had direct animal contact in live
        markets.
    b. A/21/117/311/BAODI(H7N9) was derived from five
        cultures from the initial human infectees (male and female
        ages 19 to 74) and two wild poultry isolates of a reported
        zoonotic infection of poultry industry workers in Baodi
        with direct poultry contact. It is unclear why there were wild
        poultry samples, but not culled commercial flock samples,
        even though the human infectees worked with commercial
        flocks.
    c. A/21/406/312/BAODI(H7N9) was identified in several
        subsequent human cultures (source info unknown) and

culled domestic poultry samples from the Baodi region.

d.   Source of the Paris culture was the French national health department (Sante Publique France). Source of both Baodi cultures was the Chinese Ministry of Health, Beijing. Reference historical cultures were from CDC cataloged strains.

3.   It was determined that the PARIS strain and the 311/BAODI strain were precise matches in all genetic markers. The conclusion was made that the French patient was infected by the same source as the initial Chinese factory workers. The PARIS strain and the 311/BAODI strain were significantly different genetically from the historic H7N9 samples from Bangladesh in 2010 and the earliest available sample of H7N9 from Hong Kong in 1999. The identical PARIS and 311/BAODI strains of H7N9 had significant human amino acid content not present in the reference historic cultures, indicating a significant antigenic shift of both multiple key factors from probable existing human-derived Type A strains such as H1N1, or H3N2. (See below for a discussion of H5N1) Future study is underway on this point, as well as whether the significant antigenic shift present in the two samples justifies a new strain subtype classification.

4.   It was determined that the latter culture provided by the Chinese, 312/BAODI, was different in many key aspects from the PARIS and 311/BAODI strains. It had little of the human amino acid content found in the other two strains. On the contrary, the 311/BAODI strain culture appeared to be virtually identical to the historic Hong Kong 1999 strain. The normal antigenic drift that could be expected from an Influenza Type A strain in either a wild or domestic animal environment over nearly twenty years was not present. For these and other reasons beyond the scope of this report, our office at CDC must question the sourcing and handling of the 312/BAODI strain cultures. The 312/BAODI culture appears to be anomalous to the main, earlier 311/BAODI infection strain. Chinese officials should be requested to confirm details of the 312/BAODI strain culture.

5.   A very preliminary analysis of the patterns of antigenic shift found in the PARIS and 311/BAODI indicates similarities with HA and NA factors evidenced in the antigenic shift present in the current Egyptian H5N1 strain (A/CHICKEN/ MINUFIYA/ EGYPT/ AB-K8/(H5N1)) which has achieved non-zoonotic transmission.

Analysis and comparison of these two strains' (H7N9 versus H5N1) antigenic shift should be made the highest priority by all capable laboratories.

6. CONCLUSIONS:

    A. The PARIS and 311/BAODI strains are nearly identical and present significant evidence of an antigenic shift, indicating a likely admixture of human-sourced Influenza Type A strains. These factors present a greater likelihood of potential non-zoonotic transmission than was present in earlier H7N9 strains.

    B. The 312/BAODI strain should be considered anomalous until further study and clarification are done.

    C. Genetic factors and proteins in the PARIS and 311/BAODI strains of Influenza Type A H7N9 are indicative of similar factors in Avian Influenza strains that have achieved human-to-human transmission.

Respectfully,
Nancy Cox
Branch Chief
Virology, Surveillance, and Diagnosis Branch
National Center for Immunization and Respiratory Diseases
Centers for Disease Control

———

Beijing-Harbin Expressway G-1
Northwest Border of Tianjin Province
Near Baodi, China
9:30 AM Local Time March 29th

Xi Zemin's rank of Inspector 2nd Class made him the senior police officer assigned to the roadblock on the main highway from Baodi to Beijing. He had been briefed with all of the other senior people at police headquarters early this morning. The briefing had been given by Superintendent Tong, the same provincial police commander that had taken Xi off of the influenza death cases. It seemed things had changed somewhat in the week since.

Superintendent Tong had given very little real information on the apparent crisis. Everyone attending the briefing remembered stories of similar events with the coronavirus infestation in Hubei province. It seemed this new flu was being dealt with in the same way in Tianjin province. The major difference being that Hubei was deep in central China, whereas Tianjin was virtually a suburb of Beijing. From Inspector Xi's current location on the far western border of Tianjin province, you could see the airliners coming in, descending, and heading to the northwest to the main Beijing airport.

Tong's instructions had been clear. Xi and his men, as well as the dozens of other teams, were to let nobody out of the Baodi District, and no vehicles could come in without explicit documents issued by the Chinese Health Ministry. Xi had passed on to these men and women he was directing at the roadblock that they were to give no answers to anyone asking why the road was blocked. He suspected that the face masks on all the policemen would give some indication of the purpose.

Their post was actually across the river, just outside Tianjin Province's boundary. There was an interchange there on the Expressway that allowed the police to turn vehicles off the exit and back on the Expressway heading back west. They had been told a sign was being set up farther west directing all traffic south or north on the S-271 highway, but it obviously had not been done, as they were turning around dozens of trucks and cars headed from the capital city to Harbin and other points east.

Xi Zemin had overseen the placement of a couple of large semi-trucks at an angle across both lanes of the Expressway right at the detour exit ramp. He watched the policemen telling the drivers they had to exit and turn around. It frequently devolved into a shouting match, but so far, there had been no trouble. Xi was technically in charge of the other roadblock to the east on the Expressway, blocking anybody trying to leave Baodi. That was much easier to deal with. Still well inside the boundary of the province, the roadblock simply closed off the entire highway, forcing anyone off the road. So, Xi and his men at the river only had to pay real attention to those heading east.

From his viewing position on the expressway bridge, Xi Zemin could see the patrol boats at regular intervals traveling up and down the Chaobaixin River. They were making sure nobody tried to break the quarantine of Baodi by crossing the river. Xi wondered how far south of Baodi the quarantine extended. *Was this just Baodi, or did it include southern Tianjin province, too?* Even the senior police officials at the briefing had not been told such things. Superintendent Tong had made clear that certain information was to be kept secret. Kept secret, like the deaths Xi Zemin had discovered who had never been in contact with infectious animals. It seemed to Xi that he had been right after all.

—

Karen Llewellyn ate her breakfast at the restaurant next door to her motel. It would be her last day on the road. She used her laptop to confirm the hotel reservations for this evening in Thousand Oaks, California, her destination. There was also a message saying her household goods had been routed from Atlanta to California and would be delivered on time. She had to find a place to rent before the delivery.

The drive across the country had been a strange mix of feelings. She was heading for her first assignment in her professional life in which she would not be working for CDC. Her two stops en-route had been at Army installations, first, Fort Detrick, and then the side trip to see how the government-owned contractor-operated manufacturing facility worked at Radford Army Ammunition Plant in Virginia. Both stops had been informative but had left her with major questions about what to expect in her new job in California. With that, and in general, Karen had an uneasiness about the future.

Karen Llewellyn had question marks everywhere she turned. Her new job. A new place to live needed to be found in a town she had never seen. The world situation, which she had such a store of knowledge about, but few current details. The implied disbelief and distrust the CDC had for the information the Chinese were sending out on the Baodi flu strain. The awkward situation of having her estranged husband moving back into the home they had once kept together. For the first time in many years, Karen had an unclear view of where she was in the world. Or was it she had doubts about the world she was in? She remembered the chaos the world had descended into when the coronavirus pandemic hit. She had a gut instinct that might happen again.

Some moron at the CDC information technology office had deleted Karen's email account when he got word she was leaving CDC-Atlanta, and her network connection would be canceled. She had discovered that goof the first night after she left Fort Detrick. A call to Phil Reynes had gotten her reconnected with the CDC information network and the email updates on the world influenza outbreak. And now, after Fort Detrick, Karen also had an Army email address. She now had both of them on her laptop and cell phone, along with her private email that was rarely used these days.

Karen had watched the cable news as she got ready this morning in the motel. The situation in Egypt, southeast Europe, and several other spots regarding the apparent H5N1 epidemic was bad. She saw on her Google Maps app that the location of the reported H5N1 flu outbreak in Los Angeles was just off of Highway 101 that she would be traveling to get to Thousand Oaks.

Avian flu in Los Angeles? Unbelievable.

Karen suspected that the world situation was the center of her personal emotional malaise and uneasiness. The world was speeding into the realm she had spent her entire life getting ready for, and here she was, somewhat on the sidelines, driving her Audi towards suburban California and an uncertain future. She needed to get more information on this Los Angeles outbreak. If it really was the same strain as Egypt, it could be bad.

—

Chapter 22

Jarfooz Street
Cairo, Egypt
4:48 PM Local Time April 1^{*st*}

Miriam Mansoor walked the three blocks from the U.S. Navy Medical Research Unit to the staff quarters building where the Americans had provided her with an apartment. It was an excellent place to live, much better than anything she could have expected back home. Miriam had a roommate in the apartment, but her roommate had stayed late at work tonight. So, Miriam walked alone.

Her work for the U.S. Navy, fortuitously, provided several benefits that were exceptional for a young Egyptian nurse. They issued her a cellphone so that they could reach her day and night. And, as a civilian employee for a U.S. military unit in a foreign country, the Navy let her buy things at the small U.S. Navy Exchange store in the NAMRU building. In a country bludgeoned by the epidemic and the follow-on quarantine, NAMRU employees' access to American consumer goods in short supply in Cairo was a blessing. Miriam's generous salary from NAMRU even made those goods affordable.

She was finishing her usual workday at the Research Unit and the neighboring hospital logging and cataloging blood sample results to help to get a mapping of how the influenza strain may have mutated as it passed through the Egyptian populace. Miriam, of course, had known nothing about such things before she was discharged and went to work at the Research Unit, but she had caught on quickly when the statistician showed her what to do. It was not the patient care work she had thought she would be doing as a nurse at the Research Unit, but it was interesting.

Now, walking in the afternoon sun in Cairo, Miriam could smell smoke in the air. It was a horrible stench, probably made worse as she knew what was burning. It came across the city with the prevailing spring wind from the west. The hot wind off the great western desert brought the foul smoke from the fires across the Nile. Miriam tried not to think about what was being burned in the flames, although everyone in Cairo, everyone in Egypt, knew what was in the huge pyres.

Why didn't they burn the bodies downwind from the city?

Miriam hurried to cross the street while traffic was light. She had learned that you could not count on Cairo drivers obeying pedestrian crossing rules. On the other corner of the intersection, she turned to walk the last block to her apartment. Ahead of her, she saw several people come out of one of the many apartment houses in the area. Two men carried a cloth-wrapped bundle out of the building.

As she walked closer, Miriam saw the men carefully lay the bundle at the edge of the street. One of the men bent on one knee and gently touched one end of the bundle. He closed his eyes and mouthed some words. The other man bowed his head. As she approached, Miriam heard several women crying in grief at the entranceway of the building. The men stepped away from the bundle as Miriam passed.

Miriam looked at the bundle with wide eyes. It was not large, the size of a child. The bundle was wrapped in what looked like a cartoon character printed bed sheet and tied with strips of cloth. The bundle was shaped like a child, too.

These people were laying a child's body, an influenza victim, out on the street, following the instructions given to have bodies picked up by the coroners' vans on their rounds of the city streets. Miriam had heard the instructions on the television, and people had discussed such things at the hospital. Death had become so common in Cairo that people were relegated to disposing of loved ones as one usually does the household trash.

Miriam had seen the dead at work, both at the nursing college in Minuf and here at the hospital. She had a vague memory of Leyla's body being moved out of the intensive care room she had shared with her. However, this was the first dead body she had seen out in the city. This must have been what it had been like the month before back home in Minuf. Or, maybe worse. She had missed all that when she was transported to Cairo with Leyla in the first days of the epidemic.

Miriam gave a respectful nod to the people standing near the little body and then averted her eyes. She had sent a letter home to Minuf to try and reach her family, but no response had come yet. Miriam knew from her cataloging work how bad the flu had been in Minuf and the area around her home. The little body reminded her of her two younger siblings, of whom she knew nothing. *May Allah bless them.*

———

Defense Pharmaceutical Plant
Thousand Oaks, California
7:56 AM PDT April 1ˢᵗ

Karen Llewellyn had already driven by the headquarters building of the defense pharmaceutical plant she would be assuming command of today during her drive around Thousand Oaks and the surrounding area the prior afternoon. So, she knew exactly where to go this morning, her first day on the job.

One thing that differentiated the huge building from the dozens of other commercial buildings in this commercial enclave in the northwestern part of suburban Thousand Oaks was the eight-foot chain-link fence with strands of barbed wire on the top. Compared to the usual look of a high-tech corporate building, this building gave off a slightly different aura of security. Karen had read the information packet she had received in Maryland and knew this building was a re-purposed industrial plant and warehouse that the government had acquired to house the management, scientific, and testing functions of the vaccine plant. The actual industrial manufacturing lines were in a cluster of buildings farther west in Camarillo, closer to the several high-tech greenhouses where the genetically modified plants that produced the virus-like particles that powered the vaccine were grown in the agricultural region between Camarillo and Oxnard. Karen's new fiefdom consisted of those three facilities, managed for the Army by HeptImun Corporation, with Captain Karen Llewellyn denominated as the commanding officer.

The large parking lot in front of the pharmaceutical plant building was nearly full, with a few cars still arriving. Several people were walking from the parking lot toward the guard shack at the front gate through the high fence. Having already been here on Sunday afternoon, Karen knew there was a parking spot to the left of the gate and guard shack marked with a sign "Reserved Parking – Plant Commander." Karen parked her silver Audi Q5 in that spot. She saw a Chevrolet Suburban with federal government license plates in the spot next to hers, that spot was marked 'Official Vehicle.' She grabbed her purse and cellphone from the passenger seat and got out to get her dress blue uniform jacket from the hanger in the back seat.

As she was unhooking the coat hanger from the hook above the car door, a guard from the gate walked toward her. He said in a loud voice, "That's reserved parking for the Plant Commander."

Karen finished taking her uniform jacket off the hanger and told the guard, "Yes, I see. Thank you for pointing that out." Karen had decided to wear her service dress blue uniform on this first day on the job, so without her jacket on, she was in a white blouse and small black crossover tie under her collar. The guard probably could not see her small shoulder rank epaulets on the blouse, as she was standing behind the Audi SUV. She clicked her keyfob to open the back hatch on the Audi.

Karen walked to the open hatch to get her things she was taking to her new office and slipped into the service dress jacket. She saw the guard now walk closer and come around the vehicle as he spoke, "You can't park here!"

When he came around the SUV and finally saw Karen buttoning the dark blue uniform jacket with its four gold stripes on each sleeve, with her service ribbons, professional badges, and new silver PHS Officer in Charge insignia, the guard stopped short and blinked at her. It was an impressive uniform. As she reached into the car and put her white service hat with its decorative gold braid, Karen smiled at the now-silent guard and said, "Good morning, beautiful California day for my first day on the job."

"Uh, yes Ma'am. Welcome to Thousand Oaks," the guard answered, a bit sheepishly. And, when he saw her lifting a large box out of the Audi, he added, "Can I help you with that?"

Karen smiled again and said, "I wouldn't want to take you from your post."

"That's OK, Ma'am. We have two people at the gate for the busy shift change times."

Karen handed a closed banker's box of her personal things for the office to the guard. She grabbed her briefcase, purse, and cellphone and clicked the power liftgate closed. "I appreciate your help with these things. Please, show me the way to the commander's office."

———

Los Angeles County Sheriff's Station
Lost Hills/Calabasas, California
9:30 AM PDT April 1ˢᵗ

"What are you doing here?" was the first thing Matt Relford heard as he stepped into the Operations area at the Sheriff's station. Sergeant Rick Gonçalvez stood up as he spoke. "You're supposed to be on thirty days leave, not here in uniform."

Matt Relford leaned on the front counter and said, "I got up this morning. I tried to make myself some coffee and realized I couldn't take it at my apartment. Everything so quiet. Just me . . ."

Rick blinked at Matt, trying to understand what he was talking about. His expression changed as he figured it out. "Oh, God, Matt, Yeah. I didn't think about that. About Marjorie. How is all that?"

"Kind of weird. The hospital sent her body back home to Phoenix, and they had a funeral before I got cleared out of the hospital. You know, she got hit so fast with the flu, even though she was already in the hospital on quarantine. I talked to her folks by phone, which was *mucho* awkward. I think they kind of blame me for getting her sick. I did pass the flu to her, and the hospital put her in quarantine when she drove me to the hospital."

Rick nodded and seemed to try and think of what to say next, "Yeah, I know all about quarantine. They kept me for seven days. But this is spreading fast. I didn't get it, and my wife is OK, but my daughter got it, probably from school. She's good, though. She was able to stay at home when she was sick. I guess several people in the quarantine group got the flu and Marjorie and that one gal from County Health died."

"Well, plus O'Meara, the deputy from Court Services. And three of the tenants."

Rick Gonçalvez was at the coffee pot and motioned to ask if Matt wanted a cup. Matt declined the coffee. Rick said, "That was only the start. Those three who left the trailer and that Arab dude who owns the restaurant where they worked all gave it to a bunch of people, and you probably saw the news, this New Flu, as they are calling it's spreading all over the western San Fernando Valley and Agoura Hills area. A waitress in Malibu spread it around down there. And the young guy from the trailer, the one who left early, worked at the multiplex cinema at Universal City, and they've had another bunch there. All of those are now spreading. They sent an email out from County Health last week, and it was on TV, too, that it got out of hand so fast they couldn't even try to contain it like they tried with coronavirus at first. So, they went right to extending Easter Break for some schools for three weeks . . . and all that, they call it mitigation. They're hoping it ends with warmer weather like the regular seasonal flu."

"So, how is the station doing. How many out with this shit?" Matt asked.

"We were five short at role call this morning. But, the real problem is Dispatch, with all of them sitting in one closed room for hours. Day shift was down to three yesterday, and second shift only had two last night, neither of them qualified for supervisor. We called two retired deputies in to help. We had to call downtown to get more staffing today. And nobody wanted to volunteer to come out here. They're afraid of this flu. I guess it isn't so bad downtown and out away from here, yet."

"Well. If you're short of people . . . I'm here. Tell me where you need me."

"Let me go talk to Merriman. It's his call to cancel your workers' comp leave and put you back on shift."

———

Thousand Oaks Defense Pharmaceutical Plant (TODPP)
Thousand Oaks, California
1:30 PM PDT April 1ˢᵗ

Karen had been introduced to everyone around the table as she had been escorted around the executive offices after her arrival that morning. Now all six of her senior staff sat around the oak table in the conference room that was situated between her office and the plant manager's office.

The plant manger was a HeptImun corporate executive, George Marquardt. George was a square-jawed man in his thirties with a sparse Garibaldi beard. He had taken his tailored suit coat off and put it on a chair by the wall and was now in an equally well-tailored dress shirt and silk tie. He was leading this briefing and had clearly prepared his script in advance.

"Except for the new Cairo H5N1 strain, we have properly sequenced batches of the material needed to start up the sprouting and horticultural production for the other three strains of the approved quadrivalent formula for this year's production. We are using already processed material from the plants in Connecticut and North Carolina to train the new factory crews and get production started at our Camarillo facility. We have scheduled for Captain Llewellyn to tour the Camarillo production lines and the greenhouses tomorrow afternoon. We have . . ."

Karen cut George off with a question, "When will the Minufiya strain be added to the mix, and where is that sequencing happening?"

"All that is taking place back east. Atlanta has pretty much finished the sequencing, and they are comparing their results with North Carolina's findings. Once they finish, the animal and human trials will be done on an accelerated basis. We will not be involved until they have multiple batches of properly sequenced and tested material that we can start using to make the final piece of our quadrivalent product."

Karen followed up with, "So, even though we are capable of doing the sequencing and work on the virus, we are just waiting for the labs back east to do the grunt cellular biology work, and we wait to run the production?"

"That's right, ma'am. Even though our lab is capable of handling the virus sequencing work and starting a batch for a given strain, we won't actually be doing any of the live virus work or any RNA sequencing for the seed batches, for the time being. And we have no provision for any animal or human testing at our location. We will use the seed batch of RNA material from the eastern labs to start our horticulture meshing and production. Our lab capabilities here in Thousand Oaks, for now, will just be used for QA, uh, Quality Assurance, purposes. Sonya Hayburn, our chief scientist here at the plant, will be taking you through our laboratory facilities after we finish here. Sonya can answer your questions about our capabilities in more detail." George motioned to a young-looking, and well-groomed blonde sitting at the far end of the table. Sonya Hayburn did not appear to Karen to fit any mold for a "chief scientist,' but she decided a woman in Karen's position should not make rash presumptions about a young female scientist.

Karen frowned but nodded. Karen suspected this was just one of many frustrations she would encounter. Here she was, with her own primary expertise being the DNA/RNA sequencing of virus strains, and she had a fully capable Biosafety Level 3 laboratory under her command, but she was relegated to just overseeing the factory production of vaccines that some other scientist had created.

George Marquardt continued through his overview of the current overall status of the facility and then turned the floor over to Priscilla Wooster, another HeptImun manager, to cover personnel status. Priscilla was a slim 30-ish brunette with a mousy demeanor and appearance. Sonya and Priscilla were as unalike as two young women could be, but both seemed to have HeptImun's trust. Priscilla apparently realized her area of responsibility was innately boring, so she quickly reported on the number of HeptImun employees who had transferred from other locations, the number of new hires in California, training levels, and the plans going forward to get the plant fully staffed and functional on June 1st, the target date for full operations. She finished with, "As of yesterday, the flu outbreak over in Los Angeles County has just started to impact our workforce, but we are very concerned with that, and we will report any change in that status. That's just about it for the civilian, uh, corporate employees, and I'll turn it over to Mr. Tanner for the government side of things."

It had been explained to Karen, both in Maryland and at the GOCO munitions plant in Virginia, that her contracting officer would be her 'right-hand man.' Roscoe 'Ross' Tanner, Jr. had retired from active duty in the Army as a lieutenant colonel in the Quartermaster Corps. He had then gone into civilian work for the Army at the Radford Army Ammunition Plant. He had risen to the position of contracting officer there. Now, he had accepted the offer to move to California and switch from overseeing the contract with BAE Systems, the weapons manufacturing company running Radford. He would now be in charge of the federal government's contract with HeptImun to run the Defense Pharmaceutical Plant in Thousand Oaks (TODPP). As Contracting Officer, he would be Karen's government manager of the operation at the plant.

Unlike George, who had addressed Karen using her first name, Ross addressed her by rank and last name, at least in this meeting, "Captain Llewellyn, with the final execution of the main operations contract on March 1st, TODPP was the last of the three plants to go online and, thus, we were last in line for our military and civilian personnel needs to be filled. Our TO&E only has seven total military personnel, and we are authorized a civilian civil service staff of eight. Quite light compared to most military installations, but the unique nature of a GOCO plant makes up for that, and HeptImun fulfills many of the functional needs of this operation.

"We have all of our civil service team in place. Military-wise, we only have you, the plant commander, and the senior NCO, Master Sergeant Ronald

Ghent in place. Your XO has been designated by HRC and I've checked him out with his prior commanding officer, highly recommended. He is a captain on the major's promotion list who has finished his third assignment as a medical service corps officer at Walter Reed. He is a West Point grad with a Chemical Engineering degree. He had a short TDY at Fort Detrick to get acclimatized to his new duties, including epidemiology and pharmaceuticals. He is on orders with thirty days leave en route, and he left Maryland on March 15th so that he could be here any day. The other four enlisted personnel have been slotted by HRC, and their orders have been cut for their arrival in the next month. They include a driver, a medical technician, a mechanic, and a mid-level NCO. The driver, mechanic, and technician are ostensibly assigned to carry out whatever duties you assign, but their organizational purpose is to be core staff to maintain and, if necessary, assist any temporarily assigned personnel to operate the USAMRIID vehicles and equipment."

Karen squinted at Ross and asked, "The USAMRIID equipment?"

Ross smiled, "Yes, Captain. As an add-on to the overall government contract for this plant's operation, General Harding's people convinced the Defense Contract Management Agency staff who masterminded the contract with the three GOCO contractors to include in the contract a provision for equipment to support the field deployment of a USAMRIID response team in case of a national medical emergency. That government commission after coronavirus named this as a need after seeing the weaknesses of the federal response to the coronavirus pandemic. In our case, the equipment is staged here, on the West Coast, and under your command. But in a national emergency, your boss, General Harding, can send a medical response team from USAMRIID to take the equipment and use it for an epidemic or other needs. In the back parking lot here, you have what looks like a mighty cool RV, but which is really a fully equipped field lab that can handle virtually any laboratory or diagnostic function of a regular research lab. Quite a toy General Harding bought for you. And it comes with a small bus for response personnel, a couple of supply trucks and several conventional SUV vehicles, one of which, the Suburban, we have parked next to your personal parking spot for your official travel. As part of their contract, HeptImun provides supplies and maintenance for that little side function of this plant. I forget exactly how many Army Reserve personnel the intended response team is, but HeptImun has a supply room here with personal protective clothing, supplies, medicine, bubble tents, and everything else the team USAMRIID deploys might need."

Karen raised her eyebrows and said, "Wow, I had not seen that in the briefing materials."

Ross smiled again, "That's probably on purpose. It's in the overall contract, but the Army side did not think it necessary to emphasize to your old friends at HHS and CDC that the Army had squeezed some extra military equipment out of the vaccine contract that Congress approved. And HeptImun is happy since they get paid their contract overhead percentage for all supplies and equipment provided to the government."

"A-ha." Karen nodded.

The HeptImun managers straightened their stacks of papers and did not comment.

"Does anybody have anything else right now?" Karen asked.

Everyone shook their heads.

Karen took a piece of paper out of the leather portfolio in front of her, saying, "Well, I will probably have quite a few questions as I learn more and more about this place and our operations. But, right now, I've one thing I need to bring up. And, I'm not sure if this is for Ross or if it's HeptImun's to take care of here. I'm assuming it's HeptImun."

Karen held the paper in her hand, and said, "As I mentioned to a couple of you, on my way out here, my boss, General Harding, told me to go to the Radford Army Ammunition Plant in Virginia, a GOCO plant, to see what a well-run government-owned/contractor-operated facility was like. Ross used to be the contracting officer there. My arrival at Radford was slightly different from my arrival here this morning. And, I think we need to work on what I noticed before we have our official visits from General Harding and Stephen Royce, the Health and Human Services Assistant Secretary for Planning and Emergency Preparedness, later this month. I might add that Assistant Secretary Royce is a retired Air Force colonel. Both of them will certainly notice the disparity I noticed on my arrival out front here this morning."

Karen handed the paper she held to Ross, who looked at the paper, smiled, and nodded. Karen continued to speak as Ross slid the paper across the big table to George Marquardt, "This is a print I made off the internet of a picture of the sign at the entrance to Radford Army Ammunition Plant. Compare it to the sign you have in place out front here in Thousand Oaks.

"Here in Thousands Oaks, you have a beautiful three-dimensional HeptImun corporate logo, followed by what is apparently the HeptImun corporate slogan and way down at the bottom of the sign you finally see fit to mention in much smaller letters that this is a 'Defense Pharmaceutical Plant.' However, at Radford, as well as all other GOCO plants I found on the Internet this morning, there is a bold declaration of the full name of the military facility followed by the logo of the U.S. Army, the Joint Munitions Command Logo, the military unit logo and other Army team insignias. Nowhere on the sign do you see any indication of the existence of BAE Systems, the huge multinational armament corporation that contracts to fill the 'contractor-operated' part of the Radford GOCO operation.

"I can assure you that General Harding and Colonel Royce will notice that the actual owner of this facility, the U.S. government and specifically, the U.S. Army, are not even mentioned on the front gate sign here. I'm assuming the same is true at the Camarillo factory facility and the horticultural operations buildings out west in Ventura County.

'Understanding that part of the problem is that this military unit is new and just got its commanding officer this morning, I've told Master Sergeant Ghent to get together with the U.S. Army Institute of Heraldry and come up with, posthaste, a unit logo for the Thousand Oaks Defense Pharmaceutical Plant. I will leave it to HeptImun to research the governmental and military logos that need to be in place for a proper sign out front of these military facilities. Work with Ross and the Master Sergeant on that. I don't see any problem with incorporating your lovely HeptImun trademark also. The Public Health Service logo might not be a bad idea, all considered. However, I would strongly suggest you have appropriate signs in place before the Commanding General of the U.S. Army Medical Research and Development Command and the Assistant Secretary of the U.S. Department of Health and Human Services visit their plant at the end of the month."

Karen looked around the room and then directly at Marquardt with her eyebrows raised ever so slightly. "Any questions?"

There were no questions. Karen realized she had probably come off as a bit on the officious side, but it seemed to her that she ought to make sure everyone knew what the pecking order was at the new vaccine plant.

———

Chapter 23

Bilbeis Air Force Base
Northeast of Cairo, Egypt
3:15 PM Local Time April 2ⁿᵈ

Viewers of the cable television news report relayed by the network in New York for the morning show saw a much different Shaysee O'Neil than they were used to from her earlier reporting. Gone was the pretense of her wearing a Muslim head covering, and what viewers saw was a rather gaunt-looking young woman with her hair tied back and sweat visible on her make-up free face. She was squinting in the bright afternoon sun. She also wore what seemed to be a simple white cotton blouse, quite wrinkled. Behind her, the viewers could see a crowd of people standing together in the sun with a large airliner rolling to a stop behind them.

After a slight delay in which Shaysee touched an earbud to listen to the network anchor's introduction, Shaysee said, "Yes, good morning, Maria, although it's mid-afternoon here. I'm reporting from an Egyptian Air Force base that's co-located with the Egyptian Air Force Academy. The crowd of Americans, Canadians, and other foreigners standing behind me are, like us, waiting to board a chartered flight sent by the U.S. Government to evacuate Americans and others from the Egyptian capital. We were brought here in buses from downtown Cairo this morning, apparently because, with the immense impact of influenza here in Egypt, the regular international airport in Cairo was shut down due to a lack of personnel to operate and, of course, the international blockade of most flights from Egypt. Instead, we are here at the more remote military base that's still operating.

"It's with great sadness that I report this afternoon without one key member of our team. Andre Foucault, our producer, lost his battle with this avian flu yesterday. In what was a surprisingly quick onset, he succumbed to what I'm told was pneumonia brought on by the flu. With hospitals already totally beyond capacity, even with the assistance of the United States and French embassies, we were only able to get treatment for Andre through the hotel doctor where we were staying. That medical care was not enough to save Andre Foucault, who died as the tens of thousands of other people in this country have.

"My cameraman, Mitch Dorsey, and I were not able to go into the hotel conference area where the hotel guests who were stricken with the flu were sequestered, but the hotel staff told us that Andre died last evening. Andre worked for our network for over ten years, coming to us after a long career at

France TV 2, where his reporting from the news hotspots around the world was legendary. Andre leaves his wife, Genevieve, and two teenage children behind. We will miss Andre dearly."

Shaysee paused a moment, closed her eyes, and then stared into the camera to finish, "These last weeks in Egypt have been unimaginable for me. With Andre's death, I'm brought personally to the grief that I've seen ten thousand times over in the faces of the Egyptian people facing this avian influenza epidemic and its deathly nightmare. Knowing I get to escape from this place on the aircraft you see behind me is reassuring, but I leave with the knowledge that what I've seen in the crowded hospitals and funeral pyres here in Egypt may only be starting for the rest of the world. May God bless us all. This is Shaysee O'Neil sending you my final report from Cairo, Egypt."

—

Beijing-Harbin Expressway G-1
Northwest Border of Tianjin Province
Near Baodi, China
7:30 AM Local Time April 2nd

Inspector 2nd Class Xi Zemin was back at his post for another 12-hour shift. The buses bringing his crew in from Baodi were now picking up the crew that had manned the roadblock overnight. Xi had just finished getting the status report from his nightshift counterpart. Nothing had changed overnight. He reported to the commissioner's office with his handheld radio that his team was in place for the day.

Hearing a distant rumble to the west, Xi looked up the highway, expecting to see another big transport truck that they would need to turn around. Instead, he saw a convoy of green Army vehicles heading toward him.

Dozens of huge JieFang army trucks were led by several smaller MengShi tactical vehicles. Xi walked with his senior sergeant toward the far side of the semi-truck they had blocking the highway. They waited for the Army convoy to approach them.

The sergeant asked Xi, "Do we turn the Army around too? Do we have that authority?"

Xi looked at the sergeant and shrugged, "I kind of doubt that, but . . ."

A hundred yards before the lead vehicle reached them, a figure appeared in the top hatchway of the infantry vehicle, waving a red signal flag toward the following vehicles. The convoy slowed to a stop.

When the lead vehicle stopped, a tall figure in the green field uniform of the People's Liberation Army exited the vehicle. Two more men in full battle gear and carrying assault rifles hopped out of the second vehicle and ran forward to escort the first figure.

As the man approached, Xi saw the star and wreath on the shoulder epaulet, indicating this man was a *Shao Jiang,* a general officer that Xi knew, from his own days in the Army, usually commanded an Army division. Both Xi Zemin and his sergeant quickly saluted the senior officer.

Xi loudly announced, "Sir! I'm Inspector Xi. How can we help you?"

The general returned the salute and said, "Inspector, I'm the deputy commander of the Beijing Military Region. I've been ordered to take over the security situation in your province. You're hereby relieved of your duties here and ordered to return to your headquarters."

Xi Asked, "The Army is taking over the roadblock?"

The general smiled and shook his head, "The roadblock established by your provincial leadership is ill-advised. You cannot just block a major roadway leading to our capital city. The backup and chaos your leaders have caused cannot be allowed. I've been sent to have the Army secure the corridor alongside the G-1 Expressway while allowing transport along the roadway. Baodi will remain in isolation for the time being, but Beijing will not be cut off from the East."

Xi and the sergeant looked at each other.

The general continued, "Please have your men remove these vehicles and the detour signs. Report to your superiors that you have been relieved of duties here by order of the Ministry of Defense. The Military District Commander is speaking to your provincial Ministry of Public Security officials as we speak."

"Sir, let me call in and get instructions," Xi said.

"No, inspector, you have been given your orders. Clear the roadblocks and order your men to stand down immediately." The general did not wait for anything further from Xi. He turned and headed toward the men now standing around his vehicle.

Xi turned to the sergeant and shrugged again. Then, Xi pointed to the semi-truck, "Get everything moved to the side of the road. I'll tell Baodi what has happened."

Xi Zemin thumbed the button on his radio and walked to the side of the road where his sedan was parked. As soon as the sergeant had cleared the truck from the road, the Army convoy headed past. Six of the JieFang trucks pulled to the side of the road near Xi's vehicle, and several dozen armed soldiers fanned out on both sides of the freeway and bridge over the river.

Xi reported the situation to the commissioner's office and waited for the buses from Baodi to return and pick up his men. The quarantine of Baodi was now the responsibility of national leaders and the Army. Xi wished them well.

———

Thousand Oaks Defense Pharmaceutical Plant (TODPP)
Factory Production Facility
Camarillo, California
9:30 PDT April 2nd

Karen Llewellyn was being driven down the steep grade of the 101 freeway from Thousand Oaks to Camarillo, where the main manufacturing facility for the vaccine plant was located. She rode with George Marquardt, the HeptImun manager, and his production chief, Kerry Weathers. They rode in a large Mercedes passenger van with HeptImun logos on the doors. Instead of the service dress uniform she had worn the first day, today Karen was in the Public Health Service blue working uniform that Americans had first become familiar with in press briefings about the coronavirus in 2020.

George pointed out the window as they reached the built-up area of Camarillo at the bottom of the steep hill. "You mentioned you would be looking for someplace that's furnished to rent until you got settled in the local area. I'd recommend that you check out Camarillo. They've had lots of new home and townhouse construction here in recent years. It's a short drive up the freeway to Thousand Oaks, and there are lots of nice amenities in the area. I'm in escrow on a house in Spanish Hills, which is just west of Camarillo. I can put you in touch with my real estate agent. Her company does rentals, too."

Karen smiled, "That would be nice. I need to get moving on that. I got an email that my household goods are in LA waiting to be delivered."

"I have her card in my office. I'll get it to you when we get back."

The van exited the freeway at a sign indicating they were near the Camarillo Airport.

As they turned west on the south side of the airport, George Marquardt told Karen, "You will probably have several meet-and-greet events with local politicians and movers and shakers as we get up to speed here. You should know that there was a bit of unhappiness locally about the U.S. Government being able to ignore local planning and zoning, and strict California environmental laws, to put in our factory facility on what was zoned as prime agricultural land near the airport here. Then, the brouhaha got worse when they found out the U.S. Army would have title to the land and the plant. And the Army would not be paying any property tax as a regular business would. We still have a court case going on where the Ventura County Assessor is trying to tax HeptImun on our possessory interest in doing business on the property as the government contractor."

"I did hear a bit about that from the contracting office at Fort Detrick," Karen said.

"Yeah, sort of interesting concept, if you're into that kind of thing. HeptImun's contract says we get reimbursed by the federal government for any expenses incurred to run the plant, but the Army is exempt from state taxation. So, the question is, does the Army having to pay for our tax really mean that the state can actually tax the federal government on their federal property."

"Yes, interesting," Karen said, trying to sound interested.

As the van slowed to turn into the entrance to the factory facility, Karen saw several carpenters at work on the large sign out front. The HeptImun logo was being removed.

Karen looked over to George, who smiled at her and said, "Message received."

After a brief set of introductions of Karen to the various managers and supervisors at the factory, they started a tour of the facility with Kerry Weathers leading the small group and explaining things as they went.

Just beyond the main office, they passed a door where a nurse in blue scrubs smiled at them. Weathers explained, "When we are at full strength, we will have nearly 1100 workers here, on the various shifts, so we have a full-featured industrial clinic on site. We have a nurse on duty and a contract with a nearby medical clinic to have a doctor come out as needed."

Karen asked, "What provisions for the avian flu outbreak in LA have you made?"

Weathers fumbled for an answer, and the nurse stepped up to say, "We have sufficient PPE, that's Personal Protective Equipment, on-site for all employees, as needed, so that they can continue work even in epidemic situations. And, I have test kits giving me influenza ID, you know, whether or not they have Type A and sample kits to send out to the labs to tell us what strains we have. So far, we have had four people put on sick leave and suspected of having the New Flu, as they are calling the flu from LA."

Karen nodded, "Thank you; that's what I needed to know."

Weathers nodded thanks to the nurse and continued with the tour. He showed Karen through the incoming processing rooms, where the harvested plants from the greenhouses were processed to extract the genetically modified virus-like particles that were the heart of the vaccines' ability to convey to humans immunity from the virus.

Weathers explained, "Over here we have the centrifuge and filtering stations where the mulch from the first step is processed to produce the rudimentary liquid that moves to the pharmaceutical production unit. Oh, and although we are currently planning on using the plant-based virus-like particles for this year's quadrivalent vaccines, we do have, in that area over there," he pointed to a wing of the factory where the lights were turned out above dozens of pieces of equipment, "machines capable of producing and refining cell-based virus-like particles from bacterial mulch in years when it's determined that the cell-based processes are more efficient for a particular virus strain."

They continued through the factory and into an area where robot machines were lined up. The machines were capable of filling, labeling, and packaging millions of individual vials of the vaccine to be produced by the factory. This area was not yet active.

"When will we be able to start the packaging process?" Karen asked.

"Right now, we are just getting up to speed on the production of the three vaccine types already in the mix. Let's call them, by their strain names, Perth, Mannheim, and Alberta. When the labs back east finish with the new work on the Minufiya/H5N1 strain and clear it for human use, we can quickly sprout the plants with the required genetic mods and, in a few weeks, have enough raw material to start processing mulch and the rest of our processing. We will, for the time being, begin producing the vaccines for the first three types and storing them for the addition of the key H5N1 strain that has been ordered in this year's quadrivalent vaccine. If all goes well, we should be able to start shipping vaccine for all four flu strains in late July or August."

"Wow, not much lead time to get it out. Cutting it close. Flu season starts in earnest in September, provided this current onslaught dies down a bit over the summer."

Weathers nodded, "Yes ma'am, but a place like this," he waved his hand around the factory, "cuts a good six months off the time we used to expect for a new vaccine."

Karen restrained the impulse to say anything about 'preaching to the choir.' She just smiled and nodded.

They finished their circuit around the huge plant and came to a shipping and storage area near where they had started the tour, where workers were unloading boxes from several semi-trucks at the loading dock.

Weathers said, "When the plant is up to full speed, we can produce hundreds of thousands of vaccine units per day. Outgoing shipments will be almost entirely automated, unlike the work crew here that is handling incoming equipment and chemical shipments by hand. A key factor is the modular system designed by HeptImun that all of the defense production plants will use, as well as the plants in China and the outside commercial plants using the HeptImun licensed equipment.

Weathers continued, "Over there, you can see the rows of modular metal casings that the raw material from the fields comes into the factory. Those containers and the ones used to transport the virus-like particles are all the same in every HeptImun-designed plant. In fact, when North Carolina finishes with the H5N1 VLPs, they will just ship the standard VLP container they use on their production line, and we can plug it into our machines here to replicate the VLPs and produce the vaccine. It works with either the plant-based VLP we are using this year or the cell-based bacterial VLP process. There are similar provisions for the old attenuated and inactivated viruses, but we do not expect to be using those, as a rule, in this new plant. "

Weathers walked over and put his hand on a stack of dark gray cubes with metal hinges and the HeptImun logo on it. "This is one of the VLP transport canisters. You can fill it with VLP here and ship it to China, Schaumberg, Raleigh-Durham, or the home HeptImun plant in Connecticut, and those plants could use it to recreate more VLP or use the VLP for vaccine without missing a beat."

"And, that's about it for our tour, Captain Llewellyn. Do you have any questions?"

Just as Karen was getting ready to say "No," one of the workers unloading a truck gave a powerful sneeze and covered his mouth with his hand. He wiped his hand on his pants and continued to work, grabbing another box from the truck."

Karen looked at Weathers and Marquardt, "Are you going to have anyone do something about that?"

Both men looked at Karen and blinked, not knowing what to say in reply.

Karen waited a moment, before shaking her head and walking briskly over to where the men were working. She stood away from them and motioned to get the attention of the man who had sneezed. She said, "You . . . yes, you, please walk over here." She pointed to where a forklift stood idle. "Stand by that forklift until I get back."

Then, Karen quickly walked away in the direction of the main office. In a few moments, she returned with the nurse at her side. The nurse had a face mask and gloves on and carried something in her hand. Karen motioned the nurse toward the man by the forklift. Another man had walked over near the first man. Karen pointed at this second man and directed him with hand motions to move away from the forklift.

Karen stood back as the nurse approached the man who had sneezed. The nurse said something to the man that Karen and the HeptImun managers could not hear over the factory noise. The man tilted his head back. The nurse took two swabs and twice took samples from deep in the man's nose. She put each swab into a different vial in her hand. Then, the nurse took a face mask and hooked the rubber bands over the man's ears, covering his mouth and nose.

The nurse shook one of the vials and walked over, closer to Karen. The nurse nodded her head and showed Karen something in the vial. Karen also nodded.

Karen walked back over to the HeptImun managers. "That man tests positive for Type A influenza. The nurse should have the exact strain ID back from the lab by tomorrow. If he has the H5N1 avian flu from LA, you have yourselves a problem. You told me yesterday that you have epidemic protection measures in place. It sure does not look like that to me. That man needs to be sent home to quarantine, and his co-workers need to be checked. Anything he touched needs to be cleaned, including that incoming shipment other workers will be handling. The hundreds of millions of dollars Uncle Sam gave us to make vaccines here will be worthless if your workforce gets sidelined with a bad-boy virus before you even get up to speed. Let's start acting like we are public health professionals. Right?"

Every man nodded.

"So, let's go see the greenhouses. Mr. Weathers, you need to get this mess straightened out." Karen waved toward the man by the forklift and his co-workers who had stopped working to watch the performance of the tall woman in the blue uniform.

—

Chapter 24

Thousand Oaks, California
April 3rd

Press Release

HEPTIMUN ANNOUNCES NEW VACCINE MANUFACTURING FACILITY FOR QUADRIVALENT INFLUENZA VACCINE

The Unique Government-Owned/HeptImun-Operated Facility Will Serve an Urgent Need.

—— ——

THOUSAND OAKS, CALIFORNIA (April 3rd) – HeptImun Corporation, a leading biopharmaceutical company, and leader in the development and production of cell-based and plant-based vaccines, is proud to announce the opening of a new, state of the art plant for the production of seasonal quadrivalent influenza vaccine (QIV) and other necessary vaccine products. In a unique and groundbreaking partnership with the United States government, HeptImun has been chosen to operate a government-owned facility in Thousand Oaks, California. Working with both the U.S. Department of Health and Human Services and the U.S. Defense Department, the HeptImun managed Thousand Oaks Defense Pharmaceutical Plant (TODPP) will produce large quantities of critical influenza vaccines for American and overseas needs. With the completion of construction and certification of HeptImun's flu program, the expected launch of the vaccine will be in time for the forthcoming influenza season in the USA, Canada, and Europe (October through April).

"Reaching this critical stage with our quadrivalent flu vaccine is a very exciting time for us as a company," said Bruce D. Clark, President and CEO of HeptImun. "We are convinced that bringing this novel vaccine to market will offer many advantages over current vaccines and benefits for those most at risk from the influenza virus. The current avian flu crisis highlights the need for a facility that can rapidly respond to public health and national defense needs."

HeptImun's QIV product is produced using a novel virus-like particle (VLP) technology. VLPs represent a new approach to vaccine development and production. VLPs mimic the native structure of viruses, allowing them to be easily recognized by the immune system. However, they lack the core genetic material, rendering them non-infectious and unable to replicate. In other words, they are safe and highly effective as they induce an immune response similar to a natural infection.

An alternative to egg-based and cell-based production systems, HeptImun's manufacturing platform brings many advantages, including much shorter lead time, reliability, and versatility. It currently takes only 10 to 12 weeks for the company to produce a clinical-grade vaccine, compared to 5-6 months using egg-based production methods.

With influenza viruses constantly mutating, HeptImun's rapid technology enables the creation of a vaccine that precisely matches the specific strain in circulation. During a Phase 2 study, the antibody and cell-mediated immunity (CMI) responses to HeptImun's VLP vaccine were higher than the responses using a comparator vaccine.

"We are excited to demonstrate the efficacy of the VLP vaccine during a large-scale field trial and prove the benefits of the unique immune response induced by this innovative product," said Nathalie Landry, HeptImun's Executive Vice President of Scientific and Medical Affairs.

Based in Montvale, New Jersey, HeptImun announced a major expansion project in 2018 for a new headquarters and commercial production facility to meet demand and complement its present main manufacturing plant located in Connecticut. HeptImun has already opened a related research and development facility in Fairfield, California. With the opening of the large government-owned/contractor-operated facility in the Los Angeles area, HeptImun is ready to lead in a new public health mission.

Please visit http://www.HeptImun.com for more information.

———

Topanga-Victory Urgent Care Center
Los Angeles, California
6:12 PM PDT April 3rd

Dr. Rohrbach came out of the examination room, followed by her latest patients, another family with multiple members sick of the flu. She went to the front counter, but instead of checking for the next patient's slip, she went behind the counter and pulled a large poster board sign out from behind the filing cabinet. Cyndi, the nurse/receptionist, watched with a surprised expression. The large sign, meant to be placed in the front door of the storefront clinic after hours, said:

CLOSED.

This clinic is closed—No physician on duty.

FOR IMMEDIATE MEDICAL CARE YOU SHOULD CALL
1(800) 555-4619 FOR THE LOCATION OF ANOTHER URGENT
CARE CENTER

or

IF THIS IS AN EMERGENCY CALL 9-1-1 OR
GO TO THE WEST HILLS HOSPITAL EMERGENCY ROOM
AT SHERMAN WAY AND ROYER AVENUE.

Dr. Rohrbach smiled at the two patients still waiting and slipped the sign into the lower part of the front door. She turned the door lock to locked.

"I'll be with you in a moment," Rohrbach said to the waiting patients, as she returned to the counter. She pulled two tissues from the box on the counter and motioned for Cyndi to follow her to the back room.

When they were out of the patients' hearing range, Cyndi asked, "What's up? You closing early?"

Rohrbach did not immediately answer. Instead, she held one finger up, waited, then quickly turned around and sneezed into the tissues.

After she finished blowing her nose, Teresa Rohrbach said, "Yeah, I've got this shit bad. It's been getting worse all afternoon. And, lots of chest congestion now. My lungs are literally whistling; I may need to go to the ER myself if it gets worse overnight. I took a Tamiflu and dextromethorphan and put my own flu test in the last batch we gave to the lab courier at five o'clock. I called Dr. Shiraj to come in and cover for me, and he says he has been put on full-time special contingency rotation at West Hills. All the doctors on staff there have to cover this New Flu epidemic. Some of the ICU docs are working 18-on-6-off and sleeping at the hospital. I called our corporate office in Pasadena, and they don't have anyone to cover me either. So, I told them I would be closing at six and couldn't say when I'd be back. They said they understood. It's bad all over."

Rohrbach finished with, "So, give me a couple of minutes to clean up, spray my nose, and put on a new mask; then I'll see those last people in the waiting room. Put them in Exam B. Put the lab packets we've collected since five in the dropbox so that the driver can pick 'em up in the morning. You should call Pasadena to see where or if they want you to work. "

"OK, Doc," Cyndi said. As Cyndi turned away, she gave a deep raspy cough into her elbow.

"Cyndi, forget calling about working. You stay home, too."

———

Chapter 25

Emergency Room
Grady Memorial Hospital
Atlanta, Georgia
3:12 AM EDT April 5th

Dr. Martin 'Marty' Craig finally gave up on his attempt to take an impromptu nap sitting on the rolling lab chair lodged between the medicine cabinet and the counter in the supply room. The regular bunkroom near the ER where residents, nurses, interns, and other staff could usually get some sleep during their extended work hours at the hospital had been commandeered for additional bed space for patients. Marty Craig had been working at the ER with no break since morning. He had been at work for eighteen hours and had not slept for almost twenty-four.

Marty stood up and rotated his neck, an attempt to get rid of the kink from his unsuccessful attempt to sleep with his head braced against the cabinet. Before he tried to sleep, he had stripped off his face mask and the disposable coverall they were using to treat the many flu cases in the ER. So, now that he was ready to go out again, he grabbed a new gown, mask and face shield from the cardboard boxes where they were dispensing these items. Supplies were nowhere near as short as back at the height of the first coronavirus wave. The system had learned something from the stark lesson coronavirus had taught everyone about preparedness. However, it seemed to Marty that this avian flu onslaught had hit, if anything, quicker than with the coronavirus. He had seen the first news reports from Egypt in early March, then the news of a similar outbreak in LA that must only have been three weeks ago. The first Atlanta cases had been the sick passengers at Hartsfield-Jackson Atlanta International Airport in the last week of March. Now, not even a week into April, there were around the clock new cases of seriously ill patients not only in Atlanta but every major American city.

It seemed to Marty that the culprit behind this massive influx in flu cases, compared to the earlier coronavirus pandemic, as horrible as that had been, was the much shorter gestation period for avian flu. Whereas coronavirus had a gestation period of from four days to fourteen days or more before the symptoms appeared, this avian flu, like the common flu, could start showing serious symptoms within a day of the viral infection. While the nation had weeks to get ready for the coronavirus and a couple of months forewarning of what happened overseas, the avian flu was filling Marty's ER in Atlanta less than a week after the first local case and a couple of weeks after the news from Egypt.

There was another major difference between this avian flu and the coronavirus. Unlike coronavirus that had hit the elderly and already infirm hardest, this flu seemed to hit the healthiest people the hardest. Young people with the strongest immune response were getting hit with lung-filling pneumonia and astronomical fevers. He remembered stories of the 1918 Spanish Flu that seemed to hit young soldiers and nurses the hardest.

Marty finished fitting the face shield over his coverall hood and reached under the shield to adjust his mask. He yawned and stretched his arms, together with one last pivot of his neck, to deal with the neck kink. He picked his stethoscope back up and hung it around his neck.

As he walked toward the main lobby of the ER, Marty reached into the nurses' station and pulled two nitrile gloves from the boxes on the wall. He always used large gloves, but he noticed the medium size box was empty. He was heading to go check the patient status board in the backroom when the automatic doors to the ER slid open, and a man appeared, carrying a body in his arms. Marty and a young LPN ran over to the man.

The LPN pulled an empty gurney from where it was parked by the front wall, and she and Marty helped the man lay the body, a woman in a nightgown, on the gurney.

The man, a tall, muscular black man, said, "I woke up in bed, and she was wheezing in bed next to me. She was fine when we went to sleep. Well, not fine, but not sick like this. She couldn't walk in from the car."

Marty answered, "We've got her. The nurse will be asking you for some details. The waiting room is full, so you can stay with us, but you need to stay by the wall, out of the way." One of the smaller ER bays on the side hallway was empty, so they rolled the woman in there.

The woman was mixed-race, early 30's, medium build and body weight. Her breathing was labored, and sweat glistened on her forehead. The LPN took her temperature and announced, "A little over 102."

Marty looked around the ER bay, spinning to look at all four corners. "Where's the ventilator?"

The nurse looked around also, and said, " Somebody pulled it out. I'll get another." She took off on the run.

Marty finished a quick check of all the woman's vital signs. She was cyanotic and struggling to breathe. She needed a ventilator. The nurse was taking a long time. Marty started to leave and find one himself. He looked toward the man waiting by the wall and saw him slowly topple, sliding down the wall. Marty rushed to grab the man's shoulders. Marty strained to handle the weight of the large man. He was able to slow the slide and ease the man to the floor.

The man's eyes were closed. He checked the inside of the dark-skinned man's lips for the tell-tale blueish color. He seemed cyanotic, just like the woman. Marty used the back of his gloved hand to touch the man's forehead. The man was burning up with fever. His temperature seemed worse than the woman's temperature by touch.

Since the nurse had not returned, Marty made sure the man's body was stable, leaning against the wall. He grabbed the telephone and pushed the red announcement button. Throughout the ER, speakers sounded, "Blue Assist Team, ventilator and gurney to ER 13, Stat! Blue Assist Team, ventilator and gurney to ER 13, Stat!" If there was anyone in the ER who was not critically busy, that would call them to come to help Marty with what was now two patients.

Marty looked quickly between the two patients. He turned to the gurney to move the woman's head into position with her throat straighter so he could insert the ventilator tube down her throat when it arrived.

The first nurse to respond to his announcement ran in. Marty gave her an order to hook both patients up to intravenous fluid line and get both antibiotic and antiviral meds started on both of them. The LPN finally appeared with a ventilator. An orderly with a gurney arrived. They started to work to save the couple.

———

U.S. Navy Medical Research Unit
Abbassia Fever Hospital
Cairo, Egypt
8:30 AM Local Time April 5th

Miriam Mansoor had reported to her usual workplace to continue the work on the statistics of the influenza spread but was told by the statistician that she had been reassigned. She was told they were getting short of trained medical personnel, and she would be doing the patient care work she had expected all along.

So, Miriam was back at the Intensive Care Unit of the Medical Research Unit, where she had first arrived as a patient a month before. She was following the instructions of a U.S. Navy nurse she had been told to report to and was dressing out in the full protective gear the staff in the ICU wore – pajama-like gown, mask, and face shield.

Miriam asked the nurse, "Do I need all of this," holding up the mask, "since I've already had this flu and am immune."

The nurse smiled, "Sure, you've probably developed an immunity for this strain, but when you go inside the ICU, there will be virus all around, and the only way to get clean of it when you come out is to take the same precautions as everyone."

Miriam nodded and said, "Of course, I should have thought about that."

As Miriam finished getting dressed, she asked, "I noticed the guards in the hallway when I came in. Why is that?"

The nurse said, "We have some rather high ranking patients right now. The deputy prime minister, his wife and the Minister of Health and Population are all sick and being treated here—some pretty important people. The director wanted to make sure we are fully staffed. That's why you're here. Several of our ICU team are down with the flu, too. For now, just follow me and watch what I do. You'll catch on to the main tasks we have. You ready to go in?"

Miriam swallowed and said, "Yes, I'm ready."

Miriam followed the American nurse through the air-sealed door into the ICU. She was surprised to see that there were six beds now crowded into the room where there had been two when she was a patient. The wife of the deputy prime minister was in Miriam's old bed in the corner. The woman was fully intubated with a ventilator hose. The director himself was standing over her bed. The director nodded to Miriam and handed Miriam his stethoscope.

"Listen to her lungs," the director commanded. "Listen carefully, so you can tell if it changes."

Miriam donned the stethoscope and listened. The congestion was quite obvious. The woman's heart was beating fast.

Miriam started to give the stethoscope back. The director shook his head. "No, you keep it. I want you to monitor her closely, constantly. Let us know if there is any change. For better or worse. Understand?"

Miriam nodded. It was quite a responsibility for a young nurse who originally had been scheduled to finish her residency six weeks from now.

———

Ministry of Health
Medical Products Facility
Fangshan District
Suburban Beijing, China
9:30 AM Beijing Time April 5th

Dr. Zhao Xiang pushed the off button on the speakerphone. She took a deep breath and waited for a few minutes, thinking about the conversation she had just had with the Deputy Minister of Health, Cao Jinghui, her boss and old friend.

The original purpose of the call was for her to give a status report on the four new vaccine plants under her control. The state-of-the-art plants built with American and Canadian technology but mostly equipped from Chinese factories were in varying stages of readiness. The Shanghai and Guangzhou plants, having started first, were ready and already turning out the raw vaccine for the three existing influenza strains. The home plant, here in the Beijing suburbs where she worked, was nearly ready for production and her laboratory was hard at work on the gene typing and detailed work needed to recreate a useful virus-like particle (VLP) for the new Egyptian H5N1 avian flu that everybody knew would be needed for next year. The fourth plant in Chengdu would be fully operational in May. Deputy Minister Cao had confirmed that the human tests on the avian flu vaccine, with the assistance of the Ministry of Defense, would be ready as soon as her laboratory could get the initial H5N1 VLPs in production. Xiang had wisely not asked any questions about where and how the Army would be doing human tests, or upon whom the tests would be administered. Some questions were best not asked.

The human testing of the forthcoming avian flu vaccine by the Army was not the only secret subject that had been talked around on the phone call. Xiang had also learned that the Army-led blockade of the Baodi district to the east of the capital was still in place. Most of Beijing had heard rumors of the blockade; how could they not? Nothing was to be found in the news or on the internet about the blockade. If anything was mentioned at all, it was originally called a quarantine to deal with a dangerous poultry pathogen destroying the poultry flocks in Baodi. Many had heard of the passenger buses being stopped, and passengers checked for temperatures. The stories were unclear as to why the poultry problem required humans to be checked out before leaving the area. So, the story was changed to this being an outbreak of the Egyptian avian flu, caused by foreign travelers, thus the travel restrictions in the area.

Dr. Zhao Xiang, however, knew the real answer, as did her boss. Neither of them spoke about it openly, at least not on the telephone. They both knew that the pop-up of H7N9 avian flu in Baodi in early March had been mercilessly beaten back with rapid response and shutdown of the whole Baodi district. Thousands of people had been sequestered and some transported, dozens of warehouses and factories emptied and sterilized, and millions of poultry and swine had been killed. The crackdown on Baodi was formulated by men who had learned the lessons of the Wuhan and Hubei quarantine in the early days of the coronavirus epidemic. They did not make the same mistakes a second time. Their incompetence was not going to be the source of another pandemic, and they were not going to be blamed as others had been with coronavirus. This could not happen again. Not in Baodi, a district that was only a short drive from Beijing. Baodi was locked up tight, and the truth was declared a state secret.

Both Xiang and Jinghui knew the truth about the avian flu in Baodi. It had not been the same avian flu as was now spreading like a wraith across Egypt,

Europe, and the Middle East. In the early days of the Baodi outbreak, a few leaks had made their way out of the Ministry of Health about the H7N9 strain and the very first human victims of that novel avian flu strain. This was caught quickly by the Ministry, and the story was downplayed as a strictly zoonotic transmission to a few poultry workers. The one Westerner who got caught up in the initial outbreak, the woman from France, had a clear connection to a poultry market, so that fit into the official story. The original problem in Baodi was deemed to be a case of a few sick chickens and ducks giving a few unlucky people the disease, directly animal to human. The truth of significant person-to-person spread of H7N9 had been covered up and stamped out by quick action by the Army, the Ministry of Public Security and the Ministry of Health.

The one poor woman from Paris, France, who had caught the strain in the Baodi wet market became a sort of scapegoat when the Ministry decided to start calling the Baodi H7N9 strain by its French genetic strain typing, 003/PARIS(H7N9). So, in the phone call, Xiang had just had with Deputy Minister Cao, it had been the 'Paris' strain that he had given her instructions about, never mentioning its true home locale, Baodi. If it were not so terrifying, their conversation might be viewed as comical.

He had told Xiang, "The ministry has decided it would be fortuitous if your laboratory would undertake a complete genetic typing of the 'Paris' strain with an eye on making it possible to formulate a VLP vaccine later, if necessary."

Xiang had waited a moment before following up, "Are there problems in 'Paris?' I heard that was under control."

Jinghui answered carefully, "The People's Liberation Army in 'France' thought they had the matter under control, but their *cordon sanitaire* and movement of the 'Parisians' may not have been fully effective. It seems they may have found some stray 'Parisians' in the far north of 'France,' and we want to be ready to help, again, only if necessary."

Xiang had to think about what he was saying for a moment and then added, "The ministry does know that I have several consultants from HeptImun, Sanofi, and Medicago in our plants. I assume we don't want to worry the American or Canadian, or certainly not the French, consultants with our concerns about the 'Paris' problem."

"That's is correct. Do whatever is necessary to ensure that this stays as narrowly known as possible. You can probably use the Egyptian strain workflow to cover up for the 'Parisian' issue. That might work."

Xiang had finished up the call with, "Yes, I understand completely. Consider the work started."

"Very well, good day."

That was the phone call that Zhao Xiang now sat and worried about. The HeptImun scientists were in China with the specific job of training the crews of Chinese geneticists in the process of doing the genetic typing of the flu viruses and formulation of the virus-like particles, starting with the Egyptian avian flu strain. The Chinese had not wanted to be at the mercy of the American CDC in the creation of the critical genetic markers needed for the VLP vaccine factories to work. Now, Xiang had been given the task of working out an entirely new virus gene typing for the brand new H7N9 avian flu that had struck in Baodi and was apparently threatening to break out of the Army quarantine and cause major trouble. And, she had to keep it secret from the foreign scientists and managers with whom she was working closely.

Zhao Xiang hoped Jinhui's idea of covering the creation of a vaccine for the Baodi strain and calling it the 'Paris' strain did not blow up in his face, or her face. Dr. Zhao Xiang loved her profession, but she hated her job. She wished she knew how things were really going in the fictitious 'Paris' given that it was only about a hundred kilometers away, on the far side of the Beijing metropolitan area.

—

Chapter 26

Los Angeles County Sheriff's Station
Lost Hills/Calabasas, California
7:30 AM PDT April 15th

Matt Relford quickly read through the several items on the clipboard again as he walked down the hall toward the Squad Room. He had listened to the morning briefing from the station sergeant several thousand times over his career, so he should know the routine by heart, but this would be his first time doing it himself, and he was a bit nervous.

There were many empty seats in the normally full squad room. There were also some surprised faces when Matt took his place at the podium and waited for people to quiet down.

Matt cleared his throat and began, "Good morning, everyone. I got a call from the undersheriff just after six this morning telling me that both Merriman and Gonçalvez are down hard with this flu, and they figured downtown that with our lieutenants already out, I was senior on the totem pole for now. The undersheriff said he is contacting one of the detective lieutenants from West Hollywood station to come up as acting station commander. But I will be acting day sergeant for now."

Matt took a deep breath and continued, "And yes, Undersheriff Martinez is in charge downtown. As you all probably heard yesterday, Sheriff Covarrubias was in a serious one-car accident on the 14 Freeway. When Fire got him removed from his vehicle, they found he had multiple flu symptoms besides the accident injuries. He was trying to drive back from the plane crash scene in Lancaster, while he had walking pneumonia. He must have passed out while he was driving. That can happen with walking pneumonia that you can get with this New Flu shit. He was airlifted to USC Medical Center and is in guarded condition, according to the undersheriff."

Matt looked down and read from his clipboard. "According to the latest email from the County, LA Unified School District and all the outlying districts have closed for the rest of the month of April. However, unlike the school closure we had with the coronavirus that turned out to last all the way through summer break, they are counting on this epidemic, since it should act like the regular flu, to slow down and maybe let them get schools back in session in May. So, all schools are closed. Drive by schools in your area when you're in the neighborhood and check for vandalism. Check for groups of kids someplace where they shouldn't be. Ask them to break up crowds.

"According to the County Health email, the epidemiloli . . ." Relford paused, a couple of snickers were heard, ". . . epidemiologists are saying they may be seeing the peak of the New Flu, at least for this year. They say our New Flu is acting just like the Egyptian Flu that has spread on the East Coast, and both seem to be slowing down, in overall new cases. So, a bit of hopeful info. Enough of the news, now to the details for the day."

Matt turned the page, "We are just under 70% manpower at this station. Slightly better department-wide. We are limiting ourselves to just essential tasks. No traffic enforcement except for accidents with injuries. No probation pickups or checks. No warrants, except serious felony. Cite misdemeanors, and don't arrest except for DWI and then release even those at the station after the arrest is processed and they're sober. Dispatch will run all 911 calls that are not crime-in-progress or life and death through Operations, which is just me right now, and I will decide if Dispatch will have a unit respond. Civil Division and Courts are closed, and the jail is thinking about releasing inmates to lessen the load there and free up people for patrol. We hope to get some of those people from downtown out here today, along with some deputized probation officers and park rangers, plus retirees, to fill in for our missing personnel. Follow the instructions sheet they put out on Monday – no physical contact with an obviously sick person unless a life is in danger – limit all arrests to serious crimes only – don't have any . . . well, I'm not gonna go through them all. Read the list yourself. It's on the board."

Acting Sergeant Matt Relford read through the rest of the abbreviated briefing and ended with "Be careful out there. We can't afford to lose anybody else."

——

Message/Email
Centers for Disease Control
April 15th

> From: nancy.cox@epi.CDC.gov
> To: philip.reynes@CDC.gov
>   marta.le_salles@CDC.gov
>   flu_updates@CDC.gov
>   infogroup4@HHS.gov
>   medrespgrp@us.army.mil
>   wholiaison@dc.CDC.gov
>   infogrp1419@DHS.gov
> Subj: Weekly Status Report Multi-Strain Avian Flu Outbreak
>   Analysis and Projections

UNCLASSIFIED - NOT FOR PUBLIC RELEASE

Forward within USG as needed

1. Information regarding the avian flu outbreak in March in the Baodi region of China continues to be sparse. Official reports from the Chinese Health Ministry have indicated the zoonotic transmission of the A/21/117/311/ BAODI(H7N9) and A/21/406/312/ BAODI(H7N9) strains has been limited to the previously reported cases, numbering fewer than fifty. However, current reports coming from the region of a serious outbreak of the A /MINUFIYA/EGYPT/AB-K8/(H5N1) strain, ostensibly a spread of the Egyptian epidemic to this semi-rural area of China cannot be confirmed. Strict quarantine controls on the area by the Chinese Army have prevented any outside observers from sampling or interviewing local health agencies. The single case of the A/21/836/003/ PARIS(H7N9) strain in France has been reliably confirmed to be derivative of the 312/BAODI strain.

2. After considerable study, it has been determined that the A/ Minufiya/21/04(H5N1) and A/Los Angeles/21/07(H5N1) are nearly identical and that the Los Angeles outbreak was most likely derived from the single local resident, a restaurateur, who traveled to Egypt and spread the strain in California. After a broader selection of samples were studied, earlier differences in the strain typing between A/Minufiya/21/04(H5N1) and A/Los Angeles/21/07(H5N1) have been found to be negligible. Although the popular vernacular of calling the Minufiya flu strain currently being transmitted in several European countries and the Eastern Seaboard of the U.S. as the "Egyptian Flu" and the localized epidemic in Southern California is being called the "New Flu," in reality, the outbreaks are of the same strain.

3. Final figures on the massive epidemic in Egypt are not available yet. It is estimated that total deaths in Egypt alone were upwards of 70-80,000. Corollary outbreaks in other Middle Eastern countries, southeastern Europe and Asia Minor and elsewhere, are still in progress, although seemingly slowing with the onset of warmer weather. The Minufiya strain continues to spread in several U.S. and European metropolitan areas. Lastly, the Minufiya strain has continued to hit young, otherwise healthy adults the hardest. Like the classic 1918 Spanish H1N1 influenza, young adults with healthy immune response appear to get serious pneumonic reactions that often prove fatal without intensive respiratory therapy.

4. CONCLUSIONS:

   A. The PARIS and 311/BAODI strains are nearly identical and present significant evidence of an antigenic shift, indicating a likely admixture of human-sourced Influenza Type A strains. These factors present a higher likelihood of potential non-zoonotic transmission than was present in earlier H7N9 strains.

   B. The 312/BAODI strain should be considered anomalous until further study and clarification are complete.

   C. Genetic factors, possible human amino acids, and proteins in the PARIS and 311/BAODI strains of Influenza Type A H7N9 are indicative of similar factors in A/Minufiya/21/04(H5N1) and A/Los Angeles/21/07(H5N1) avian influenza strains which have achieved human-to-human transmission.

   D. A/Minufiya/21/04(H5N1) and A/Los Angeles/21/07(H5N1) strains are deemed to be the same strain, although, to date, the Los Angeles outbreak does not seem to be as deadly per capita. However, that may just be a result of the difference in medical care available in the U.S. compared to Egypt. Studies are in progress to see if any strain genetic drift may explain the decrease in lethality. Initial estimates that a vaccine may be available for the Minufiya/Los Angeles strain by August seem to be possible, which at six months would be a record for a new vaccine from initial strain ID to production.

Respectfully,
Nancy Cox
Branch Chief
Virology, Surveillance, and Diagnosis Branch
National Center for Immunization and Respiratory Diseases
Centers for Disease Control

———

Defense Pharmaceutical Plant
Thousand Oaks, California
1:10 PM PDT April 15th

Over the lunch hour, Karen had changed from the blue working uniform she usually wore at work to the sharper looking short-sleeved summer white uniform worn by the Public Health Service. She also decided to wear the white trousers with the uniform, instead of the skirt that was optional for women.

With shoulder epaulets, service ribbons, and qualification badges, she figured the sharp-looking white uniform looked a little better for the television interview that was scheduled for the afternoon.

She had gotten a call from the Public Affairs Office at Fort Detrick the afternoon before. They were making sure Karen and the HeptImun staff in Thousand Oaks were ready for the cable television news team that was arriving for a report on the new vaccine plant. That call was followed in rapid succession by a call from Assistant Secretary Royce's office and then Jared Bentley at the HeptImun headquarters. A press release from HeptImun's publicity team had started the process, and both General Harding and Jared Bentley had volunteered Captain Llewellyn as the perfect figurehead to represent the multi-agency and multi-location defense pharmaceutical plants. Royce's office was calling after a head's up call from Harding. Royce and Harding were, apparently, old friends.

Karen and George Marquardt were in her office discussing the press visit when Master Sergeant Ghent stuck his head in her door, announcing, "They're here, at the front gate."

Karen nodded and gave one last look to the write-up they had prepared to cover the essential aspects of the facility's mission and the science behind it. She wouldn't be reading the script, but it was nice to have already gone over the essentials before she was interviewed.

Karen looked at George, "This will be a first in my career. I'm used to being in the back room. You sure one of you corporate types wouldn't be better for this?"

"Nice try, Captain. But I have very clear instructions from my home office that Captain Llewellyn is to be the face of this operation. I heard from them that the decision was from General Harding."

"Well, it seems like I don't have a choice. Let's go."

They met the four-person news team in the building's lobby. Karen recognized the reporter at once. The pretty, young woman was looking the part of a television reporter more than the last time Karen had seen her reporting on TV from the airbase in the Egyptian desert. "Ms. O'Neil, welcome. I'm Captain Karen Llewellyn, the commanding officer here. I saw your reports from Cairo. I'm surprised you're out of quarantine already."

Shaysee O'Neil smiled and said, "Yes, they flew us to March airbase from Cairo and kept us in quarantine for ten days. If we tested clean, they let us go, and the network figured since I was already in the Los Angeles area and people knew about my earlier reports on the flu that I should do this, too. Finally, a little bit of good news about the influenza pandemic."

"Yes, indeed. Let's go into the conference room where we can make introductions all around and talk about what you want to hear from us."

After the introductions and exchange of background information, they set up the camera in TODPP's laboratory with Shaysee interviewing Karen on camera. The large room of high-tech equipment with technicians in lab coats made a perfect background for the interview. Karen's white military uniform matched up perfectly with the laboratory setting and her technicians in lab coats.

Shaysee started, "I'm here with Captain Karen Llewellyn, the Commanding Officer of the new Defense Pharmaceutical Plant in Thousand Oaks, California. Captain Llewellyn, can you give us an overview of this plant and its purpose."

"Yes, certainly. This plant is one of three defense pharmaceutical plants put in operation this year, with two more planned for next year. The idea is to harness the technological power of America's fantastic pharmaceutical industry, but make sure that the effort reflects the best plan for the protection of our nation in times of national emergency, like the coronavirus outbreak or the current avian flu pandemic. The defense pharmaceutical plants are each operated by a different major medical products company, in our case HeptImun Corporation. The plant itself is owned and controlled by the federal government. All of this state-of-the-art technology you see around us is owned by the American taxpayers but operated by the brightest minds in American industry. The contract to run the plant is handled by the U.S. Army, and I'm assigned as the commanding officer with overall management authority over the vaccine production."

"But you're not an Army officer, Captain; you're a U.S. Public Health Service officer, a medical doctor and genetic scientist, I understand. How does that fit in with an Army facility?"

"The federal government decided after the coronavirus pandemic and the year-long struggle to come up with a vaccine while people died for lack of a weapon to fight the contagion, that it needed to have a better system to rally America's resources to fight any future viral pandemic. The government decided to use a system the Army had used for over a century to manufacture critical armaments for the military, but in this case, to manufacture vaccines using a government-owned and contractor-operated factory. It brings the best of both worlds, corporate logistics and manufacturing expertise with the government's ability to direct important events of national interest as it deems best. In our case, the Defense Department and the Health and Human Services Department agreed to have the Army handle the contracting and organizational support, but to put an experienced Public Health Service officer in charge of each plant. It seems to be working well."

"So, what exactly do you do here, and how is a vaccine created?"

Karen walked over to stand in front of a table filled with laboratory equipment, included several beakers connected by tubing with greenish-gray fluid bubbling within them. "A vaccine that's used to give a person immunity to infection from a virus, or from a bacteria, contains an antigen that does the magic. Antigens are substances, like a protein or some other chemical marker, that mimics a characteristic of the virus and causes the body to produce an immune response to protect itself. The antigen is masquerading as a virus, and the body's natural immunity system learns how to protect against future attacks from the actual disease. In classic vaccines, like polio, smallpox, and some influenza vaccines, the antigen they used was a dead or weakened amount of the actual virus. That process had some obvious inherent dangers. However, with modern genetics research, we have learned to recreate the genetic markers of a virus so that the body can react to that genetic marker, instead of the actual virus itself. We call that a 'virus-like particle.' Once we develop the virus-like particle that can cause the human body to develop an immunity to a particular strain of virus, we can generate large quantities of that genetic marker in other living organisms that can be filtered, processed, and used to make an effective vaccine."

Karen pointed to the beaker of bubbling gray liquid. "Here is a good example of that. In this beaker, we have a bacteria that has been genetically modified with bits of the DNA and RNA genetic code of the influenza virus. This bacteria is not dangerous to humans. In fact, it's similar to the bacteria that every human has in their digestive tract to help digest food. When you take a commercial probiotic food supplement, you're swallowing a cousin of this bacteria. But, this bacteria soup we have growing here has the genetics to create those virus-like particles that the human body uses to develop an immunity to the actual influenza disease."

Karen picked up a sealed bottle of clear liquid. "After 24 to 48 hours in the growth medium, the bacteria soup is filtered and processed to remove the primary bacterial material and just leave the virus-like particles, as we have here in this bottle." She held up a small bottle of clear liquid. "In this bottle, we have virus-like particles of just one of the four influenza strains that we will have in the coming year's flu vaccine. And besides the bacterial method, we can also grow plants that sprout quickly and also produce the virus-like particles. For this year's four strains, we will be using the plant-based virus-like particles for each of the four strains we are working on."

"Four strains?"

"Yes, we will produce what we call a quadrivalent vaccine, capable of protecting from the four flu strains we have determined are most likely to be a problem for the coming flu season. For influenza, we name the strains after the locale where the influenza strain was first found and which then move around the world as the virus spreads. For this year, they are Perth, Mannheim, and Alberta, and now with the avian flu rearing its head, we have Minufiya, for the city in Egypt where the avian flu started in March."

"So, you do not call this Egyptian Flu?"

Karen shook her head, "No, we avoid that kind of thing, and in general, we would likely just call it avian flu or like the swine flu we had back in 2009. Labeling a strain by its city of origin is just a label used by the scientists for accuracy. We try not to blame it on its country of origin. It was the coronavirus, or COVID19, not the Chinese virus, despite what the president back then tried to nickname it."

"So, when will the vaccine be ready for the avian flu that's ravaging the world and is now spreading across America?"

"We are working on the first three strains as we speak and should be in production of the complete quadrivalent vaccine later in the summer. We hope to have the raw materials for the avian flu from the labs back east that are doing the genetic work on the avian flu in a couple of months."

"So, you can't work on the avian flu at this plant?"

"By plan, we have the full capability of handling everything from initial genetic typing to production of any influenza strain. However, to ensure safety and uniformity in this rush to put out a vaccine for a new strain in record time, the CDC labs in Atlanta and the defense pharmaceutical plant in North Carolina are making the initial virus-like particle mix for the new avian flu strain and running the animal and human testing. We will then replicate those proven particles and make our own vaccine."

"And when will the vaccine be ready for shipment?"

"If all goes well, we can start shipping the vaccine before the start of the next flu season next September. We will be shipping millions of vaccine doses in a few months."

"By September, that's a long time. The avian flu is filling up hospitals in America as we speak. Hundreds are dying right now."

Karen nodded, "Yes, that's true. But getting the avian flu vaccine ready and shipped in about six months after it was first discovered in Egypt, will be a miracle in itself. That process took a year or more in the past, sometimes several years. Please remember how everybody was screaming for a vaccine from coronavirus for many months before it was available. And, the good news now is, the avian flu seems to be acting like the traditional seasonal flu and is slowing its spread as summer approaches. And, since the avian flu is a close cousin of the other Type A influenza strains, we do not have to start over from scratch as we did with coronavirus. We know our existing flu vaccine manufacturing process, and its primary components are safe, just waiting for the new particles. The new virus-like particle process makes it safer than the decades-old methods of using dead virus cells in a vaccine, much safer and quicker. We can only hope that this scourge slows down and hides for a bit before we are ready with our vaccine in the fall, as the latest word about it seems to indicate."

"Thank you, Doctor Llewellyn." Shaysee turned to face the camera. "Now, let's take a look at the factory area where the vaccine will be made."

The cameraman lowered the camera and turned out his fill light. Shaysee took a deep breath.

"How was that?" Karen asked.

"You were great. I can see why DC said for us to come here. I think you just got a side job as the government's vaccine spokeswoman. Viewers will love you."

"Oh, God, I hope not. This is not my thing. Give me a DNA strand to unravel rather than on-camera work any time."

———

U.S. Navy Medical Research Unit
Abbassia Fever Hospital
Cairo, Egypt
6:30 PM Local Time April 15th

Miriam was changing the bedpan of one of the six patients in an ICU room when the strident steady tone of a heart monitor went off across the room. She sat the dirty pan on the floor and raced across the room to the bed where the alarm was sounding. One of the young American navy doctors ran into the room and joined her. Miriam quickly stripped off her dirty gloves and donned a new pair. The doctor was listening to the man's heart.

When the doctor shook his head and took the stethoscope away, Miriam motioned to the crash cart by the bedside and looked to the doctor for a decision. He nodded, "Let's try."

Miriam quickly turned on the unit, spread gel on the defibrillator paddles, and handed them to the doctor.

"Clear!" he announced.

Miriam stepped back from the bed. The defibrillator thumped, and the patient's body jerked. The even tone continued, no blips from the heart.

"Up a hundred."

Miriam turned the knob.

"Clear!"

Another thump. The steady tone continued unabated.

"Clear!"

After another thump, the doctor looked down at the patient. The fifty-year-old man was already fully intubated and on oxygen via the ventilator. Now, his heart had stopped. There was nothing else to do. The doctor handed the defib paddles back to Miriam. He checked his watch for a time and pulled the blanket up over the patient's face.

The Arab Republic of Egypt would need a new Minister of Health and Population. He was the fourth death since Miriam had started working in the ICU. It probably would not be the last.

—

Chapter 27

Defense Pharmaceutical Plant
Thousand Oaks, California
9:05 AM PDT April 17ᵗʰ

Karen's cell phone gave a custom musical ringtone she had not heard in a long time. She did not need to look at the screen to know it was her husband, Marty.

"Hello, there," she said.

"Yes, hello. I saw you on TV."

"Wow, at times like this, an ER doc with enough time on his hands to watch TV?"

"Yes, good point. I didn't watch it on TV. Marcia recorded it, and she had Danny send me the link for her Instagram post about it."

"Yeah, I've heard about my appearance from several people. Apparently, General Harding is happy with me, too."

"It did my heart good to see you. I was proud of you. You were terrific."

"Umm . . ." Karen paused, not knowing how to answer that. "How are you holding up? Is this as bad as COVID19 was?"

"In some ways worse, in other ways not. This hasn't reached the sheer volume of the height of COVID yet, but the cases are a lot different. We're getting lots of healthy, young people with horrible temperatures and lung failure. Their lungs are filling up with fluid, just like the med school stories of the original 1918 flu epidemic. And, the older folks don't seem to be getting the brunt of things like with coronavirus. Kids are getting this avian flu bad, too."

"I saw on the CDC daily recap email that it seems the growth is slowing, maybe starting to take a seasonal turn. You seeing that in the trenches?"

"Well, probably the fact that I finally got to take a lunch hour off today and call you is an indication of that. It has been hell here for, like, three weeks. It might be slowing."

"We can hope."

"Yeah. And other than your newfound stardom, how are things going out there?"

"Good, kind of what I expected. I finally rented a furnished condo in Camarillo. That's near where we have our factory production line, five miles or so from the headquarters and laboratory here in Thousand Oaks. The shipment of my stuff from Atlanta arrived, but I haven't had time to unpack. I was lucky that the VIP visits that were originally scheduled for this month were postponed because of the avian flu. Both the Army medical and HHS VIPs have other problems on their minds. One local congresswoman did stop in with a local TV station crew so she could take credit for locating the plant in her congressional district."

There was a slight pause before Marty continued, "I wanted to ask. When things slow down for both of us a bit, do you think . . . I mean have you thought about whether you and I can try to see about . . ." his voice trailed off.

"Yes, Marty, like I said when we talked before I left. I wouldn't mind you coming out for a visit. Maybe in the summer. You're probably going to be busy until this epidemic breaks, and I'm still getting up to speed. My busiest time is going to be getting the vaccine out for the fall flu season."

"I understand, I just wanted to let you know I was still hoping, you know."

Master Sergeant Ghent knocked on Karen's door and poked his head inside the door.

"I gotta go, Marty. Somebody just came in," Karen said.

"OK. Call me when you can."

"Right."

When Karen put down the phone, Ghent said, "Sorry to interrupt you."

"It's OK. Just a situation report from my husband in the ER in Atlanta. What's up?"

"Your XO has arrived. Captain Cameron would like to see you."

"Ah, yes. Glad he finally made it. And, if I can ask you for some sage Army wisdom since you have more experience in the Army hierarchy than I do, I could use some advice on what exactly I should be asking an Executive Officer to do. I thought about asking that before. Basically, an assistant manager, right?"

Ghent gave a slight nod, "Yes ma'am, sort of assistant manager, but also a bit of alter ego for the CO. If your XO is doing his job, and I'm doing mine, you shouldn't have to sweat the small stuff. A good XO lets you look at the big picture without hassling about the details."

Karen nodded, "Thanks, noted. Send him in."

Karen was sitting at her desk in her usual blue working uniform. She remembered reporting to General Harding at Fort Detrick, so she remained seated.

There was a single knock on her door.

"Yes? Come in," she answered.

An officer in the Army pink and greens dress uniform entered and closed the door behind him. He was medium height, with closely-cropped, dark brown hair. Karen recognized the Medical Service Corps insignia on his lapels. He had two-rows of service ribbons and a Combat Medical Badge, probably from the Afghan service that Karen had seen in his records. Oddly, he wore a medical face mask. He walked in front of Karen's desk and saluted.

"Ma'am. Captain Robert Cameron reporting for duty."

Karen returned the salute, "Please have a seat, Captain."

When he was seated, Karen asked, "How did your trip go? I assume you drove."

"Yes ma'am. I got in last night."

"Do you go by Robert, Rob, Bob?"

"Rob, Ma'am."

"Yes, and in informal settings, please call me Karen. We're going to have minimal military staff, and things will probably be mostly informal. But, there will be times where formal protocol will be needed. Understand?"

"Yes ma'am."

"I noticed you're married with two children. Did they drive out with you."

"No ma'am. By the time we got cross-country to my wife's folk's house in Joplin, Missouri, both my wife and one daughter had this flu. So, we decided to have them stay with her folks there while I continued out here. I'm about seven days into my ten-day waiting period without getting the flu, so that's why I have this mask on, just in case I get some symptoms. I don't want to be shedding virus around my new duty station."

"Yes, I was going to ask about that. How are your wife and daughter?"

"Betsy, my daughter, seems to be snapping out of it fine. My mother-in-law says my wife, Meredith, is pretty sick. Not bad enough for the hospital. High fever, chills, coughing. I had to ask her mom because Meredith won't complain about how she feels."

"We could have given you some extra time to report."

"I thought about that but decided to continue. My wife has our other car there. So, she can drive on out when she gets better and when I've found a place for us here."

"If you need any help getting settled, please let us know. Our HeptImun staff seems to have good contacts in the local business community. You planning on renting or buying?"

"I probably want to buy something here. We sold our house in Bethesda, so we need to buy something to do the tax thing on the capital gains by buying again in the tax year."

"Ah, yes." Karen paused for a moment. "Captain, uh, Rob, I read through your military file, the 201 file, I think you call it. I saw you were top ten percent graduating from West Point. That lets you take your pick of officer corps branches. You picked Medical Service Corps. My husband, who is Army Medical Corps himself, once told me the Medical Service branch is kind of low on the totem pole of choices for new Army officers, usually the domain of underachieving ROTC grads, not top of the class Academy grads who usually choose combat arms or military intelligence or such. Leaving the question . . ."

Rob Cameron smiled, "Yes ma'am. Valid question. My answer is that military officers on the promotion list for O-4 are the largest segment of the officers selected for free medical school education at the Uniformed Services University Medical School or the civilian contract schools. For ten years running, Medical Service Corps officers have been slightly more successful in getting admitted to medical school than combat arms officers, even though the combat arms branches have many times the number of officers. So . . ."

Karen nodded, "And, I suppose, for an officer hoping to get selected for medical school, being XO of a military command running an important defense pharmaceutical plant would be a nice ticket punch, whereas other officers might consider it not so much of a prime career opportunity."

"Yes ma'am. And once you get a chance to know me, I'm hoping a letter in my file from an O-6 Public Health Service officer-in-charge might be a benefit. Not to mention the amount of information I can absorb around here."

Karen smiled, "Sounds like a plan. Welcome to the team." She stood up to come around the desk and shake hands.

—

Los Angeles County Sheriff's Station
Lost Hills/Calabasas, California
6:25 PM PDT April 17th

Matt Relford finished the twelve-hour shift as acting operations sergeant at the Malibu/Lost Hills Sheriff's Station. Everyone was doing extended shifts until the staff shortage from the flu ended. Rick Gonçalvez was back to work after a relatively short time off the job, but Captain Merriman was not. Merriman's heart had succumbed to the stress of labored breathing with the flu, and he had passed away.

Gonçalvez was wearing captain's bars as acting station commander, which was a two-step promotion for him, even if just a temporary acting captain. You got paid for your 'acting' rank. Gonçalvez had told Matt to wear sergeants stripes as Rick's 'acting' replacement as day operations sergeant.

Matt left the parking lot at the sheriff's station driving east on Agoura Road. He did not take the first turn toward the freeway and continued east, intending to go to the Albertson's supermarket at Las Virgenes since he knew he had nothing to eat in the refrigerator back at this apartment. He was dead tired.

Matt's Subaru was stopped at the light at Lost Hills Road when he saw two transit buses stopped with their emergency blinkers on and a crowd of people standing nearby. Something was wrong. When the light changed, he pulled around the buses and parked in front. Since Matt was in uniform, the crowd of onlookers parted to let Matt approach and see what was happening.

The two bus drivers and two other people were trying to carry a woman off the bus. The woman's body was limp. Behind them, a small child was crying and trying to get to the woman being carried.

"What happened?" Matt asked.

One of the uniformed drivers answered, "She was passed out in the seat, another rider told me. I think this is her kid. I radioed it in to our Dispatch."

"Lay her on the bus bench," Matt ordered, waving an arm to get people to move.

As they laid the woman on the bench, Matt could see she had her eyes open but was breathing in quick short breaths. Matt had seen this before, the people in the trailer. The little girl ran to stand by the woman on the other side of the bus bench.

"I think she's sick," said the bus driver. The crowd backed up several steps at hearing this but kept watching.

Matt knelt on one knee by the woman. He reached to touch the woman's forehead. It was hot.

Matt keyed his shoulder microphone, and since he was off duty, he said, "Dispatch, this is LASD body number 16146, off duty. Over."

"Roger, 16146, Dispatch, over."

Matt continued, "My 10-20 is at the intersection of Agoura and Lost Hills. I need an on-duty patrol, paramedics and an ambulance at this location for a female, age 25, who is 10-45 Bravo, breathing difficulty, severely ill. And we need to call Child Services, a child, age 3 or 4 is accompanying the women. Over."

"Wait, over."

A moment later, Matt heard a familiar voice, the sergeant who had just relieved him at the station, "This is Lima 2-One-Hundred, Relford, that you?"

"Roger that. Over"

"What's going on? Over."

"Young Asian woman with a child. She passed out on a transit bus. They took her off the bus right here near the station. She is really sick, having trouble breathing. We need medical response and probably Child Services for the kid. Over."

"Roger, out."

"Can I leave now?" the first bus driver asked.

"Yeah, I'm outa here too." The other bus driver headed toward the other bus.

"Wait, before you go. Any idea where she got on the bus?" Matt asked the first bus driver.

"I'm pretty sure it was in Westlake. By that big daycare center on Westlake Boulevard and Agoura."

"OK, thanks, Yeah, you can go. But put in a report to the transit authority on this."

"Of course."

A heavy-set older woman dropped a shopping bag and purse on the ground near where Matt knelt by the woman, "I think this is her stuff from the bus."

Matt nodded and smiled, "Thanks for helping out. That was good of you."

The woman added, "She was really sick and coughing on the bus. I changed seats cuz I didn't want to get sick. You should be careful, too. This flu is horrible."

Matt nodded again. He knew that.

Most of the waiting crowd got on the two departing buses, leaving Matt, the sick woman, and the crying child waiting for help to arrive. The only good thing was that Matt did not have to worry about getting sick from this woman. He had already had this stuff. That thought made him think of Marjorie. Matt hoped this young woman would not wind up like Marjorie.

He heard a squad car from the station chirp its siren to cross the intersection behind him. The little girl had stopped crying and was watching Matt intently while holding her mother's hand. The flashing lights of the squad car reflected in the girl's wide, unblinking eyes. He heard the rapidly warbling siren of a paramedic van exiting the freeway, coming their way.

———

Chapter 28

U.S. Navy Medical Research Unit
Abbassia Fever Hospital
Cairo, Egypt
7:10 AM Local Time April 29ᵗʰ

Miriam Mansoor waited in the classroom with perhaps ten other nurses. They had all been told to assemble here, earlier than usual. The nurses were mostly Egyptian, but there were two American nurses also. The American nurses were wearing different uniforms than Miriam had seen before; they were in gray and blue camouflage shirts and trousers. The Egyptian nurses had all been handed new, dark blue jumpsuits to be put on after the briefing. They were all, apparently, going somewhere today.

Doctor Ghariid, the Research Unit medical director, came in, followed by an American Navy officer in a white uniform that Miriam had seen before around the Research Unit. When the officer appeared, the two American nurses started to get to their feet, but the officer quickly said, "At ease," and the nurses sat back down.

Dr. Ghariid went to the podium, "Good morning, thank you for coming in a bit early this morning. We have pulled all of you from your usual assignments for special duties today, which will require a little travel, so we needed the early start.

"Let me start by introducing, for those of you who may not have personally met him before, the Commanding Officer of the U.S. Navy Medical Research Unit Number Three, Captain Jonathan Rogers, Jr., for a few words."

Captain Rogers came to the podium and looked around the room. "I want to give all of you my personal thanks for the fantastic job you have all done over the last few months. All of you on our medical staff have played an indispensable role in fighting this tragic epidemic. The entire NAMRU team should know that I received a call from the Egyptian president himself, asking me to thank you for your service and courage in helping in this fight.

"On that point, I would also like to give you the good news that it appears the flu outbreak is slowing across Egypt. Except for a stubborn hotspot in Alexandria, the influenza seems to be following the typical pattern of retreating in spring and summer months. Similar reports are coming in from other countries. If that turns out to be accurate, it will indeed be a blessing. If we are given a break over the summer, we may be able to get an effective vaccine against the avian flu to the people before the flu season starts up in earnest again next fall. If we cannot get the vaccine out before the flu comes back, I can't even imagine what a full season of the avian flu will be like, here or around the world.

"What we are asking you today is to start on the important job preparing that vaccine for use by the citizens of Egypt and the people of the whole world. I will let Dr. Ghariid explain and give you your instructions. Once again, thank you all for your service. Have a safe trip today."

Captain Rogers nodded to Ghariid and left the room. Ghariid came back to the podium, and said, "The job of preparing a vaccine for use is an effort of thousands of people in many countries. The World Health Organization is gathering data from around the world. Laboratories in many countries, including here at NAMRU are, right now, striving to come up with an effective antigen against the avian flu. But, before the vaccine can be produced and distributed, it must be tested. The vaccine must be both safe and effective. Once the vaccine is formulated, it must go through both animal and human tests. The human tests will take place in several countries, including Egypt. To be sure that the vaccine is effective in the human tests, we must be sure that the persons who will be the test subjects have never had the avian flu and have never even been exposed to it. They cannot have been exposed because they cannot have already developed antibodies to the virus. We need to know that the vaccine successfully caused their bodies to produce the right antibodies to the avian flu.

"As you might guess, given the massive epidemic that has hit Egypt, it might be difficult to find enough people who have not been exposed in any way to the virus. But we think we have an idea. When the avian flu broke out in February, the Egyptian Army had two regiments of its special forces troops deployed to eastern Libya on an anti-terrorism and peacekeeping mission. Within the last two weeks, those two regiments have been withdrawn from Libya and have returned to a base southwest of Cairo. With the ongoing fighting amongst the Libyan factions, there was little commingling of people in Libya with citizens of other countries that were hit by the avian flu in the last two months. Those two Egyptian regiments have, unlike the rest of the Egyptian military, had no cases of the avian flu.

"The Egyptian leadership has put the base where those two regiments are currently stationed under strict lockdown quarantine. It has been agreed that the two to three thousand soldiers there will be the perfect group to test for the antibodies and then, those who have not been exposed will be perfect test subjects to get the first doses of the test vaccine.

"NAMRU will be coordinating the Egyptian testing of a number of new vaccines which will be formulated in America and other countries. Today, you will be starting that important work by taking blood samples from a couple of thousand special forces soldiers. After we get the blood test results, we will have an accurate list of who will get the first vaccine, which you will go back to administer in June or July, and then resample their blood a few weeks later to check for antibodies. The only weak spot in this proposal is how to keep two thousand young men away from their families, friends, and other temptations for the two months until they get the vaccine shots." The nurses laughed. "The Army will have its hands full with that.

"So, please get dressed for field work. The bus to take you out to Faiyum and the trucks with your supplies will be waiting for you in the east courtyard. You should not need much for the trip; it's just for today. The weather is supposed to be nice, and we will provide food. You should be home in Cairo by early evening. Please let your families know you might be a bit late this evening. Thank you all."

Miriam sat and thought for a moment. She turned to the nurse next to her and said, "Two thousand soldiers divided by ten nurses. That means we each have to do two-hundred blood draws today? Is that possible?"

The other nurse looked at her, raised her eyebrows and shrugged.

———

Emergency Room
Grady Memorial Hospital
Atlanta, Georgia
08:48 AM EDT April 29ᵗʰ

Dr. Marty Craig was reading the patient status whiteboard in the ER when he felt his cellphone vibrate in his pocket. He checked the screen and recognized the 301 area code for Maryland. It was the same area code as his Army Reserve unit at Fort Detrick, but he did not recognize the number.

He answered, "Hello?"

"Lieutenant Colonel Craig?" a woman's voice asked.

"Yes, this is Martin Craig."

"This is Major Sarah Morton. I'm the adjutant for General Harding, your wife's commanding general."

"Yes?" Marty's voice conveyed his uneasiness. "Good morning."

"Doctor Craig, we just received a call from your wife's XO, Captain Cameron, letting us know that early this morning, Captain Llewellyn was transported from her quarters to the St. John's Regional Medical Center, near there. She was ill with the flu. The general remembered your wife saying that you're still down in Georgia and asked me to call you. I got your number from USAMRIID's S1."

When Marty did not immediately answer, Morton continued, "Captain Cameron says she left work after only an hour yesterday. Before she left, she had the nurse at her command do an influenza test on her, which they were able to do right there in their lab. It came back that she has the avian flu that's circulating in LA. Captain Cameron says she called the ambulance herself shortly after midnight this morning and called him when she did. I guess if anyone knows when it's time to call for help with this flu, it's your wife."

"Do you know her current condition?"

"I tried to call and could not get any information. General Harding called back and identified himself as an Army doctor, and they told him she was in serious-to-guarded condition. I assume you know what that means since you're a physician."

"Yes, I do."

"If we get any more information, we'll let you know immediately. Is this the best number?"

"Yes, this is my cell. Thank you for calling," Marty said. "Wait, you said she is at St. John's Hospital?"

"Yes, I Googled it. St. John's Regional Medical Center is the biggest and the best hospital they have in that area. It's in Oxnard, California, that's O-X-N-A-R-D."

"Yes, I know, I went to med school in LA. Thank you again for calling." They hung up.

Marty stood looking at the blank cellphone screen for a long while. He knew the medical jargon well. If a hospital was listing an avian flu patient using the term "serious," that most likely meant she was in severe breathing distress and probably intubated. Adding "to Guarded" probably meant she was better occasionally but remained serious. He had entered that same note too many times in the last month.

Dr. Martin Craig decided he had two calls he needed to make. First, he would call the Grady ER coordinator to get taken off rotation for a week or so. Next, he would call Delta Airlines. Before his last conversation with Karen, he had already checked and figured out Delta had the most direct flights from Atlanta to Los Angeles. This was not the way he had intended to reconnect, but he would go to LA and make sure Karen was alright.

—

Chapter 29

101 Freeway
North of Downtown
Los Angeles, California
10:45 AM PDT May 2ⁿᵈ

The message for Acting Sergeant Matt Relford to break free from his shift at the Lost Hills-Malibu Sheriff's Station and drive downtown for a meeting at Sheriff's HQ had come in with only an hour to spare before the time of the meeting. Matt was supposed to meet with the undersheriff. He had talked to the undersheriff when he had received the call to take over as acting sergeant to cover while Rick Gonçalvez was laid up, but he had never met the undersheriff personally. With about 10,000 deputies and another 8000 civilian employees, the LA Sheriff's Department was a big place, and Matt Relford was not in the same circle of acquaintances as Undersheriff Guy Martinez. Matt was not sure what such a meeting could be about. He assumed it was to make his temporary promotion to sergeant permanent. He had been on the promotion list to sergeant for several years, but the promotion had been tied up in budget cuts and hiring freezes. As he thought about the meeting, Matt remembered that this was not a meeting with the undersheriff, it was with the acting sheriff. Word had spread in the department that Sheriff Covarrubias had lost his battle with the flu and his car crash injuries and had passed away the week before.

The 101 was not as busy as usual mid-morning on a weekday. Matt took the Broadway exit and turned right and right again to park in the 'official business' parking structure next to the Hall of Justice, where his meeting was. Matt had been to LA Sheriff's headquarters many times in his career but rarely ventured to the executive office area. When he mentioned his name to the receptionist, he was directed to a wood-paneled waiting room. One other deputy, a sergeant, was already there waiting.

Matt knew the sergeant, Ned Pujols, having worked with him many years before. Matt shook hands with him and asked, "You have any idea what this meeting is about?"

"Not a clue. You?" was the answer.

Matt shook his head and took a seat.

The sergeant pointed at Matt's sleeve and the three chevron stripes, "When did you make sergeant?"

"Acting," Matt explained.

"There is a lot of that."

Matt nodded.

In a few moments, a woman came in with a sheriff commander star on her khaki uniform collar. Matt recognized her as the former captain who had run the promotion exams at Personnel. Here was another promotion.

"Sergeant Pujols," the new commander, Nowak, announced. She motioned for Pujols to follow her. "Sergeant Relford, I'll be with you in a moment."

Matt sat and waited. In about ten minutes, a stocky woman in a sheriff lieutenant's uniform came in and sat down. She and Matt nodded to each other. Matt remembered seeing this woman at the North County Jail in Castaic. They exchanged greetings, with each looking at the nametag of the other.

The commander reappeared with no sign of Pujols. The commander asked Matt to go with her and told the lieutenant she would be back.

Matt followed the commander to a small conference room. She sat near a stack of maybe twenty file folders and pointed Matt to a chair at the end of the table next to her. She took the top folder off the stack. When she opened the folder, Matt saw his picture inside. It was his personnel record jacket. The commander silently turned pages and double-checked things with a paper she pulled for a pile nearby.

At last, the commander turned to Matt and said, "This meeting will be a two-step process. First, I will explain what's going on, and then you will go in to meet Sheriff Martinez, who will explain the details as it pertains to you."

Matt noticed she called him Sheriff Martinez, not Acting Sheriff Martinez, nor Undersheriff.

The commander closed the sheet of paper inside Matt's record jacket and took a sip of water from a paper cup on the table. "Like everyone else in the department, I'm sure you're aware of the impact this avian flu has had on the department. That sentence probably sounds peculiar to you as you were one of our first cases. In reality, it's much worse than most people realize. The department was already short of sworn deputies and people in senior officer ranks, after the coronavirus deaths plus the freeze on hiring and promotions put in place to deal with the budget shortage after the financial fall-out from the coronavirus. Now, this avian flu has hit Los Angeles like a sledgehammer. For some reason that I'm sure a brilliant scientist will figure out someday, the Sheriff's Department and LAPD have been hit with a higher percentage of both avian flu cases and flu deaths than the population at large. About one percent of our sworn deputies and officers succumbed in the last two months to the flu. And, this has hit our senior officers disproportionately, for the same unknown reason. Your area, out west, and out in Lancaster/Palmdale, plus in the correctional facilities, were particularly hard hit. You may have heard that last week, Sheriff Martinez convinced the Board of Supervisors that this lack of people in senior leadership positions in the department was a danger to public safety, especially as this avian flu threatens to continue and perhaps hit us again in the fall. He threatened to start emptying the Main Jail and Twin Towers and shut down Court Services if he did not have enough leaders to protect the public. Just making temporary acting promotions was not working. The department needed stability and leadership.

"The Board of Supervisors passed an emergency ordinance, effective immediately, authorizing the Sheriff to ignore normal civil service rules and make permanent promotions for qualified officers to fill the vacant senior officer positions, as he sees fit. You already had your papers in for promotion to sergeant for some time and probably would have made it, if not for the promotion freeze. You also had applied for a lateral to the detective bureau. You had glowing recommendation letters from Merriman, Jackson, and Moldonado. To make a long story short, besides giving you a few weeks off to recuperate, this flu epidemic is going to give you a permanent promotion. I'll let Sheriff Martinez tell you about that. Let me see if he is done with the previous person."

She got up and knocked on a door on the far wall of the conference room. She looked in and then walked back to the table. She handed Matt his records jacket and said, "Sheriff Martinez is ready for you."

As Matt opened the door, he saw the sheriff was already walking toward him with his hand out. The sheriff took the personnel jacket from his hand and then shook hands with him. He noticed the five stars on Sheriff Martinez's collar.

"Please have a seat, sergeant," the sheriff indicated a chair in front of his desk. He went and sat behind the huge desk. "Give me a moment to look through this."

"Yes sir."

After thumbing through the file folder, the sheriff nodded his head and gave an expression that he was satisfied with what he had read. "Sergeant Relford, I don't recall having met you before. I came up through the ranks out at Temple Station, which is a bit out of your stomping grounds. I've been meeting many new faces recently.

"First, I want to express my condolences on the loss of your fiancée. I know there is nothing I can say that will make things better, but I wanted to mention that."

Matt pursed his lips and nodded, saying nothing.

The sheriff continued, "I don't have a lot of time, and I know Commander Nowak already filled you in, so let's cut to the chase. When I had Rick Gonçalvez in here to give him his captain's bars, I asked him for his advice on whom he knew in the department who could help me out with my leadership vacancies.

He did not hesitate one second in giving me your name. I had Commander Nowak check you out and make some calls for me. Hearing the results, I had her put you on my list."

The sheriff turned his office chair to face Matt directly, "You have everything I need right now. You finished your B.A. degree in Law Enforcement from Cal State Northridge. You have nearly twenty years of spotless service in both patrol and corrections. A couple of people who I really trust and admire said great things about you. I see in your performance evals that ten years ago, Commander Moldonado offered you a sergeant's slot at the Jail if you would turn down your pending transfer to Patrol."

Matt tried, unsuccessfully, not to react to that. He had no interest in Corrections. But Matt had never had a good poker face.

Martin gave a small smile and said, "Yes, I know how most patrol deputies think about Corrections. Remember, I was a patrol type for most of my career. But, everybody is aware of the somewhat sordid history of leadership at the LA County Jail. Now, that problem is made worse by the losses we have had in the leadership there and elsewhere. I have not helped things, either. Seeing which senior officers I had available in Corrections to promote from within given the flu losses and the firings a few years back, I actually decided the best thing for the department was to ask two of them to retire early to clear out the deadwood, so to speak.

"Oh, and I forgot to mention. The ACLU and the County Public Defender have teamed up to sue Los Angeles County, alleging that the current avian flu infection rate for inmates at the Main Jail and every one of the branch jails constitutes unconstitutional 'cruel and unusual treatment.' And, confidentially, I'm not sure I disagree with them. It's bad. I promised the Board of Supervisors when they confirmed my appointment as Sheriff that I would make changes needed to correct things.

"Which brings us to you. I realize that going from Patrol in Lost Hills-Malibu to working back at the Jail may not be what you hoped for. However, in these bad times I need to ask you to 'take one for the department' and help me out at the Jail."

Matt cut the sheriff off, "Sir, I'm not sure getting these stripes permanently could make up for going back there. I did nearly nine years there and earned my way out."

Sheriff Martin laughed out loud at this. Matt blinked at him, a bit in shock at the sheriff's reaction.

The sheriff continued, "I didn't say anything about sergeant's stripes. And, it's those nine years of sterling corrections experience I'm counting on. And, ten more in the field. Commander Nowak is our guru of human relations data, and she tells me that if you had taken Moldonado's offer of sergeant at the Jail when he offered it, you would be a captain by now. At least a captain, she says, given the difference in promotions between Corrections and Patrol. So, given our losses from this god-damned flu, and the Jail's bad reputation—I need bold new leadership at the Jail—here is my offer."

The sheriff picked something up off his desk, stood, and walked around to stand next to Matt. The sheriff held his closed hand out, palm down. Matt stood up.

"I'm asking you, for the good of the department to which we both have devoted our lives, to take these and report to your new boss at the Main Jail tomorrow morning."

Matt held out his hand, palm up. Matt's brow was furrowed. The sheriff dropped two single silver star rank insignias in the palm of his hand.

"Commander?" was all Matt could say.

"Yes, I have a gut feeling that you're a good match for this. The Board gave me the authority to follow my gut. And that gut feeling is confirmed by every officer Commander Nowak called about you."

"Who will be my new boss at the Main Jail?" Matt asked.

The sheriff shook his head, "I'm not sure just yet. I have a set of double stars still on my desk that are waiting to find their owner."

Matt thought for a moment and then moved the stars to his left hand and reached out to shake the sheriff's hand. The world which had gone weird with coronavirus and, now, had gone crazy with this avian flu and had cost him Marjorie, had just thrown Matt Relford a new curve.

As Matt exited the Hall of Justice, his head buzzed with a jumble of thoughts. Two thoughts were foremost. First, how do you handle 18,000 inmates crowded into the largest jail system in the world in an age of deadly pandemics? His second question was, what on earth had he just done?

When Matt reached the squad car in the parking garage, his thoughts turned to more practical questions. When he had removed his old Deputy II stripes on the shirt he wore today, he noticed that the fabric was faded a different color under the old double chevron. That was fine when he sewed the new sergeant triple chevron over the discoloration. But, now, he would have nothing on his sleeves, just the new star on each collar. He decided that since he was downtown already, he should stop into Zavin's Uniforms and pick up some new shirts for his various sheriff department uniforms, and a few more silver stars. He figured he would wear one of the new shirts when he dropped the squad car off at Lost Hills. The reaction to his new rank at the station should be interesting. Besides, he needed to thank Rick Gonçalvez for his good words that had gotten him promoted. Then again, Matt might live to regret this promotion.

———

U.S. Navy Medical Research Unit
Abbassia Fever Hospital
Cairo, Egypt
4:10 PM Local Time May 2ⁿᵈ

Miriam Mansoor had been correct in her suspicion that one day was not enough time for ten nurses to take blood samples from two entire regiments of soldiers. On top of that, one of the regiments was not in the loop about the blood tests, and some of the soldiers were out training in the desert that first day they went to Haiyum. So, the Research Unit had scheduled a return trip this week, with five additional nurses and phlebotomists borrowed from the Abbassia Hospital staff.

The second trip earlier today to Haiyum had been shorter, and they returned to Cairo early. Miriam was changing out of the blue jumpsuit into her usual white nurse's dress in the nurses' locker room when the secretary for the head nurse came up and handed her an envelope.

Miriam's heart leaped when she saw the envelope. She had not seen an answer to the letter she had sent to her parents in late March. Her hopes dimmed when she read the return address. Instead of her parents, the return address on the letter was from her father's brother, Miriam's uncle, Anwar Mansoor. The envelope was addressed to the address here at the Research Unit Miriam had given in her letter. Her uncle was a sundries merchant in Minuf and was getting on in years. The envelope and the note inside was written in disheveled Arabic handwriting.

Dearest Niece Miriam,
It is with great sorrow that I write to you. I am sorry to tell you that your parents did not survive this plague. We were so happy to get your letter and to know that you had survived. Allah be praised.

The Magistrate's Office in Minuf brought your brother and sister to us to care for, as is our duty and joy. The children send their love to you, their sister. They are excited to hear that their beloved sister is employed at such an important institution in Al Kahira.

The Magistrate reports that there was not much left of your parent's property after the disturbances ended in Minuf. The thieves and brigands pilfered the property of the unfortunate dead. Allah be praised, our home was safe, and my wife and children survived.

My son, Hakim, followed the Magistrate's instruction and collected a trunk of papers, pictures, and small things that were not stolen from your parents' house. Your aunt, my dearest Badriyah, will save the items for you to share with your brother and sister when they are of an age to care about such things.

Please write to us to let us know you have received this and to tell us how you fare. We all look forward to seeing you again.

Blessed be,
The loving brother of your father,
Anwar ibn Mahmud al Mansoor

Miriam sat on the bench in the locker room with the letter in her hands. Sanniya, Miriam's roommate in the Research Unit's employee housing, came up behind her and announced, "Two of the soldiers passed me notes with their names and addresses. Did you get any?"

Sanniya tried again, "Miriam?" but she stopped when she saw the tears in Miriam's eyes. "What's wrong?"

Miriam handed Sanniya the letter. Sanniya read it and handed it back. There was nothing to say.

"Miriam, finish dressing and let's go home. You can't just sit here on the bench."

Miriam sighed deeply and nodded. At any other time, she would be bragging to Sanniya about the note with name and address she had collected from not just a mere soldier but a handsome young officer. Such things did not seem to matter to Miriam now. But she was glad she had Sanniya to walk home with and talk to tonight. Miriam missed everyone back home.

———

Intensive Care Unit #3
St. John's Regional Medical Center
Oxnard, California
5:19 PM PDT May 2nd

After the horror stories that everybody had heard during the coronavirus crisis, this was the perfect nightmare. Karen Llewellyn awoke lying in a hospital bed. An oxygen tube wrapped across her face. A figure in a hooded medical jumpsuit with a full face mask and face shield looked down at her. Her head ached, and her lungs hurt. Her dry mouth and dreadfully sore throat pained her with each breath. But . . . she was breathing on her own. She seemed to remember when that was not the case. She tried to speak but only croaked. The figure standing over her reached and gave her a sip of water. That helped.

"Was I intubated?" she asked.

"Yes, you were. But you're better now," said the caregiver, a man. His voice seemed familiar. She was confused.

Her vision was not exactly clear. Eyes that had not opened in a long time do not focus well. She struggled to see behind the glare of the face shield on the caregiver.

"Marty?" she asked.

"Yes. How are you feeling?"

Karen thought a minute and answered, "'Like death warmed over,' I think is the term."

Marty shook his head, "Not exactly what I need to hear right now. You had us worried."

"Where am I?"

"St. John's in Ventura County."

"How did you get here, and dressed out like that?" Karen asked.

"General Harding had me called. And, when I heard your condition, I knew I had to get here. Then, it turns out the medical director here was my best friend at UCLA med school. He approved temporary privileges for me."

"What day is it? How long was I . . . ?"

"This is your fourth day. I think. I've sort of lost count myself."

"You've been here the whole time."

Marty nodded. "This is nothing unusual for us real doctors. You ivory tower doctors don't know the joys of sleeping in chairs and stealing patient meals from the meal cart. I've gotten good at marathon hospital slumming over the years."

After a pause, Marty added, "You had us worried. You were on full ventilator with oxygen for the better part of two days. Bilateral edema. You scared the . . . out of me."

Karen wrinkled her forehead, "And General Harding called you?"

"His adjutant. Then, once your Army buddies like Rob Cameron heard I was here, I became information central about Captain Llewellyn's condition. Then, after the TV report, I . . ."

"TV report?" Karen asked.

"Yeah, that reporter who did your cable TV interview last month found out about you from somewhere. She did a human interest story about the beautiful military doctor who was trying to save the country with her vaccine, but was now fighting for her life in the hospital from the very avian flu she was hoping to save the country from."

"Oh, God!" Karen tried to put her hand on her forehead, but stopped when she felt the IV tube.

Marty continued, "I refused to talk to the TV crew on camera, but they managed to get a shot of me slumped on a bench with my head in my hands, trying to get some shut-eye. They put that in the TV segment, too, and identified me. Then, the calls really poured in. Phil Reynes called me. I got chewed out by your mother for not calling her. Now that you're out of the woods, and as soon as I figure out how to recharge my cellphone, I have plenty of promised return calls to make."

"Thanks for coming, I guess."

"You guess?"

Karen smiled, "No, ignore that. Thanks. I'm just having a hard time taking all this in."

"Yeah, I understand. Now, you should get some non-chemical sleep. You have been through a lot." Marty started to leave.

"Wait, you said you talked to Rob Cameron. Is everything OK at the plant? You know . . ."

"Yes, Karen, I'm sure everything is fine. Lotsa big boys and girls there can survive for a few days without their heroic captain. This is why God invented XOs. Get some sleep."

Karen nodded. She reached out to where Marty's hand was on the bed rail and squeezed his hand.

—

Chapter 30

Staff Conference & Training Room
Twin Towers Correctional Facility
Los Angeles, California
9:00 AM PDT May 5th

Leona Madigan was the stocky woman Matt Relford had met in the Hall of Justice waiting room before he had gotten his four-step promotion and reassignment. Leona had become the new owner of the twin star insignias the Sheriff mentioned he had on his desk. Her promotion had only been three steps, from lieutenant to chief. She was the newly appointed chief of the LA Sheriff's Custody Services Division.

Chief Madigan looked around the room at her senior officers in charge of the Los Angeles County Jail facilities handling the nearly eighteen thousand prisoners. "It doesn't seem to make sense. Everybody is telling us how the current avian flu epidemic seems to be dying down, probably lessening like the regular seasonal flu. However, they also say it will be back next fall. But the infections of our inmate population seem to be getting worse. Our in-house hospital is full. All of the medical wards at every facility we run are full. The LA County-USC Hospital jail ward is full, and they have many non-dangerous prisoner avian flu cases in their regular infectious disease containment areas. The non-hospitalized prisoners with avian flu still in the main lock-up areas are sequestered by themselves. Every one of those sick prisoner groups is growing. Why are the jailed prisoners with avian flu not synching with the seasonal drop in the flu, like everywhere else? Plus, our custody deputies are still dropping from this flu. Any ideas? Is it simply crowded conditions?"

There was silence at first, and then Chief Madigan saw the new head of the Twin Towers Jail facility lift his hand to get her attention. She nodded and said, "Matt, you have any ideas?"

"I think I might," Commander Matt Relford said. "Many of you have probably heard that I had the misfortune to be among the first handful of people catching this avian flu in March here in LA."

Matt saw several people nod their heads, including Chief Madigan.

Matt continued, "Besides the unwelcome fifteen minutes of fame that brought me, it did put me in touch with one of the top experts in influenza. Dr. Hector Cristobal is an infectious disease doctor at Cedars-Sinai Hospital, and he teaches at USC. When I was recuperating from the flu, he came in to talk to me. Originally, he intended just to come in to offer his condolences on the death of my fiancée from the flu and apologize for his staff not being able to save her. I told him I didn't blame anyone, except for maybe myself for bringing the flu home from work. He stayed to talk with me for a while. Hector turned out to be a very brilliant man, he told me some amazing things about the flu <u>and</u> the coronavirus. He literally wrote the book on the coronavirus crisis when it was over. He won some big award for that book. Anyway, I was amazed at what he knew about diseases. Even though I talked to him back at the start of the avian flu here in LA and very early in the epidemic in Egypt, he told me exactly what he expected to happen here and in the rest of the world. Everything he told me turned out to be right on."

Matt paused and continued, "Yesterday, I saw the ugly figures from here at the Jail that Leona . . . Chief Madigan just asked us about. I remembered how Doctor Cristobal had told me that the avian flu would probably rest over the summer. He said that was natural for flu viruses. I figured I needed to call Doctor Cristobal and ask him some questions.

"I got ahold of him by phone, told him who I was, and he remembered me. I told him what my new job was and explained our situation. I asked him why our prisoners weren't getting a seasonal flu break like the rest of the world is."

Matt waited a second before continuing, "Doctor Cristobal's answer to me was that the avian flu probably wasn't dying down in the jail because it isn't summer in the jail, despite the calendar on the wall. He said that the usual thinking about seasonal flu that it dies down when people stop getting crowded together indoors is not really the main answer. Of course, it will always be crowded in jail, but Doctor Cristobal said that close quarters is only a small part of the answer. He said that the predominant theory about why influenza is seasonal is that environmental factors affect the virus itself. First, the virus is deathly allergic to ultraviolet light, the light that comes from the sun, gives you a suntan, and increases its brightness in summer months. When people go outside in the ultraviolet light of summer, the virus cannot survive on their hands and face, and those people's sneezes and coughs produce the contagious droplets we have all heard about, but the flu droplets die in the direct summer sunlight. Next, the flu virus flourishes in cool, dry weather, like the weather that's almost everywhere in the winter. The flu virus hates the heat, and heat plus humidity is even worse for flu because the moist, humid air conducts the warmer temperatures better than dry air. Flu spreads much slower in hot, humid weather.

"Doctor Cristobal asked me if the LA jails were air-conditioned. I said yes and mentioned the lawsuits some jurisdictions have had about jails being too hot and having poor air conditioning, bad circulation, and high humidity. Doctor Cristobal said cool temperatures and low humidity, like most commercial HVAC systems produce, create perfect breeding grounds for flu viruses.

"He said that if you combine cool temperatures and low humidity along with lighting fixtures that produce very little ultra-violet light, it pretty much creates an environment in a place like the jail where it's never summer. He said that most of the standard fluorescent light bulbs, like we use in the jail, are specifically designed with phosphor coatings inside the tube that absorbs all the ultraviolet light. So, the avian flu is not acting like the seasonal flu for our inmates and our staff. Inmates and staff spend most days and nights in an artificial winter-like existence where the flu virus thrives."

"Did Dr. Cristobal give you any specific advice, besides those obvious issues?" Chief Madigan asked.

Matt nodded and smiled, "Better than just advice. Doctor Cristobal offered to come down here, maybe with a couple of his USC graduate students to do a survey, tour the various jail facilities, sample the environmental factors, look at the lighting, maybe study prisoner outside rec hours and perhaps interview our medical staff to see if we could diagnose a way to convince our flu germs to take a summer break."

Leona raised her eyebrows and pointed her finger at Matt, "Commander Relford, I want you to make that happen."

———

Infectious Disease Treatment Ward
St. John's Regional Medical Center
Oxnard, California
4:30 PM PDT May 8th

Karen Llewellyn sat on the edge of her hospital bed in a new, blue jogging suit that Marty had bought for her at the Walmart across the street from St. John's Hospital. She could not go home in Marty's rental car in the same pajamas she had worn for the ambulance ride ten days before. Marty stood waiting for her at the end of her bed. They were listening to a young nurse give Karen her discharge instructions.

Karen's nurse, Kimberly, was reading from a stack of papers in her hand. "Typically, a healthy person is no longer contagious with the flu virus five to seven days after the onset of illness. So, you should be free from shedding the virus by now. But, just to be sure, we recommend against going back to work or meeting unnecessary people for another week after you're discharged. Usually the flu virus . . ."

Marty interrupted the nurse, "You can probably skip the virus advice. Karen is an expert on flu viruses."

Kimberly turned toward Marty, pulled her glasses down on her nose to stare at him. "I'm quite aware of who Dr. Llewellyn is. I saw the TV report about her. It made quite a splash here at the hospital. In fact, I have my cellphone in my pocket to ask my famous patient to do a selfie with me after I finish with her discharge papers. However, the bottom of this paper is a certification that I sign as a medical professional, swearing I've properly informed my patient of the parameters of her illness and her instructions when she leaves. I try to do my job correctly. OK, doctor?"

Karen looked at Marty and gave a little snicker.

Marty raised his hands in a gesture of surrender and said, "Point made, I apologize."

Karen and Marty listened to Kimberly read the rest of her pile of papers.

———

Camino De La Mimosa
Camarillo, California
5:45 PM PDT May 8th

Marty parked in front of Karen's rented condo in Camarillo. He rushed around to open the door for her. She went inside first. On the way to the front door, Karen reached to pull up her sweat pants.

"Don't lose your pants, Captain," Marty jeered.

"Either I've lost some weight, or you bought the wrong size."

"Probably the former, I didn't see you eat anything for the first six days."

"Sounds like a new book, The Avian Flu Diet."

Karen sat on the couch in the living room. Marty did not sit down.

"You need me to go buy anything while I'm here?" Marty asked.

"No, I should have everything I need here. I've gotten pretty handy at ordering what I need from Whole Foods delivery. What are your plans? You going to stay around for a while?"

"Despite the fact I've hoped for an invitation like that for a long time, no, I can't. Danny says they are still on twelve-hour shifts with the avian flu in Atlanta. My ten-day absence has strained the ER system beyond its limits. "

"Hmm, too bad. We've made some progress these last few days. I trust you're coming back for a visit soon." Karen sounded sad.

"Of course. We can talk about the future when you get on your feet and back in your groove."

"So, when you leaving?"

"It's about two hours to LAX, plus rental car return. I just about have the time I need to leave now and catch the Delta red-eye flight to Atlanta."

"Umm-hmm." Karen pushed herself off of the couch—awkward and a bit weak getting to her feet.

Marty said, "Remember to call your mother. I promised her I would tell you that. She threatened to come out here and nurse you to health herself if she didn't hear from you that you're alright."

"I'd better call her." Karen looked at Marty and spread her arms wide. "Nurse Kimberly said no kissing for my fourteen days. But, a hug won't hurt."

It was hard to end their hug. It had been a long time.

———

Thousand Oaks Defense Pharmaceutical Plant (TODPP)
Thousand Oaks, California
8:00 AM PDT May 16th

Karen decided to look her best on the first day back to work after her illness, so she wore her summer whites uniform. She was feeling good, a bit weak still, but good nevertheless.

She parked in her CO's parking spot and picked up her things to bring inside. When Karen rounded the back of her Audi, headed for the gate, she came face to face with a young woman in an Army Class A uniform, also headed for the gate, who stopped and saluted Karen. The soldier was in her 20s with a broad, Slavic-looking face, and her pale blonde hair was cut short. The woman, a Specialist 5, wore numerous award and campaign ribbons and a Combat Medical Badge above her left pocket.

"Good Morning, Captain Llewellyn."

Karen glanced at the soldier's nametag, "Good morning, Specialist Kuchma. We were expecting you."

"I got in the week before last, while you were out."

"Yes, I got some of this flu."

"I know. I saw the report on TV."

Karen rolled her eyes, "Seems everybody did. So, why are you in a dress uniform, we usually wear utility uniforms to work. I'm just in this to get back in the office groove after being away."

Kuchma smiled, "Kinda the same for me, Ma'am. Master Sergeant Ghent said you'd be here today, and I wanted to make a good first impression."

Karen smiled, "Mission accomplished. Let's go." She walked toward to gate, followed by Kuchma.

Both women showed their TODPP/DOD employee badge to the guard at the gate and clipped the badge to their uniforms. They headed for the front door.

"So, Specialist Kuchma. I read that you're assigned as our medical technician?"

"Yes, ma'am. I have a dual MOS. I was a medic for my first tour. That's where I got these," she indicated her campaign ribbons and badges. "Then, I re-upped for more schooling and qualified as a medical technician."

"Well, we are glad to have you. Our work here should be interesting."

The automatic front door opened, and Master Sergeant Ghent was standing in the doorway. He saluted Karen. She saluted back.

"Master sergeant, you always manage to be here at the door when I come in. How so?"

Ghent smiled, "Well, ma'am, one of my assigned duties is facility security. So, it was easy to review the guards' operating procedure manual and make sure that every time the CO passes through a gate at any of the three facilities, in or out, they send a text message to Plant Security, which is me."

"I see."

Kuchma took off her hat inside the door and said, "Nice meeting you, ma'am. Good morning, master sergeant." Kuchma headed off down the main hall.

Karen and Ghent headed to the right down the executive office hallway.

Karen asked Ghent, "Where does Kuchma work?"

"Well, when Kuchma was introduced to Sonya Hayburn as a medical technician, Sonya assumed she belonged in the lab and gave her an office there, even though Kuchma is Army staff, not HeptImun. Hayburn didn't understand that a medical technician in the Army is a medical caregiver, not a repairman. Captain Cameron and I did not argue with Sonya, and it has kind of worked out well."

"Sounds good to me. What's on the agenda for today?"

"A briefing to get you up to speed on happenings while you were gone. And, we need to start work on the public outreach meetings we are supposed to do with news media, politicians, and important SoCal people."

"Yuck, not my forté." Karen said.

"You could have fooled me on that. You seem to be a natural."

———

Chapter 31

3rd Floor Control Room, Tower One
Twin Towers Correctional Facility
Los Angeles, California
9:00 AM PDT June 14th

Sheriff Commander Matt Relford stood watching out of the shatterproof glass surrounding the control room overlooking two floors of the Twin Towers Jail. From the panels and multiple-video monitors to his right, the unit duty sergeant and two assistants watched security cameras and controlled the electronically-operated doors on the multiple window-enclosed hexagonal-sectioned prisoner units that surrounded the common area on these two floors. The two-stories of cells he could see here were duplicated on the several different levels of the two double-columned jail buildings that Matt was now in charge of. Another commander was in charge of the nearby Main Jail building. Both answered to Chief Leona Madigan.

Elsewhere in this building, the single-person high-security cells were clustered in smaller groups with no common area. The design of the Twin Towers building had been state-of-the-art penal architecture when it had been built in the 90s. In the age of viral pandemics, the building design Matt was looking at meant that two-hundred-plus prisoners all faced inward to a single common area where they ate and congregated 24 hours a day.

The twin eight-story buildings meant getting groups of prisoners to daylight for the limited period of outdoor time they were scheduled for was difficult at best. The newly installed banks of light fixtures producing whitish-blue ultra-violet light for the common area were what he had come here to inspect.

Matt heard the elevator open, and footsteps approach him. He turned to see Leona Madigan walking up. "Morning Chief."

"Morning, Matt. Christie said you were up here."

"Yeah, she seems always to have a good handle on where I am. Not sure how she does that."

Leona laughed, "Really, Matt? You haven't figured that out yet. The duty sergeants and watch officers are all listening on Security Common circuit. They have nicknames for every senior officer. As you or I move through the building, they announce our moves to everyone else. When I just came in here, they passed the word that Elvira was on 3-1-North with Dillon. Your efficient young admin assistant merely has to check with any duty sergeant or the watch officer and ask him where Dillon is."

Matt looked questioningly at the Chief. "Elvira and Dillon?"

"'Elvira' Madigan and Matt 'Dillon.'"

Matt laughed, "I've still got some things to learn here."

"How are things this morning?" Chief Madigan asked.

"Getting better. We are down to 75% capacity, and the complaints about not having A/C are fewer. Only three new flu cases yesterday and today. Staff numbers are up to snuff. I was checking out our pretty new lights."

"Well, I have some good news. The sheriff just called. He just got out of a closed session with the Board of Supervisors discussing the lawsuit. They agreed to the interim settlement with the ACLU and Public Defender. The work plan for our operations, capacity, and physical plant changes worked out. County Counsel said that the report from Doctor Cristobal made all the difference. That convinced everyone we are on the right track to controlling the flu in all our jail facilities. The sheriff told me to make sure you knew he gives you full credit for that."

Matt did not say anything at first. He just nodded. Then, he added, "Now, we better hope that the scientists come up with something to stop the flu from coming back in the fall."

"Yup, they say on TV that they have a vaccine in the works. Should be ready by September."

Matt shook his head, "That's OK for staff, and most of the people we have in lock-up. But I read that only about forty percent of people in general in the U.S. get the annual flu shot. Even after the coronavirus scared the shit out of people, the initial big numbers of people getting the coronavirus vaccine dropped a lot the next year."

"Yeah, some people never learn," Chief Madigan said.

Matt added, "And the people that are our primary clientele in here are slower than most to learn life's lessons."

———

Jiandong Restaurant
Jinjing Street
Baodi City, China
6:20 PM Local Time June 14th

Xi Zemin smiled when he saw Yang Xinru's head pop up over the hedge outside the restaurant. That was how she usually looked to see if Zemin had arrived first at what had become their favorite restaurant.

When he had been removed from the disease-related cases back in March, he had felt more comfortable with calling Xinru up and asking her out. Xinru continued to work on the flu deaths but had increasingly felt uncomfortable talking about them with Zemin, especially after the older woman Xinru worked with had succumbed to the disease. Xinru and Zemin whispered about the disease between each other, but like most people in Baodi, nothing was spoken in public. The only difference was, Zemin and Xinru knew exactly why everyone was silent about the disease and then about the movement of working-class people from the Baodi area to the food and agricultural jobs farther north.

Zemin was already at the table when Xinru walked up. He started to stand for her, but she reached over and pushed his shoulder down, kissing him on the forehead. Zemin liked how she did little things like that.

Zemin asked, "So, how is everything?"

Xinru beamed, "Everything is great! Better than great. My parents send their regards. They enjoyed meeting you last week."

Zemin nodded, "And I enjoyed meeting them. And your brothers."

"And you, Zemin," Xinru asked, "how is work?"

"Good, not so many problems since the Army finally left. The soldiers on their pass into town were real problems."

Xinru nodded, "Yes, I had my share of improper comments on the bus from the soldiers."

The two ordered their meals and side dishes. When the waiter asked if they wanted anything else with their meal, Zemin ordered a bottle of wine. Not the traditional rice wines, but a grape wine from down south.

Xinru raised her eyebrows after the waiter left, "Wine, Zemin? That's not our usual. Is this something special tonight?"

Zemin smiled and double-checked that the small velvet box was still in his coat pocket, "Yes, perhaps tonight will be something special."

Inspector Xi Zemin had thought about this a lot, and he thought that 'Xi Xinru' would be a beautiful married name for this lovely young lady across the table.

———

Base Gymnasium
153rd 'Thunderbolt' Regiment HQ
Egyptian Army Base Haiyum
Haiyum, Egypt
9:15 AM Local Time June 14th

Things were much better organized today than for Miriam Mansoor's first two trips to the sprawling military base at Haiyum. The medical officers at the U.S. Navy Medical Research Unit had held a training for the nurses and phlebotomists, as well as for the clerks who were assisting them. They now stood at the sixteen tables spaced around the gymnasium floor. The NAMRU staff had explained how a double-blind medical study worked and how they were part of a multi-national testing program to select the candidates for the vaccine to fight the avian flu that had ravaged Egypt and the other countries. The trainers said that the vaccines being tested came from medical laboratories and factories in all major countries, except the Russia and China, who were doing their own testing of avian flu vaccines. The soldiers they would see today had all tested negative to prior exposure to the H5N1 avian flu virus.

Each clerk had a new laptop computer with a database program running. Each table had a new pneumatic injector unit instead of the old fashioned hypodermic needles. Each table also had a supply of multi-use vaccine supply tubes with a generic vaccine batch number listed on the labels. Nobody in the field test knew which vaccines were which, but the people compiling the test scores knew which batch numbers represented the vaccine products of Sanofi, Merck, Inovio, HeptImun, Mitsubishi and the other vaccine producers. One of the batches would be placebos to test the accuracy of the testing procedures. Miriam felt sorry for the people who got the placebos. She hoped her table was not one with many of the placebo vaccines. No one knew which were placebos; that was the essence of a double-blind study.

The doors opened, and hundreds of Egyptian special forces troopers jogged in and lined up at the various tables. They all had their outer shirts off and stood in their t-shirts. Miriam smiled at her first soldier and read off the batch number on the first tube of vaccine she inserted in the injection gun. The soldier handed the clerk a slip of paper with his unit, serial number, and name to enter into the database. The clerk typed in the information on batch and identity.

Miriam was careful to warn every soldier to "Stand still, don't move!" before she pushed the injection trigger button. A loosely placed injection, or a patient who moved, could cause the powerful pneumatic injector to slice the skin, instead of making a bloodless, needle-free subcutaneous injection.

As Miriam fell into the routine of her work, she got to thinking about what she was doing here. She was very proud of her work. It seemed that she was part of something great. She was part of a world-wide effort. The soldiers seemed to appreciate her work, and her, even as they grimaced from her minor act of torture. As she worked, Miriam kept her eye out, looking at the soldiers, but she did not see the man she was looking for.

—

Thousand Oaks Defense Pharmaceutical Plant (TODPP)
Thousand Oaks, California
1:30 PM PDT June 25th

The TODPP staff officers' full professional qualifications had been spelled out in the public relations brochures they had been handing out at the many public orientation sessions that had filled their calendar in June. Captain Karen Llewellyn, U.S. PHS, MD, DSci, stuck her head into her executive officer's office. Captain Robert Cameron, U.S. Army, BSChemE, (*USMA '13*), was typing on a laptop computer.

"Can you break free for a couple of hours. You're invited on a field trip to get out of the office for a while," she said.

Rob looked at her and made a sort of 'sure, why not?' gesture, and said, "Field trips are fun."

Rob was wearing his regular office uniform, the camouflaged Army ACU uniform; he grabbed his baseball-like utility cap to follow Karen. She was in her corresponding uniform, the medium-blue PHS informal operational dress uniform (ODU).

Specialist Jerome Ali, the enlisted Army driver who had arrived at the plant in mid-May, was leaning against the Chevy Suburban parked in the 'Official Vehicle' parking spot. When he saw his CO and XO exit the plant building, Ali quickly ran around to open the rear door for Karen, making sure he did not bump the door into her Audi, parked next to it. Ali was in the same uniform as his XO.

Specialist Ali saluted Karen when she approached. She returned the salute. Since the Public Health Service was a corps of only commissioned officers, Karen was not used to dealing with enlisted personnel, but she was getting used to how her Army subordinates expected her to act. Rob got in the backseat of the Suburban with Karen.

Behind the wheel, Ali asked, "Where to, Ma'am? Master Sergeant Ghent just told me I'd be driving you. Didn't give a destination."

"The 'Toe-Dip' Camarillo factory, main entrance."

Once they were on the road, Cameron asked, "What's up?"

"Kerry Weathers called to tell me they had harvested the first crop with the VLP particles North Carolina sent us. I want to see the freeze-drying and start of the processing of the plants. They should be ready to purify some of the actual VLP by the end of the week," Karen said as Ali accelerated onto the northbound freeway.

Rob said, "I need to study more of the details of our process. I've been getting up to speed on the contract and the financial end and don't know much about the science end. What exactly is the crop you mentioned they just harvested?"

"Don't be hard on yourself. It's a really complex process the various vaccine companies use. And since corporate and university research grant money from the Feds is usually tied to product licenses, the U.S. government has its choice as to which companies' recipes we can use. Our factory has the capability of doing either plant-based or cell-based vaccine production. Current plans are to use plant-based VLP production for all four of the different vaccines we will put in our quadrivalent vaccine mixture. We are already in plant-based production for the first three flu vaccine parts, just waiting for word on the H5N1 avian flu piece. That is, we will use plant-based if it turns out the plant-based avian flu VLPs are as effective as the cell-based VLPs some of the companies are using. We will find out that when we get the results of the human safety and efficacy trials that have started worldwide this week. Anyway, getting back to your question, our greenhouses are full of hydroponically grown *Nicotiana benthamiana,* that is like a primitive Australian cousin of the tobacco plant. Scientists discovered quite a while ago that *Benthamiana* plants had several characteristics that made them good test subjects for experimentation.

"One of those characteristics is that it can be encouraged to sort of become a plant 'zombie;' to lose itself and take on the genetics of other living things. We have learned how to study the genetics of virus germs and create a *Benthamiana* plant that goes zombie and creates little pieces of itself that have the outside structure of a virus, but none of the internal working of the virus. That's the virus-like particle. The human body recognizes the virus-like surface features of the actual virus that the *Benthamiana* is mimicking and develops an antibody to what it perceives as a danger. *Voila!* A vaccine."

Karen continued, "There are also bacteria cells that can create similar VLPs, and we have a separate factory line to produce those cell-based VLP vaccines, if necessary. But the difference between a greenhouse with thousands of pounds of *Benthamiana* and a stainless steel kettle growing fifty gallons of bacteria makes plant-based production a bit more efficient. However, the flip side of the equation is that brewing the kettle of bacteria takes a couple of days, whereas sprouting and harvesting the plants takes several weeks."

Rob said, "I saw you do the TV spot about the bacteria back in April just before I arrived. My introduction to Captain Llewellyn was on the TV in my Kansas motel."

"God, don't remind me. Those TV reports are haunting me."

Karen finished with, "So, today they will be freeze-drying the first crop of plants and starting the processing to break the plants down until all that's left is the tiny piece of genetic code that our bodies think is an avian flu virus."

"But, I thought we could not start making the vaccine until the human testing was finished and the drug approved."

Karen nodded, "Right, this is just a test run to make sure our local version of H5N1 VLPs is working right. And, if HeptImun's recipe for the avian flu vaccine is finally approved after testing, then we will be slightly ahead of the game. We'll have this one batch finished and our first vaccine ready to use, probably for our workers. If not, we will quickly switch recipes to one of the other company's, or CDC's, vaccine recipe that the U.S. government already has a license to produce. If all goes well, we will start shipping the vaccine by August."

The Suburban turned into the parking lot at the TODPP Camarillo factory. Ali parked in the Commanding Officer's parking spot and rushed around to open the door for her. Karen and Rob headed into the building, and Ali started to wait by the Suburban.

Specialist Ali called after Karen and ran up to her to ask, "Uh, ma'am. What you were talking about seemed really interesting. Is there any chance I can come with you and see how they do that?

Karen smiled at him, "Of course, Specialist, what we do is, indeed, fascinating. You're part of our team. Come on in."

—

Central California
Late June

The drake and his mate had started the trek south from the sun-warmed tundra and marshlands south of Nome, Alaska as soon as their four baby ducklings were strong enough to make the trip. Their trip down the Pacific Flyway through British Columbia and the Pacific Northwest had been directed by the instincts of the flock of Northern Pintail ducks they traveled with. And the drake's mate had memories from the year before. The drake's instinct was worthless for this trip, as his memories, and his parents' lessons were half a world away in the Far East. But, the drake did know that you flew south in the spring until you found a good place to live.

Nature had provided the Pintail duck family and their cohorts with many prime feeding areas as they headed south from Alaska toward the Lower Colorado River Delta of the female's memory. Part of what allowed the Northern Pintail ducks to range across the entire planet was their broad diet. They could eat almost anything; grasses, insects, seeds, small animals and fish, and their favorites -- aquatic and wetland larvae. They had fed on the seaside wetlands along the Pacific coast, the grain fields and marshes of the Columbia River Valley, and a dozen other excellent habitats.

Something told them they were getting close. In late June, they now flew over the green and golden fields of California. Breaking from the phalanx of other pintails for a while, the six members of the drake's family circled down to a large pond surrounded by verdant grasslands far below.

The pond was a wonderful habitat for the ducks. The only residents of the pond and green fields around it were two large white geese and three horses. The huge, oafish geese were friendly, or at least non-hostile, to the ducks, and the horses produced large amounts of horse feces that attracted big black horseflies. The horseflies laid eggs in the horse droppings that hatched weekly into juicy horsefly larvae that the Pintail ducks truly loved. The area near the pond had another asset for the ducks. Nearby, there were hundreds of rows of grapevines that had dropped many grapes to the ground the autumn before. Those grapes had now dried in the warm sun, and the well-fertilized vineyard soil was covered with thousands of raisins, as well as the slugs, snails, and worms which ate this vineyard refuse. The drake and his mate decided this pond was a fine place to raise their four ducklings and spend the summer, fall, and early winter before the brood would head north again when spring approached.

The drake was no longer sick from the influenza that had killed his siblings and the other ducks at Dakouten Zheng back in February. His mate was also healthy again, as were their ducklings. But the nature of all wild ducks was to have the various influenza strains remain viable in their system. Over time the viruses they naturally carried sometimes changed genetically, morphing, and combining with other strains. The H7N9 virus that had killed the drake's siblings and the Chinese factory ducks was still there. These Pintail ducks that carried it were no longer in danger from the disease. However, like the domesticated ducks in China, the Pintails' new neighbors, those oafish geese, were not safe.

—

Thousand Oaks Defense Pharmaceutical Plant (TODPP)
Thousand Oaks, California
1:30 PM PDT June 25th

Karen Llewellyn saw the foreign phone number and ID of Zhao Xiang on the cellphone screen. She thought a second, accepted the call, and then said, "Doctor Zhao, Joan, so good to hear from you."

"Yes, Karen. I had meant to call you, but, you know, the press of getting the plants online has been overpowering. And, I'm sure I'm preaching to the choir, as you say, on that. And I saw a news clip on the internet about your bout with this flu yourself."

Karen shook her head as she answered, even though Joan could not see her, "Yes, it seems like everyone saw the story about my hospital trip."

"But, the same website had a link to your other interview at the new vaccine plant. You seemed to be a natural in front of the camera."

"No comment on that," Karen decided to change the subject. "How are things with your plants. Are you up and running?"

"Oh, yes, all four plants are producing to some extent. Probably like you, we are waiting for the clinical trials and final lab results of the Egyptian Flu vaccine. Are you working on that, too?"

Karen thought of how to answer that, "Well, we are getting our production line ready to produce, but we were not involved directly in the VLP creation for the H5N1 nor the production of the vaccine for the animal or human trials. That was handled by the existing vaccine producers back east and by CDC. They predict a result in record time. Thank goodness. How about you?"

"Oh, we were right in the middle of it. The HeptImun process for VLP analysis and creation worked like a charm. We produced in our main plant the vaccine that was sent to be used in the human trials."

Karen asked, "How are your human trials being done? Are you involved in that? Our FDA and CDC have the reins on human trials for us."

There was a pause before Joan Zhao answered, "Our Ministry of Health, my employer, handles that, but they are assisted by our Defense Ministry, the Army."

"I see . . . that makes sense, some of the militaries in the western countries provide the test volunteers, too. But I guess in most armies; it really isn't a voluntary thing. No doubt."

"No, probably not," Joan said. "You know, Karen, I was thinking. I have your business card from back at CDC, and the cellphone, thankfully, still worked for this call. But, if I wanted to mail something to you, I don't know, research material or whatever, where would I send it to get it to you there at your new plant."

Karen gave Joan Zhao the full address of the plant in Thousand Oaks. Dr. Zhao 'Joan' Xiang also gave Karen the same information, her main office at the pharmaceutical plant outside Beijing. They agreed to exchange emails also. They both signed off the call with promises to keep in touch and compare notes on the vaccine production process.

As Karen Llewellyn thought about the call afterward, she remembered her talk with the two CIA men back in Maryland last March. Karen had promised to contact those two if she had any further contact with Dr. Zhao. The call was 'contact,' but it probably had nothing of intelligence interest. Karen made a note of the call in her journal and sent a quick email to the email address on the CIA agent's card. Probably nothing more would come of that.

—

Chapter 32

Base Gymnasium
153rd 'Thunderbolt' Regiment HQ
Egyptian Army Base Haiyum
Haiyum, Egypt
11:15 AM Local Time July 5th

This would be Miriam's last trip to Haiyum. The NAMRU team was there for the final check. They were taking final blood samples from the soldiers who had been given the vaccines. The blood tests would confirm if the soldiers' bodies produced the proper antibodies in response to the vaccines. If the right antibodies showed up in the soldiers' blood samples, the world would have an avian flu vaccine. So, the nurses were back with thousands of needles and blood vials.

By mid-morning, Miriam's hand was getting a bit sore from pushing hundreds of rubber ended glass collection vials into collection tube holders, She had to stick the companion label to the vials on the sign-in sheet where the soldiers entered their names and serial number. Her routine was interrupted when there was a commotion at the front of the line to her table. An officer had butted into the head of the line, and the enlisted men muttered their complaints but wisely let him be.

Miriam finished with her current patient and waited for the officer to sit down at her table.

When he sat down, Miriam smiled and said, "Good Morning, Kariim."

The handsome lieutenant blinked and said, "You know my name?"

The lieutenant spoke the citified dialect of Cairo. Miriam hoped her country-girl accent was not too noticeable. "Of course, I do. You gave me the little note with your name and address when I was here back in May."

"But, you did not contact me."

"You and your men were quarantined on base for two months, out here in the desert, so you would not get the flu. Not much reason to contact you."

"But, you remembered my face and knew my name."

"Yes, but later in the day you handed me your note, I also got word my parents died in the epidemic, so I had much on my mind."

"My condolences on your loss. My grandfather and a niece died, too."

"Yes, we have all lost someone in this horror," Miriam said with a catch in her voice. "But, I did keep your note and remembered you and your name. I found a picture on the internet of you and your father when you graduated from the Academy in Abbassia. That's quite close to where I work. I hear your regiment will be getting leave now that the medical tests are finished. I thought maybe I would give you this if you showed up again." Miriam reached into the pocket of her NAMRU jumpsuit. She handed 1st Lieutenant Kariim Al Beshry a slip of paper on which she had already printed her name and the number of her NAMRU cellphone.

The sergeant who Kariim had cut in front of in line cleared his throat loudly. Kariim glared at the sergeant and then smiled at Miriam. "Yes, thank you. I have leave in two weeks."

Miriam smiled back and pulled Kariim's arm across the table and felt for a vein inside his elbow. *Back to work.*

———

Rue de Pyrenees
Paris, France
8:30 Local Time July 13th

The writers, advertisers, and staff of the *Journal Gastronomique*, which was one of Maximilien Tauty's primary publishers, had a longstanding tradition of a reception on the Saturday evening closest to Bastille Day. All of the writers, chefs, and food lovers in general who contributed to the popular gourmet publication brought their own *spécialité* to a massive buffet that was enjoyed by all. Invitations to outsiders to the buffet party were much prized and hard to come by. Some people flew in from across Europe to attend.

As Maximilien was best at savoring and writing about gourmet foods and not so great at preparing them, it always fell to Marguerite to make the Tauty contribution to the gourmet buffet. Marguerite's *Terrine de Foie Gras Frais de Canard* was legendary. She would make a generous quantity today to bring to the soiree on Saturday.

The primary ingredient for her *spécialité* was in her huge Gaggenau deep freezer. Max spared no expense in the kitchen equipment he bought for Marguerite and enjoyed showing visitors around, as though he used the gourmet equipment himself. Max was a master at presenting an excellent gourmet façade.

The box had been in the freezer for months, waiting for today. Marguerite pulled the large DHL Express box out from under the other frozen foods that had accumulated on top of it. She had plenty of time to thaw the two and a half kilogram block this morning and prepare it this afternoon. The DHL box still had the shipping and customs labels Max had filled out and given to the gourmet food dealer they had paid to ship it in dry ice back to France for them. As was always the case when Max sent food purchases home from overseas, he had simply named the contents on the customs label as '*aliments emballés*' with a value of ten Euros. 'Packaged foods' with a nominal value almost always avoided any customs inspection.

Inside the box, she found the several empty foil packets that had once held the dry ice that had kept the delicacy fully frozen on the express shipment to France. The original dry ice had long since evaporated into CO_2 in her deep freezer, but the main plastic pouch was still frozen rock hard. Marguerite could not read the Chinese lettering on the pouch, but the contents looked fine to her. She put the pouch in warm water to thaw for several hours.

The pouch was nearly thawed when Marguerite came back to it. Opening the pouch, she inspected the contents. The individual pieces were not large enough nor fatty enough to pass for Class A product in France, but since she would be pureeing it, the size and shape of the lobes did not matter to her. The secret of her *foie gras* was in the recipe and preparation. This much duck liver would certainly cost many hundreds of Euros in France, even at Class B. The price Max had paid for it in China justified the trouble of shipping the pouch home to France. She set about removing the veins.

Marguerite continued with her signature, but simple, recipe; cream, white pepper, fine sea salt, honey, plus the two secret spices that were the *pièce de résistance* of the recipe. As she pureed the livers, she thought momentarily of the day she had purchased the duck livers in Tianjin Province. It had been on the trip where they had inspected those horrible little chickens hanging by their feet in the market, the chickens that had given Marguerite that dreadful bout of flu back in March. She hated the memory of her illness and put it from her mind. She made no connection between the flash-frozen duck livers in the sealed plastic bag and the live chickens in the market. Marguerite had forgotten that she had inspected, by hand, some sample duck livers in an open pan before Max had paid for the shipment of the sealed pouches.

When she finished adding the ingredients, she made sure and mixed the resulting paste for several minutes in her food processor. Then, she put the puree covered in a rich golden *glacé* layer and creamy white gel base in several long tin pans that would form the loaves that would be inverted for serving. Then, Marguerite sat the tin pans into a bath of hot water to gel them. As per the warning in the recipe she had found so many years before, Marguerite carefully followed the instruction to ensure the mixture was gently raised to a temperature of 60-65 degrees Celsius to kill any bacteria. For the secret to Marguerite's legendary *Terrine de Foie Gras Frais de Canard* was hinted at in its name, in the word '*Frais.*' Marguerite's foie gras was different from the usual practice of baking the foie gras puree. Baking the *foie gras* changed the texture, heating up the fats that provided the great flavor, and additional ingredients, like eggs, were needed to make the baked version smooth and solid. Marguerite's *Terrine de Foie Gras Frais de Canard* had its beautiful texture because it was 'fresh,' not baked. And, it was indeed legendary.

Unfortunately, influenza is not a bacteria; it is a virus. Many viruses, such as influenza, require a temperature of at least 75 degrees Celsius to be killed for certain.

———

Beaumont Family Ranch
Santa Ynez Valley
Santa Barbara County, California
11:30 AM PDT July 16th

Inga Beaumont watched as her daughter, Heather, carried her bags down the stairs where her friend Chelsea was waiting for her. The two friends since childhood were dressed nearly identically in tank tops and jeans. With matching long blonde hair, they could have been sisters.

"Two bags? The college orientation is just an overnighter. You really need two bags?" Inga asked.

"Mom! Really. I can handle it. And it's two nights. We'll be home on Tuesday. Right? And besides, one of them is mostly my laptop, charger, and stuff."

Inga nodded, "I still can't believe you two both got accepted at the same college."

Chelsea smiled at Inga and then at Heather and said, "Yeah, it's really neat. And UCLA was both of our top choices. I guess we are kinda blessed."

"Make sure you feed your geese before you go. Your father and Mark are up at the Fair today with that pig, and I do not feed geese, nor do windows." Inga smiled at her humor and added, "And we still have to figure out what you're going to do with those birds. Mark is going to be busy with football practice, and neither your father nor I want to be stuck with goose-sitting duties while you run off to UCLA."

Inga turned to Chelsea, "Chelsea, you got geese when Heather did, what did you do with your geese?"

Chelsea frowned, "Well, Harry got eaten by a coyote. And, my Mom found a guy over in Solvang who raises poultry and sells fresh eggs for a living. He took Hermione for us."

"Interesting, I'll call your mother and see if I can get his name. That sounds good with you, Heather?"

Heather paused for a minute and then said, "Yeah. Maybe, but don't do anything until I get back, and we talk about it."

"Of course not. You girls need to get going. It's easily a three-hour drive to LA. And, afternoon traffic into Los Angeles is horrible." Inga reached to hug Heather.

Heather added her bags to Chelsea's in the trunk of Chelsea's BMW. They both headed across to the Beaumont barn to feed the geese pair.

———

Emergency Situation Office
Epidemiological Branch
Sante Publique France
Paris, France
10:47 AM Local Time July 17ᵗʰ

The first emergency request for influenza strain typing hit the French government laboratory on Sunday afternoon. By Monday morning, there were dozens of samples waiting to be tested. The samples came in from across the Paris metropolitan area, and later from all across France.

The influenza strain in all of these new test requests was not difficult to identify; the French had seen it before. They had identified a single case last March. The problem was that it was a rare strain, and its appearance *en masse* in Paris was frightening and confusing. The strain of influenza the tests identified was A/21/836/003/PARIS(H7N9), the avian flu strain previously only found in zoonotic cases where a human got infected from an animal. The H7N9 case in March in Paris had been traced to foreign travel by the French citizen to a wet market and poultry in China. The strain was also called by its Chinese acronym, A/21/117/311/BAODI(H7N9).

By Monday afternoon, the contact tracing investigators for *Sante Publique France* had concluded that every person behind the H7N9 samples had attended the *Journal Gastronomique* buffet on Saturday evening in the Monmarte section of Paris. The suspicions about *Journal Gastronomique* were confirmed late Monday afternoon when the French public health officials were contacted by their counterparts in Cologne, Germany, and Milan, Italy. Patients in Cologne and Milan, who showed H7N9 infection, were asked about any foreign travel, and they mentioned their trip to Paris over the weekend.

More evidence poured in. By mid-morning on Tuesday, one intrepid Parisian detective had brought into the laboratory one buffet attendee's take-home boxes that had been collected for a couple who could not attend in person. Samples were tested, and by Tuesday afternoon, the *foie gras* was clearly found to be the culprit behind the infection. Questioning of hospitalized *Journal Gastronomique* staffers gave the contact tracing team the name of Marguerite

Tauty as the chef behind the *foie gras*. *Journal Gastronomique* was able to give the authorities a definitive list of who had attended the buffet on Saturday. Notice and warnings about the adulterated *foie gras* were sent out.

———

University of California, Los Angeles
New Student Orientation Meeting
Westwood, Los Angeles, California
9:00 AM PDT July 17th

Heather and Chelsea lined up to get their bag of information from the sign-in table. They had checked into the dorm the night before and were now starting the two days of meetings and tours of the campus. The dorm was mostly empty for the summer and had been opened just for the freshman orientation. They would stay over in the dorm again on Monday night and drive back home late Tuesday afternoon.

Chelsea was first in line and smiled at the upperclassman who handled the morning registrations, who said, "Hi, I'm Jeb, I'll be your resident advisor for your stay. Your name?"

Chelsea told him. He checked a list and gave her a marker pen to fill out her full name on a nametag. Jeb gave her an bag of information, brochures and UCLA paraphernalia.

As Chelsea moved away from the table, Heather stepped up. Heather was writing her name on the tag when she felt the sneeze urge hit her and paused. She quickly bent to the side and sneezed into her elbow as everyone had been taught to do doing the coronavirus crisis. She dabbed her nose with the back of her hand. She apologized for her sudden sneeze and handed the marking pen back to the registrar.

As they walked away, Chelsea looked at Heather and asked, "You have tissues?"

Heather shook her head, "Forgot to bring them. This cold just came on."

Chelsea opened her shoulder bag and handed her BFF a packet of Kleenex.

They spent most of the morning in orientation briefings in a large, auditorium-like lecture hall with perhaps 150 incoming UCLA freshmen in attendance. They were served lunch in the dorm cafeteria.

In the afternoon, the larger group was broken up into groups of twenty or fewer depending on their prospective major. These groups would get briefed by academic departments. Since Chelsea and Heather wanted different majors, they split up for the afternoon.

By the time they got back together at the dorm for dinner, Heather asked Chelsea, "You have any more tissues? I'm out."

"No, that was my whole supply. But, there is a branch campus book store that sells stuff like that over by the Engineering Building. We can hit there before we eat. Boy, your nose is all red. You're doing a real Rudolf."

Heather nodded, "It feels like it. You lead, I have no idea where Engineering is."

———

Emergency Situation Office
Epidemiological Branch
Sante Publique France
Paris, France
3:12 PM Local Time July 18th

Michel Dormer, like other French Public Health investigators, continued to work around the clock on the outcome of the Bastille Day *foie gras* disaster. The list of buffet attendees was complete, given the elite nature of an invitation to the event. More and more of these culinary elites took ill, and many soon passed away. Marguerite Tauty was hard to track down, however. Unknown to Dormer, she was away from home, back at *Hôpital Tenon,* where her husband, Maximilien Tauty, was deathly ill. One of the H7N9 samples in the Paris lab belonged to Maximilien.

What looked like a final clue was uncovered when the young secretary in Michel Dormer's office who filed the case notes for *Sante Publique France* was proofreading the report about whom had been sickened in the disastrous Bastille Day buffet aftermath. She noticed the last name of Maximilien Tauty was the same as the name of the woman who had been the patient in the original March H7N9 case. Now, with added importance, Michel Dormer searched for and found Marguerite.

Dormer interviewed Madame Tauty in an office near the waiting room in *Hôpital Tenon,* where she awaited word on her husband. Marguerite Tauty was distraught when she heard that Dormer assumed some connection between her and the sickness. He had not yet discovered the truth about the source of the duck livers when he mercifully paused questioning her when they got word that Marguerite's husband, Maximilien, had died in a room down the hall in *Hôpital Tenon.*

Inspector Dormer spoke with Madame Tauty again the next day at home. He had one final, and gently worded, question for the new widow, Marguerite Tauty. Her answer presented the complete connection between the H7N9 outbreaks in Paris, both in March and July, with the goose livers in the Baodi wet market. What had happened was clear—contaminated food linked to China.

Unfortunately, the death rate from the Paris *foie gras* H7N9 cases quickly climbed toward the World Health Organization's figures for previous animal-caused human cases of H7N9, about 30%. In a few days, the French culinary scene was devastated. *Journal Gastronomique* had to close its editorial offices. Of 187 cases of people who had gotten H7N9 from the adulterated *foie gras*, 53 people eventually died. Duck liver and *foie gras* prices plummeted. *Foie gras* was removed from most menus.

The only good news was that H7N9 had never been known to pass from human to human. Every case in WHO records had clear and unmistakable evidence of purely zoonotic contact. Animals had been the cause of every human H7N9 infection, including the Baodi ducks behind Marguerite Tauty's *foie gras*. Health authorities in France and the seven other European countries who had H7N9 cases from buffet goers were thankful for this fact. This fact had also been the basis of the initial conclusions made by the Baodi Health Ministry workers dealing with the deaths of Yunan Qiuyue and her co-workers and neighbors in February.

———

Beaumont Family Ranch
Santa Ynez Valley
Santa Barbara County, California
5:50 PM PDT July 18th

Despite their plan to share the driving, Chelsea drove the whole way back from Los Angeles. Heather had sat out of the UCLA campus tours that morning and had fallen asleep for most of the 'UCLA Bruins' team spirit building movie that had ended their freshman orientation. Heather's impromptu nap in the back row of the auditorium was punctuated by her sneezes and coughs. Heather reclined the BMW's passenger seat and slept much of the way home.

Inga Beaumont saw the car drive up and stood at the front door to welcome the girls back. When she saw Chelsea walk around to open the door for Heather and then Heather walking feebly around the car, Inga ran out to them.

"What's wrong, dear?" Inga asked.

Heather did not answer, so Chelsea said, "She's got something. She's been mostly out of it all the time we were there. Has she had coronavirus?"

"She didn't get COVID, but she had the corona vaccine, both annual shots. She had her flu shots too. This might be that New Flu from LA. They say it wasn't part of this year's flu shots."

Heather finally spoke, "I feel like shit. I need to get to bed. I ache all over—arms, legs, even my butt aches."

"I'll get her stuff from the car," Chelsea volunteered.

Inga put her arm around her daughter, and they walked slowly to the house. Inga said, "This is just awful. Mark is sick, too. And your father already left for his meeting in New York. I'll have to drive both of you to the doctor in the morning. I'll get you to bed and give you some Tylenol. That should help."

—

Chapter 33

Policlinico di Milano
Milan, Italy
7:30 AM Local Time July 20th

Anna Maria Bertolucci walked up the steps at the Milan Polyclinic. This was her first day back at work after taking three days off for her sister's wedding. She took the stairs and not the elevator thinking the vertigo of the elevator ride probably would not mesh with her queasy stomach this morning. Anna Maria had been the maid of honor at the wedding yesterday. She had partied magnificently at the big wedding celebration that had gone into the wee hours of this morning. As the maid of honor, she had drunk a lot of champagne and had danced with dozens of men. Such were the duties of a maid of honor. Her hangover was dreadful. She should have taken another day off.

Anna Maria finally climbed to the third floor of the hospital, to the Intensive Care Unit, where she worked. She put her things in her locker and donned her white lab coat that identified her name and her position as Respiratory Therapist. She dropped into the chair in the back of the nurses' station and laid her head back on the wall.

"Anna, you look like hell!" said her friend Gina, an ICU nurse.

"I look better than I feel. Too much partying last night. I'm not used to that." Anna Maria looked at Gina and asked, "Anything big going on today. How'd that one guy I intubated on Monday do?"

Gina shook her head, "We lost him on Tuesday. They said he got sick from something he ate in Paris over the weekend."

"That wasn't food poisoning; he had pneumonia."

"Whatever, you've got those two breathing therapy patients that you need to hook up and test."

"Right. I'd better get started. Those old people are so slow to do what I say," Anna Maria said as she stood up.

Anna Maria stood and, as Gina watched, slowly swayed in her stance. Gina saw Anna Maria's eyes roll up, and her head tilt back. Gina grabbed her and struggled to set Anna Maria back in the chair.

When Anna Maria did not immediately open her eyes, Gina laid her hand on her friend's forehead. It was hot to the touch. Her pulse was rapid.

Gina grabbed an electronic thermometer and ran it down the side of Anna Maria's face. Anna Maria opened her eyes.

Anna Maria said, weakly, "Wow, this is some heavy hangover."

Gina shook her head, "This isn't a hangover. Your temperature is 39. You're really sick. I'm getting Dr. Fonseca. Just sit there."

———

Thousand Oaks Defense Pharmaceutical Plant (TODPP)
Thousand Oaks, California
10:30 AM PDT July 21st

Karen Llewellyn was in the conference room with her senior staff, both HeptImun and Army, going over status reports and production milestones. The H5N1 avian flu vaccine production had cleared FDA approval. They had all four of the plant-based production lines busy in Camarillo. Their lab in Thousand Oaks was busy checking quality control on the interim manufacturing steps of the final vaccine, and they were just now packaging the first quadrivalent vaccine. They were all jubilant that they were getting ready to ship the vaccine in just under five months from the first avian flu cases in Egypt and LA. It was an amazing feat for modern medical science and engineering.

The conference room door opened. Rodney Ghent stepped into the room and waited for Karen to acknowledge him. Karen held up her hand to get Kerry Weathers to stop his report.

"Master Sergeant?" Karen questioned.

"We just got a call on the commanding officer's line. Your secretary asked me to take it while you were busy. It's Dr. Charlene Reed. I told her you were busy in an important meeting, but she insisted that this was extremely urgent, some sort of an emergency she said you needed to know about."

Karen remembered Charlene Reed as being the Public Health Officer for Santa Barbara County. TODPP had held a series of public official's orientation visits at the plant back in June to acquaint the movers and shakers in local politics and medicine around Southern California with the work of the new plant. Some federal bureaucrat had put such public outreach work on the contractual workplan for HeptImun and TODPP, so it went on Karen, Rob and George Marquardt's to-do list. Dr. Reed had been invited down from Santa Barbara to one orientation session, and she and Karen had spoken at length after the session finished. The two female MDs had considerable common ground and interests, mainly a public health career.

"Urgent, huh? That's odd, coming from her. Let's take a ten minute break, so I don't miss anything important here. Sorry, Kerry." Karen realized that nobody else knew who Dr. Reed was, but Karen did not fill them in.

Back in her office, Karen pushed the blinking button on the telephone, "Doctor Reed, nice to hear from you. What's up? They said this was urgent."

"Yes, Captain Llewellyn, I'm sitting on top of what is clearly an emergency and I think you may be uniquely able to help me out."

"Yes?"

"When we were there at your plant, you mentioned your laboratory was designed to be able to give real-time reverse transcriptase and all the related PCR testing to identify specific Type A flu strains, including, if needed, the rare novel avian flu strains. You said your lab's abilities in that area were, by design, almost on a par with CDC's."

"Yes, we have the ability, but it isn't part of our current work. If I hear where you're going, I have to say we aren't in the business of running virus strain testing."

"Yes, Doctor, I understand that, but, if you will hear me out, I think you will agree we have a unique and tremendously important problem."

"OK, tell me."

"On Wednesday morning, two teenagers, brother and sister, were brought into the hospital ER in Solvang. That's a small town in central Santa Barbara County. That hospital is pretty much just an ER with no patient rooms. They send admitted patients to the main hospital in the city.

"Both patients were very ill with flu-like symptoms. Onsite testing was done, and they had Type A influenza, but the strain did not match any strains their local testing could identify. It did not match the H5N1 quick testing kits that have come out for the LA avian flu strain. Both teens were transferred to the hospital in Santa Barbara by ambulance. The ambulance with the male patient had to intubate and ventilate him on the way. They are both in infectious containment rooms at Cottage Hospital downtown.

"Blood samples were taken to identify the strain involved. They sent them overnight express to the California state lab, VRDL, in Richmond, California.

"The Viral Labs are always backed up, so with overnight shipping and waiting for them and their backlog, it took the better part of two days for the report. The report on the 15-year-old boy was influenza Type A with 'inconclusive strains,' and they requested new blood work done. But for the 17-year-old girl, the strain typing using their polymerase chain reaction assay, testing came back as close in essential genetic typing to PARIS/H7N9. The same bug as that woman in Paris last Spring, the zoonotic strain in northern China, and the new outbreak that's being reported in Europe this week. I understand even the Chinese are using the Paris appellation for the identical strain. VRDL wants a new sample on the girl as well to double-check the H7N9 result."

"Wow."

'Yeah, 'wow.' We got that info this morning. We have ordered new blood work to be sent to both VRDL and, this time, CDC, but that could take several days, like before. Especially, cross-country to CDC. We probably have VRDL's attention now and maybe CDC's also, but they will take up precious time."

Karen spoke up, "H7N9 is strictly zoonotic. I saw in the CDC email this morning that the Paris outbreak was from tainted animal product in food, according to reports. The old Chinese H7N9 strain came from a commercial poultry source. Do you have an animal vector for these kids?"

"Hold that thought about 'strictly zoonotic.' But, in answer to your question. Our contact tracing specialist interviewed the mother of the two teens. The family has both poultry and swine at their ranch. And these kids are the animal caretakers."

"So, what's your point on strictly zoonotic."

"The first two patients came in two days ago. Yesterday and last night, eight other teenagers from the Santa Ynez Valley came into clinics and hospitals. Seven of them were in a football practice with the first boy on Monday. In fact, all of the boys were in one-on-one blocking drills with the first patient, according to the coach. The eighth new patient was a friend of the first female patient who rode with her to a college event in LA over the weekend. All of them test positive for Type A; negative for H5N1 or any other strain we can type match here. All eight of the new patients are very sick, a couple in serious condition."

"Any animal contact for them?"

"For the girlfriend, yes, same poultry as the first girl. No animal contact for the seven football players."

"Have you checked on the poultry and swine on the ranch?

"That's a problem, too. Everything gets worse as we peel back the layers. The forensic team we sent to the ranch found two lethargic, sick geese. We have them in quarantine and available for testing. But, there was no sign of the pig that the mother mentioned; the pigsty was empty. Checking back with the mother, we found the boy had sold the pig at the County Fair last Sunday. VRDL only accepts human samples for testing and suggested we try the U.S. Department of Agriculture laboratory in Omaha as a place that can confirm H7N9 in the geese. H7N9 is rare in American poultry flocks, so few places do it. We are trying to find out where the pig went after the fair."

"So, you think you have ten patients with non-zoonotic H7N9 and need help getting real-time testing for that strain. Right?" Karen asked.

Reed said, "Yes, Doctor, but I'm not done with the scary stuff yet."

"Really, what else?"

"The college meeting the two girls went to was an orientation at UCLA for about 150 freshmen students from all over the state and maybe the country with a two-night stay over in the dorms. The County Fair last Sunday was attended by hundreds of people, maybe thousands. And, the father who drove his son to the fair last Sunday with the son's prize pig left Tuesday by air for a corporate shareholders meeting, or somesuch, in New York City, attendance there unknown, the airline he flew on unknown. The mother is trying to reach him by phone. So, we may have possibly hundreds of contacts . . ."

"I get it. Let me make some arrangements for . . ." Karen stopped suddenly and then exclaimed. "Oh, God!"

"What?" Charlene Reed asked.

"An alert from CDC just popped up on my cellphone. They report that a health care worker in Milan, Italy, who treated one of the Paris H7N9 victims, has tested positive for H7N9 with no contact other than with the now-dead patient."

"'Oh, God' is right? Do you think there is some connection between our cases and Paris? All of it coming out the same week?"

"No idea about that. You've convinced me. I'll make arrangements to do your tests. I'll send someone up to bring the samples back. I may come up myself. Where should we go? Both to get the samples and to go someplace to get a good look at the situation?"

"The County is activating its Emergency Operations Center. That's on Cathedral Oaks Road, right off Highway 154. If you're coming here, I'll get the new samples sent up from the hospitals and out in the Valley."

"How many samples are we talking about?" Karen asked.

"Well, ten current patients are for sure, already sampled. Then, we have at least 23 football players who were in the Zone of Likely Contact at practice Monday, plus the mother, and then about seven health care workers before they got into full protective mode. I don't want to overburden your generosity of helping us. The book says that if we have a suspected novel avian flu virus, we need to quarantine and test everyone with close contact for the five days before symptom onset."

"I understand that and don't worry about asking for too much. I will have to check on our lab's current supply status. We will do whatever we can," Karen assured Dr. Reed.

"Thank you."

"Oh, one more thing," Karen paused before finishing, "you need to realize that I need to report what I'm doing up my chain of command. That could highlight your problem to a lot of people, including the media in all likelihood. That's just the nature of the beast."

"I understand completely. This is one time when that's not a worry. I can use whatever help I can get, and that help won't come unless the right people know about this."

"Right. On Google Maps, it looks like you're about an hour away from here. We'll have help there sometime over the lunch hour." Karen exchanged cell phone numbers and email addresses with Dr. Reed and hung up.

Karen thought for a moment and then printed out a couple of copies of the new CDC email and the Google Maps page for the Santa Barbara County EOC. She saw that it was well over the ten minutes she had told the staff to wait in the conference room. She quickly opened one of the binders the Operations people at Fort Detrick had given her to check some things. Then, Karen went across the hallway and asked Ghent to come with her to the conference room.

In the conference room, Karen did not take her seat; she stood next to where Rob Cameron sat. "Sorry that took so long. We had a lot to discuss.

"George and Kerry, without hearing everything you have to report, it seems you have things well in hand, and our primary mission of making the quadrivalent vaccine is on track. The one input I have for you now is to ask if you have thought of giving your employees the first doses of the new vaccine. Get them protected while they protect everybody else. I trust you will keep things moving and let me know if anything specifically needs my attention or decision. One of TODPP's secondary missions has reared its ugly head. I need to go deal with another problem."

She handed a copy of the CDC email to Rob, "Captain Cameron, while I'm out this afternoon, you will be in charge. I want you to respond to this email. I've forwarded a copy to your AKO email so you will have it to reply to and forward. Write this down."

Cameron opened a notebook.

Karen looked at the other copy of the email she had and said, "Reply to this email but make everybody on the original email a 'CopyTo:' addressee. Your primary 'To:' addressees for your email will be, General Harding that is, Commanding General, USAMRDC; next, Operations, USAMRDC; and probably, Commanding General, Army Medical Department, that's AMEDD; and also send it to Commanding General, USAMRIID."

"Here's my text, you can edit to make it read right," Karen spoke slowly and waited between sentences so that Captain Cameron could transcribe correctly. She used their newly-coined jargon 'Toe-Dip' when she spoke of 'TODPP.' "Commander, TODPP has been requested by Public Health authorities in Santa Barbara County, California to assist in an emergent public health crisis. Ten persons have been identified with possible . . . no, make that probable . . . identified with probable non-zoonotic, that spelling is N-O-N dash Z-O-O-N-O-T-I-C, H7N9 influenza infection. That's Hotel 7 November 9. Ten persons aged 15-18 hospitalized in serious condition. Thirty-plus potential additional local contacts, plus possible spread to Los Angeles, New York City, and Central California. Contact tracing assistance will be needed for local agencies. Investigation ongoing. Infection is similar to current H7N9 crisis in Paris, France, parenthesis, (see message below). H7N9 was previously exclusively zoonotic, with an extremely high mortality rate, circa thirty percent. No known connection between Paris and Santa Barbara incidents. Unless otherwise directed, TODPP will assist Santa Barbara with on-scene testing and epidemiological advice. Recommend USAMRIID and CDC consider appropriate response assistance to local authorities and testing support to TODPP Commander, TODPP requests Ops, USAMRDC, in their discretion, assist TODPP in the issuance of appropriate OPREP reporting of emergency situation per this message. You got that?"

"Got it," Rob answered.

"Sign it yourself as Executive Officer, TODPP. Put your Army cellphone and email on as a point of contact. List Master Sergeant Ghent as field operations contact, with his contact info."

Karen now turned to face HeptImun's laboratory manager, Sonya Hayburn. "Sonya, I need you to make sure that we have our equipment and supplies we need for viral and serology blood and nasal swab tests. And ensure everything is working and your staff is ready to handle it. I realize it isn't our specialty, but the design book for this place says we have the capability. Focus on being ready to test for H7N9. It's an avian flu cousin of H5N1 and a bit trickier to identify because it has a wider normal mutation range. H7N9 plays tricks genetically. By the way, TODPP's commanding officer, yours truly, wrote her doctoral thesis on H7N9 and its cousins, so she can probably answer some questions if you have them. If there is anything we don't have for the lab, send someone into LA to get it, now, this morning. Tell George, and he'll arrange to get you whatever you need. Charge everything to an emergency operations account Ross will get you. You have six hours to get ready to test maybe forty-plus samples for H7N9. Can you do that?"

"We can. Piece of cake," Sonya said, perhaps a bit too flippantly.

"Oh, and Sonya, You need to find out what, if anything, is different between doing a viral blood and throat culture tests for humans and on a goose. Call the USDA Lab in Omaha, Nebraska, and tell them our situation and ask for advice. And get Omaha's address where we can send backup samples for them to confirm. Tell them it's a national emergency and you are at an Army lab if you need to impress them to get them to move. I'm sure they will be intrigued that a goose is in the middle of a national emergency. At 6 PM today, you need to be ready to tell me whether a goose or human blood, nasal, or sputum sample has H7N9 flu. And your people may be working into the night. OK?"

This time, Sonya was not quite so flippant with her "OK."

Karen turned to Ross, "I need you to dust off the emergency clause in our GOCO contract and make sure HeptImun gets paid for everything I'm telling them to do."

"Yes ma'am."

Karen turned to Ghent, standing by the door, "Master Sergeant, make sure Lyudmila, uh, Specialist Kuchma, has whatever she needs to transport forty-plus Biosafety Level 3 blood samples and nose swabs back here. And, if necessary, whatever she needs to draw a blood sample from a goose if they have not already done that for us. She might need specimen containers for goose organs if Sonya calls and tells us that's how you do a virus test on geese after she talks to Omaha. I kind of remember that's how you sample poultry viruses, but that might have been when they are already dead. It sounds like our geese are alive still." Karen paused to think, 'It will be you, Kuchma, Ali and me on our trip north, utility uniforms. Make sure Sergeant Riddell knows what's going on, but he is staying here to help Captain Cameron if he needs anything. Here is the map of our destination." She gave Ghent the Google Maps printout. "We'll take the silver Suburban. Make sure we have four sets of PPE, that's suits, masks, face shields, and multiple gloves, in case we need it. Probably won't need PPE today, but Kuchma might. We should be wheels up at 11:30. We'll eat lunch on the road, maybe drive-through in Ventura. Uncle Sam's treat. Understood?"

"Yes ma'am."

Karen realized the HeptImun people were all staring at her with shocked expressions.

Karen smiled at them, "Hey people, look lively. This is where we earn our salaries."

—

Inmate Reception Center
Los Angeles County Jail
Los Angeles, California
11:19 AM PDT July 21st

Jeb DeVries had sat in the holding cell at the Los Angeles Police Department's West Los Angeles Station for several hours. The alcohol buzz that had gotten him arrested had long since dissipated. He had no idea where they had towed his slightly damaged VW Passat. He did not remember much about the accident he had caused on Pico Boulevard early this morning or the breathalyzer test the cop had given him afterward. He had been read his rights, thrown in the holding cell, loaded in an LAPD van, and was now being delivered to the Los Angeles County Jail to wait for court. Jeb was in awful shape, hungover, despondent about his DWI, and sick.

The week had started out great. Jeb, as a grad student, was due to be a resident advisor for the coming year at UCLA and had started the week by handling the sign-up of the new freshmen for their orientation at the dorm he would be working in. Mid-week, he had been invited to what seemed like it would be a great party in Hollywood Heights, along with several fellow grad students. The Thursday night party, from what Jeb could remember of it, had, indeed, been great -- good music, lots of food and drinks, and a few celebrities in attendance. His drive home afterward to Westwood had not been so great. Hence, his present predicament.

Jeb and the other two prisoners being transferred from LAPD custody to the Jail had been restrained with handcuffs and leg manacles for the trip across town. Inside the door to Jail Reception, the restraints were taken off, and they were put in another holding cell. More waiting. Jeb sneezed several times in the holding cell. His fellow prisoners frowned and moved away from him, as everyone did after living through coronavirus. He had nothing to wipe his hands with or blow his nose. His nose was really runny, and he felt a chill.

Finally, Jeb had his civilian clothes taken and bagged, and he was given an orange jail jumpsuit to wear. He was brought to a counter where he was again fingerprinted, photographed, and had the contents of several papers read to him.

The deputy finished with, ". . . and if you have not posted bail prior to your court session and the judge does not order you released on your own recognizance, you will be returned to Jail and incarcerated as a regular prisoner until a future court date. You have a right to an initial court session within 72 hours, including court holidays and weekends. Do you understand the rights and the information I've given you about posting bail? If you do, please sign here on the dark line by the big 'X.'"

As Jeb reached for the pen to sign the paper, he had another urge to sneeze. He sneezed quickly into his hand, but the pen was in his hand. The sneeze left a slimy deposit on the pen and the counter. The deputy cussed at Jeb and handed him two of the paper towels they use at the counter to wipe off the fingerprint ink.

Jeb wiped his hand and the pen with one towel. He used the other towel to blow his nose. He did not clean off the counter, and the pen went right back on the counter. The deputy held up a trash can from under the counter for Jeb to put the paper towels in. Jeb followed another deputy's instructions to head for the Jail's reception center housing cell he would stay in until the first court date.

As he walked away, Jeb had a momentary flash of *déjà vu* that his sneeze at the jail counter was the same thing that had happened with that girl that had sneezed when he handed her the pen at the freshman orientation sign-in last Monday. Life was strange.

—

Chapter 34

Emergency Operations Center (EOC)
Santa Barbara County
Santa Barbara, California
1:04 PM PDT July 21ˢᵗ

Specialist Ali drove the TODPP Suburban into the parking lot of the Santa Barbara County Emergency Operations Center. It was a modern, one-story building, standing on a hillside by itself, overlooking the city of Santa Barbara below. Ali saw some empty parking spaces near the walkway to the building and drove up there. The open spaces were all marked 'Official Vehicle Only.' A Sheriff black-and-white patrol car was parked in one of the spaces. Ali thought for a minute and pulled into the closest space. The Suburban had U.S. Government plates.

As everyone was getting out of the car, Ali motioned to Karen Llewellyn to see if she wanted him to come in. She pointed to him and made clear he was to come inside. Karen, in her blue duty PHS uniform, was followed by the three soldiers in camouflage. Specialist Kuchma carried a laptop case with her.

On the way up the walkway, Karen's cellphone chimed loudly. She took out the large-screened cellphone. An urgent notice indication flashed on the screen.

"Hold up a minute. I need to read this," Karen said as she stopped walking to read the email on her cellphone.

She found that her military superiors at the U.S. Army Medical Research and Development Command (USAMRDC), Fort Detrick had just issued an Immediate Precedence OpRep report based upon the information Karen and Captain Cameron had sent them. General Harding agreed with Karen's concern. Every U.S. Government entity that was involved in public health and security issues now knew what was happening in Santa Barbara County. The OpRep report put in a lot more background about the Paris H7N9 incident and the events in Europe than Karen had told Captain Cameron to put in his email. The picture painted by the OpRep's language was somewhat jarring. Karen had a momentary thought that maybe she had gotten ahead of Charlene Reed and the local people. However, Karen had warned Charlene that this might happen. Jarring or not, the OpRep report was true.

Karen and her three soldiers were asked to show their IDs and sign in by an older gentleman at a window in the front lobby of the building. "You here for the meeting about the flu? It has just started, I think. Go right on in. On your right at the end of the hall." The man pointed.

The room at the end of the hall turned out to be a large room with huge screens across the far wall and rows of computer laden desks facing in arcs toward the screens. It looked like what one would envision an 'Op Center' to look like. Several people were working at computers and talking via headsets, but there was no meeting going on.

Walking into the room, Karen saw that one of the glassed-in conference rooms at the rear of the bigger room was full of people. She led her crew over there. Dr. Charlene Reed came out of the room to meet them. Charlene had a face mask on.

"Dr. Llewellyn, thank you for coming." Reed started to shake hands, then reconsidered and held her hand back. "We just got started. Let me introduce you, and we can recap."

Karen smiled and circled her finger around her face, asking with the motion why Reed was wearing a mask.

Reed answered, "We decided, just as a caution, that anyone who had been up in the possible Zone of Contact up in Solvang should wear a mask. Better safe than sorry."

In the meeting room, Dr. Reed introduced Karen as "The Public Health Service doctor from Ventura County I mentioned to you." Reed then quickly pointed around the room and introduced the County staff and political leaders who were assembled, perhaps twenty people.

Everyone sat down, and a tall man with a graying crew-cut wearing a polo shirt with the County logo on it stood at the podium. He had been introduced as Charlie Witherow, the Emergency Management chief. "OK, recapping. As of this morning, we have eleven patients in the hospital, all teenagers. Four of them are up north at Marian Medical Center and seven down here at Cottage Hospital. Two of those patients, Patient #1 and Patient #3, are in serious condition on a ventilator with respiratory problems. The others are in varying stages of illness; all have high temperatures and the usual flu symptoms. Patients #1 and #2 are brother and sister, and Patient #3 is a friend of the sister.

"Coach Nielsen has given Public Health the names of a total of 31 football players who were at practice with Patient #1 and Patients 4 through 11 last Monday. I'm not sure if that's 31 total or 31 plus 8. Jeff will update all of those when he shows off the new contact tracing software in a minute. Mrs. Beaumont, the mother of the first two patients, is in a quarantine room at Cottage. She was able to get hold of her husband in New York. Mr. Beaumont is in his hotel in New York, apparently also sick, waiting for the New York health authorities to contact him. Mr. Beaumont is now designated Patient #12-NY. Dr. Reed has contacted her health department contacts in Los Angeles to get them working on the contacts of Patients #2 and #3 at the UCLA campus. That's out of our hands.

"The sheriff's team is working to contact all of the potential Santa Ynez Valley contacts and seeing if there are any other high school contacts besides the football team. Santa Ynez High starts the fall semester early and is scheduled to begin classes in the second week of August. There is some discussion as to whether that's wise or not. We don't know yet.

"We have contacted the Santa Maria County Fair people and let them know about the situation with Patient #1's prize pig. Fortunately, the purchase of an award-winning pig is a big thing, and they have the purchaser's information. The pig's new owner is a commercial agriculture company in Visalia. Authorities in Tulare County have been contacted to go get the pig and track the human contacts. Unfortunately, the Santa Maria Fairpark has both swine and poultry in the same show building, and there were several hundred animals that are potential influenza vectors in that building over the weekend when Patients #1 and #12-NY had their pig at the fair. The fair people estimate there were well over a thousand visitors to the animal husbandry building. Probably impossible to individually track, so if tests on the swine are positive, we may need to make a public announcement to get people to quarantine themselves.

"The geese belonging to Patient #2 have been collected and are in the County Animal Services quarantine facility in Buellton. We are still trying to get them tested.

"That's all I have, for now, Jeff?" Charlie stepped away for the podium and sat down.

A young man with thick glasses wearing a t-shirt with the Santa Barbara County seal on it set a laptop on the podium and clicked something that made the wall-sized screen behind the podium light up with several colored circles and shapes connected by lines.

The young man explained, "We have set up our software package that FEMA and CDC produced to track an epidemic and trace contacts across multiple locations in an epidemic. This was one of the big advances after the coronavirus crisis showed we had insufficient ability to manage and track the spread of a virus, and one agency didn't know what the others were doing."

As Jeff spoke at the podium, Karen saw Specialist Kuchma open her laptop and activate it.

The man continued, "This is a graphics-based information program. You can see every agency involved in a particular epidemic effort. The icons have different colors and shapes to identify whether an icon is local, state, federal, hospital, or whatever. Here," he used a mouse cursor to point to the central green circle, "you can see us in Santa Barbara. And here are our two hospitals involved. And here is LA and Tulare Counties, who have logged on to our network, which is on FEMA's cloud. You can click on any icon and make menu choices to see whatever you want about what an icon's agency is doing. If I click on our icon and choose Contact Tracing or Patient Status, you get a head's up display of all eleven local patients and the one we have designated #12-NY, which, when New York logs on, will move over to their Patients list."

A woman, who had been introduced as a county supervisor, raised her hand and spoke, "You have thirteen patient icons showing. What does that mean?"

Jeff looked at the screen, quickly spotting icon '#13,' which he clicked on. He highlighted an information flag attached to the new icon. "Hmm, it seems Cottage Hospital has admitted Mrs. Beaumont, the mother of Patients #1 and #2, to the hospital. She is sick, too."

Jeff went back to the main screen, "This FEMA/CDC software also works as a communications conduit. We will have it at all of our County stations, the hospitals have it, and you can quickly contact any entity in the network nationwide by voice or video by going to the Comms screen and clicking who you want to talk to or chat with. You can transfer any data or documents instantly through the network." Jeff clicked to show icons identifying three California county agencies and two hospitals involved.

Jeff excitedly announced, "There, see that! The Feds have joined our incident network." He clicked on a blue rectangle icon on the left of the screen.

A window showing a young female in a camouflage uniform appeared. When Specialist Kuchma waved at her laptop, the soldier in the video window on the front screen also waved.

Kuchma spoke to her laptop, and her voice came over Jeff's computer on the podium. "This is great. I can use it to send you the blood sample information when we get it this evening."

Jeff smiled, "Exactly, this is what the system was meant for."

After a few more speakers outlined their individual office's duties and status, the meeting broke up, and Dr. Reed took Karen's group out to the main room to talk about the patient sample process. They sat at one of several tables set up around the room for group chats.

Dr. Reed told them, "We have all eleven patients blood and nasal swabs boxed up and ready for you. We just got the four new samples from the hospital in Santa Maria. We are working on the football teams samples. If you have time, we will get the samples from Mrs. Beaumont. It's sad to hear she is sick, too. That means her entire family is now sick from this."

Karen said, "Yes, it is. It is probably not the last sadness that comes out of this. While we are here, should we . . ."

Karen was interrupted by Charlie Witherow, who walked up and asked, "Captain, do you know anything about the Army issuing a nationwide alert about this? I just got a call from Sacramento asking about it."

Karen nodded, "Uh, yes. My higher headquarters issued what they call an OpRep, which is their report of this incident. I saw that they had issued it just before we got here. Sorry, if that's jumping the gun on you. This is your show here; we are just here to help."

Witherow smiled and shook his head, "Damn, Ma'am, don't apologize. I called this into the State's Emergency Management watch officer at 7:30 this morning, and I haven't heard hide nor hair from them until they got the alert from DC. Now, they are asking me what they can do to for us and do I need help tracing the contacts. You did us a great service by rattling the cage on this. Thank you."

Witherow walked away, and Karen continued, "Uh, I was just saying . . . what's the status of samples on the geese? I have my staff working on the process to do those tests, too."

Reed answered, "Yes, just before you got here, I heard from the vet in Buellton. They have new gullet swabs and blood samples from both geese. The geese are still alive, but, of course, they will eventually need to be put down, after we finish testing. The samples are heading on the 101 down from Buellton to here as we speak."

"Good, now what else do we need to do while we're here? Oh, and you might want to hold off as long as possible on putting down those geese. They could be a key piece of evidence as to how this started."

Kuchma cut in, "Captain Llewellyn, you should probably take this video call on my laptop via the incident network. Some Colonel from USAMRIID wants to talk to my commanding officer. It's a Colonel Hal Kessler."

Karen took the laptop to another table to talk to her old friend, who was the Army's senior viral expert. He had a lot of questions.

———

Ministry of Health
Medical Products Facility
Fangshan District
Suburban Beijing, China
8:05 AM Local Time July 21st

Dr. Zhao Xiang met her old friend at the door to the administrative building where her office was. "Jinghui, I appreciate you driving out so we could talk about everything. Our telephone calls about this have been less than helpful at times. There is only so much you can do to talk around the details of a very technical issue."

Deputy Minister of Health, Cao Jinghui, nodded. "You're correct there. But, we learned with what happened to Liu that the Central Security Bureau has extensive 'ears.' And, their knowledge level on those very same technical issues is limited. They misunderstand when people are speaking of essential things that must be discussed."

"Do you want to go talk in my office first, or go directly out and see the production facilities?" Xiang asked.

Cao Jinghui laughed and shook his head as though Xiang had said something very foolish, "No, Xiang, talking in your office would probably be worse than talking on the telephone." He stared into Xiang's eyes with a lift of his brow to make his point about not talking freely in her office. The telephones and the walls had ears, especially in suburban Beijing.

She nodded. They continued their walk, out toward the pharmaceutical production building.

"Tell me, Xiang, How is your father? Is he enjoying his new posting?"

"I received an email from him last week. He likes the broader range of contacts he has in Geneva and is getting into the routine of working with an international organization. My mother is not so happy there. She doesn't speak French nor German and was quite happy back in London."

Jinghui nodded, "Yes, that's an issue I had not thought about. Your father is close to the top of the pecking order. Perhaps there is a spot for him back home here."

"I doubt it. All of the top spots in Beijing at the Foreign Ministry go to people from the outside, the political people, not career diplomats."

"I suppose so." Jinghui changed the topic, "Is everything we talked about with the new vaccine in order? The newest vaccine, that is."

Xiang answered with a questioning tone in her voice, "I think so. But, I could use some clearer information on what we are facing. You're always trying to tell me about the problem with terms like the recipe from Paris, and the Army in the 'north of France.' I understood the France and Paris references. You mean the Baodi flu strain is no longer a problem only there?"

Jinghui answered, "The Army cracked down pretty hard in Baodi. Baodi is supposedly clear of the H7N9. But they had to move many people in Baodi farther away from Beijing both to protect from the spread and to keep the problem under wraps. They moved many of the factory workers north to Changchun. The big company in Tianjin that owned the factory and farm where the problem started had company plants and farming operations up there in Changchun. They cooperated in covering up the problems in Baodi. It was not in their interest to publicize their poultry problems."

The deputy minister continued, "But now, the H7N9 is spreading in the north of Changchun. There is a good chance it will become an epidemic in all of Heilongjiang province and maybe the entire Dongbei region. It has hit the ethnic groups on the Russian border particularly hard. The area is remote, so word has not leaked out, but it's probably only a matter of time."

Xiang shook her head, "That's unfortunate. The strain is bad news. I'm glad you asked me to start the vaccine work when you did last April. The Army's testing for us seems to have been conclusive, but their methodology of testing does not meet normal medical protocols. We have converted their data to something more recognizable to the medical community, as we assume we will have to show it to the West, eventually. With the news this week from the real Paris, not our codenamed city, the West will need our help, since they probably have not started work on a vaccine."

Jinghui shook his head, "Do not get ahead of the Leadership, Xiang. Yes, we will obviously not let thousands or millions in Europe and elsewhere die when we have developed a vaccine for H7N9 already. But, the Leadership wants to be careful that we do not get blamed for the outbreak like we were for coronavirus. Such a horrible insult to China cannot happen again."

"But, the morons in Hubei were, indeed, responsible for coronavirus getting out of hand. And, if we do not act as soon as we can, this H7N9 avian flu could make coronavirus look tame. It's a real killer."

Jinghui stopped walking and put his hand on Xiang's shoulder, "Be careful, Xiang. You have done a magnificent job getting this H7N9 vaccine ready. Let us carefully watch what happens elsewhere. At the appropriate time, the Leadership will make sure the right thing is done. Hopefully, if not, we may try something else. For now, get your production lines working to produce what we need to deal with our own H7N9 epidemic in Dongbei and also make sure H5N1 does not come back in the fall. Oh, and we need to produce enough of both the annual vaccine and the Paris vaccine to distribute within the government and the military on a first call basis. We need to make sure our leadership infrastructure and our friends are protected if things get out of hand. Let me know when I can have people pick up three of the 10K lots of each vaccine. OK?"

She nodded. Jinghui had emphasized 'our friends' in an odd way.

Jinghui continued, "You have raised a good question about how we present the evidence that we have already produced this vaccine to the rest of the world. I will discuss that problem downtown. They may want to send some of their experts out to get your advice on how this should look to the West. You probably have a better feel for how the western companies view the vaccine production business. Just heed my advice and be circumspect about how you talk to anyone besides me about your concerns."

Jinghui removed his hand from her shoulder and took a deep breath, "Now, Xiang, show me the production. I understand the regular quadrivalent vaccine, including H5N1, is being produced by the plant-based method, and the 'Paris' strain is being produced with cell-based methods. Correct?"

Dr. Zhao Xiang nodded and also took a deep breath. She then turned toward the rows of kettles where thousands of gallons of bacteria were growing virus-like particles within them – H7N9 virus-like particles.

Xiang turned to Jinghui and said, "It's rather ironic that the strain we have nicknamed as the 'Paris' strain, has really become the Paris strain."

———

Debussy Waterfront Hotel
Seaport District
Manhattan, New York City, New York
3:15 PM EDT July 21ˢᵗ

Derek Beaumont had been confused when his wife had called. She had told him yesterday that both of their children were sick and in the hospital. He had promised her to fly home as soon as he could extract himself from the acquisition meeting with the Wall Street bankers and venture capital firm.

Now today, at lunch, he had come back to his hotel room with a headache and fever himself. His wife had called him and tried to explain that she was sending him a doctor. *What?* That had been odd. She had then put some doctor in Santa Barbara on the phone who had explained the situation.

Derek was not happy about somebody from NY Public Health coming to his hotel room. Nothing about that was appealing to a wealthy executive like Derek Beaumont. Now, here they were.

Four people were in his hotel room. They were all in protective suits, masks, and gloves. Derek could see two police officers in face masks standing guard at the hotel room door. He had tried to make a call to tell the people at the buy-out negotiations that he would not be back in today, but these people had told him not to call his business associates. They said they would have some of their people go down to the venture capital firm themselves.

God, what a mess!

The Public Health team was helping Derek put a hooded jumpsuit on over his clothes and a full mask on his face. It was not a cloth mask and face shield like theirs, Derek's mask was a full face covering, like a gas mask, that filtered his breath as he exhaled. Derek's suitcase, laptop, cellphone, and all of his property, like his shaving kit, was being bagged in large orange bags. Everything else in the hotel room -- telephone, blankets, desk lamp, TV remote, phone book, everything – was also being bagged in red bags with bio-hazard symbols on them. They put all of his bagged property on the bottom of an ambulance gurney that they had just rolled into the room. They apparently expected Derek to get onto the gurney for the ride to wherever they were going.

Derek Beaumont acquiesced to getting on the gurney. He was not feeling well at all.

———

Santa Barbara County
Emergency Operations Center
Santa Barbara, California
3:15 PM PDT July 21ˢᵗ

The Ops Center had filled with more people since Karen and her team had arrived. Ghent and Ali were huddling with a few sheriff's deputies over by a map of the County. Kuchma was talking with her new buddy Jeff near a computer console that controlled the big view of the FEMA software schematic that now showed on the large main wall screen in the Ops Center.

Karen and Dr. Reed had been explaining to an assistant county executive officer and three county politicians why H7N9 was different from normal flu and the H5N1 avian flu that had circulated earlier in the year and now threatened to start up again in the fall. Their listeners had been, of course, incredulous when they heard the historical mortality rate of H7N9 in the various animal-related human cases that had occurred over the years. It was hard to imagine an influenza outbreak with a death rate of 30%, but that was the WHO statistics.

Karen's cellphone went off, and she broke free from the group to take the call. "Hello, Marty. This is not a good time to talk. I'm pretty busy right now."

"I bet that's kind of an understatement. I'm quite aware of what a busy girl you have been today."

"What do you mean?"

"I got an email from my Army Reserve detailer at HRC at Ft. Knox telling me I was being activated and should contact the travel office at Fort Detrick to arrange the earliest possible travel arrangements for me and my reserve response team to assemble in, of all places, Thousand Oaks, California. I was instructed to collect some forward-deployed USAMRIID gear and wait for further instructions per CG USAMRIID. I called Hal Kessler, and he explained it to me."

Karen was quiet for a moment, "Well, Marty, you said in May you wanted to come back out for a visit. Here you go, a visit to the Golden State at Uncle Sam's expense."

"Cute, Karen. Is this as bad as Hal Kessler indicated."

"I'm not sure what he said, but this is the real thing. About as deadly as a virus gets. I'm up here in Santa Barbara now, with my team, waiting for blood samples we can take back and analyze."

Marty said, "I saw on CNN that they have dozens dead in three countries. Is this the same stuff?"

"The preliminary blood test here says yes, same H7N9 strain as in Paris, last spring and now. That's why the locals asked for help. This is not an easy viral strain to ID. And, we've got three or maybe four Zones of Contact with potentially hundreds of contacts to trace. They need all the contact tracing help they can get, here, in LA, and now it seems like New York. Oh, and add Tulare County California, too. We just got word there is a pig that may be a vector up there in a pig-feeding lot with a couple thousand of his pig buddies."

Karen saw a man in a khaki uniform walk into the room, carrying a cooler chest. Dr. Reed stood up and motioned to Karen. The goose samples had arrived.

Karen said, "I've got to run. Our samples just arrived from the poultry vectors, and we need to get on the road. I'll call you when I can. I'll give my driver your number to make contact so we can pick your people up when they fly into LA, OK? We have your vehicles for you; you won't need rentals."

"OK, it seems like most of us can make it in tonight. But, our team's Intel guy, Geof Sands, is vacationing in Cabo San Lucas. My flight comes into Burbank at 19:55. That's a little closer to you than LAX."

"Alright, when you get details on when people are getting in, call Captain Cameron, and he will arrange hotel rooms for your people. Although, you'll probably all be coming up to Santa Barbara as soon as you get your gear from my parking lot."

"Hotels for all of us? Me included?" Marty asked.

"This really isn't the time for that . . . but no, I'll find a place for you." Karen said.

"Sounds good. See you tonight."

———

Inmate Reception Center
Los Angeles County Jail
Los Angeles, California
4:35 PM PDT July 21ˢᵗ

Jeb DeVries had been able to post bond, so the judge had ordered him released. He had not had a chance to see an attorney yet, so his arraignment was delayed. He signed a promise to appear for the next month. Now, he had been sent back to the Jail Reception Center to get his civilian clothes and possessions and be released.

Jeb had to wait a bit in the holding cell before being released. He was sick. It had been getting worse all day. The bailiff at court had given him a mask to wear because of the courthouse rules about prisoners who were coughing or sneezing. He still had the mask but did not have it over his face because his frequent sneezing would just goop up the inside of the mask, and Jeb had nothing to clean his nose.

The holding cell for prisoners was crowded. At last, he was brought to the counter where a plastic bag with his property and clothing was given to him. He looked through the receipt list that they asked him to sign to acknowledge his property being returned.

"My cell phone is not here," Jeb complained.

The deputy grabbed the list, read it, and said, "No cellphone on the LAPD list of property when you were booked in."

Jeb must have left the cellphone in his car. He asked, "Where's my car?"

"If you were arrested for DWI by LAPD, they towed your car to one of several different lots. There should be a number on the paper attached to your ticket where you can ask about your car. Are you done now, or you want to stay here and talk all night?"

Jeb sneezed again. He put on his clothes in a changing booth and was pointed to the release door. Outside, many people were waiting for rides at a taxi stand with no taxis present. There was a bus stop, but he did not recognize any of the bus numbers. But then, Jeb DeVries was not a frequent bus rider. He had his Passat, usually. Now it was somewhere in an impound lot. Jeb knew nobody at UCLA that he wanted to call, explain a DWI arrest, and ask for a ride to Westwood.

Jeb saw Los Angeles Union Station in the distance, south of the Jail. He knew there was a Metro Line station there, and he could connect to the E-Line, which would take him out to Westwood and his resident advisor apartment in the dorm at UCLA.

Jeb was miserable on the walk over to the Metro station. Fever, chills and body aches were getting worse. From the D-Line train he caught at Union Station, it was an easy transfer to the E-Line and the long ride west.

He had forgotten to buy Kleenex at the shop in Union Station, so Jeb had nothing to wipe or blow his nose when he sneezed while riding on the Metro car. Of necessity, he wiped his hand on the seat. His cough was getting worse, too. It was Friday rush hour now, and the Metro car was full heading out of downtown.

There were taxis waiting at the Westwood/Rancho Park Metro Station. Elite Westwood was much better territory for drivers to pick up taxi passengers than the Jail was. Jeb took one of the taxis. The taxi drove him past the intersection on Pico Boulevard, where his journey to the Jail had begun early that morning.

What a day!

——

101 Freeway
Santa Barbara/Ventura Counties, California
4:00 PM PDT July 21st

The ride back to Thousand Oaks was busy. Everybody except Specialist Ali, who was driving, spent much of the time on their cellphones.

Captain Llewellyn called Cameron to check on how things were going at TODPP. He had been handling calls from several federal agencies who had seen his name on the original email he had sent out. Having seen the set-up in Santa Barbara, Karen asked Rob Cameron to have the HeptImun people create a miniature version of an Ops Center in the training room HeptImun used for new employee briefings and the like. Karen had Specialist Kuchma call HeptImun's IT person to give him details on getting the FEMA/CDC epidemic tracking software set up on the big screen in the training room. Kuchma also took Karen's and Ghent's cellphones and installed the FEMA/CDC app so that they could get into the crisis management network anywhere.

Master Sergeant Rodney Ghent's name had also been on the email, so he also got calls, mostly just people on the original email, looking for information. Two calls were from news media. At Karen's suggestion, the media inquiries were told to call the Public Affairs Officer's desk at the Santa Barbara Ops Center. Karen had picked up the County PAO's business card when Charlene Reed had walked her around to introduce her to people. At Kuchma's suggestion, Ghent started suggesting to government callers that they should sign onto the FEMA/CDC network. Ghent was also in touch with his assistant, Sergeant Riddell, who had started the process of getting the incoming Reserve personnel routed from the LA airports up to Thousand Oaks. Ghent estimated they would need fifteen hotel rooms with two beds for the Reservists overnight, and he called Ross Tanner, who reserved enough space at the business suites hotel near TODPP. It was Friday evening, so the business-oriented hotel had openings.

Karen also had a long conference call with Phil Reynes and Nancy Cox at CDC. They wanted to hear everything Karen could tell them about the situation in Santa Barbara. Karen promised to keep them in the loop as the TODPP lab got firm results on the strain samples. They, in turn, promised to test the existing samples from Santa Barbara that were already at CDC, but which nobody had made a high priority until the OpRep arrived. Karen asked Phil and Nancy for any information CDC might have on the situation in Europe. Everybody wondered if the two H7N9 events were connected. Philip Reynes said he would call his Chinese contacts to see if there was anything new with their H7N9 outbreak last spring. Word was that five *arrondissements* in Paris had been issued curfews and were in lockdown until the French health authorities could track the attendees of the buffet, now six days ago. Both Paris and Milan were in a medical reaction mode they had not seen since the coronavirus crisis. For some reason, despite the two deaths and multiple hospitalized patients, the situation in Germany did not seem as bad as it was in France and Italy.

———

Intensive Care Unit
Santa Barbara Cottage Hospital
Santa Barbara, California
5:15 PM PDT July 21ˢᵗ

Mark Beaumont was a big guy, even at just age sixteen. With his father's muscularity and his Swedish mother's height, Mark had the stature expected of a blocking tight end. That was the position he had been practicing for the previous Monday afternoon. It had been the first day of on-the-field drills for the varsity football squad in Santa Ynez.

Now, Mark's size was a problem. The hospital staff struggled to turn him head to foot on his ICU bed and then flip him over on his stomach. The ICU bed could be tilted down at the foot more than it could at the head. Mark had been intubated and ventilated since he arrived in the ambulance two days before.

Now, the anesthesiologist directing the ventilation procedures on Mark had ordered him flipped and tilted as much as possible, as a last-ditch effort to get his blood oxygen levels up. The theory was that the on-the-stomach, head-down positioning of a patient on ventilation maximized both the expansion of the lungs as the ventilator pumped oxygen, as well as the possibility of drainage of the pneumonic fluids now flooding his lungs.

With Mark in his new position, the doctor rechecked everything. The orderly had strapped Mark's hips so that he did not slide down on the highly tilted bed. Oxygen was on 100%, and oximeter set to alarm at any further blood oxygen drop. The drugs keeping Mark in a coma while the ventilator pumped were properly set in the IV. All the doctor could do now was wait. He had done everything he knew how.

———

Thousand Oaks Defense Pharmaceutical Plant (TODPP)
Thousand Oaks, California
7:14 PM PDT July 21ˢᵗ

George Marquardt had done an excellent job with Karen's idea for the training room. By the time Karen and the three soldiers returned from Santa Barbara, the training room was now an operations center and had the FEMA/CDC program projected on the wall and several large-screened computer stations on the classroom tables. On the sidewall, there was even a large, full-color display of the new TODPP unit crest logo that Master Sergeant Ghent had designed. Karen had not seen that before and was not sure whether that was new for the Ops Center concept or if it had been in the training room before and was just Marquardt's way of making up for the signage complaint she had expressed to him. Karen's initial positive reaction at the gungho HeptImun response this afternoon was tempered a bit when she remembered that everything HeptImun Corporation did was repaid to them at a cost-plus basis by the government. Even so, they had done an excellent job.

When they had arrived in Thousand Oaks, Karen had followed Sonya and Specialist Kuchma to the laboratory area. The Biosafety Level 3 lab was in a separate secure area apart from the quality control lab HeptImun used to support its vaccine production. Sonya had that secure lab in operation now with airflow protection and full entrance and exit decontamination procedures in place. Karen watched through the viewing windows and listened on a speaker as Sonya and two of her lab techs took the samples out of the two sealed transport tubs Kuchma had given them. Kuchma asked Sonya if she could watch the sample test process, which Sonya allowed.

"Let me know as soon as you get anything," Karen ordered as she turned to leave.

Sergeant Riddell and Specialist Ali had each done one trip to the airports in Los Angeles to pick up incoming USAMRIID reservists. The training room had also become the gathering place for the people when they showed up. Karen and Rob Cameron welcomed them. One of the tables at the back of the room now had pizza and sodas on it. Karen suspected George Marquardt was behind that, too.

The first of the blood tests had taken about an hour and a half before Sonya felt comfortable with her conclusions that the first five tests they did were definitely H7N9. Sonya sent Kuchma to Karen with printouts of the PCR and genetic logs that Karen quickly confirmed. Patients #1, #2, #3, #10, and #13 all had H7N9 in both blood and nasal swabs.

Karen called Dr. Reed and told her the news. Rob Cameron contacted the duty officer at USAMRDC in Maryland and gave him the information to put out an update to the OpRep report. Kuchma entered the information into the FEMA/CDC software. So, everybody involved soon knew that the three members of the Beaumont family and the other teenage girl in Cottage Hospital, and one of the football players in the hospital in Santa Maria, California, all had a vicious new form of avian flu that, until this week, had never been know to transfer from human to human. Within the next two hours, the TODPP laboratory added several more of the football players and both geese to the H7N9 diagnosis list.

The TODPP people and the reservists now watched the software display as they waited for others to arrive. Some of the USAMRIID people were epidemiological specialists who were very familiar with the FEMA/CDC software. One of them, Chief Warrant Officer Morrison, showed Kuchma how to change the viewing window to a geographic map, instead of the flowchart style presentation. As they watched, they now saw Los Angeles County, Tulare County, New York City, USAMRIID, and CDC/Atlanta had all entered the network. CDC had also made a subheading entry that allowed everyone to get information on the H7N9 situation in Europe. Morrison also showed Kuchma how to load the DNA/RNA typing from their H7N9 tests as backup documents for each patient. Now, everyone network-wide could see the defining genetic patterns of the target virus.

Around 8 o'clock, Karen got a call from Marty. She left the room to take the call. All he wanted to tell her was Ali had picked him up in Burbank, and they were on their way. When Karen came back in the room, Kuchma waved for Karen to come over where Kuchma stood next to a USAMRIID warrant officer operating a software screen.

"You should see this, ma'am," Kuchma said. She pointed at the big screen.

The warrant officer was showing the screen with the graphics of the Santa Barbara patients shown on it. He circled the mouse pointer over two of the little stick figure icons on the chart. Patients #1 and #9 now had a small black 'X' overlaid on them.

"Does that mean what I think?" Karen asked.

Kuchma nodded, "Yes ma'am. It does. The Beaumont boy and one of the football players are gone."

"That's not all. Look here, ma'am," Morrison moved his mouse pointer. "Patients 14, 15, and 16 just showed up in Santa Maria."

"More football players?"

He shook his head, "No ma'am. The notes put in by the contact tracers in Santa Barbara says they are two of the fair judges and a veterinarian who worked at the County Fair last weekend."

"So, this is spreading across California."

"Worse, Captain Llewellyn, New York City has confirmed two of the father's banking contacts are sick, too. They've established a Zone of Contact for the New York City cluster, too."

Karen had learned Ghent's trick with the gate guard, and she got a text message when Ali brought Marty to the front gate. She went out to meet them.

Specialist Ali was carrying a large suitcase. Lieutenant Colonel Craig carried his carry-on, which he quickly switched to his left hand since he was wearing the Army's short-sleeved summer uniform. Both Marty and Ali saluted Karen.

"Good evening, ma'am. Colonel Craig explained that you two don't need any introduction," Ali said with a slight smile.

Karen saluted back, "Yes, good evening. Can you put his bags in my office? We have pizza in the training room. Get some. We'll be inside in a minute."

Ali took the carry-on and headed into the building.

There was a moment of silence after Ali left. However, the awkward moment was explained by the fact that as a young wife of an Army officer, Karen had learned about the Army rule against 'pubic displays of affection in uniform.' Standing outside the building at night was not public, but given their recent history both of them refrained . . . Marty turned toward the door and put his arm around the small of Karen's back, and the two walked inside.

"How are things?" Marty asked.

Karen shook her head, "Just as bad as we feared. Our suspicions confirmed. Two teenagers are dead already. Three more patients here, two new ones in New York. Both geese vectors test positive. Swine vector is probably positive since three of the new patients only had contact with it. One of the dead and seven patients here and two in New York had human-only contact."

"Are my people here?"

"Most of them. Nice bunch. Working well with my people. Your Intel guy, Major Sands, called USAMRIID from Houston, they relayed the info to us. He got a flight from Mexico to Houston and will be in LA in the wee hours tomorrow. Come on in, and we can give you a status report."

Marty Craig shook hands with several of his team. Karen introduced him to Cameron and Ghent. George, Ross, and Sonya came into the room. Karen introduced them to Marty, too.

Karen asked, "So, Sonya. You just taking a break, or . . . ?"

"No ma'am, unfortunately, not a break. We finished. All blood samples and all swabs except five that were inconclusive are positive for H7N9. We repackaged the remaining samples for shipment to CDC and USDA Omaha. Sergeant Riddell will deliver them to the UPS Express Gateway at LAX tonight."

"Well, good work switching gears so quickly and efficiently."

Ross and George both started to talk at the same time, but when they paused for each other, Kuchma spoke up from upfront on the computer. "Ma'am!" Kuchma was waving her arm to get Karen's attention.

Everyone turned to Kuchma, and she turned to Morrison, "Mister Morrison, show them."

The USAMRIID warrant officer clicked an icon on the main screen and announced, "Los Angeles County just logged onto the FEMA network. They immediately entered a newly confirmed H7N9 patient into the system. It seems UCLA Medical Center has in-house strain typing capabilities, and their patient's flu strain matched what we entered for our Patient #2 precisely, the same exact RNA. And the LA County contact tracing people already linked Patients SB#2 and SB#3 to LA#1 as all three being in the same college dormitory for some event last Monday. We officially have a multi-location human-to-human spread of fully-identified H7N9. With New York, Santa Maria, Santa Ynez, and now Los Angeles, we have confirmed four-location, multi-state spread of a previously non-circulating novel virus. That meets the CDC definition of 'outbreak,' next stop epidemic."

———

Chapter 35

Newspaper Pressroom
Kölner Zeitung
Cologne (Köln), Germany
10:45 AM Local Time July 22ⁿᵈ

The pressroom of the *Kölner Zeitung* newspaper occupied an entire floor of a modern high-rise building in downtown Cologne. The editors' offices around the periphery of the huge room looked out on the desks of dozens of reporters, assistant editors, and copywriters that filled the open floor. Everybody was busy. There were a few vacancies, though. The Food and Beverage Editor's office and the nearby desks of some of his staff were empty. That was strange. It was a few hours away from the press time for the newspaper's big Sunday edition.

Then, something odd happened near the elevators on that floor. A dozen uniformed police officers exited the elevators and took up station, blocking the elevators and the stairways. Every officer wore a protective face mask and shield. Then, another dozen persons in full-body protective gear came out of the elevators. The newspaper's staff photographer started snapping pictures.

The crew in protective gear spread out across the office, handing employees two-page questionnaires and face masks. The crew explained that everyone must answer all questions completely; each person was read a pre-printed set of instructions. Nobody was allowed to leave until cleared by the crew—no excuses. The statement was to be given under penalty of perjury. The questions included identification, home address, known illnesses, their current health status, a list of places they had gone in the last week, and names of people they had been within two meters of in the last week.

Herr Günther Rechtmann, a stout man with a Prussian mustache, saw what was going on in his pressroom and stormed out of his corner office demanding answers from the first of the invading crew he approached. The young woman he challenged simply gave Rechtmann a copy of the form and a mask. She read to him from the instruction card that was being read to everyone. She told Rechtmann to go back to his desk and sit down. She turned away to go to the next employee.

Günther Rechtmann was the publisher of the newspaper and was not used to being ignored, not in his own office, not in his own building. He grabbed the arm of the young woman to turn her around to face him, and he again demanded a full explanation of the intrusion. That was a mistake.

Several officers of the North Rhine-Westphalia State Police standing by the elevators rushed to confront Rechtmann. He had assaulted an inspector of the Ministry of Health carrying out an official investigation. Rechtmann was quickly separated from the young woman, manhandled to the floor and handcuffed. The intrepid staff photographer caught everything on camera. The Sunday edition would have a copy of this picture on the front page.

The picture would accompany the cover story that explained the events in the newsroom. It had started with the deaths of the *Kölner Zeitung's* Food and Beverage Editor and his wife. The hospitalization of several co-workers and neighbors of the editor and his wife soon followed. The well-known German culinary editor and his wife had been invitees to the *Journal Gastronomique's* buffet in Paris the weekend before. The efficient bureaucrats of the North Rhine-Westphalia State Ministry of Health quickly started epidemiological contact tracing. The focus of their work soon pointed to a common workplace of several of the people hospitalized in Cologne with H7N9 influenza. Many of them worked for *Herr* Rechtmann.

The Sunday edition of the *Kölner Zeitung* was late going to press. Some of the reporters' and editors' unfinished work on their desks was illegible after being sprayed down with disinfectant after the personnel interviews by the Health Ministry workers were completed. Several of the key people necessary to get the Sunday edition out were unavailable. Anyone who admitted to having spoken directly to the late Food and Beverage Editor or the other newspaper staff who were already in the hospital were involuntarily moved to a nearby hotel for seven days of quarantine courtesy of the State of North-Rhine Westphalia. Günther Rechtmann was among them.

———

Thousand Oaks Defense Pharmaceutical Plant (TODPP)
Thousand Oaks, California
7:35 AM PDT July 22nd

The back lot at the plant headquarters building in Thousand Oaks was busy. The morning's schedule had been set before everyone departed the evening before. Specialist Jerome Ali, driving the small Army passenger bus designated for the team, picked up the 22 soldiers who had stayed at the hotel right on schedule at 6:45 AM. Karen had brought Marty in before that. George Marquardt had his supply staff ready to unpack the supplies and equipment in storage for the USAMRIID team. Ross Tanner and two of his accountants were there to double check that everything specified in the contract addendum and equipment lists was correct and ready to use.

Marquardt also had the food truck contractor that usually provided mid-shift meals for the workers at the factory and greenhouses ready to provide anyone, whether soldiers or HeptImun staff, with a hearty breakfast. Like Ross Tanner, George Marquardt was well aware of what the emergency contract clause considered an allowable operational expense. Food for deployed troops and essential personnel, whether pizza or breakfast burritos, was an allowed expense.

On the early morning ride from Karen's Camarillo condo to Thousand Oaks, Marty had explained to Karen the make-up of his team. The USAMRIID response teams were the product of the early days of the coronavirus crisis when many locales struggled with the triple needs of medical response and infrastructure, infection contact tracing and similar epidemic response duties, and physical control of quarantine areas. There was one team made up of active-duty soldiers at Fort Detrick and five teams that consisted of Army Reservists. Each team had medical personnel, intelligence and information specialists, and military police officers whose job it was to advise local authorities in a time of epidemic crisis. The Army teams were not only experts in their individual fields, but they were also trained to know who to call in the government hierarchy to get an immediate response to problems. The coronavirus crisis had shown the national leadership that, in a pandemic, knowledge of epidemiology, crisis management and, emergency medical organization was beyond the scope of many local and even some state government agencies. These response teams were the Army's answer. The FEMA/CDC software was a corresponding crisis response tool to fill the need for interagency communications, contact tracing, and epidemiological information management that had been woefully weak in the initial stages of coronavirus. FEMA, CDC, the Army Corps of Engineers, the Public Health Service, and other federal agencies all had many new functions that had grown out of the brutal lessons learned from COVID19. Karen's assignment in the national vaccine production program was another example.

Marty's team was designated as USAMRIID Response Team Three. The team had done their two-weeks summer reserve training just a month before in June at Fort Detrick. They had trained on identical equipment to that pre-positioned at TODPP for them. The USAMRIID headquarters staff had called Santa Barbara as soon as the word went out Team Three was to be sent to help out. The active-duty USAMRIID team and two of the other reserve teams had been deployed earlier in the year to respond to the H5N1 outbreak. It was Team Three's turn. Now, it was just a matter of making sure their gear was ready and heading to Santa Barbara.

As Karen watched the outfitting process, she was amazed at the supply chain for the Response Team Three emerging from her pharmaceutical plant's storerooms. The chief of her uniformed gate guards appeared with three 9mm semi-automatic pistols and ammunition that were designated for the Military Police officers on the team, but which had been in storage in the gate guards armory for their sidearms. While Karen looked on, Major Geof Sands was asked by a HeptImun logistics clerk to sign for a high-tech satellite telephone. Sands immediately proceeded to test the secure Iridium SatComm device with a check-in call to the National Military Command Center (NMCC) at the Pentagon. He then made two other calls to let their immediate commanding officer at USAMRIID and General Harding's staff know Team Three was online and capable of secure telecommunications.

There was one problem that came up as Team Three got ready to deploy to Santa Barbara. As Ross Tanner had mentioned to Karen when he first told her about the USAMRIID response team equipment at their location, several of their enlisted personnel were ostensibly assigned to TODPP to be there if needed by the response team. Those included the driver – Specialist Ali, the medical technician – Specialist Kuchma, and a vehicle mechanic whose personnel slot still remained empty four months after the military unit was organized. Lieutenant Colonel Craig and his expert team were mainly officers and had been told in their training at Fort Detrick that enlisted personnel to support their mission would be assigned by the host command upon deployment.

Now, Response Team Three was driving seven vehicles, including the huge laboratory 'RV' vehicle to the scene of the crisis and they expected to find a driver and a mechanic to drive the supply truck and passenger bus for them and a medical technician to 'man' the laboratory vehicle and support the team's medical mission. Craig brought the problem up to Captain Llewellyn, who turned to Ross Tanner for advice. She did not relish losing the services of Kuchma and Ali. Ross found an answer to the problem in the myriad of Army paperwork that was his realm.

Karen was back in her office when Ross Tanner came in with several thick documents and an Army Regulation manual. "I had never dug into this before since the problem never arose. But, it seems the TODPP TO&E has . . . "

Karen interrupted, "TO&E? You mentioned that before. What's a TO&E?"

Ross Tanner swallowed and thought how he could explain the complicated Army system of unit organization and supply to a commanding officer who had never heard of such. "Ma'am, let me give you a fast and dirty explanation, but if you have a few spare weeks sometime, I can explain the system the Army uses to assign people and equipment to a unit. A deployable, combat unit like an infantry battalion has a proposed list of officers and enlisted to be assigned and equipment to be delivered to carry out its combat mission—that's called Table of Organization and Equipment, or TO&E. A regular, non-combat unit, like a military fort, say Fort Detrick, or an administrative office has its list of people and equipment —that's called a Table of Distribution and Allowances, or TDA. They are pretty much the same thing, but because one, TO&E, is meant for combat and deployment, the essential missions of the Army, it has more clout.

"So, when General Harding and his subordinates at USAMRIID managed to get support for the Response Teams thrown into the defense pharmaceutical plant proposal, they also managed to get the Response Teams designated as a deployable unit, which it is, a unit meant to deploy to fight a pandemic. Smart idea. So, TODPP has both its administrative TDA and it has a TO&E to support the deployable 'combat' troops, the Response Team. Kuchma, Ali, and our missing mechanic are all assigned here because the Response Team needs them when they go to 'war.'

Karen asked, "So, I'm sunk? They get my people?"

Ross smiled, "Not necessarily, ma'am. One more piece to the puzzle. There is a corollary document called a Modified TO&E, which is meant to show the perfect situation of what a unit needs when heading into battle. That infantry battalion in peacetime has its TO&E people and equipment assignment, but when it gets orders to deploy to Afghanistan, everybody tries to get it up to full combat strength, that is, its MTO&E. Getting a unit up to deployment strength is the highest priority in the Army, both for personnel and equipment."

"Yes, and . . . ?" Karen was uneasy with all the acronyms.

"As a key part of the response team deployment, TODPP and its sister plants have an MTO&E, too, that gives you everything some post-coronavirus Army staffer conceived might be needed in the event of another pandemic crisis. Cutting this short, if you can get your major command to invoke your full MTO&E status, you can get not only your missing mechanic, but a dozen or so other people, like a junior officer whose job is to get critical supplies to the response team. Also, Kuchma has been great getting the FEMA software working and helping out in the laboratory, but that is not her job. Your MTO&E has a senior non-commissioned officer in a computer support and communications slot and a senior MOS 68K medical laboratory specialist who is supposed to run that 'RV' laboratory in the parking lot and interface with your lab at TODPP. Kuchma is actually supposed to be helping your husband treat patients. You need to invoke your full MTO&E to handle this emergency that has been dropped in your lap. It doesn't directly answer the issue with Kuchma and Ali, but it gets both you and the Response Team more people."

"What do I need to do and what are my chances of getting it approved?"

At this, Ross Tanner smiled, "Ma'am, you and I have both met General Harding. Can you imagine what his reaction will be to one of his subordinate commanders announcing she is going into battle and needs her full, official allotment of battle-ready troops? It will be fun to watch the assholes and elbows flying when the General gets that bit in his teeth. In this current climate with people keeling over dead in the streets of Paris and Milan, Fort Knox will be falling all over themselves to cut emergency orders to fill your slots and keep that from happening here."

"Fort Knox?" Karen did not get the reference.

"Fort Knox is where the Army Human Resources Command is."

"What do I do to get started?"

"Just give me the word, and I will go spoil the Saturday afternoon golf game of Harding's S-1."

Karen was going to ask what an S-1 was, but she just said, "Do it."

———

Topanga-Victory Urgent Care Center
Los Angeles, California
12:17 PM PDT July 22ⁿᵈ

For Dr. Teresa Rohrbach, it was a typical day, the usual mix of medical problems. Skinned body parts and a broken ankle from the newly re-opened skateboard park on Victory Boulevard seemed to be the most common. It was a relief to have a few months when the rush of avian flu cases had slowed down. The corporate office assured staff that the new batch of flu vaccine that included avian flu was due to arrive in late August. That was hopefully in time to prevent a horrible return of flu season, which, in the San Fernando Valley, always seemed to come with the start of the school year.

Teresa had warned the corporate office that she would be taking the first two weeks of August off. She had plenty of vacation time saved up. She and her partner were scheduled to take a ski trip to New Zealand and Australia, to catch the southern hemisphere winter. Living in Southern California, Teresa missed the weekly ski trips of her youth in Colorado. It would be fantastic. Thinking about the time away put Teresa in a good mood.

Teresa went to get the next patient slip from Cyndi. When their last name was called, Teresa saw what seemed to be a mother and teenage daughter get up and walk toward her. The mother had her arm around the daughter as she walked, and the girl was coughing. Teresa reached her hand over the counter, and, with much-practiced routine, Cyndi handed Dr. Rohrbach three face masks.

Teresa put one on and handed the other two to the patients, "Please put these on."

Dr. Rohrbach directed the patients to the exam room and put on new gloves.

Since they were relatively busy, operating without a duty RN at the storefront clinic, and Cyndi had not pre-screened the pair, Dr. Rohrbach did the interview and vitals. The girl had a temperature of 102° F. and complained of sinus congestion, cough, body aches, phlegm, and painful breathing. Teresa was sure this was *déjà vu* of the thousands of avian flu patients she had seen earlier in the year.

Dr. Rohrbach went to the supply cabinet and got one of the many Avian Flu QuickCheck test kits they now stocked. Teresa gently lifted the girl's mask and made the deep twist with the swabs to get the nasal culture. The dual swabs came back as positive for Type A influenza, but negative for H5N1. She quickly ran a second test—same result. Not H5N1.

This seemed like the classic symptoms of the H5N1 avian flu they had been hit with in March, but then it could also be a strong case of the old seasonal flu. Rohrbach needed to go through the standard flu symptom questions with the girl.

"Have you been around anyone who was obviously ill in the last week?" she asked.

The girl thought and then shook her head.

"How long have you had these symptoms?"

"Coupla days, ya know, two."

"Have you been in any large groups of people or around people you did not know in the past week?"

The girl thought, coughed into the mask, and then nodded, "Uh, Yeah, I went to my freshman orientation meeting at UCLA on Monday."

"How many people was that?"

"Coupla hundred, maybe."

Rohrbach finished the questions and noted all of the answers on the iPad. The flu questions panel would automatically go to the LA Health Department. She unlooped her stethoscope from her neck. She listened to the lungs and heart in front and then the lungs from the backside. She asked the girl to cough while she listened.

With the cough, Rohrbach heard the classic rattle and whistle of pneumonia. She asked the girl, "Describe for me again what the pain in your lungs feels like."

"OK, when I breathe in, I can't get a full breath, and it hurts inside my ribs when I try harder. It's like I can't quite catch my breath."

The girl had given the textbook answer—the textbook answer for pneumonia that requires hospitalization. With the high temperature, the cough, the raspy lungs, and the painful shortness of breath, Dr. Teresa Rohrbach had no choice not to write a referral form for sending the girl to the Emergency Room at Northridge Hospital, the closest ER to the family's home. Dr. Rohrbach added an instruction in the hospital referral for the referring physician to be copied on the hospital's diagnostic testing. Teresa Rohrbach wanted to know what this girl had.

———

Emergency Operations Center (EOC)
Santa Barbara County
Santa Barbara, California
1:30 PM PDT July 22nd

The Santa Barbara County people had been waiting for the arrival of Lieutenant Colonel Marty Craig's Army Response Team. After general introductions, the county crisis leaders gave an update of the current status of the various aspects of the crisis.

Dr. Charlene Reed briefly discussed the patients. The number of dead stood at two. The number of sick had risen by four since Marty had last heard the figure. A football coach and another player, a waitress at a popular Mexican restaurant near the high school, and a farmworker from Los Olivos were now probable infectees—they needed testing to confirm. The farmworker worked for the vintner who had the contract to manage the Beaumont's vineyard acreage. Reed had the four new blood samples ready for the response team to test, as soon as they got set up.

Tulare County officials had located the former Beaumont pig, or rather the corpse of the pig. The Tulare County Agriculture Commissioner and several people from the California Department of Food and Agriculture visited a swine feeding operation in Visalia. The owner regularly supported the Future Farmers of America by purchasing FFA-raised, prize-winning pigs from the state's county fairs. The young pig's body was found in a pen with several sick pigs. The state inspectors immediately issued an order to cull and dispose of over 1400 pigs. The hazardous waste facility in Kettleman City was designated as the site of the mass porcine disposal. Since the state inspector had signed the order, the State of California would be sending a check to the owner of the pigs.

The fieldhouse at the community college in Santa Maria had been outfitted to handle the massive contact tracing effort that the connection to the County Fair in Santa Maria now required. Volunteers and people sent in by the state were working to find possible infectees and trace their contacts. They thought they had a handle on the high school football players, their families, and local contacts in Santa Ynez, but the huge numbers possibly involved up in Santa Maria at the County Fair were daunting. The Fair Board had not been able to help much, as they had no idea which visitors had toured the animal sheds, other than registered animal exhibitors and a few employees. The county epidemiologists were now grappling with the question of whether making a public announcement of the possible infection at the Fair would gain them more value than it would cause harm by people trying to escape the area or hide their identity to avoid a quarantine order or a kill order for a family pet.

The job of contacting the Fair's registered animal exhibitor's became a grueling task, hampered by incomplete sign-in lists. Like in Tulare County, when Santa Barbara health inspectors and animal control wardens contacted the exhibitors, they had to enforce the mandatory kill order. Hundreds of beloved pet pigs and families' laying hens and prize roosters had to be put down. Since local county fairs were scheduled to allow exhibitors to compete at multiple nearby fairs, the gruesome visits by animal control wardens spread into several neighboring counties.

After the arrival briefing at the EOC, the county, state, and Army personnel now working in the County Ops Center broke into separate interest groups. Major Geoffrey 'Geof' Sands, the Army Intelligence officer, who had finally arrived from Mexico, and the two Military Police officers gathered with the Office of Emergency Management, Sheriffs, and Santa Maria Police personnel to study a map to peruse possible boundaries of quarantine zones if that alternative became necessary. They also spoke with an attorney, to compare federal and state law to discus the best legal lever to enforce possible quarantine orders.

The people at the EOC working on the medical testing problem went to the parking lot and toured the Army's mobile testing laboratory, along with Dr. Charlene Reed and Lieutenant Colonel Craig. It was eventually decided that the most pressing testing need was in Santa Ynez, where they might be able to use on-scene testing to eliminate many of the people who had already been put under quarantine-at-home orders because of contact with the Beaumont family or the football team. The mobile lab would be deployed to the government building campus in Solvang. If the testing was completed in the Solvang/Santa Ynez area, it might move to Santa Maria, where the need for H7N9 testing was potentially far greater, but which, for now, was impossible to manage and design a responsive testing program for. Everyone had learned in the coronavirus crisis that massive random testing did little to manage the big picture of a pandemic; you had to design a testing program and pattern, along with coherent contact tracing, that let you control the spread of the disease.

—

Chapter 36

Emergency Situation Office
Epidemiological Branch
Sante Publique France
Paris, France
8:05 PM Local Time July 23rd

Inspector Michel Dormer was working late, although it seemed, more and more, his efforts were for naught. It seemed to be a losing battle he fought.

It seemed to Dormer that part of the problem was a general misunderstanding by the public of both the scope and the cause of the problem. In the last ten days, there had been a massive release of information about the deaths and illnesses caused by the new flu virus. But for the public, especially the French public, word that people were dying as a result of what they had eaten implied this was food poisoning. The fact that this particular flu virus had never been transmitted from one human to another had also been explained in the myriad of reports on television and in the newspapers. All told, the public was not ready to absorb the information that had come out midweek when news of the first secondary infections started to filter out. The media itself, which had sensationalized the initial deaths, had backpedaled on reporting the first few cases of spread to other people.

The French Public Health system had greatly expanded such functions as case contact tracing and epidemiological investigation after coronavirus. But Michel Dormer and his co-workers were not ready to take on the bizarre way this viral outbreak was released on their countrymen. Often, case tracers followed an initial patient or a few initial patients deriving from one core incident or an occurrence in a new community. And in many cases, those initial cases were common people whose lives were easy to categorize and trace. Such was not the case in this disaster.

When the first word of the spread alarmed the health officials, they reacted as they had with coronavirus and with the avian flu the spring before. Five of the twenty *arrondissements* in Paris had been issued curfews and were initially placed in lockdown. But it quickly became evident that H7N9's spread had nothing to do with geographic location nor the character of the neighborhoods in Paris.

With the outbreak of H7N9 in Paris, there was not one Patient #1, nor a few; there were 187 Patient #1s. And they did not come from any given locale. Their only commonality was attendance at a buffet dinner in Monmarte that Saturday evening. From there, they split to a hundred-fifty plus different homes, walks of life, cities, and even countries. And they were not common workers, at least most of them were not. They included celebrities, politicians, the ultra-wealthy, foreigners, jet-setters, famous restaurateurs, and many people who did not appreciate adverse publicity nor French health inspectors poking into their lives. Most of those types of people were, however, willing the talk to investigators when they, their loved ones, and those around them started sickening and dying. The additional downside of all of the initial infectees being grouped as being those considered the French culinary or social elite was that many of them had lives that included extensive public contact through their restaurant customers, their fans, their fellow airline passengers, etc. And, the *Journal Gastronomique* was not the only entity with upscale parties the week after Bastille Day.

With 187 initial infectees, each of which turned out to have 5, 10, 20 or more contacts in the next few days before they got sick enough to no longer be adding contacts, there were thousands of contacts that French authorities, like Michel Dormer, had to trace before those contacts, too, added new contacts. The manner in which the new H7N9 flu presented itself added to the problem. It seemed to be almost immediately infective of a new victim, making them capable of further shedding virus and infection to others the very next day. But the disease progression sometimes took several days to blossom with symptoms. So, there was a period of from two to five or six days when contacts could spread the disease before they were immobilized with symptoms. The buffet invitees were able to fly or drive back home and spread the disease before they were bedridden. Most were eventually bedridden, though; there were very few who showed limited symptoms, unlike the experience with coronavirus.

Michel Dormer had initially tried to keep contact tracing maps on the walls of his office with the cases he was working on marked with pushpins. Within a few days, during which initial buffet attendees had passed H7N9 to the next contact and then they to the next, Michel Dormer had a shelf of binders and dozens upon dozens of computer database entries containing his current contacts' information. His pushpins were obsolete. Each of his co-workers at *Sante Publique* had the same problem.

The real-world impact of this geometric progression of H7N9 cases was profound. The death rate from the Paris *foie gras* H7N9 cases quickly climbed toward the World Health Organization's historical figures for previous animal-caused human cases of H7N9, about 30%. In a few days, the French culinary scene was devastated; the higher a restaurant's Michelin rating, the more likely it was to be closed, by missing owners and employees. *Journal Gastronomique* had to close its editorial offices; it had no staff who were ambulatory. Of 187 cases of people who had gotten H7N9 from the adulterated *foie gras*, 53 people eventually died. Prices plummeted for duck meat and, specifically, duck livers. *Foie gras* was removed from most menus.

A short time after the initial incident, Paris and France were transported back in time to the worst days of the coronavirus. Hospitals were filling up. People were dying. People were scared. And this horrid disease, H7N9, had a significant difference from coronavirus. Whereas coronavirus had left a large number of people asymptomatic and seemed to attack the elderly and infirm the hardest, leaving most youths apparently immune from its worst effects—this H7N9 had a much higher hospitalization rate, overall, and its mortality rate was plague-like. And, it attacked the young and healthy with abandon. Also, whereas with coronavirus or Egyptian Flu, people were shocked at a mortality rate of two or three percent, with H7N9 a mortality rate an order of magnitude greater unbelievably manifested itself.

Although initially slow to pay attention to H7N9, the French public soon got the message, perhaps too late. H7N9 was assigned, by popular usage, the obvious moniker, '*grippe parisienne.*' *Sante Publique France's* employees were instructed not to use that nickname, but it soon became necessary in order to make sure people knew what they were talking about. 'Parisian Flu' was soon adopted worldwide to refer to H7N9. Certain Chinese officials had been ahead of their time, but for the wrong reasons.

Sante Publique's contact tracing efforts for H7N9 were soon limited to new, remote outbreaks. General epidemic mitigation measures, like quarantine, social distancing, and stay-in-place orders, were started. Inspector Michel Dormer could not disagree with that decision. His young, public-spirited co-workers in the case tracing division had been thinned by an abnormally high rate of disease. Michel Dormer knew his job was futile in most cases; it did no good to trace thousands of persons who multiplied their number every few days. Maybe, if they ever got this onslaught under control, they could return to contact tracing to clean up the remaining cases.

———

Hotel Via Granada
Palma, Mallorca
Balearic Islands, Spain
9:12 AM Local Time July 23rd

The paramedic handed Angela Spinetti her new husband's passport, from which the paramedic had just copied the information. Behind them, the other paramedic strapped the recent bridegroom to the ambulance gurney.

"*Signora* Spinetti, I understand you just arrived in Mallorca from Italy. Has your husband been in contact with anyone in the last week who was sick?"

The paramedic spoke slowly in his best Italian, as he knew the young Italian woman did not speak Catalan or Spanish well.

"My mother called me and said my sister is sick, in Milan," Angela said. "She was at our wedding, *di giovedì, ah, jueves.*"

The paramedic frowned at this. "Your sister, she doesn't work at the hospital, does she?"

Now Angela frowned, "How did you know that? She is a respiratory therapist."

"*Madre Sagrada!*" the paramedic cussed. He turned to the other paramedic and let forth with a long stream of excited Mallorcan Catalan that Angela could not understand. The other man shook his head.

Both paramedics reached into their equipment valises and pulled out face masks. They put the masks on, and the first man handed one to Angela.

"Why? What's wrong? Why this?" Angela asked. She put the mask on.

The paramedic looked understandingly at Angela and thought of how to say this, 'On your honeymoon, you have probably not been watching the news. But, there was a story on TV last night, about the bad, new avian flu in Paris, and one man who died in Milan and how one of his hospital workers was sick with it, too."

Angela's eye expressed her shock, but her hand to her mouth movement did not work, given the mask.

"*Signora* Spinetti, if you want to come to the hospital with us, you need to change your clothes, quickly." He pointed at her outfit.

Angela Spinetti *née* Bertolucci looked down and finally noticed she was still in the silky red nightgown she had put on the night before. Her new husband had already fallen asleep before she had exited the bathroom and come to bed in her trousseau nightgown. She had snuggled into bed with him, and they had awoken with him feverish and sick.

———

Veterans Memorial Building
Solvang, California
10:45 AM PDT July 23rd

The big Army laboratory vehicle was parked in the parking lot of the Veterans Memorial Building in Solvang. The 'building' was really a small complex of buildings, a police station crewed by sheriffs deputies, a small pubic library, a branch courtroom, a large auditorium used for community gatherings, and several meeting rooms, used by the VFW, American Legion and various civic groups. Two large canopy tents with red cross emblems on them had been set up on the grass with tables to handle testing and immunizations of the seasonal flu vaccine that the Army had brought with them from Thousand Oaks. The meeting room closest to the laboratory vehicle in the parking lot had been taken over by Public Health to handle the staff working on contact tracing and testing. The building was about a mile from the high school that had become the center of attention for the H7N9 outbreak in the Santa Ynez Valley area.

Specialist 5 Lyudmila Kuchma had been released from her duties in Thousand Oaks by Captain Llewellyn to assist the response team. As an experienced field medic and trained medical technician, she was perfect for helping the doctors and nurses with the testing, including taking blood tests. As a certifiable computer geek, she was at home making sure the information they gathered was entered correctly into the crisis data system.

Kuchma was working at the computer with the FEMA/CDC program running when Chief Warrant Officer Morrison and Lieutenant Colonel Craig came in with Dr. Reed. They gathered around her to see the current status screen.

Before anyone could say anything, CWO3 Morrison asked Kuchma, "What's all this?" He pointed to a stack of four, large, hardcover books, sitting next to the keyboard.

Kuchma patted the stack of books, "Oh, I walked through the lobby next door this morning, and the public library auxiliary women had a cart of almost new, hardcover books that had been donated for fundraising. They were selling them for a buck a copy. I picked up four, can't tell them from new, bestsellers, two are first editions. Good deal.'

Kuchma saw Morrison give Craig a skeptical, sideways glance, to which she said, "What?"

Morrison gave a little shake of his head, "Uh, Lyuda, second-hand books on a cart in the lobby of a public library in a city in the middle of a viral outbreak are not necessarily prime collectibles. You don't know where they came from. And they certainly shouldn't be in the team's work area."

"Jeez, you're right—I should have known better. I'll throw them out." Kuchma said.

Before anyone could say anything, Dr. Craig spoke up, "That's not necessary. I love books, too. Tell Deavers out in the lab that I said it was alright to put them into the autoclave on the dry heat setting for five minutes. That should solve the problem."

Kuchma nodded, "Thank you, sir. I won't make that mistake again."

"So, what's the status?" Craig asked.

Kuchma clicked on the circle representing the Santa Ynez Valley contact tracing and patient status. She pointed with the mouse as she spoke. "Not really my place to make conclusions, but things look pretty good. The sheriff lieutenant in charge of Solvang police came in twenty minutes ago with his report. I told him I would enter it into the FEMA program, so the EOC and everybody else would have it. The morning check of all people in home quarantine was completed. A few were still sick, but nobody needing the hospital. The sheriff made sure the sick people were on the medical visit list. The one group of 'runners' they had, the Pederborg family, was traced to their grandparent's house in Vista, California. Last evening, the San Diego sheriff contacted them, explained that violating quarantine is a crime in California and ordered them to stay put in Vista until cleared by San Diego Health. Mr. Morrison?"

Morrison reported, "Good turnout for the morning testing at 9 o'clock. Twenty-nine people in all. Fourteen were on the contact list and came in as they were asked. Fifteen were locals asking for testing either because they thought they might be contacts or they were sick. Deavers is still running the twenty-nine H7N9 tests. The five people who reported they were sick tested positive on the regular QuickCheck kits for the existing avian flu. Those five were told to see a doctor and were told about the public sick call at the Chumash Tribe medical clinic every afternoon at three. All twenty-nine accepted the free current quadrivalent vaccine. Still a lot of confusion among people about the fact that the annual quadrivalent flu vaccine we are giving them is not for the H7N9 flu outbreak we are worried about. So, as Specialist Kuchma said, things are actually looking good in Solvang/Santa Ynez. On existing patients in the hospital, just the five in Santa Maria and eleven patients in Santa Barbara. Well, plus the two deaths. Five H7N9 cases are at home under full quarantine with twice-daily medical visits. No new H7N9 cases, all obvious contacts traced. Just waiting for seven days without any new H7N9 cases. If we clear that hurdle, our Zone of Contact here may be clean."

"You want me to tell you about the Santa Maria stuff?" Kuchma asked as she switched to the different circular icon on her screen.

"No, Dr. Reed and I are heading to the EOC, and we'll get that info there. But, how is everything else on the network?" Craig asked.

Kuchma answered, with a flash of her screen, "Not so hot. The New York Zone is getting new hits from the financial meeting. Plus, New York reported their first probable connection with the Paris outbreak. Some network node labeled as 'HHS/DC' showed up last night. They seem to be tracing contacts of the Beaumont guy's airplane flight last Tuesday. One-hundred forty-one named contacts with location data, thirty-six with names but no locations yet on the TSA passenger lists. One flight attendant from First-Class on that flight is sick in Atlanta. Her pilot on a later flight to Miami made an emergency landing in Atlanta when she passed out in flight. HHS/DC entered unpopulated Zones of Contact for the flight attendant's two flights after the one to New York with Beaumont. Everyone on the Atlanta flight got self-quarantine orders. Tests on the flight attendant are pending, but she is really sick.

"Los Angeles Zone of Contact is popping up with contacts like zits on a . . ." Kuchma quickly thought better of her comment and just added, "Los Angeles has lots of contacts from the UCLA thing. Many are outside LA, too."

Craig said, "OK, keep up the good work. I may stop back in this evening. Kuchma, let me know how the new Baldacci novel is. OK?"

Kuchma smiled sheepishly, "Yes sir. I will."

———

Policlinico di Milano
Milan, Italy
11:30 AM Local Time July 23rd

The staff members of the third floor ICU were in shock. They were accustomed to death. Death was part of their life. These veterans of the coronavirus contagion in Milan remembered back when many of their co-workers had succumbed to that disease. That was supposed to be in the past. Times were different now, or so they thought. Now, one of their own had become the second person in this hospital to die from a new contagion.

Anna Maria Bertolucci had died while connected to one of the ventilators she had used with her patients so many times. She had been young and healthy, but that seemed to have been the problem. Her youthful, healthy immune system had kicked in to fight the H7N9 flu virus, but it had gone too far, too fast. When Anna Maria's immune system tried to flush the flu germs from her lungs, her lungs filled with fluid, and she, quite literally, drowned on her own immune response.

The Polyclinic's ICU staff did not have much time to reflect on the death of Anna Maria. They had four new patients that all had been tested as having the H7N9 virus. One of those patients was Vincente Bertolucci, Anna Maria's great-uncle. Two of the other new patients had also gone to the Bertolucci/ Spinetti wedding the previous Thursday. The fourth patient was a tourist from France.

———

Chapter 37

Inmate Transfer Entrance
Twin Towers Correctional Facility
Los Angeles, California
7:09 AM PDT July 24th

Matt Relford was with Dr. John Morganeau, the medical doctor in charge of the LA Jail medical program. They were on the platform usually used to load buses and vans to transfer prisoners to other jail facilities, prison, or court. This morning, two ambulances were backed up to the stairs with doors open, waiting for patients to transport. A black coroner's van was parked between the two ambulances. Chief Leona Madigan's Sheriff Department sedan passed through the guarded gate to the back lot at Twin Towers and pulled in to park next to one of the ambulances.

Madigan got out and walked up to the two waiting men, "Two ambulances, I thought you said . . ."

Relford cut in, "When the prisoner in 4-3 South reported his roommate was dead at daybreak, the shift sergeant saw the roommate was very sick too. They started a room by room call-out to check on the other prisoners on that floor. They found another sick prisoner after I called you. They are waiting to get the coroner's crew and that body out before they bring the two sick ones down. The coroner has to take photographs of the body and cell for the autopsy report."

Morganeau added, "I checked both of the sick ones myself, clearly candidates for the hospital. Beyond our in-house capability. They are going to USC Med."

"I thought the USC Jail ward was full," Madigan said.

Relford answered this, "It is full. I checked these two out. They are recent arrestees, booked Friday. Neither is hostile nor dangerous. One is gang-related, but his current charge is non-violent. They meet the standard in the lawsuit settlement for immediate release of prisoners with medical needs. I had the compassionate release paperwork done, and these two will be going to USC as regular patients, not prisoners."

"And the dead guy, what's his story? Contacts with the other two?" Madigan asked.

Relford answered, "Felony prisoner. Gang member. A frequent guest here. He has been here for six weeks this time. He had a court hearing Friday. One of the sick guys is his gang member roommate, so he definitely had contact.

He may have had contact with the other sick one either in transport over to court or in the holding cell, here or at court. They were on the same floor, but the dead guy was on lockdown for gang safety reasons. But, the three could have a common, third party contact, too."

The doctor added, "I checked the dead guy's medical record. He is a Mexican national. Significant drug use history, multiple medical problems, a couple serious. Likely candidate for the flu to hit hard."

"So, are all three of these avian flu, you know New Flu?" the chief asked.

"No, Chief. We did the QuickCheck kit for avian flu on all three. Positive for flu, but definitely not the avian flu, H5N1." The doctor sounded positive.

"So, what's this? The same stuff they are talking about at UCLA and up in Santa Barbara? Or over in France?"

"Could be. We have done blood and nasal tests on all three. The samples will be at the County Health lab in Downey when they open this morning. Under the ACLU lawsuit settlement, the County lab is supposed to do the jail's flu tests first in line, even though they are balking at that given this new crisis. So, we should know what this is soon."

Madigan turned to Matt Relford, "What do you plan for facility status?"

Matt shrugged, "Not much choice. Full lockdown for Twin Towers while extraction teams in full PPE check every prisoner, quick health check, and temperature. Segregate any positives. I called in the off-duty deputies, but it's prime vacation season with people out of town. 4-3 South will be scrubbed and sprayed as soon as we can move those prisoners somewhere else. And they cannot go in with other prisoners, so I have to clear another floor before I move them. Then, wherever I stash the 4-3 South people I have to disinfect afterward, too. A big daisy chain of prisoners moving around, hopefully, nobody else sick pops up. Captain Marquez is doing one of the contact tracing plans Dr. Cristobal taught her how to do. She has already pulled the prisoner lists for everywhere these three have been for their time here, and she is starting to compare everything. Oh, and you need to invoke a no transfer order between all jail facilities until we figure this out. Let's try to keep this out of the Main and branch jails."

Madigan nodded, "Yes. Let me know what you find. I need to go call the Sheriff. Matt, double-check we are doing everything Cristobal and the settlement guidelines say we should be. This smells like big trouble."

"Of course, Chief."

———

Hôpital Tenon
Salle d'Urgence
4 Rue de la Chine
Paris, France
10:35 AM Local Time July 24th

Ambulances could no longer drop off patients at the *Hôpital Tenon* Emergency Room drive-through lane. There were several inflatable tents now standing in the drive-way outside the ER. These tents were the ER now, where triage of the dozens of incoming patients took place. The actual ER had been converted to an Intensive Care Unit, one of many created around the hospital. The street behind the large hospital, Rue Pelleport, had been closed to through traffic and marked as one-way traffic only. It now had a lane for ambulances and one for private vehicles and taxis dropping off patients. Both lanes were crowded. Family members dropping off a patient could not go inside with their loved one, after filling out a next-of-kin form, they were given a slip of paper with a phone number to call and find out the patient's status, "in a few hours."

Farther south on Rue Pelleport, two large white trucks were parked behind the hospital. Power cables from the hospital ran out to the trucks. The cables supplied power to the refrigeration units in the trucks. From time to time, workers in full protective gear carried white plastic, fold-out coffins from the back door of the hospital to store in the trucks. At regular intervals, one of the trucks was driven off somewhere and replaced by another.

———

Thousand Oaks Defense Pharmaceutical Plant (TODPP)
Thousand Oaks, California
11:30 AM PDT July 24th

Captain Karen Llewellyn was staring intently at several rows of RNA sequence markers on a computer in the HeptImun QA lab when Rob Cameron found her. Sonya Hayburn and two of her technicians worked nearby.

"You're a hard person to find. Never would have thought of looking back here for you. Ghent told me your hiding place," Cameron said.

"Sorry, I apologize. Sonya called me to see this. I know a lot is going on. It's just that I worked on this yesterday, and Sonya found something she thought was important. What's up?"

"You worked on Sunday in the lab?"

"Yeah, you can take the military officer out of the lab, but you cannot take the lab geek out of the military officer."

"I suppose so. Things are happening fast, personnel-wise. That was a stroke of genius for Harding's people to file an annex to the OpRep on the H7N9 virus to highlight the request for full military personnel fulfillment. That pretty much meant that everybody important in the government saw a two-star general telling Army Human Resources that the unit deployed to fight the virus in California did not have all of the people the Army says it needs. With the *60 Minutes* report on the Parisian Flu fiasco on Sunday night, it was pretty certain to get a reaction."

"And?"

"Ghent and I just fielded that first two calls from people getting their orders changed by HRC. A military police sergeant in Georgia thought he was going to Germany, already sent his household gear there, got an emergency orders change to report here ASAP. And a doctor at Fort Drum, in New York, got immediate orders to report here. He thought he had another year in upstate New York."

"Another doctor and an MP to be on our staff?" Karen asked.

"Yes ma'am, I went to look at this MTO&E that Ross Tanner was talking about, and it has a slot to represent just about all of the functions on the USAMRIID response team. It's really set up to make sure you can support the team when it goes to the field. I talked to Ross, and he says HRC thinks they can have an answer to every empty billet on the modified list this week."

"Now, you and I need to make sure we put them to good use."

"That shouldn't be a problem. What was the status report on the network this morning?"

"Well, Santa Barbara is looking good, but Los Angeles is really falling apart. And there are bad outbreaks in several cities. The FEMA network says it seems to be from both LA, the Beaumont guy on the plane, and in the banking meeting, and now they are getting people from Europe. Several hotspots all over the country. I talked to Marty last night, and he kind of thinks his team may be pulled from Santa Barbara and moved to LA. Marty says two more reserve response teams have been called up to go to New York and Phoenix."

"Phoenix? What's with Phoenix?"

Karen nodded, "That was on the FEMA network. Apparently, a UCLA alumni group in Phoenix had sponsored several of the UCLA freshmen from the Phoenix metro area who were supposed to come to that orientation and hired them a rental van, a little RV, to drive to LA together. Eight of them drove between Phoenix and LA in the RV last week, and all of them got the flu from UCLA. The alumni group had a congratulatory dinner for them the evening they got home. So they have a little hotspot of twenty-plus H7N9 patients in Phoenix plus their family and community contacts. They had a couple of deaths very quickly, both were students. That hotspot is just getting started, but the congresswoman in Arizona heard about the Army Response Team and asked to have one sent to Phoenix."

Cameron shook his head, "The saga continues." He motioned to the work Karen had been looking at when he came in, " So, what is it you're all working on back here."

Karen turned her monitor so Rob could see it, "I told you that I had worked on the H7 family of viruses as my graduate work. I chose that influenza virus family because of their unique genetic factors, weird mutations. Plus, a morbid history of this disease in humans. After the first news on H7N9 in China and Paris last March, I dusted off my old notes with a thought of how it might be needed, but my pending move out here intervened. Now, I happen to be in command of a pharmaceutical plant that has the theoretical capability of working on a vaccine for H7N9. And, as of Friday, I have multiple samples of the actual virus back in our Biosafety area. Sonya and I are doing some initial work looking to see a route to making virus-like particles for H7N9. Of course, our abilities here are limited, compared to the big corporate labs or back at CDC, where they have a team of scientists, but plans for this place called on us to have the capability. I thought I would give it a look-see."

Cameron smiled and said, "Oh Yeah, that reminds me. One of the personnel billets listed on our MTO&E that Ross Tanner found is for an Army officer MOS 71E, Clinical Laboratory Scientist. Ross says HRC at Fort Knox is cutting orders sending an assistant professor in molecular biology at West Point out here. You and Sonya will have an Army officer joining you in the scientist ranks soon."

Karen raised her eyebrows, "That may be good and bad news. Good, that I would love to have him, or her, but bad that he or she is probably pissed at losing a professorship and getting sent out to the boonies to join our little band."

"I don't know ma'am; it seems like Uncle Sam bought you guys a nice bundle of scientists' toys to play with. And you have a mission that seems pretty damned important right now."

———

9ᵗʰ Floor Hallway
Grady Memorial Hospital
Atlanta, Georgia
7:30 PM EDT July 24ᵗʰ

"This is what it feels like to die," Emilie Porter thought. *"I must be dying."*

She had little time to think before another painful spasm of coughing hit. She had coughed so much, so often that her ribs flashed with pain in every hacking shake. She could not cry out, as she had no air to make any sound. It was not only her ribs—everything hurt. She could feel her heartbeat in the pulses of pain from the pressure behind her eyes and in her head. But, her heartbeat meant she was still alive.

Emilie's life had devolved down to a progression from one misery after another. She knew she was in bed, a hospital bed. But she seemed to be in a hallway, not a room. Many people in those blue bodysuits and masks walked past her, shoes sounding on the floor, and an occasional blue person stopped to check on her. The bright light fixture above her head hurt her eyes. She could not turn her head away from the light. Every fiber of her body ached. She could never catch her breath. If she breathed in too much, there was pain in her chest, and the coughing hit again.

Time was meaningless. She had nothing to measure how long she had been like this. Sometime before, she had asked one of the blue-suited people where she was. "In the hospital," was the worthless answer from a female voice. "Where is the hospital?" "Atlanta." That had made no sense. *How did Emilie get to Atlanta?* She remembered being at work, on a flight from New York to Miami, not Atlanta. Emilie knew no one in Atlanta.

More coughing, worse coughing. It squeezed the last air out of her lungs. With no air, she could not cough; she could only shake with spasms in empty lungs. The spasms made her head explode. *God, it hurt.* Emilie tried to breathe, struggled to draw in air. The painful light from above her faded for a moment, everything faded out, and then a siren went off. It was loud enough to be a siren but higher, a piercing whine, a painful whine, and it was from nearby. The siren was in her bed.

Another blue-suited person did something with Emilie's finger. The siren went silent. Emilie coughed again.

Emilie felt the bed moving. It bumped into something—more coughing. Now, the bright, overhead light was gone. That was better, but Emilie still could not breathe.

Someone lifted Emilie's head up and turned her, so her chin was pointing up, with something behind her neck. Her jaw was pulled open. She coughed again. She had to spit a choking glob out of her mouth. She did not care where she spit.

Then, a warm/hot cloud of feeling moved from her arm to her shoulder and chest. The aches seemed to stop as the warm cloud moved. Just before the warm cloud brought a release of pain in her head, Emilie felt something pushed into her mouth and down her throat. Then, nothing.

—

Chapter 38

Little Mermaid Statue
Mission Drive
Solvang, California
10:30 AM PDT July 25ᵗʰ

Shaysee O'Neil stood waiting for the signal from the network for her to start her report. She stood in front of the statue and fountain of the Little Mermaid on the corner of the main intersection in Solvang, California. The Little Mermaid was a replica of the original statue in Copenhagen, symbolic of this small city's Danish roots. Her cameraman and two producers were with her. Shaysee watched the monitor held by one of the producers and listened for her cue in an earphone.

The producer was also listening, and he gave Shaysee his estimate of when to start with a countdown on his fingers, three, two, one . . . fist.

Shaysee took her finger from her earphone, pulled down her face mask, and started, "Thank you, Josh. Today, I'm reporting from the picturesque little town of Solvang in the heart of California's lovely Santa Ynez Valley. But, this beautiful area is also ground zero for the new outbreak of the H7N9 avian flu virus that's ravaging Los Angeles and now, New York and other cities across the country, not to mention around the world. I had the opportunity yesterday afternoon to speak with Professor Ernst Holveg, a professor emeritus of biology at Stanford University and author of a book on the history of pandemic disease. Doctor Holveg explained to me the reasons why this current avian flu virus, now also called the Parisian Flu, is different from other flu strains and why we need to pay special attention to this growing epidemic."

Shaysee waited a few seconds while the network rolled the recorded interview with Holveg. He gave details on the history of H7N9, including several poultry-caused outbreaks in China since 2003 that had killed hundreds of people with a mortality rate of thirty percent of those infected. He ended by comparing the history of the coronavirus pandemic with what could be expected from the new virus.

Shaysee O'Neil waited, watching the monitor for the recorded interview to end and then continued, "Here in the Santa Ynez Valley, the Parisian Flu outbreak started with a single family who owned a pair of geese, who, like ducks and chickens, can carry the H7N9 influenza virus, but unlike humans, do not die from the flu strain. All four members of the Beaumont family were sickened by the flu. Sadly, the sixteen-year-old boy succumbed last week. Before the boy's death and before coming down with symptoms of the disease, the father traveled to New York, and the daughter traveled to the University of California campus in Los Angeles. Thus, this deadly avian flu strain that started out here is now spreading in the two largest cities in America, as it has in France.

"Here, in the Santa Ynez Valley, a dramatic official response to the flu outbreak seems to have limited the spread. Local health officials called in the assistance of an elite team of first responders from the U.S. Army who brought this," Shaysee waited until a recorded video appeared, "state-of-the-art mobile laboratory which was able to provide immediate, on-scene testing of possible victims." A video of people waiting in line for vaccine shots from a soldier in a camouflage uniform ran. "This quick response and testing capability allowed them to limit the spread locally to twenty people, fifteen of whom have required hospitalization and sadly, as of this morning, five of whom have died. The original teenage boy, two of his schoolmates, one boy and one girl, a farmworker and a local veterinarian have all succumbed. We can see that those five deaths give this outbreak in coastal California nearly, but not quite, the same thirty percent mortality rate Dr. Holveg mentioned for the earlier animal-spread outbreaks in China. Local officials and the U.S. Army's first responders declined to be interviewed for this report. This tight-knit community is reeling from all that has happened in these two short weeks.

"With a mortality rate second only to that of the deadly Ebola virus, this H7N9 avian flu, Parisian Flu, is truly frightening. Our reporter, John Mathias, will tell us how the officials in Los Angeles are handling the dreadful prospect of such a horrible pestilence in our nation's second-largest city."

Shaysee waited for the red light on the camera to turn off and then handed the microphone to the cameraman. She and her producer would have to work on how to get someone relevant to be interviewed for her next report. She needed a soldier or a doctor to interview with her.

———

Rue de Pyrenees
Paris, France
3:30 PM Local Time July 25th

Health Inspector Michel Dormer received a text message from Lieutenant C. V. Blanchette, who identified himself as a homicide detective with *La Police Judiciaire*. Blanchette asked Dormer to meet him at an address that Dormer recognized from the week before. There was no further explanation in the text message.

Arriving at the elegant apartment building, Dormer flashed his health department inspector's badge, and the policewomen at the crime scene tape let him in. He was directed to Blanchette in the dining room. Except for the *Médecin Légiste* gurney carrying a bagged body, the room was the same as it had been the week before when Dormer had come here to ask the last few questions of the recent widow, Marguerite Tauty.

Dormer introduced himself to Blanchette, a studious looking man with thick bifocal glasses and curly gray hair. They showed each other their badges. Both of them were wearing face masks. They did not shake hands, both because of the pending epidemic, and the fact that Blanchette was wearing rubber gloves.

Blanchette unzipped the body bag on the gurney, and Dormer identified the body as Madame Tauty. Dormer explained when and in what context he had last seen the dead woman.

Detective Blanchette explained that the Tauty's Nigerian cleaning lady had found Marguerite Tauty sitting in an overstuffed chair in the sitting room off the dining room. She had apparently been dead for a day when she was found. She was dressed in an evening gown. An open bottle of Romanée-Conti wine with a partially consumed glass was sitting nearby. The curtains were drawn open, showing a magnificent view of the Paris skyline. The formal dining table had been set for two, and an obviously magnificent dinner, now cold, had been laid out. Only one plate had been eaten from, and Madame Tauty's lipstick was on that place setting's water glass. She had provided an entrée serving for an absent guest also. Margeurite had given herself and an unseen guest a superb final meal. The wine glass by the other place setting had a full serving of the grossly expensive Romanée-Conti in it, too.

Two empty prescription bottles for powerful opioid pain medication had been found by Blanchette's forensic crew in the bathroom. One bottle had just been refilled in Maximilien Tauty's name, three days before, which was after his death. Blanchette expected the autopsy to show the pills as Marguerite's cause of death. It would have been a sleepy, mellow death, in a comfy chair, with a beautiful view, after an excellent meal. Marguerite Tauty had everything well planned.

The reason Inspector Dormer had been called to the suicide scene was on the far end of the big dining table from the last supper dishes. Marguerite Tauty had placed an ornate silver tray in plain view on the end of the table. On the tray were three things, a single white rose, a sheet of Marguerite's personalized stationery inscribed in nearly calligraphic handwriting, and Inspector Michel Dormer's business card. He had given her the card at their last meeting, along with his words that if she thought of anything else to call him.

Marguerite had decided Michel Dormer could tell everyone exactly why Marguerite Jocelyne Tauty *née* Gouveia had decided to end her life. It also seemed that her tying Inspector Dormer to her death was a bit of retribution, or perhaps supplication. That made sense, too. He had explained her culinary misdeed to her. Dormer's official report on the cause of what people now called the Parisian Flu had identified Marguerite Tauty and her *foie gras* to her fellow *Parisiens*. The story had run in the newspapers and on television the morning before her death. So, Inspector Michel Dormer being given special notice by Marguerite Tauty of her death seemed apropos.

The ornate inscription on Marguerite's suicide note was simply,

Pardonne-moi s'il te plait,

La femme qui aimait Maximilien

[Forgive me please, The woman who loved Maximilien]

—

Chapter 39

"Already?" Karen asked her husband, Marty, "I thought you would be up there for weeks."

"We all did," Marty said from the Skype screen on Karen's computer. "With the initial reports and the possible numbers involved, it looked like it would be a long haul. But, it seems we caught it in time, at least for the local area here. The local health department gathered up the initial infectees. You helped get the critical testing right away. The real break was up in Santa Maria with the Fair.

"It turned out only the three people who actually had physical contact with the infected pig caught the virus. Two of the fair's judges and the veterinarian who inspected and cleared the pig to be registered for the competition caught the virus, and just the vet died. The Animal Control people and State Ag department came down hard on other exhibited animals. Lots of them were put down. Which is sad, but it may have kept the viral spread from happening. The Ag people have many of the culled fair animals waiting to be tested. That may tell us if there was any virus amongst the animals."

"So, you're not waiting for the waiting period to run before clearing out?" Karen asked.

"No, Dr. Reed and her team have a handle on things. They have all the potential contacts traced, and if any of them come down with symptoms within seven days, they know what to do."

"And, you think USAMRIID will be sending you to LA?"

"That's the tentative from Hal. We will break free here tonight and tomorrow morning and assemble back in T.O. with you to resupply and find out where we are needed in the big city."

"Well, we're ready for you. General Harding got a good response from his demand for personnel. I have at least ten new people already and a couple more inbound. Two enlisted military police sergeants, a medical doctor, a supply officer, a mechanic, another driver, and two medics are waiting to hook up with you. Oh, and a lab technician, too. I've got a Ph.D. microbiologist who showed up from West Point on Wednesday, who has pretty much taken over my notes on H7N9 and thinks he can finish his own blueprint of the virus' RNA to start work on a virus-like particle mesh that might work for a vaccine. It's like Christmastime in the human resources department."

"That's good. Things look bad in LA. They are back to temporary morgues in hospital basements there."

"Where do you think you might be sent in LA?"

"No real idea. Los Angeles already has several very sophisticated university and government labs that can track and test for H7N9 and treat the disease as much as is possible for now; they don't need us for that. The Los Angeles County Health people and the HHS team that's working on the case tracing I see on the network seem to know what they are doing. They don't need any input from my little band of men and women; they need time and a few good breaks. Our team specializes in going in and helping with medical, testing, and tracing work and training of locals in a finite, critical location like we did here in Santa Barbara. I'm not sure where in Los Angeles that might be."

"Well, I guess we'll see you tomorrow, then?"

"Looks like it."

"Oh, and Marty?"

"Yeah?"

"Since I've got you two new medics and a driver, I want Specialists Kuchma and Ali back."

"We'll see, Captain Llewellyn-Craig, we'll see."

Karen realized the use of her hyphenated name was an intentional zinger from her husband, but she ignored it.

———

Topanga-Victory Urgent Care Center
Los Angeles, California
10:12 AM PDT July 28th

Every morning they received a shipment in the delivery van from the corporate offices of the urgent care center chain in Pasadena. It brought supplies and paperwork from the home office. This morning it had brought something different, two large signs, pre-printed in bold, red and black letters, for them to put in the front windows of the storefront clinic. The signs read:

NO WALK-IN PATIENTS
Due to the ongoing health emergency,
We must ask all patients to call ahead to
(818) 555-4710
for an appointment before entering this clinic.
If this is an emergency, please contact
the nearest Hospital Emergency Room, or call 9-1-1.

It was the same sign that they had eventually had to put up with the New Flu back in the springtime and back in the days of coronavirus, but this change, with the H7N9 flu, had come much sooner. It seemed that everyone was getting used to a new reality and saw the merit in responding quickly.

Dr. Teresa Rohrbach agreed with the home office on the signs. There was little she could do for the slew of patients that had started to come into the clinic. Most of them had the same set of symptoms. Symptoms she could do little about. She did not even have the promised vaccines for the old avian flu, and she certainly had nothing but general advice to give the patients with the new H7N9 flu. She did not even have a way to get a test for them, other than waiting for several days.

Teresa had been relatively busy that morning with call-in 'telemedicine' calls. Quite often, the final advice she gave was something like, "I think you need to check with the ER. The symptoms he has indicate your son needs to be hospitalized." The alternate advice was, "Stay home, keep everyone indoors, stay hydrated with lots of clear liquids, no alcohol, and take acetaminophen, that's Tylenol, for body aches and pain. Call back or call 9-1-1 if your symptoms get worse or you have trouble breathing."

In better times, Teresa would have administered Tamiflu or one of the similar antiviral drugs, but the flood of H7N9 cases had depleted the supply of antivirals. She had nothing to use to treat this flu.

Teresa and Cyndi now sat together behind the counter drinking sodas. The phone had been quiet for a while. The cellphone in Teresa's labcoat pocket buzzed. She looked at it and clicked an icon.

After reading her cellphone screen, Dr. Rohrbach said, "I don't fucking believe it!"

"What?" Cyndi asked.

"My vacation is off."

"Why? What happened?"

"It seems New Zealand has closed themselves off to all foreign travel. Our travel company just sent us refunds for the airline tickets and the reservations at the ski resorts. I've been dreaming of my ski vacation Down Under for months."

"Didn't New Zealand do that back with coronavirus, too."

"Yeah, I think so. I saw a TV show that said New Zealanders had a totally different outcome from coronavirus because of it. I just never thought . . . That sucks, but I guess I can't blame 'em."

The clinic phone line rang. Cyndi answered. She listened to the phone, asked a couple of questions, and turned to the computer to log the telemedicine call. She then turned to Dr. Rohrbach. With a rolling motion of her hand, Cyndi indicated to Teresa that it was another call like the others, someone with symptoms they had no answer for. Dr. Rohrbach took the call. Since it was an existing patient, Cyndi and Dr. Rohrbach could charge the telemedicine call as an office visit.

———

Thousand Oaks Defense Pharmaceutical Plant (TODPP)
Thousand Oaks, California
8:29 AM PDT July 29th

"No! Not again. Who got the idea that public relations and television appearances were part of my job description, anyway?" Karen Llewellyn stated as firmly as she could.

The man on the phone answered, "Well, the easy answer to your question is that my boss, who happens to be your boss, too, says it's in your job description. General Harding really liked what you did last time in April, and he says the country needs to know where they stand, to get a feeling that there is some hope as they face more of these disease horror stories. He thinks you're perfect as the face of the government's effort to fight this thing. When the television network called Harding's boss, the head of the Army Medical Department, she apparently thought so, too. Between the two of them, that's five stars that say this is your job."

"So, what can I possibly say that's hopeful? This virus is spreading fast, everywhere. It's killing one in four people who get it, the last count from LA and New York."

"I have some ideas on that, That's my job," the public affairs officer from Fort Detrick said. "I've already sent you several possible script ideas to your AKO email address. I want you in the same white uniform with all your ribbons you were in before. You standing in the lab last time was great. It looked like you knew what needed to be done. Do that again, but I'd like to see you add a shot in front of your factory machines that are churning out a vaccine for the American people."

Karen cut in, "But, that vaccine is for last spring's virus, not this one. People are already confused about that."

"Exactly, tell them that you and your people are already making a vaccine that will stop that last flu, just six months after the last virus hit us and before it hits again this fall. With any luck, you will be working to do the same thing for this new Parisian Flu virus, too. All they need to do is buckle down, protect themselves, follow instructions, and America will win this coming battle, too."

"I don't want to give them false hope."

"Are you sure you can't do it again, get a vaccine for this Parisian stuff, as we did for the Egyptian Flu."

"No, but . . . We could lose thousands, probably millions in six months. We were really lucky last time, that summer intervened and slowed the Egyptian Flu."

"Then, if there is a chance you could do it again, it's not false hope. It's just plain old hope, hope that someone who knows what she is doing is fighting for them."

"God . . . ," Karen sighed.

"If you want to invoke Him, that might work too. Couldn't hurt."

Karen waited a moment before asking, "When will they be here?"

"The TV network rep in New York said the news team is in LA already. When he heard the general wanted you to do this, he said he would call them. They probably are already trying to reach you. I'd say they'll be there this afternoon."

"Well, I'd better go then. That white uniform you like is at home, in the ironing." Karen hung up.

—

Front Entrance
Main Jail
Los Angeles, California
10:10 AM PDT July 29th

Having got the call that Sheriff Guy Martinez was on his way, Chief Leona Madigan and Commander Matt Relford were waiting at the front doors to the Main Jail when an unmarked black Ford Expedition outfitted with emergency lights drove up. It was driven by a uniformed deputy. The sheriff got out of the side door. The sheriff held the door open for someone, and a well-dressed black woman got out. The two walked toward Madigan and Relford.

When they reached them, the sheriff motioned to his officers, "Supervisor Gillems, I don't know if you know Chief Leona Madigan, our Jail Chief, and Commander Matt Relford, who runs Twin Towers and is our lead officer for dealing with the flu problem at the jail. Chief, Commander, you probably recognize Supervisor Letisha Gillems, the County Supervisor for District 3.

"Supervisor Gillems had a meeting with me this morning, and I mentioned your idea for relieving pressure on the jail and saving lives. She asked if she could come along and see for herself."

Gillems stepped forward to shake hands but pulled back her hand when she remembered the new societal vogue during the flu outbreak of no contact.

With the politician now in front of him, Matt could see the sheriff now give a quick facial expression of apology to Leona for having brought a politician on a 'sheriff's business' meeting.

Leona spoke, "We're happy to show you our idea . . . our project, or rather Commander Relford's project. I think his plan will kill several birds with one stone. I'll let him lead us out and explain while he goes." Matt saw Leona give him a firm look—a warning from the chief.

"This way, please," Matt said as he turned toward the jail access door across the lobby. "To keep from having to walk all the way around the Main Jail building, we need to cut through the first floor, and that requires we go inside the lockdown area, not an inmate residence area, just the admin part of the main jail that's controlled access in case we need to bring an inmate up here, for administration, legal or other reasons."

A deputy at the door buzzed them in and took the badge numbers of the three officers and gave a visitor's pass to Gillems. He handed each of them a mask, explaining it was required inside the jail. As they put their masks on and walked away, Relford heard the deputy quietly announce into an intercom, "Elvira, Dillon, and Nottingham entered M-1." Matt smiled to himself.

Relford walked them through a maze of office hallways. At one point, a work party of inmates in green jumpsuits cleaning a hallway and guarded by a deputy quickly stepped back to allow the VIPs down the hall. All had masks on.

Matt realized from Leona's warning look that the presence of the politician would require him to present a lot more information than would have been necessary for just the sheriff. He quickly thought of all he needed to explain. At the end of a long hallway, they passed through another guard checkpoint and emerged outdoors into a large parking lot.

Matt started his presentation as they walked across the parking lot, "Although we have a maximum population in all jails of just under 20,000, we already started to reduce that last spring when we were dealing with the first wave of avian flu and had to drop our inmate population. The numbers started to creep up over the summer before we were hit with this latest attack of the flu. Unlike back when we had to deal with coronavirus, when we were able to undertake a release of inmates over several months, this time, the jail was hit immediately and hard. We have figured out that a worker at the UCLA dorm at the center of our outbreak in LA was arrested by LAPD for DWI, and in just a few hours in our reception center, he managed to infect several inmates, who went to various places in the general inmate population. In the crowded jail, it spread like wildfire, even with the environmental changes for flu prevention we had in place. Within that first week, we had several dozen sick in many areas, and much of our Main Jail and Twin Towers were within the Zone of Contact, as the experts call it, of the flu. One inmate died on that first

Monday morning after news of the flu outbreak in LA hit. It was one of the first Parisian Flu deaths in LA. We had a horrible mess, and we could not start releasing prisoners to decrease the danger, because our mass of possibly sick prisoners had, itself, become a danger to the outside world."

They turned the corner of a raised parking and utility building, and, to the south and west, they could see the entire downtown LA skyline, Union Station, and the railroad switchyard.

Matt continued, walking them toward the tracks, "We tried to figure out a way to move healthy prisoners between the two buildings of Twin Towers, the Main Jail and outlying facilities, but we did not have enough room anyplace to sort out the healthy and the sick. We had new sick every couple of hours. Then, our deputies started getting sick. We needed a place where we could move hundreds or maybe even thousands of prisoners who were not sick, or preferably had been tested as not infected, so we could get them out of the crowded jail areas where the flu was rampant. If we had a prisoner who was not dangerous and who passed a ten-day quarantine, we could actually let him go, as required by common sense and the ACLU court order, and solve our problem and the prisoner's predicament. So, I came up with this."

Matt stopped at the west wall of the main jail parking structure and pointed out across the railroad tracks. There, on the far side of the railroad tracks, was a huge vacant lot. It was covered by dozens of cement floors and foundations of demolished buildings. Almost the entire area was, thus, paved by jumbled cement relics and trash. The huge lot seemed to be a set from a dystopian sci-fi movie. They could see several construction trucks and machines in operation. Fencing was going up on the outside of the lot, tall fencing topped by barbed wire. Some areas were being scraped clean of refuse by road graders and city street sweepers, and some asphalt was being laid down. Several big green National Guard trucks were parked near where rows of large white tents were being set up, dozens of white tents.

Matt explained, "That's about five acres. It was supposedly meant for urban renewal, the site of several old factories and warehouses, but there is some issue about pollution underground that would have to be fixed to excavate and build. But, we just need it as is, flat and wide-open. It's bounded by city streets on four sides and by the railroad on the jail side. Utilities, both water, and electricity, are available in the old connections of the former buildings to the streets. There was a big homeless encampment over to the right there, off of East College Street, but Public Health already closed that down as a health hazard in this epidemic. The lot was listed for sale, had been for years, and the owners were happy to get a cash rental tenant like the County for a ground lease for six months. In about 72 hours, we should have a healthy, secure living area, out in the open, summer air, that can take as many of our healthy prisoners as we can find. We should not have many security problems with the prisoners as they will understand that if they stay here for ten days, they will be healthy, and we will release them. We call it the College Street Jail Annex."

Gillems spoke first, "Don't you need to get County Board of Supervisors approval for a project of this size?"

Sheriff Martinez gave a slight cringing expression, but Matt had an answer, "No ma'am. The County Real Property office has the authority to sign any real estate rental contract under twelve months without Board approval. The tents are free from FEMA. They have thousands out in Riverside, in storage for emergency housing for the Big One earthquake in California, when it comes. And, County Counsel Harrison says the sheriff has constitutional and statutory authority to manage any temporary facilities needed for law enforcement in an emergency. Your Board and the Governor declared that emergency last week. And, no environmental study is needed for an emergency response that has life and death impacts. The sheriff also has the authority to ask the National Guard for assistance. Oh, and we thought that if we get the jail problem solved, this will make a great site for a pop-up emergency hospital, a pre-built tent city, and ready to occupy. We will have an information item on your Board agenda about the project the first Tuesday in August."

Gillems watched the activity beyond the tracks for a minute, nodding her head slowly, and then said, "Anything else you need for your project, Commander Relford?"

"Well, yes, ma'am, if I could find some way to test the prisoners for this H7N9 flu, I could release them before the full ten days and speed everything up. Everybody is desperate to do the flu testing on the sick people that are flooding the hospitals. So, nobody will help Sheriff Martinez to test several thousand hopefully healthy prisoners, no matter how important the security and lifesaving issue is that we try to explain to them, even with the ACLU court order that says the jail tests come first. Getting prisoners out of a death trap takes second fiddle to testing for Parisian Flu in hospitals."

Matt Relford continued, "I remember back when the ACLU sued the county and the sheriff in April, they had a cute line they told the judge and put in all their press releases railing against the County's inability to protect prisoners from the flu. Their mantra was, 'Getting sent to the County Jail should not be a death sentence.' We have already had 143 prisoner deaths in not even ten days. Bottom line, if I could get some influenza testing here, I could save the lives of hundreds or thousands of men locked in a jail where we currently have a 22% mortality rate if they catch this new Parisian Flu."

Supervisor Gillems turned to the sheriff and his officers, "Let me see what I can do about that."

———

Chapter 40

Camino De La Mimosa
Camarillo, California
5:45 PM PDT July 29th

Karen pulled the Audi into her garage and clicked the garage door remote to close the door. Marty went to get the groceries they had stopped to get from the hatchback, and he got his suitcase to bring inside. He had returned from Santa Barbara just that afternoon. He drove home with Karen as soon as his team was ensconced at the hotel in Thousand Oaks for the night.

"Let's hurry. I don't want to miss this," Marty said.

"We're still fine. Shaysee said she would be in Los Angeles at the scene of the UCLA dormitory for her intro to my story on the 6 o'clock program, that's 9 PM in New York."

"I wish I had been there to see this live. I saw Shaysee when she and the crew were leaving, and we just arrived."

"She told me how she had met up with you in Solvang, and you refused to give her an interview."

"Standing rules for the Response Teams, nobody talks to the media, you refer everything news-wise to the locals." Marty set the groceries on Karen's kitchen counter.

"No such protection for me." Karen had the TV remote, turning on the screen and cable box, and pushing the record button. She sat down on the couch, and Marty sat next to her.

Karen and Marty sat through the interminable top of the hour commercials. Soon, the cable network anchor appeared and gave the network's standard introduction about 'breaking news at this hour.' The anchor introduced stories and reports from reporters in Paris, New York, and at the White House. Ten minutes passed. More commercials.

Finally, the anchor said, "And from Los Angeles, we have Correspondent Shaysee O'Neil reporting from the focal point of the Southern California outbreak of this Parisian Flu, the campus of the University of California, Los Angeles. Shaysee?"

Shaysee O'Neil appeared, wearing the same business suit she had on in Thousand Oaks that afternoon. "Yes, behind me you can see the dormitory at UCLA where the two girls from Santa Barbara, who had already been infected by the Parisian flu, attended an orientation for incoming students just twelve days ago. At that orientation, the two girls had contact with hundreds of other students, who, after two days, left UCLA to go to their hometowns, across California, and even across the United States. We know now that those hundred-plus students spread this H7N9 Parisian Flu to hundreds of other people.

"Within days, the flu outbreak had spread in exponential numbers to thousands. We have seen tonight the reports of the massive effort to trace and control the spread of this monstrous flu across the country. But, besides those efforts, which at times seem hopeless in their complexity of tracing thousands of people, we have a word of hope about some people who are still striving to fight this dreadful disease in the trenches, the medical trenches as it were, and find a cure for it. Today, I had the opportunity to talk with Public Health Service Captain Karen Llewellyn-Craig, the commanding officer of the federal government's state-of-the-art vaccine plant here in Southern California, who is among those leading the nation's efforts to find a vaccine to treat and prevent this Parisian Flu."

Marty did a mental double-take when he heard Shaysee introduce Karen. Marty had been with Karen since his return and had seen her today in the white summer uniform, but he had never noticed something on her uniform that he now saw when she appeared on the television screen with Shaysee. The small black name-tag on Karen's uniform was the old one she had worn years before with her hyphenated married name on it.

Marty had no time to think about the name now, as Karen was onscreen. Shaysee introduced Karen with, "Captain, I understand the Army's Response Team that has returned from a seemingly successful trip to Santa Barbara today, operates out of the pharmaceutical plant here in Thousand Oaks that you command."

As Karen started speaking, a computer graphic with the network logo appeared in the corner below her picture, naming her as 'Capt. Karen Craig, U.S. Public Health Service.' The TV production crew had further modified her name.

"Yes, the Army's Medical Response Team Three is actually commanded by USAMRIID at Fort Detrick, Maryland, but their equipment was pre-staged here at our plant, from which they deployed at the first notice of the H7N9 flu outbreak in Santa Barbara County. Response Team Three, working with local public health authorities, followed standard pubic health epidemic response guidelines precisely, they surveyed the local situation, traced the contacts who had been exposed to the flu, hospitalized those infected, quarantined those exposed, and provided expert, immediate testing to make sure the virus was trapped and prevented from spreading. They managed to quickly control the spread of the disease in Santa Barbara County. It was a textbook case of how we can all, in every community of this country, get together and fight this disease and keep it from spreading. Trace, test, treat, and control—that's the mantra.

Shaysee's face appeared to say, "And Captain, I understand you had some personal interest in how the Army's Response Team Three did in Santa Barbara. Is that correct?"

Karen's face reappeared, and she smiled a slightly embarrassed smile and nodded, "Yes, my husband, Lieutenant Colonel Martin Craig, is the officer in charge of Response Team Three. I'm very proud of how he and his team managed to turn the tables on this flu virus in Santa Barbara. They stopped the Parisian Flu from spreading."

Shaysee's voice asked, "What else are you doing to fight the flu virus?"

Karen and her name graphic appeared in front of a scene in the laboratory. Sonja Hayburn and an Army officer in a major's uniform were working with several civilian technicians in the laboratory. Karen explained, "Here at Thousand Oaks Defense Pharmaceutical Plant and our two sister plants in Illinois and North Carolina, as well as at a dozen or more commercial virus research facilities across the country, we are working to find a vaccine that can stop this H7N9 flu in its tracks. Just last March, we found ourselves facing a similar situation with the H5N1 avian flu that hit Egypt so hard. We, in a coordinated effort between these dozens of medical research facilities, were able to start production of a vaccine that will prevent the H5N1 from coming back with its deadly scourge this fall. It took us only six months from the initial outbreak to shipment of the first vaccine."

The scene changed to Karen standing in front of the vaccine assembly line in Camarillo, "Now, we are in full production of millions of doses of vaccine against what people are calling the Egyptian Flu. We don't like to use that name, but that's what people know it by. Just like they are calling the H7N9 flu, Parisian Flu. To make it clear as to what I am talking about, I will use the popular terms for each of these avian flu strains. Those millions of doses of the Egyptian Flu vaccine will be in clinics and doctors' offices in time for the coming flu season." The picture changed to Karen running her hand through a bin with tens of thousands of sparkling vials of flu vaccine.

"This vaccine we are making now, won't stop the Parisian Flu, but it will mean the end of the Egyptian Flu, and in only six months, that's record time. Historically, getting a new flu vaccine was a multi-year task. With a little luck, we will be able to do the same with Parisian Flu. I know how hopeless it may seem as we hear of people dying by the hundreds and perhaps thousands from this disease daily. But, I can assure everyone, that if people across the country can follow the instructions of their local public health authorities, avoid unnecessary contact with others, wash your hands, stay home, be vigilant and support their local governments as they trace this horrible disease, that any community can be as successful as Santa Barbara County was in fighting the H7N9 flu virus. We can beat this thing. There is hope!"

The view of Shaysee at UCLA returned, "And those are the words of hope from Captain Karen Llewellyn-Craig, one of our nation's leaders in this fight against the deadly Parisian Flu. From Southern California, this is Shaysee O'Neil reporting."

Karen hit the mute button and turned to ask Marty, "Aside from the name thing. What did you think?"

"I'm wondering what happened to the young woman I used to know, the one who said her happy place was all by herself in a laboratory. That woman we just saw was something else. She was fantastic. Where'd that come from?"

"That came from two generals telling me to come up with a message of hope."

"Mission accomplished."

"Thanks."

"And, the name thing, I like that, too."

Karen gave a smirking smile, "I figured that since you keep showing up in my life, I ought to get used to it. It has been my legal name for most of my adult life." She flicked her finger on the nametag above her right pocket.

"Personally, I like it," Marty repeated.

Karen had put her cellphone on the arm of the couch. The cellphone rang. She looked at it and gave a curious expression, "Hello?"

Marty watched as Karen listened and then answered, "Thank you, sir. I appreciate you saying that. Your PAO helped me with some of the ideas for what I said."

She listened again, "Yes, sir. He is right here with me now. As I said, I'm proud of him, too."

She waited again, "I'll tell him, sir. His team members are all back here now and can't wait to get to their next assignment. In the words of one of the medical technicians, she is amped to get going."

One final wait, then, "Yes, sir. Thank you for calling."

Karen put the cellphone back on the arm of the couch. She turned to look at Marty.

"That was Harding, I assume," Marty said.

"Yup. He liked my TV appearance even more than last time. And, he told me to tell you that what your team did in Santa Barbara was in the highest traditions of the Army Medical Corps. He also said that his idea about creating the Response Teams seemed to have worked."

Marty laughed, "Well, I guess we can let him take credit for that. I wouldn't know. But as Yogi Berra once said, 'a winning team sells lots of ballcaps.'"

Karen stood up, stretched, and asked, "Can you start supper while I go upstairs, get changed, and showered?"

"OK, I can start supper. Or, if you need any help upstairs, I can help there, too."

"Showering?" Karen asked.

"Yeah, just offering. It has been a while."

Before Karen could respond, her cellphone rang again. She picked it up, looked at the number calling, and then answered, saying, "Hello, Mom."

—

Chapter 41

Thousand Oaks Defense Pharmaceutical Plant (TODPP)
Thousand Oaks, California
8:30 AM PDT July 30th

Karen Llewellyn was at her desk reading emails and status reports on the viral spread from CDC. She had stopped in to check the status screen for the FEMA/CDC network with Marty when they arrived, so she was not wholly shocked at the bad news from every corner of the country, and Europe. Paris, Milan, and now, the Barcelona area seemed to have massive increases in H7N9 every day, and even aside from those hotspots, Europe was reeling. Much of Europe had gone into quarantine and social distancing reminiscent of the worst days of coronavirus.

Karen's intercom buzzed, and her secretary announced, "Major Chen is here. He says you asked for him."

"Yes, send him in."

Major Anthony 'Tony' Chen came into Karen's office. She stood and motioned him to the small conference table near the windows. "Let's sit over here. Ross Tanner and George Marquardt will be joining us soon. I wanted to have a chance to talk with you beforehand."

Tony sat on the near side of the table. Karen took her usual spot at the head. Tony was wearing the Army camouflage work uniform. He did not necessarily look the part of a PhD microbiologist.

Karen began, "We haven't had a whole lot of time to talk since you arrived, given all that has transpired. Are you getting settled?"

"Yes, ma'am. Although it was quite a shock to me to be pulled out here just when I was getting in the groove at West Point, it seems my wife looks on this move as manna from heaven. She grew up in West Covina. Her family is all out here."

Karen asked, "And here at work, are you getting a grasp on what we need to do. I realize you have switched gears radically from human genome work and teaching college to our viral RNA work."

Tony nodded, "Yes ma'am, it's different, but not so much so in its essence. The notes you gave me and the report on how they did the H5N1 VLP construction to create the vaccine in Atlanta and North Carolina this year, have all helped. But, when I started to research the history of vaccine work on this new H7N9 specifically, there are some questions."

"Yes?"

Tony turned in his chair to face Karen, "I understand our goal is to replicate the success of the H5N1 vaccine with the H7N9 virus, but I have found twenty or more already existing vaccines aimed at H7N9. People all over the world have been working on a vaccine for this virus for decades."

Karen nodded, "That's true. With H7N9's horrible mortality rate when it has been spread by animal-to-human contact, it has been the classic nightmare the world virologists have used to scare themselves for years. I'd guess WHO has registered twenty or more Candidate Viral Vaccines, that's CVVs, pertaining to H7N9. But, the important part there is that they were mere 'candidate' vaccines, the best hopes of various researchers using existing vaccine methodology. Most of those were never tested and were made with various random strains, not the one we need from this year. Also, those candidate vaccines WHO registered are almost entirely made using the old inactivated or attenuated virus methods."

"Why is that a problem?" Tony asked.

"Those methods of vaccine making, using a dead virus cell or one that has been so chemically altered that it can no longer infect a human, that is, attenuated, or inactivated viruses, have been the basis of many of the viral vaccines' successes until recently. They can have a real downside—when you put a virus cell, even one you think is dead or inactive, inside a human being, it can be deadly.

"In the 1950s, the race was on to create a vaccine against polio. It's remembered as the race between Doctors Salk and Sabin for whose vaccine, one from inactivated poliovirus and one from attenuated poliovirus, would rid the world of polio. You're familiar with that, no doubt."

"Sure, basic 20th Century medical history."

"Well, that effort gave us the vaccine world we are stuck with today. In 1955, a company called Cutter Laboratories created tens of thousands of doses of inactivated polio vaccine for a test on American school children. The problem was that the poliovirus in the vaccine was not fully inactivated. Out of 120,000 doses of the vaccine distributed by Cutter Labs, 40,000 children developed a lesser form of the disease, with fever and non-paralytic symptoms that did not involve the central nervous system—56 developed paralytic poliomyelitis—and of those, five children died from polio. Polio caused by the vaccine."

Karen took a breath and continued, "That disaster, we call it the Cutter Incident, changed how we work with vaccines. Since then, we have learned that you go slow with inactivated or attenuated vaccines. Tiny test groups at first. Triple check every step of the production and testing. Then, you do testing over a period of years, first animal, then human, making sure everything is safe and effective. You do not put a real virus cell, dead or otherwise, into the human body unless you're damn sure of what it's going to do. The Cutter Incident is why people take years to make vaccines."

"I see. But we are shipping the H5N1 vaccine in six months."

"Right. Therein is the reason you and I are here. This year, we used our VLP method, which produced a vaccine without any virus in it. There was nothing deadly in it. We were able to test it for efficacy within months and not wait years to see if it was safe."

Tony smiled and nodded, "And, now we need to do the same for the virus from Santa Barbara."

Karen said, "Yes, Santa Barbara and Paris, and Northern China. CDC has finished their genetic analysis, and they say the two, or three, samples are so very close they had to come from a common source. A source we have no idea about."

"A mystery for somebody's graduate thesis someday, huh?"

Before Karen could answer Chen, the intercom announced, "Mr. Marquadt and Mr. Tanner are here."

Since Karen was not at her desk, she shouted toward her door, "Send them in."

George and Ross came in, greetings were exchanged, and they took seats at the table across from Tony.

Karen started, "So, what's up? From Ross' request to set up this meeting and have Tony here, too, it sort of sounded like you have a little conspiracy in the works."

Ross said, "Not a conspiracy, just an excellent idea we both think you will love. I'll let George explain; this is mostly from his people at HeptImun. George?"

George crossed his arms and said, "I need to lay some groundwork for this explanation, particularly for Tony, who is new to our GOCO system. The government has three defense pharmaceutical plants and plans for two more next year. They are all run by different major pharmaceutical companies, experts in vaccine production. But the government wanted a common core to the five plants, interchangeable systems, and processes. They bid out for one company to have the design/build contract for all five plants; same set-up, same equipment, same testing, same everything. HeptImun won that design/build contract. We also got permission to build four more of the same plants for the Chinese, but that's irrelevant for this.

"HeptImun built the plants to our specifications and turned them over to our competitors to run under their own contract with the government. This one here in California, we run ourselves under our contract with the government.

"OK, each of the plants was designed on government specifications to do certain standard things the government wanted all of the plants to do. All of the plants are also supposed to be able to work on the initial creation and testing of new vaccines. That was planned for in the blueprints, but not implemented until an emergency called for it. When Egypt blew up this year with the avian flu, everyone saw we needed a new vaccine for the H5N1 avian flu virus in record time. Lots of commercial companies immediately went to work on it, and the government decided to test out its new Defense Pharmaceutical Plants and see if they could produce a VLP vaccine. Our plant here was not quite ready to operate back in early March, but the plant in North Carolina was. However, that plant was run by a corporate competitor who was just getting used to the equipment and layout HeptImun had designed for that plant. It was agreed that the VLP vaccine experts from HeptImun, who had designed the North Carolina plant, would help the other company get up to speed and produce a VLP candidate vaccine to test against Egyptian Flu.

"We, and our competitor, and the gurus at CDC, were enormously successful. And FDA cleared us after efficacy trials, without lengthy safety studies. The result is now being produced at all of the three Defense plants and several private company plants, here and around the world. With HeptImun's standardized equipment and process, all three defense plants and even the four in China all use the same raw material packaging, the same quality control, and the same product packaging. Our competitor in North Carolina is now up to speed on the use of the plant and does not need the HeptImun experts to show them how to create new VLPs. So, HeptImun was getting ready to send our experts to our new Research and Development Center in Fairfield, California, to work on HeptImun's own in-house VLP program."

George now turned toward Karen, "But, enter Public Health Service Captain Llewellyn, who, when faced by a novel avian flu virus appearing near the plant she runs, told her contractors to start looking at how they could test for the new virus and she even opened up the mothballed laboratory areas where the specifications for the plant called for a possible VLP experimentation and production program. Said PHS captain and her trusty contracting officer pulled some strings and got people reassigned from the government to come help." George motioned toward Tony Chen.

"The contracting officer and the contractor's manager discovered that Captain Llewellyn's plant had a standby, proforma sub-contract just like the one that had been used in North Carolina to create the VLPs to fight the Egyptian virus. That standby contract to make a new VLP could be pulled out and used if needed. It just happens that HeptImun has a team of experienced VLP makers just now getting ready to move from North Carolina to Northern California."

George cracked his knuckles and finished with, "The contracts manager who works for Captain Llewellyn's boss in Maryland is ready to fund the subcontract for VLP experimentation and production at her plant in Southern

California. The expert team from HeptImun is ready to change their moving plans from Northern to Southern California. The good captain's plant in California is already working on the H7N9 VLP problem and has a doctoral-level scientist, wearing the right uniform, who can act as the government's manager of the program to attack the Parisian Flu virus from Thousand Oaks. All we need is for the commander of the plant to tell her contracting manager to get the ball rolling."

Karen Llewellyn thought for a long time, "I like the idea. But this is a huge thing. I'd like the three of you to come up with a written plan, outlining the costs, the steps necessary, and all the details so that I can look at it, and I can send it to General Harding, and maybe HHS, too. They may have other ideas. Sounds good, but we need to be sure of what we are doing. When can we have that?"

"Ma'am, I'm already working on it. I talked to Jared Bentley about this idea yesterday afternoon, and he said he wanted the same thing to give to HeptImun's executives."

———

Office of the Police Commissioner
Baodi City, China
9:30 AM Local Time July 30th

Xi Zemin had just returned to his desk after finishing a theft report from the warehouse district of Baodi. He saw a figure appear at the door to the office he shared with the other criminal investigators. He had not seen his fiancée, Xinru, in her Health Ministry work uniform since the spring when he had worked with her on the disease deaths. Now she gave Zemin a sweet smile as she walked into his office. She was carrying a clipboard and a large brown satchel on a strap over her shoulder.

Xinru walked into the office, but instead of coming over to him, she turned to the sergeant whose desk was near the door. Zemin could not hear what Xinru said to the sergeant, but she checked her clipboard, turning a page, and she found something on the page. She pulled a pen from her pocket and checked something off of her clipboard page. Xinru said something else to the sergeant. He made a face, and she spoke again. The sergeant stood up, unbuttoned his uniform tunic, and bared his upper arm, turning it toward Xinru.

Xinru had put her big leather satchel on the floor. She pulled two glass vials and a needle from the bag. Xinru proceeded to give the sergeant two hypodermic shots in his arm. She ripped open an alcohol wipe package and wiped his arm, before putting a small flesh-colored bandage on each of the two punctures.

Xinru proceeded around the whole office, giving each one of Zemin's co-workers two shots and checking each employee off a list. She finally came to Zemin's desk. He was ready for the shots.

As she gave him the first shot, he asked, "Why shots in the office, we usually go to the clinic as everyone does? And why two shots?"

Xinru spoke quietly, so only Zemin could hear, "Special orders from the ministry. Every civil servant to get two shots, the annual flu shot, and a special one. The Ministry of Health sent us a separate shipment and instructions. The workers, the general public, will get their shots later."

"A special one? Why?"

Xinru did not answer; she just whispered, "We can talk tonight. Something is going on in Beijing."

———

Thousand Oaks Defense Pharmaceutical Plant (TODPP)
Thousand Oaks, California
1:41 PM PDT July 30th

Karen Llewellyn-Craig had gone to lunch with Marty and had heard the orders he had received for his team that morning. Now, she sat in as the Geof Sands, the Intel major on Marty's team who acted as the Operations Officer, briefed the Response Teams' members in the training room/ops center.

Sands explained, "Our team's deployment was requested by the Governor's office in a call to DOD, which flowed down to us this morning. The Los Angeles County authorities have a significant problem at the jail. They have something like ten thousand prisoners in three large jail buildings in the heart of downtown LA. The first death at the jail was within 24 hours of the news of the outbreak, and it has gotten progressively worse since. When we spoke with them this morning, they had over 200 deaths and between one and two thousand sick. They have lost count of the sick ones."

A Google Earth view showed on the screen. "This is the area. For reference, here is the 101 freeway. The Main Jail here. Another big jail building called Twin Towers, here and here. The central jail hospital, really just a clinic with beds, is here. They have another medical ward at the USC Medical Center and a clinic with beds in each building. Several outlying jail facilities, several thousand other prisoners, aren't our problem. At least right now.

"If you look over here to the west, there is a five-acre vacant lot they are doing an emergency modification on to become a tent city. Their plan is to use the tent city to shuttle healthy prisoners out of the central jail buildings. They apparently plan on releasing the healthy prisoners, let them out of jail, rather than keeping them in a set of buildings where the H7N9 is out of control, and they already have a 20% mortality rate. They don't have any existing buildings with enough free space to sort out the healthy prisoners, hence the tent city. They will need to keep the supposedly healthy prisoners for ten days before they release them to the outside world. They cannot release a prisoner who they don't know is not infected. If they mistakenly send a prisoner to the tent city who turns out to be infected, they need to either send them back into the jail or treat them there.

"They have limited medical support on-site. Their custody deputies are getting sick by the dozen, too. They have been augmented by one National Guard military police company and mutual assistance police from various cities. Construction of the tent city is almost finished.

"Our mission is to provide both medical support and testing support so that they can get these thousands of men out of a death trap jail. Any prisoners we can clear with a negative H7N9 test can be released before the ten-day quarantine period, freeing up space and getting healthy people out of this hotspot.

"For right now, until we have feet on the ground, our plan is to have the testing van located here," he pointed to the map, "in the open parking area between the two main jail buildings. Our medical people will be split between the existing jail medical locations and a tent in the tent city. We are talking thousands of tests with our one lab van. We will be giving the prisoners and staff the new annual flu shots at the same time. We cannot forget the Egyptian Flu threatens to come back this fall. We will need heavy-duty resupply of test kits, vaccines, reagents, and maybe medical supplies if our hosts run short.

"Luckily, it's within driving distance from here. A little over an hour. Our supply people and drivers will be busy. Our MP staff will assist the jail crew working on tracking the infection inside the jail. They say they had a good handle on that until the spread got too bad."

Sands turned to Marty, "Colonel Craig, do you have anything to add?"

"No, good job. I will be going to the jail as soon as I can break free here. You will all be on the road this afternoon. We will have our existing team, plus the new folks the plant here can supply us. It's possible we may be living in a couple of those tents for a while. No more cushy hotels until we can make arrangements. I understand hotels in downtown LA are closing. Depending on the traffic, we might be able to commute into downtown. I'll do my best to keep us from having to stay on-site. Anyone else have anything?"

"Uh, colonel?" Master Sergeant Ghent spoke up from the back of the room. "This announcement is both for plant personnel and response team, for as long as you're here. I need to let you all know that two of our contractor staff in the Accounting Office down the hall have tested positive for the Parisian flu. Since we have it inside the building, until we can disinfect the building, the entire building will be a mask only zone. And our free pizza table will be replaced with boxed lunches. Gotta be careful."

Ghent finished with, "Everyone here needs to check with Specialist Kuchma for their masks and to get their temperature taken. We may be taking full blood tests; I haven't been able to ask Captain Llewellyn about that yet."

Karen shook her head and headed over to talk with Ghent.

—

Chapter 42

Topanga-Victory Urgent Care Center
Los Angeles, California
8:30 AM PDT July 31ˢᵗ

Dr. Teresa Rohrbach pulled the 'Closed – No Physician on Duty' sign from behind the filing cabinet. It was the same sign she had used when she had gotten the New or Egyptian Flu back in April, but she now put it up for a different reason. Cyndi, her last remaining staff person, had called in sick early this morning. Teresa had gotten the message forwarded from Pasadena while she was having breakfast with her partner, Rosemary.

Teresa and Rosemary had discussed the situation the night before. Rosemary was a registered nurse who worked for a plastic surgeon in Reseda. After seeing the evening news stories about the massive overcrowding in LA hospitals and understaffed ICUs trying to cope with the glut of Parisian Flu patients, they had both decided to make a call to West Hills Hospital and, as an MD and surgical RN, to offer to go on duty today at the hospital. The call from Pasadena about Cyndi had just made things easier for Teresa to tell her regular employer about her decision. Her urgent care physician supervisor said he had heard the same from many of the urgent care company's medical staff. In a crisis like this, there were more important uses of doctors and nurses than handling a store-front urgent care center, especially an urgent care center that could do nothing for nearly all of its frantic patients.

Teresa and Rosemary had each already cleared their schedules for the next three weeks for their aborted ski vacation, so their employers should have been ready for their absence at work. The next three weeks were certainly not going to be the expected vacation. And, this was probably going to be longer than three weeks.

Teresa slid the closed sign into the slot on the door and locked up. She wondered when, if ever, she might be back here.

Rosemary was waiting in the car for Teresa. Both were in white medical scrubs. The employee scheduler at West Hills had been so happy to get their offer to sign on, that he had promised them they could work the same shifts. But, the scheduler had explained that as of yesterday at West Hills, those shifts were twelve hours on, twelve hours off, and one day off every ten days until further notice. For Teresa and Rosemary, it was just like old times; they had met each other doing shift work at West Hills. They had both switched to medical office practice to be able to have a normal life together; now, they were back on those interminable shifts again. Life was strange. They both felt good about their decision, though.

———

NYU Langone Medical Center
Manhattan, New York City, New York
10:40 AM EDT July 31ˢᵗ

"The nurse just brought me your discharge paperwork to sign. I wanted to stop by and tell you that since you're out of the ICU now, we could let you stay on a few days to rest up. Our regular rooms aren't as crowded as the ICU. You've been through a lot," the physician said.

Derek Beaumont shook his head, "No, I absolutely have to get back to California. I finally got through to my wife. I need to get back."

"How is she doing?"

"Inga's on the mend. Still in the hospital, but they managed to treat her with the antiviral drugs, she never needed the ventilator, like me. Inga is distraught about losing our son. But she says our daughter has problems. Heather has nearly recovered from the flu, but psychologically she's a wreck. She lost her brother and her best friend, Chelsea. They have her sedated. She's freaking out. She saw a news report on TV that named her as the person who spread the flu to everybody. I can relate to how she must feel like a modern-day Typhoid Mary."

"My condolences on your son."

"Thanks, my wife says the mortuary is holding his body since the whole family is in the hospital. That's part of why I need to get back, too."

The physician tried to change the topic, "Say, how did that big business deal that you said brought you to New York turn out?"

"Ppffftt!" Derek said, making a motion of a crashing airplane with his hand. "I tried to call the offices of the arbitrage firm where we were negotiating, and the recorded message says the New York office is closed due to the health emergency, please call the Boston office. I tried calling my other contacts on the deal. The people that I could reach all treated me like I was some kind of pariah. I guess many of the people in our all-day negotiating sessions got sick."

"Yes, I saw the report that Wall Street was Ground Zero for the spread of the Parisian Flu in New York."

"Yeah, and everyone knows the name of the man who started it. I can relate to my daughter's feelings. Her trip to UCLA seems to have even been worse than mine to New York. I just went on one airplane flight. Her college classmates went on dozens."

The physician stepped forward and offered his hand to Derek, "Well, good luck. I hope everything turns out alright for you and your family."

Derek hesitated at taking the handshake, "I thought we weren't supposed to shake hands in this flu."

"In the last two weeks, these hands have stuck things down your throat and up your wazoo. I think they can shake your hand, too."

They shook hands, and the doctor left the room. Derek continued to pack his suitcase.

The hospital had sent Derek's clothes to a commercial cleaner, and he was transferring his clothes from the cleaner's bundle to his suitcase. All of his other personal items had a chemical smell like pine tar to them. Somebody had disinfected everything that had come with him from the hotel to the hospital in the orange bags.

The nurse brought copies of his discharge paperwork to Derek. She also handed him a face mask.

"Why do I need this? Aren't I immune?" he asked.

"Yes, you're immune to the Parisian Flu, but nobody else is. Everybody in New York is under mandatory mask orders. The Uber or taxi driver won't let you in the car for the ride to the airport without a mask."

Derek Beaumont took the mask.

———

Main Jail Parking Lot
Los Angeles, CA
8:10 AM PDT Aug 1st

Lieutenant Colonel Martin Craig stood waiting on the upper level of the parking structure in front of the Main Jail building. Four large white vehicles stood nearby. One was the large mobile laboratory vehicle Craig's team had brought with them to LA; the other three were semi-trailers. Craig could hear the refrigeration units of the semi-trailers running. A deputy stood guard at a canopy tent near the trailers. Four prisoners in the green jumpsuits of jail trustees sat in lawn chairs under the canopy, waiting for something.

Marty Craig saw a figure crossing over the street from the Twin Towers to the east. It was Marty's usual contact, Commander Matt Relford. The two men had been continuously conferring since the Army Response Team had arrived.

They did not shake hands when Relford reached Craig. They just nodded to each other.

"Everything on track?" Relford asked.

"Yes, it seems so. We got the glitch in the reagent delivery squared away. The distributor in LA is just delivering to us here instead of driving everything to Thousand Oaks for them to send to us. And thanks for cutting the red tape for us at the hotel. That's a perfect place for my people. Walking distance."

Relford asked, "What are our numbers?"

"We have trained two of our medics to help the lab technicians, so we are running tests around the clock. They just sent 210 on a list to the tent area of prisoners who tested negative, but 36 failed and need to come back. And the tests direct from your two hopefully 'clean' Twin Towers floors were coming in overnight last night. It's not quite as clean as you hoped. Running almost 60:40 when I checked last. And, those sixty percent on that clean list will need to test negative again before you can let them out of the tent area."

"Understand, but it's better than . . ." Relford stopped talking when they heard a forklift transmission whining on the ramp behind them from the lower level of the parking structure.

Both men turned to watch the forklift. It had just picked up a load at the lower deck entrance to the Main Jail.

On the forklift was an extra-wide wooden pallet. On the pallet lay four black rubberized body bags. The forklift driver was also a prisoner/trustee. He nodded to Relford. The forklift lowered its load next to the farthest semi-trailer. The four waiting jail trustees slowly stood, in no hurry, and walked over to unload the pallet. One of them lowered the trailer's liftgate to the ground. He flipped the lever to open the rear of the trailer. The four trustees loaded four more bodies into the impromptu morgue.

"How many does that make?" Marty Craig asked.

"I'm not sure if those four are in this morning's figure or not. We passed six hundred dead." Relford answered.

"I heard a morning news program before I left the hotel that Los Angeles city figures are twenty times that," Marty said.

Matt Relford shook his head and looked over at Marty Craig, "But, the six hundred number is on my personal tally of failures."

———

Thousand Oaks Defense Pharmaceutical Plant (TODPP)
Thousand Oaks, California
11:17 AM PDT August 1ˢᵗ

Captain Karen Llewellyn-Craig was sitting next to Specialist Kuchma, looking at the rapidly more congested national map of the nodes entered into the FEMA/CDC software. Every state had multiple nodes, indicating an active hotspot for the Parisian Flu. Kuchma clicked on the Statistics icon and the national figures for total probable cases, positive tests, deaths, and recoveries popped up. Karen read it and shook her head. It was now much worse than coronavirus had been at this stage, not quite three weeks after the first case. H7N9 was spreading faster and had a much higher, and more egalitarian, mortality rate. Every age group and every locality was getting hit with the 'Parisian Flu.' *God, I hate that name.*

"And, those are current numbers, right?" Karen asked.

"Yes ma'am. They come right from the node reports."

Karen saw Tony Chen come in the room out of the corner of her eye. He walked over and gave her a thumbs-up sign.

"Everybody OK'd it?" she asked.

Tony nodded and smiled, "Yes ma'am. Ross says to tell you that both generals gave their OK and that Assistant Secretary Royce and CDC were on board, too. I listened in to the call from CDC and some guy named Reynes said for us to tell you 'he told you so.'"

Karen smile at Phil Reynes' comment. As Reynes had predicted in his office months before, Karen did seem to be in precisely the place she should be at this moment in history.

"OK, Major Chen, go talk to George Marquardt and Sonya Hayburn. Find out about the arrival of the HeptImun team. Get the VLP lab set up fully. You have a VLP design program to run."

"Yes ma'am."

"Just a sec, Major," Karen said, turning to Kuchma. "When I decided not to send Specialist Kuchma with the response team to LA, I told her we would be doing interesting and important stuff right here. Lyuda, go with Major Chen, you're his military assistant to help keep all those new HeptImun civilians toeing the line."

Kuchma smiled, nodded, and followed Chen out.

Karen watched them leave. She turned back to the screen on the wall showing the mortality statistics. She had a very sobering thought. Even if her team could produce an H7N9 vaccine in the same timeframe as had been done back east with the VLP-based Egyptian Flu vaccine, it would still be six months before a vaccine was available. And those six months would be in the height of the annual flu season. Egyptian Flu had taken the expected breather during three summer months of the six months needed to make a vaccine.

How many millions will die before her team might be able to create a new vaccine for the Parisian Flu? That is IF they were able to create a new vaccine or create it in the same timeframe. *Yes, millions will die, even if we succeed.*

Karen went back to her office to reread the research papers and lab manuals she had collected on VLP research, design, and production. She would soon have people to do that, but Karen could not sit idly by waiting for millions of people to die. She needed to be doing something.

———

Santa Barbara Cottage Hospital
Santa Barbara, California
12:14 PM PDT August 1st

The hospital was crowded and off-limits to visitors to limit the spread of the virus, the spread both inside and outside the hospital. That had been enormously frustrating to Derek Beaumont when he returned to Santa Barbara, anxious to see his wife and daughter. Now, they were scheduled to be released from the hospital, and he had to wait in the circle drive out front of the hospital.

Derek had arrived by plane the evening before at the nearly deserted Santa Barbara airport. He had parked his Mercedes in the close-in parking, thinking his stay in New York would only be two or three days. That had stretched to twelve days with his hospital trip. But, in the near-empty airport, the gates of the parking lot were open, and Derek avoided an overtime ticket. That mattered little in the scale of things these days. Not wanting to return to the empty family home over the Santa Barbara foothills by himself, Derek had spent the night at a motel on State Street near the hospital.

Derek finally saw Inga being wheeled out of the hospital. He jumped out of the car and ran to her. Inga tried to smile at Derek, but that effort failed. Inga looked as though she had lost weight. Her piercing blue eyes blinked from a haggard, expressionless face. Derek lifted her out of the wheelchair and to her feet. He helped her toward the car's passenger seat. He thanked the wheelchair driver and got back into the car.

Derek looked across at Inga. She turned her head to face him. Derek realized that he could think of nothing appropriate to say to his wife. All words failed him.

At last, he said, "Heather should be down anytime."

Inga nodded.

"Have you been able to see Heather yet?" Derek asked.

Inga nodded again, "They took me down to her room the day before yesterday. We were on the same hallway after she got out of the ICU. She couldn't talk that day. I think they had her drugged." Inga's voice seemed deeper than Derek remembered, her accent thicker.

Inga continued, "I got to talk to her yesterday a bit. She is really broken up about all this. And she seems very weak. She was very sick; the doctor says we almost lost her, too."

Inga sobbed at this. Derek pulled a tissue from the car console and reached across to her.

"They said you were sick, too. They wouldn't tell me much about that. I thought I was going to lose everyone," Inga cried again.

When she could speak again, Inga asked, "You were in the hospital in New York?"

Derek nodded.

"How long?"

"Until yesterday. I flew here as soon as they let me out."

"You know all about Mark?"

"Yes, the doctor here in Santa Barbara called me once I woke up in the hospital back there. When he called me, Heather was still very sick. He would not say much about her, either. And, then you were sick, too. I was . . . . I also talked to the . . . uh, mortuary yesterday, about Mark."

Inga blinked at him, "Oh, God, yes. I forgot about that, the funeral."

"Let's not . . . now. They told me a bit about that. They will call us at home tomorrow. There's Heather." Derek got out of the car.

Derek was shocked at how his daughter looked. Her face had no color. Her long, blonde hair was plastered to her head and neck. Her gaunt face looked ethereal, almost ghostlike. Derek really did not see any recognition when she looked at him.

Inga got out of the car. She hurried over to help Heather stand up. Inga hugged Heather, but Heather barely moved her arms around her mother. Derek opened the rear car door, and when Inga let go of Heather, Derek put his arm around her. Heather ignored his attempt to hug; she just climbed in the car, silently. Derek reached in to buckle her seatbelt. When he reached across her body, Heather smelled odd, hospital smells, sweat and illness. Not like Heather.

The awkward silence when Inga had got in, was magnified with Heather. No one said anything as Derek drove off.

As he signaled to exit the freeway to the highway over the mountains, Derek asked, "Do either of you need anything before we head home." That was a standard question when the family headed away from the city toward their rural home, but today it sounded very odd.

Derek looked over, and Inga shook her head. Heather did not answer.

When they settled in for the trip over the mountains, Heather finally spoke, "Where's Mark?"

Derek did not know what to say. *Didn't she know Mark was gone?* Mark looked over at Inga. She was looking at him, also perplexed at the question.

"I mean, where's his body?" Heather explained.

Derek was relieved at her added words, but now he had to answer. "At the mortuary, the funeral home, in Santa Barbara."

"The one where we had Grandma's funeral?" Heather asked.

"Yes," Derek said.

"What about Chelsea?"

"I don't know. We can call her mother," Inga said.

After a long pause, Heather asked, "Will we have an open casket for Mark, like Grandma. So we can see Mark again? At his funeral?"

Unfortunately, Derek had already heard the answer to that. "The social distance rules won't let us have a regular funeral. No visitors. But they say we can view the body; the immediate family can. But, viewing is only for a moment, and you can't touch the body. No final kiss, touch, or hand-holding. Because of the virus, possibly on the body."

Heather thought about this for a while, then she said, "But all of Mark's immediate family have had this stuff. We don't have to worry about the virus anymore."

Derek was amazed at his daughter. He had thought of her as being delicate emotionally. He had been worried about her. But, here she was dealing with the practical side of her sibling's death, thinking about obvious things he had not thought about, until now.

Heather was going to be alright.

"We can talk to them about that. If it's important to you," he said.

"OK," Heather said.

After another long wait, Heather asked, "What about my geese and Mark's pig?"

Derek had spoken to the Public Health woman about that. "Honey, they are gone. They are where the virus came from."

Another pause. Heather asked, "How'd they get the virus?"

"I don't think anybody knows that."

After another thoughtful wait, "So, my geese are taking the rap for all of this. Mrs. O'Leary's cow is replaced by Miss Beaumont's goose as history's animal villain?"

Yes, Heather was going to be alright.

—

Ministry of Health
Medical Products Facility
Fangshan District
Suburban Beijing, China
9:10 AM Local Time August 3rd

"Madame Director, you really need not have come out to check on this yourself. We have all four shipments complete—as directed." Her logistics manager seemed to be insulted that she had come out to inspect the outgoing shipment herself.

Director Zhao Xiang nodded to him, "I, too, have my superiors. Mine instructed me to make sure, personally, that this important shipment went out, on time and as directed by the Ministry."

The logistics manager nodded his understanding. The bureaucracy required certain things from everyone.

Zhao Xiang looked the manager in the eye, "So, we have a complete selection of each of the 'special' production materials to each plant, Shanghai, Guangzhou, and Chengdu. And a quality control test shipment to our HeptImun contractors, as well. Three crates to each, via air-freight."

"On that, Madame Director—we usually do not send such large shipments using international air-freight services. They are so expensive, especially for the shipments inside China."

Zhao feigned frustration, "I fully realize that. This is so important they, the people at the ministry, want immediate email confirmation. The domestic shippers are not good at that."

Zhao did not add that this was intentionally not being sent via a domestic Chinese company. There were other reasons for that.

She walked between the four rows of crates. She casually checked each address. Shanghai, Guangzhou, and Chengdu, plus the last to the HeptImun address in California.

"Very well, Madame Director, all is complete. Will there be anything else?" the logistics manager asked. He seemed anxious for his boss to leave his turf.

"No, that will be all. Good work." Director Zhao took a deep breath.

I hope this works.

———

Chapter 43

Thousand Oaks Defense Pharmaceutical Plant (TODPP)
Thousand Oaks, California
6:00 PM PDT August 4ᵗʰ

Like most nights recently, Karen was sitting at her office desk when the evening newscasts came on. Karen had the cable news program streaming on her desk computer as she prepared to eat one of the boxed lunches from the training room. It was still a bit odd to her for the prime time news programs to come on three hours earlier in California than they had back east. Stacks of reports sat on her desk, begging to be read.

The network anchor opened the broadcast with "Breaking News at this hour. Sources in the administration report very worrisome news that several cabinet members and possibly other administration officials have become infected with the Parisian Flu strain. The White House Press Office refused to comment on the reports. Here is our White House reporter, Renata Christy, with more."

Renata appeared, with an evening scene of the White House exterior behind her, and said, "There was a confirmed sighting of a limousine carrying the fender placard of the Secretary of Defense on the grounds of the Walter Reed Army Medical Center in suburban Maryland, outside Washington DC, the day before yesterday. Pentagon officials would not comment on rumors of the Secretary of Defense being ill." A 'file photo' of a black limousine with a Department of Defense seal on the front was shown.

Renata's voice continued, with a video from New York, "Several other cabinet-level agencies have been silent when asked about planned events by cabinet officials running those agencies being abruptly canceled or rescheduled. A planned visit by the Health and Human Services Secretary to the huge temporary hospital in New York City was handled by an Assistant Secretary." A view of the White House re-appeared.

"When the Parisian Flu crisis hit, the White House quickly invoked social distancing and disease protection measures in the White House. All visitors and press representatives have been subjected to stringent temperature and symptom testing before being allowed access to the White House and again before having access to the President."

A video of a smiling Filipino man, in a white serving jacket, delivering pieces of cake to Cabinet members was shown. "Sources who requested to remain anonymous have reported that two stewards employed by the White

House kitchen are believed to be sick from the Parisian Flu. One of those stewards is believed to be the person in this White House video showing an impromptu birthday party the president gave for the vice-president on her birthday last week. The birthday party was held prior to a Cabinet meeting on the health crisis response."

Renata narrated another video, saying, "The president appeared fine in this appearance today with the incoming Federal Reserve chairman. However, the vice-president has not been seen since her birthday party, and the vice-president's children are reported to have been absent from their private school in Georgetown this week."

Karen shook her head in consternation at this report. She reached for the box lunch. She paused and reached for the squirt bottle of hand sanitizer she kept on the front of her desk. Karen then opened her sandwich.

———

Avenue Henri Barbusse
Paris, France
4:13 PM Local Time August 4th

Inspector Michel Dormer rechecked his notebook before he went up the rickety staircase. The building smelled of some ethnic cooking. He could not identify the ethnicity. From the neighborhood, Dormer guessed it was Balkan or Syrian.

The address had come up on identification and work permit documents from three different patients who had been found on the streets or in public areas in the late stages of the flu. Two of the three using this address had died. The *Sante Publique* workers had been unable to get any family or employment information on the now-deceased patients or the one survivor, besides this address. Following a pattern of previous cases, it was suspected this might be one of the many black market 'hostels' where illegal immigrants or refugees were gathering during the quarantine to wait out the disease, but if they got too sick, the other residents delivered the unfortunate roommate to a public place to be someone else's problem. The first floor seemed to be a long-closed storage area; the apartment number found on the documents was marked as being up the stairs.

From experience, Dormer expected the worst. These immigrant hovels were always bad. And, if they had sick people inside, it could be horrid, if not lethal. Dormer had thick rubber gloves on, and a full face shield and mask like the street cops wore.

As he approached the top of the stairs, Michel Dormer was honestly concerned about the stability of the creaky old wood of the stairs and the upper landing. This building was ancient.

At the top, he listened. He heard a radio, with a tinny sound to it, playing rock music, somewhere inside. He knocked.

No answer.

He pounded his fist on the door and announced, "*Health Department*." Still no answer.

Since this was a health and safety inspection, not a criminal investigation, Dormer had the right to demand entry, or if nobody was present, to enter uninvited. He tried the doorknob. It turned easily, and the door swung open without his doing anything. He announced himself again. Still no answer.

The pungent food smell had, indeed, come from this apartment. But now that the door was open, it was clear the food smell was not fresh cooking; it was old and spoiled. But, the smell of putrid food was overpowered by the foul stench of death. It was unmistakable. Even through his mask, the smell nearly made him gag.

An antique, rotary light switch by the door worked. A bare bulb in the front hallway went on. Dormer made his announcement one more time and walked into the apartment.

The door to the first room on the right was ajar. It was dark inside the windowless room. Dormer took his penlight out of his pocket. He flicked it on to show the inside of a bedroom. The room had furniture inside that was as ancient and dilapidated as the building. There was a bed in the far corner. It appeared to be occupied.

"Hello?" Dormer shouted.

No movement. No sound from the room. Dormer walked over, nearer the bed, and shined his light. The bed had three people in it: two men and a woman. The woman's eyes stared wide open at the ceiling. Flies were everywhere in the room. All three were dead. There was no need to check for their vital signs.

Dormer used his light to make sure his exit was clear, and he quickly left the room. The room across the hall was the same, only it merely had two bodies, both men, in two single beds. This room had the radio playing in it, playing for the dead. Dormer turned the old turquoise plastic clock radio off.

The bathroom was empty. From the smell, it had not been cleaned in ages. The toilet had serious need of a plunger.

The kitchen was also empty. Several wooden crates of spoiling fruit sat on the floor. The crates looked like the farmers' market bins where old produce was collected for disposal. Clouds of tiny fruit flies circled. From the large pile of empty water bottles, Dormer assumed the water supply to the apartment was inoperative. That also explained the toilet's problem.

The final bedroom door was closed. It opened with a shove from Dormer. Light came in the open, curtainless windows. Three more bodies occupied the two beds in this room, one man by himself and a couple with arms entwined. They were all adults, and they appeared to be either Balkan or Arab. Dead several days. In the better light in this room, Dormer could see the features of the dead were bloated and misshapen from putrefaction. The smell was overwhelming.

In the crib in the far corner of the room, Michel Dormer was confronted by a tiny body. It was a baby, a girl, skinny and laying without a diaper in a pile of maggot-ridden excrement. When Michel Dormer flashed his penlight on the baby's body, her eyes opened, startling Dormer.

The baby made a pitiful sound—not a cry, just a gurgling whimper. She just lay there and blinked at Dormer.

Inspector Dormer took out his cellphone and made three quick speed dial calls. Help would be here soon.

The humanity in Dormer demanded that he get the baby out of the maggots and filth. He looked around and pulled a raincoat from a hook on the wall. He folded it on the floor out in the hallway, away from the worst of the putrid smell. He lifted the baby from the crib. Her limp neck and limbs flopped as he lifted her up. He carefully supported her head. She still made no sound.

He laid the baby on the folded raincoat. He thought of what to do next. In the kitchen, he found one of the water bottles that was not completely empty. He grabbed a soiled dishtowel from the kitchen sink. It was better than nothing.

He went back into the hallway and kneeled by the baby on the raincoat. With water and the towel, he did his best to clean the filth from the baby. He was still working at that when the paramedics shouted from the door of the apartment.

The *Médecin Légiste* crew, who were next on-scene, having answered Dormer's cellphone call, had to do most of the work here, given the number of dead bodies. Dormer had to compile a report on this obvious immigrant flophouse. His *Sante Publique* report would conclude that the Parisian Flu had, at last, sickened everyone in the apartment, and they had each, in turn, succumbed to the disease, in their beds. There were only two survivors among the residents of this address, the one living patient whose identification documents had led Dormer here and the little baby girl. As it was also one of his department's duties, Dormer filed a *Writ of Condemnation* on the building for health violations. This place was beyond hope.

———

Chapter 44

Thousand Oaks Defense Pharmaceutical Plant (TODPP)
Thousand Oaks, California
8:00 AM PDT August 5th

Karen Llewellyn had arrived at the plant early this morning. She went to check on Tony Chen, whom she found in the newly opened office space between Sonya Hayburn's QA lab and the Biosafety lab at the rear. Office and equipment space for the VLP creation effort had been designed into the TODPP blueprints, but the space had not been opened and outfitted for work until this week. The HeptImun VLP research team members were arriving from North Carolina every day. Tony Chen was making sure the team was ready to work. Both Chen and his assistant, Lyudmila Kuchma, had arrived as early as Karen.

Karen was now, at eight o'clock, at her desk, preparing to read overnight emails and check the new statistics on the FEMA network. Her personal cellphone went off.

The cellphone showed an international call, country code 44 and area code 18. Karen was not sure, but she seemed to recall 44 as being England. She took the call and answered, "Hello?"

After a tone sounded, a young woman's voice with a British accent announced, "Reading Exchange. One moment, ma'am. Your caller will be connected."

After more tones, she heard a familiar voice, "Hello, Karen?"

"Joan?" Karen asked. It was Joan Zhao.

"Yes, Karen. I'm glad I reached you, and before you say anything, please listen to me. I need to explain this call." It may be Karen's imagination, but it seemed that Joan was speaking with a much more pronounced British accent than Karen remembered from speaking to Joan in person. Joan continued, "I'm making this call to you with the assistance of one of my friends from graduate school. You do remember me speaking of my grad school days, correct?"

When she and Karen first met, Joan had spoken of graduate school in England. Her grad school friends had given 'Joan' her English nickname, instead of her real given name Xiang. So, Karen answered, "Yes."

"OK, for reasons that will become obvious to you in the next few days. I need to be careful about what I speak about on this call. Even though I'm calling you through a supposedly secure Internet VOIP connection, it is possible this call could be heard by the wrong people. So, I'm going to give you my message by referring to things we both know about rather than speaking directly. Do you understand, dear?"

Joan was clearly mimicking a British speaker's accent and inflection. Karen answered, "Yes."

Joan continued, "This call should reach you at the start of your workday at the beautiful kitchen designed for you by our mutual friend in Connecticut. It is just before midnight where I'm calling from." Joan was telling her she was calling from the Far East. "As you know, I have an identical kitchen, also designed in Connecticut."

Karen thought a moment. The only connection she had with Joan regarding Connecticut was the HeptImun corporate plant. Karen took out a pad and pencil to start taking notes on this call.

Joan continued, "Please remember the kind of restaurant where we ate that evening with the handsome gentleman from Connecticut. That type of restaurant is the same as the subject matter of this call."

Jared Bentley had taken Joan and Karen to a French restaurant.

Joan explained, "I know that the chefs in your Connecticut-style kitchen are working to create the recipe for that type of food. I saw a YouTube clip of the television interview where you talked about your hope of creating that recipe. By the way, you were *mahvalous* on TV," Joan had the accent parody down well, "I need to let you know that I, too, am working on that recipe. In fact, I've been working on the recipe far longer than you have. And, I've discovered the secret ingredient that works in the recipe."

Joan waited a moment before continuing. "Two days ago, I boxed up an early birthday gift box for you. I sent you a few of those wonderful little soup tureens from Connecticut. They have the secret ingredient inside. I also sent a wee bit of the *entrée* I made with the recipe I concocted. That food in your gift box is ready to eat. I've already done a market analysis on the food made from my secret ingredient, and the marketplace loves it. It placates hunger and digests well."

Joan waited a moment and continued, with a distinctly more serious tone to her voice, "Since you're a *Cordon Bleu*-trained chef yourself, I know that you would be horrified at taking credit for another chef's recipe and secret ingredient. However, in this case, I must insist, in fact, I beg you, that you take full credit for the recipe yourself and do not disclose beyond your own kitchen where you got the secret ingredient. Is that clear, Karen?"

"I think so."

Joan added, "I sent your birthday gift via kraut express. The gift box should arrive at your kitchen later today or tomorrow. The delivery schedule will come to your email. Please do not feel the need to confirm to me that you received it; the kraut shipping company will let me know that. And, it would be better if we do not say anything further about this until we can meet in person. I thought that since we are both such loyal Doctor Who fans, we could meet and talk at the Doctor Who fan convention this fall. Do you think we might do that?"

Karen had to think a moment on that, "Yes, that sounds like a plan."

Joan finished with, "Alright, it would be better to make this call as short as possible. I hope you can figure out my message. I think it will be clear when you see your birthday gift. I wish you well, my friend. Good Luck!"

The line clicked off with a modem-like warble.

Karen thought about the call for a moment before she went back and added to her notes the few lines at the beginning that she had not taken notes on before.

The more Karen thought about the call, the more brilliant she realized Joan Zhao was. Zhao was obviously concerned the call might be intercepted by Chinese security or counterintelligence people. So, she had devised a conversation that never identified either of them except by first name. The sound of Joan's voice had seemed flawlessly British and had come to Karen through Britain, apparently relayed from a Voice-Over-Internet-Protocol service in Reading, England. The real topic could not be determined by a listener without access to Joan and Karen's own memories. A listener on Karen's end might understand the reference to the television interview, but nobody in China would. A listener who actually knew either Karen or Joan might be able to reconstruct the message, but a random intercept of the call would tell a listener nothing. Karen pulled a yellow highlighter pen from her drawer and marked the words of doublespeak from Joan in her notes.

Graduate school—Karen's workday in her kitchen—Connecticut—Joan's identical kitchen from Connecticut—French restaurant—handsome gentleman from Connecticut—the subject is French—create a recipe—TV interview—Joan's previous work on the recipe—a secret ingredient—birthday gift box—Connecticut soup tureen—sample food—market analysis on secret ingredient—placates hunger and digests well—keep the real chef and recipe secret—kraut shipping company—Doctor Who—fall fan convention.

Doctor Xiang 'Joan' Zhao was, indeed, brilliant. It would be impossible for anyone listening in to the VOIP conversation to understand what Karen Llewellyn understood Joan Zhao to be saying. Joan had been working on a solution to the French/Parisian Flu virus for a long time. She was sending Karen a HeptImun-designed VLP shipping container with Parisian Flu VLP in it, along with a sample vaccine that had already been tested and found safe and effective. The shipment was coming via the pejorative 'kraut' (DHL) air freight and would arrive in California soon. Karen was urged to keep Joan's part in the vaccine's U.S. production secret and to take credit for it herself. Lastly, Joan was suggesting they might meet personally at the WHO Global Partnership meeting that had been scheduled in Geneva in October to discuss the status of the avian flu health crisis.

Karen had no idea of where to start on this. If there was anything that qualified for the CIA's concern regarding her contact with Joan, this was it. This was far outside of Karen's zone of comfort. Karen needed help.

———

8th Floor
Grady Memorial Hospital
Atlanta, Georgia
1:48 PM EDT August 5th

The phone number rang several times, then Emilie heard, "Flight Personnel Services, how can I help you?"

"I'm Emilie Porter, employee number 214701. I'm the flight attendant who got sick on Flight 918 from Newark EWR to MIA a couple of weeks ago."

"Oh my, I heard about that. How are you doing?"

"I'm much better; it has been kinda rough. They are getting ready to discharge me from the hospital, and I need a little assistance."

"How can we help you?"

"Well, I need help with several things. I guess I passed out on the flight, and they made an emergency stop in Atlanta for me. But, here in the hospital, I have not been able to track down my personal property. No luggage, no purse, no I.D., no credit cards. It's pretty much just me in a hospital gown, in Atlanta, a place where I know nobody. I was wondering if the airline can help me. I don't have my cellphone to contact my scheduler or anybody else with the airline who knows me. I have no way to get back to my home base, Los Angeles. And, apparently, the world has gone crazy with this Parisian Flu nastiness while I was out of it in the hospital. Nobody here at the hospital in Atlanta has any idea on what I should do to put things back together. I was wondering if the airline can track down my stuff and get me a ticket back home, if I can come up with an I.D. to get on a flight. My bag might have been left on the flight when they dropped me off. The captain on that flight was Gordy Jenkins. Can you help me reach him? He might know where they put my things."

"Just a moment. Let me check on him. He should be on the crew scheduling list."

Emilie waited for the personnel employee to come back on the line. It took a long time.

A different voice came on the phone, "Emilie?"

"Yes, who is this?"

"I'm Jessica Fordham, the flight attendant supervisor here in Chicago. We've probably met many times at training."

"Yes, I remember."

"Lisa in Flight Personnel forwarded your call to me. I'll take over and get you some help. We'll get you out of Atlanta and back home. I'm afraid I can't check with Captain Gordon Jenkins about your luggage and personal property. Who else was on that flight with you?"

"Why can't you reach Gordy?"

After a pause, Jessica said, "Captain Jenkins passed away last week. He got the flu himself and died back in New York? Who was the 2nd Officer or another flight attendant on your flight?

———

College Street Jail Annex
Main Jail Complex
Los Angeles, California
9:15 AM PDT August 5th

The strange call from Karen had come in right at 9 o'clock. She had called to ask him to come back to Thousand Oaks as soon as possible so she could talk to him about "something important she didn't want to talk about on the phone." She had asked that he bring Geof Sands, the Response Team's Intel/Ops officer with him, along with the Response Team's SatComm secure communications device. Karen had bluntly refused to answer his question as to what was happening. Marty Craig had no clue as to what his wife, a medical doctor and vaccine plant manager, needed with a Military Intelligence officer or a secure satellite communications link.

Lieutenant Colonel Martin Craig stripped off the surgical gloves and the paper surgical gown they used in this tent medical clinic. He stuffed the refuse in a red bio-hazard bin. He cleaned his hands and arms in the sanitizer and put on his ACU shirt and hat that was hanging on a chair. He waived to the nurse and two medical school students who were assisting in doing the testing and sick call at the clinic for the prisoners being housed in the tent city. He had told them he would be leaving after he got the strange call from Karen. He showed his ID to a deputy as he exited the prisoner area of the tent city.

The three tents used by the Army response team were just outside of the gate in the tall fence that surrounded the prisoners' tents in this tent city jail annex. The supply trucks, passenger van, and a couple of the regular SUVs used by the team were parked by the tents. As Marty approached the first tent, he saw a lanky black soldier stand up, put on his hat, and come out to meet him.

Specialist Jerome Ali saluted Marty and said, "Good morning, sir. Sergeant Johnson told me you wanted a ride back to T.O. I'm ready whenever you are."

Marty saluted Specialist Ali back, "This isn't screwing up your schedule, is it?"

Ali shook his head as he looked at his cellphone to check the time, "No sir. Not at all. We have a good schedule posted for all of the supply runs and crew transport. And Sergeant Johnson always has an extra driver ready to cover stuff like this. Is the black Suburban OK?"

"That's perfect. We have to stop over at the lab and pick up Major Sands and some gear from the lab."

Marty got into the front passenger seat of the big SUV and buckled his seatbelt. Ali started the engine and made an entry on a clipboard he slipped in between the seats.

Marty had been in this SUV a couple times before. It was a brand new. You could still smell the 'new vehicle smell.'

"This isn't exactly your standard-issue Army vehicle is it, Specialist?"

Ali laughed, "No sir. This a damned sight nicer than an Oshkosh tactical vehicle. But then again, the 101 freeway isn't Afghanistan either. Master Sergeant Ghent said that since this was purchased as part of the HeptImun contract that the gear isn't MILSPEC, but off-the-shelf commercial."

Marty nodded.

As he left the tent area and turned toward the Main jail, Ali asked, "Will you be coming back with me this afternoon?"

"No idea. I hadn't planned on leaving LA today. My wife . . . uh, the Captain, called and needs to talk about something. I may be coming back. I don't know. Please check with me before you make your return run."

Ali laughed, "Must be tough calling your wife by her name and rank." After a pause, Ali asked, "Say, sir. If I'm not out of line asking, isn't there a rule against having married people in the same unit, ya know, nepotism, or whatever?"

Now Marty laughed, "No, or I mean yes, but no. There is a rule against having a relative in the chain of command, but my team and I aren't assigned to the pharmaceutical plant, so I'm not serving under my wife. My direct commander is a bird colonel back at Fort Detrick."

They turned left between the Twin Towers and the Main Jail and turned up the parking ramp to where the laboratory vehicle was parked. They had to wait for a forklift coming down the ramp.

"Ah, I understand. That makes sense," Ali said. "Sir, I was wondering, how are we doing here at the Jail? Are we able to help them get the healthy guys out?"

"They are starting to be able to release the ones we test as free of the virus. But, it's slow. Our little lab van was never meant to test thousands of men. We've got people working day and night. That's most of what you drivers are hauling in, the supplies to do testing and the medicine and vaccine for the prisoners."

Ali pulled up near the laboratory vehicle and added, "Yeah, I see they just closed those truck trailers doors. I saw inside yesterday. They had hundreds of bodies in there. That is downright spooky."

"Yes, it is, but that has just started. In that Twin Towers side of the jail," Craig pointed across the street, "much of one of those towers is nothing but sick prisoners. Close to fifteen hundred of them. It's so bad they got the medical students from USC to come in to help treat prisoners. And they have a couple of hundred sick deputies, too."

"Jeesh!"

Major Sands had seen them drive up. He exited the side door of the lab vehicle, leaning back in to say something to somebody inside. He slung a large laptop sized olive drab case over his shoulder. He put on his ACU hat and trotted quickly to the Suburban. Sands was trim and handsome, but more than a half-foot shorter than Marty Craig. Marty had, of course, met Geof's lovely wife since most of their Reserve unit came from the Georgia area. Together Mr. & Mrs. Sands looked like a perfect, beautiful, soap-opera couple. In uniform, Major Geof Sands was a perfect recruiting poster for a Military Intelligence Corps officer, albeit small-sized.

Geof got in the rear seat and set the SatComm case on the seat, buckling in to the rear passenger seat behind Ali.

"What's up?" Sands asked. "I had to pull out of a couple of meetings."

"Really no idea," Craig said. "Karen called and said she needed you, me and the secure Iridium unit ASAP. She refused to talk on the phone. She was pretty clear with her 'drop everything' order though."

"That is downright weird. With all due respect, that is." Sands opened the case on the seat and handed the plug-in end of a charging wire to the front seat. "Plug this in the dash. If Captain Llewellyn-Craig needs to use our secure comms, we need to make sure its fully charged up."

Thousand Oaks Defense Pharmaceutical Plant (TODPP)
Thousand Oaks, California
10:30 PM PDT August 5th

The four Army officers sat on either side of the small conference table by the window of Karen's office. Karen took the armchair on one end of the table. Marty and Major Geoffrey Sands were on her right. Captain Robert Cameron and Major Anthony Chen on her left, their backs to the window. Karen took a deep breath, squared a file folder on the table in front of her and looked around into the four men's faces.

Karen started off with, "I'm not completely sure how to start this. But I found a paragraph in the 'Commanding Officer's Handbook' I was given that says I need to start a briefing by explaining the classification. I'll probably get this wrong, since my asking you what classification we are dealing with is one of reasons for this meeting, but let's go with what I am saying is probably Top Secret."

Karen was looking at Geof Sands when she said 'Top Secret' and she saw his eyebrows furrow.

She continued, "Something has fallen into my lap that is of obvious huge national security importance. This is way above my paygrade and mostly outside of my area of expertise. I need you gentlemen to advise me on what I should do. It gets quite complicated."

Karen opened the file folder and set a computer-printed picture on the table so each man could see it. It was a head-and-shoulders portrait of an attractive East Asian woman. She explained, "This is a picture I got off the internet of Doctor Zhao Xiang, who goes by the English nickname Joan. I'll use Joan when I speak of her as she is a personal acquaintance of mine. Joan is an official with the People's Republic of China's Health Ministry. Specifically, she is director of their VLP vaccine production program and she runs four vaccine plants similar to, if not identical to, this one here. Her four vaccine plants were, in fact, designed and built by HeptImun Corporation, our contractor here in Thousand Oaks."

Karen sat another picture on the table, "Just to give you an idea of Joan's status in the world and within her home country, here is another picture I pulled off the internet just now. This is a picture of Joan and her father, Ambassador Zhao Yesui, formerly the PRC's ambassador to Great Britain and currently their ambassador to the World Health Organization."

Karen again looked around the table as she said, "At precisely eight o'clock this morning I received a telephone call from Joan. The call was routed from its apparent source in China, through a Voice-Over-Internet-Protocol, VOIP, connection in Reading, England. I was told it was a secure connection, but that Joan was worried the call might be heard by, quote, the wrong people, close quote."

Karen saw every officer at the table had a dark expression on their faces.

"Joan Zhao started off by warning me that she would be speaking to me without identifying each other and she would use personal references that she and I would understand, rather than speaking directly about a subject. She asked me if I understood and I said I did.

"Joan Zhao then proceeded to use an affectatious British accent and many references to a French restaurant we had gone to together, plus culinary terms, kitchenware and various totally offhand clue words that she knew I would understand to convey what was a truly creative message to me. I have my notes of the actual message if you want to see it, but that is not important. What is important is that I was able to precisely understand her intended message."

Karen took a deep breath and said, "Joan's secret message to me was that she had been working for months on a VLP vaccine for what we now know as H7N9, Parisian Flu, and she had completed a successful VLP design and production of the vaccine. Most importantly, she wanted to send her formula and the raw materials for the vaccine to me, even though that was apparently not approved by her superiors in the Chinese government, since she warned me to keep her sending me this windfall a secret."

Marty cut in with, "Your kidding, that is unbelievable."

Tony Chen, added, "Seriously?"

Several of the men spoke at once. Karen raised her hand to silence them.

"Wait!" she said. "You haven't heard the best part." She pulled a paper out of her file. "This is a courtesy email I just received from DHL Express at LAX telling me my three-part air express shipment from China will be here in Thousand Oaks between 12 and 3 this afternoon."

Karen had to, again, shush the spontaneous outbursts of all four men. When they got quiet, she said, "So, your mission has multiple pieces. You need to tell me how to handle this highly classified information. You need to tell me who I tell about this, and how. You need to tell me how I make sure this isn't a Trojan Horse. You need to tell me how I safeguard whatever is on that DHL truck. You need to tell me how I test and verify whatever is on that DHL truck. And, if this bizarre fantasy is really true, you need to help me do what is necessary to save millions of lives with this vaccine gift Doctor Zhao Xiang wants to give us."

———

Thousand Oaks Defense Pharmaceutical Plant (TODPP)
Thousand Oaks, California
1:12 PM PDT August 5th

One of the few things that the group around Karen's table that morning had reached agreement on was that the actual contents of whatever was in the inbound DHL Express truck would probably change the answers Karen needed. They also agreed that they probably did not need any outside assistance for the delivery and probably could not properly notify any higher government office prior to the delivery sometime after lunch.

Geof Sands declared that both the call from Doctor Zhao and any result following that call should be classified as Top Secret–Sensitive Compartmented Information (TS-SCI), insomuch as it was, in its very essence, sensitive intelligence information involving a foreign official and government. Further, the subject PRC government official's life was probably and seriously at risk based on the contents of that telephone call. Geof opined that as soon as they had knowledge of what was in the shipment they had to call both Karen's commanding general and the Defense Intelligence Agency (DIA). Karen mentioned the two CIA types she had encountered who were interested in Joan. Geof and the others agreed that DIA had primary jurisdiction over this incident as it impacted an Army unit, but that the CIA would probably get involved eventually. DIA could tell whomever they wanted inside National Intelligence circles.

With Geof's guidance, Karen also decided that the people who were going to be informed about this needed to be strictly limited to those who had a firm need to know. For example, she would need the help of certain HeptImun people with the incoming shipment, but they did not need to know anything about the bizarre story behind the shipment and its source. They did need to understand that the relationship between the shipment and China was classified—highly classified. That would make working with HeptImun people awkward this afternoon.

All four of the Army officers had current, updated DOD Top Secret clearances. Karen had been told in her Ops briefing at Fort Detrick that, as a commanding officer, her clearance was also Top Secret. Since they, all five, had actual knowledge of the sensitive information, it would be up to DIA to handle the special clearance the TS-SCI information would require later on. A quick check with Ross Tanner indicated the HeptImun senior staff had all been granted contractor's Secret clearances as part of the government contracting process. As a retired Army officer and supergrade civil service employee, Ross also had proper clearance. With Geof's OK, Karen briefed Ross on most of what was going on. As her 'right hand man' the contracting officer was essential to getting things done at TODPP.

After the meeting, everyone had preparatory tasks to take care of quickly.

Tony Chen asked Sonya Hayburn questions about tests that could be done for biological contamination or hazard in a shipment and what tests would be needed to verify the quality of an incoming shipment from a plant similar to a HeptImun plant. His refusal to explain why he was asking the questions frustrated Sonya. Likewise, Rob Cameron's direction to George Marquardt for an empty room with a secure lock on it near the shipping dock was complied with, but the lack of reasons behind the request rankled George. Geof Sands' post-meeting tasks involved figuring out the correct contacts and secure communications connections he would make in DC when the situation became clear. He also had some concerns about physical security.

Both Karen and Marty quickly searched the records of the March through June process of approving the Egyptian Flu VLP vaccine to see what was involved. How could a new, unproven vaccine be made useful. Of course, if this accession was real, they would have help at every level to get any resultant vaccine approved. However, Karen needed to know the ground rules so she could explain things properly to General Harding when she called him. Of course, until the shipment arrived, Karen would not know if this bizarre Chinese connection was real or not. But she had no reason to doubt Joan's call was genuine.

Karen sincerely had cause to wonder, if Joan Zhao's 'gift' were real, what would be the pathway to save those millions of lives that would otherwise certainly be lost in the next six months to the Parisian Flu. How would they handle an unapproved, untested vaccine—at least, unapproved and untested in the American system of things. Underlying those practical questions was the core secret, could they find a way to get the vaccine into production and still protect the woman in China who might be a true hero.

Karen and Rob had made arrangements with the HeptImun managers to handle the shipment when it came into their facility. George, Kerry Weathers, and Sonya had also been told to standby for a call from Karen to assemble at that room Rob had asked for, again without explanation.

Now, precisely in the middle of the three-hour window the DHL email had given her, Karen got a call from the shipping manager that the DHL driver wanted a 'Mrs. Karen Llewellyn Craig' to come sign for a signature-only shipment. Karen called George to get his managers together, she called Tony Chen, and she went to the training room where she knew Geof, Rob and Marty were conferring.

Marty, Geof, Rob and Karen were met by Tony and Sonya on their way to the back of the building. Tony was carrying a spray bottle in his hand. Sonya had some type of flashlight. In the cavernous Shipping and Receiving bay,

George and Kerry were waiting. The HeptImun managers were surprised at the phalanx of Army officers Karen brought with her merely to sign for a shipment. George, with a frown, pointed Karen toward an open roll-up door. Outside, a large yellow and red DHL delivery truck was backed up to the loading dock. Three solid-looking wooden palletized shipping containers, each slightly smaller than a clothes washer, sat on the dock. The DHL driver had a computer tablet in his hand. Two HeptImun shipping employees with a hand-operated pallet jack and hand tools stood waiting.

Karen walked up to DHL man, who asked, "Are you, Mrs. Craig? I need ID for this shipment."

Karen showed him the DOD employee badge around her neck. After a second of hesitation, he accepted it and gave her a digital pen to sign the shipping receipt on the tablet's screen. She thanked him, took the paperwork he offered, and he left. Karen saw the shipping employees were looking at the shipping documents attached to the three boxes.

One of them pointed to Karen, "We need to compare the invoice numbers and enter the manifest info into the ledger. You know, these are air-freight from China."

Karen held on to the papers and said, "Not just yet. Move these into the room we asked for earlier."

The men looked nervously to Kerry Weathers, who motioned for them to do as Karen asked.

When they walked around the corner to the room, they found a military police sergeant from the Response Team standing guard at the door, armed with a 9mm pistol in a holster. He came to attention, but did not salute as Karen entered the room.

It took three trips with the pallet jack to get the crates into the room. When they were finished, the employee with the hand tools asked Karen, "You want me to do the inventory and open them?"

"Just a second," Karen said as she turned to Tony and Sonya, motioning them toward the crates. Both Tony and Sonya put on colored goggles and rubber gloves. They circled each crate in turn, with Tony spraying a mist of what seemed to be blue-green liquid on the crates and Sonya holding a light wand with a telltale purplish/blue haze of ultra-violet light above where Tony sprayed.

When they finished the last crate, Tony told Karen, "They are clean—no bio-hazard."

Now Karen motioned to Geof. He faced both the shipping employees and the three HeptImun managers and said "Before we do this, all of you need to understand that this is a federal government facility. This shipment and what is in these containers is highly classified. At least Top Secret, maybe compartmentalized higher than that. None of you are to talk about this with any other employee, except as needed for government work. Nobody is to tell anyone including your spouse about what happened today at work. You do not tell anyone outside this room. This shipment and any connection to China is Top Secret. Got it?"

Geof and Karen looked in turn to all five HeptImun employees. They each nodded their understanding.

As an afterthought, Karen said to the man who has spoken to her, "Don't put these in your regular shipping ledger. Talk to Ross Tanner about how to handle classified property receipts. Open them up!"

When the first lid was unbolted and loosened, Karen said, "Leave the lid on. Open the others."

The workers followed directions.

When all three lids were loose, Karen said to the men, "OK, that's good. Thank you. You can leave. Remember what Major Sands said about classified information."

The men looked sideways at Weathers, who again motioned for them to obey Karen.

"Close the door on your way out," Karen ordered.

When the men had gone, Karen walked to the boxes and said, "Let's see what we've got."

Everyone stepped forward to see. Tony and Rob lifted the top off the first crate. They saw a cardboard bankers' box of documents on top surrounded by plastic peanut packing material.

Karen asked, "What's in the document box?"

Tony lifted the box out. Everyone gathered closer.

Tony sat the bankers' box on the corner of the crate and opened the box. He read a few of the stack of papers and said, "Sonya, come look."

Sonya took a stack of papers. She shook her head in amazement. Then she reached for another, and said, "These are standard HeptImun quality control report documents, the same forms our people are trained to use to test product coming up from the Camarillo plant or shipped in from Schaumberg or Raleigh. Only the handwriting is mostly in Chinese, but some is English. We got reports just like this, on these same forms, only in English, when North Carolina sent us the first Egyptian Flu VLP to start production. This is someone telling us a VLP, and raw vaccine shipment passed a HeptImun home plant quality control. What on Earth?"

Karen motioned to the crate, "What else?"

With the lid of the bankers' box and with Rob's help, Tony scooped the peanuts out on the floor. They looked down into the crate.

Kerry Weathers announced, "That's a HeptImun shipping container for vaccine packaged for distribution. That size is probably the 10,000-dose container. We use it to transship to other HeptImun facilities and warehouses. From this, the vaccine will be packaged for distribution."

"Tony, what does it say?" Karen asked. Everyone could see the container was labeled in Chinese.

Tony pushed more plastic peanuts from the lid of the interior container and read slowly, "My Mandarin is out of practice, but I read that as 'Ten thousand doses – H7N9 – monovalent – 10 ml/10 dose vials, Do not freeze. Temperature range 5 to 37 Centigrade.'"

The HeptImun managers looked shocked. Karen pursed her lips and said, "Next crate."

The second crate was packed with pre-shaped polystyrene foam panels that fit precisely over cube-like gray metal cases, hinged at the back and with a clasp on the front sealed with a thin wire and lead seal.

Karen looked at Kerry Weathers, "Kerry?"

Kerry smiled at Karen, "Captain Llewellyn, I'm guessing you already know what those are. Those are the standard HeptImun transshipment containers we use for cell-based virus-like particle transport."

"Cell-based, not plant-based?" Karen seemed surprised.

"That's right. I can tell by the size. Plant-based VLPs are shipped in 3-liter containers. That plant-based VLP is powder-like, so it's lighter. The cell-based VLP with the bacterial culture is liquid, so it comes in a smaller container, but is the same weight. Each one of those can stock fifty of the bacteria production kettles, which take about 48 hours to complete, and each one of those kettles produces another container of raw VLP mulch. Those can be used to make new VLP stock or purified and filtered to produce raw vaccine. The twelve VLP containers in this box would supply one of our cell-based production lines to get started. This would have our entire cell-based factory lines in Camarillo, the ones we have inactive now while we work on the plant-based side, up to production level in about a week."

George Marquardt blurted out, "Karen, is this for real? How in the living hell did you . . ."

"Let's see what's in the last box," Karen said, ignoring George.

Tony Chen and Rob lifted the lid off of the last crate. It again had form-fitting packing. Below the packing layer was a six by six pattern of metal cylinders, the size of large soda bottles. The crate looked like three layers deep, or 108 flasks. Tony lifted one cylinder out of the box. They could see the HeptImun logo on the side. By the way Tony held it, they could see it was full. Karen looked to Kerry.

Kerry nodded, "Those are raw vaccine, concentrated. After initial filtering and purification of the VLP sludge, we use those to transport the raw vaccine to the final stage where is it mixed with adjuvants, preservatives, other strain vaccines, and inactive ingredients, you know, filler; then, it's pasteurized, sampled, tested and packaged in vials. In these crates, you have the raw materials of HeptImun's entire cell-based VLP vaccine factory process."

George tried again, "Is this really H7N9 Parisian Flu vaccine?"

"That's what we are going to find out," Karen said. She pointed to the three crates, "Sonya and Kerry, take one sample of each of these, raw vaccine, VLP and end product. I want them tested every which way you can. Make sure what we have here. Make sure it's pure, no contamination. Tony, get one of the raw VLP containers back to the Biosafety and VLP lab. Get the VLP experts to work on it. I need answers tonight. Make sure this VLP is a good H7N9 clone. At the same time, start antigen testing to make sure it's acting as influenza VLP should. Everybody who works on this should be given the same classification talk Geof gave. This cannot get out—lives are at stake. And, for you HeptImun people, that includes, for now, your superiors at HeptImun. You DO NOT tell anyone at HeptImun about this until I get permission from my superiors to do that. Understand? This does not go beyond the walls of this building unless I say otherwise. Tony and Geof, make sure the HeptImun VLP people know that, too."

"That's not possible. We . . ." George's objection was cut off by Karen.

"George, when we get back together shortly, I'll explain what's going on. Well, maybe part of what is going on. There is a good reason for me ordering that. That is not negotiable. That is an order." She stared at him until he nodded.

"Once all of you get your people working on the assignments I gave you, meet me back in my conference room. I'll give you a call about when to meet."

As an afterthought, Karen added, "And George, everyone is probably going to need lots of those box lunches and drinks for a late night. Nobody goes home until I get some answers."

George, Kerry, and Sonya stood together, figuring out who would do what. Tony Chen took one of the VLP cubes with him and left.

Karen thought for a moment, and then pulled her cellphone out of her pocket and took several pictures of each crate, as well as the contents of the bankers' box, including close-ups of the labels on the containers.

Karen turned to Marty, raised her eyebrows in her usual expression when perplexed, "We probably need to bring the document box with us?"

"Got it," Geof announced.

Geof took the box and stopped a moment to give the MP at the door some orders. The three officers walked with Karen up the main, central hallway back toward her office.

None of the four said anything, until Karen finally said, "Wow!"

Marty replied, "Wow, indeed."

"What do I do first?" Karen asked, somewhat rhetorically.

"I don't think you have any choice," Marty said. "You're a military commander. Your first duty is to make sure your superior officer knows what you know. Then Geof needs to get the spooks involved. That Iridium phone we couldn't figure out why you wanted is going to get a workout this afternoon."

———

Chapter 45

General's Quarters
Family Housing Area
Fort Detrick, Maryland
5:04 PM EDT August 5th

Tom Harding got out of his Buick Enclave. The ride home from work was short, but he still had his usual spasm in his back when he stood up after sitting. He was not getting any younger. He was in his Class A uniform, having met today with a group of Congresspersons concerned with the Parisian Flu and the Army Medical commands' actions in the crisis. Since the higher medical headquarters were in Texas, Harding's command, a short drive from the Capitol, was often the scapegoat for briefing DC VIPs on Army medical matters. Harding took his uniform jacket, briefcase, hat, and cellphone from the rear seat and headed inside. His wife would probably have the family dinner started. Their three college-age children were still in town for summer break from college.

His cellphone rang when he was halfway to the front door of the expansive, white-columned General's Quarters at Fort Detrick. The throbbing ringtone indicated it was one of his subordinate commanders or his staff calling him. Sarah Morton had set up his cellphone with different rings to tell him who was calling. Sarah was a great adjutant.

Harding pressed his thumb to the sensor and looked at the caller's name, "This is General Harding."

"Yes, General, this is Captain Morales, your watch duty officer."

"Yes."

"We have an incoming secure SatComm communication for you, Sir."

"From whom?"

"It is Major Geoffrey Sands, the S-2 of USAMRIID Response Team Three. He says he is calling on behalf of the Commanding Officer of Thousand Oaks Defense Pharmaceutical Plant. They have immediate importance, highly classified, sensitive compartmented information for your personal eyes only."

"What the fuck? SCI from a vaccine plant?"

"General, will you be coming back here or taking the call at your residence? I have them on the secure line now and need to give them the right number to call you."

Harding answered, "Fine, tell them to call me back on my residence Iridium number. Have them give me five minutes to get inside and get the phone unlocked and running."

"Yes sir."

Harding dropped his uniform jacket and hat on the table by the front door. His wife came out of the dining room and started to say something. Harding brusquely waved her away, told her, "Not now. You and the kids go ahead and eat. Something came up," and headed into the den. He slid the heavy oak door closed in his wife's face.

Harding moved the family picture frame behind his desk off the wall and entered the combination for the large wall safe. He moved several folders of documents over and removed a case the size of a laptop from the safe.

He set the Iridium secure phone up on his desk and plugged the charging cord into the outlet on his desk lamp. He sat in his chair with the phone handset in front of him and waited, wondering whether he had time to get some iced tea from this wife. He did not.

He picked up the handset, depressed the answer button, and said, "This is Major General Thomas Harding, this is a secure line. Who is speaking?"

"This is Captain Karen Llewellyn-Craig."

"Good afternoon, Captain."

"Good afternoon, sir. I'm sorry to bother you. I know it's after hours there. But, something enormously important has happened here. I need to brief you on it."

"And, it needs to be done right now via secure phone?"

"Yes sir. I think it does. And, I expect it may take some time. Maybe ten to fifteen minutes with the questions you're probably going to have. And sir, I believe we should consider this to be Top Secret–Sensitive Compartmented Information. That is why it needs to be secure communications, sir."

Harding shook his head, amazed at what he was hearing, "Highly classified information about a vaccine plant?"

"Yes sir, that is what we have. And, sir, I have my senior officers here in my office with me. I'd like to put them on speaker phone so they can hear any questions you might have that they can answer better I can."

"Certainly, but have them identify themselves and give me a moment so I can get something to take notes first." From experience, Harding knew he would want notes on this call. So he pulled out a leather portfolio with a pen.

The general gave the go ahead and Marty Craig, Tony Chen, Geof Sands and Rob Cameron all identified themselves by name, rank and duty position.

"OK, Captain. Go ahead. What have you got?"

"Yes, General, something has occurred here that is enormously important to our country and the world, and it involves a foreign country and, frankly, matters of national security way above my pay grade. I need to explain things to you and get your direction on what to do."

"Very well, Captain, proceed."

Captain Llewellyn-Craig told Harding about Dr. Xiang 'Joan' Zhao, her position in the Chinese Health Ministry, and the details of the call that morning from China via England. She explained about the crates that had arrived and the potential importance of this to the Parisian Flu crisis. Harding had several questions, to which the Captain gave direct, knowledgeable answers.

As she finished, Captain Llewellyn-Craig added, "Oh, and General, when I was there at Fort Detrick, I met with two CIA types who were interested in my meeting with Joan Zhao. I promised to contact them if I had any further contact from her. So, she is on someone's intel radar screen. I discussed that with Major Sands and he says that since this directly involves an active duty U.S. Army facility, the DIA has primary jurisdiction, even though CIA seems to have an ongoing interest."

"I would agree with that."

"Yes sir. Major Sands, with your approval will be contacting DIA after we finish with you."

"Good idea. I will probably be talking to them, too, after I speak with my Ops and S-2 Chief. And my people will definitely be calling you back, too."

"Yes sir, we assumed as much. And anyone needing to call us should use the Iridium number for USAMRIID Response Team Three. Toe-Dip does not have a secure phone."

"Toe-dip?"

"Uh sir, yes, my plant, T-O-D-P-P."

"Ah, yes. Gotta love a new acronym." Harding summarized his thoughts verbally, "So, Karen, absent contrary information, we should assume this is legit. And, assuming so, this could save millions of lives in the next six months. You're damned right; this is important, possibly as important as anything could be right now. On a separate platter, the woman who helped us out deserves to be protected. It is really her who is saving those lives, and we can't give the Chinese hierarchy anything that would bring harm to her. The Chinese government cannot be trusted, never could. What they did with coronavirus, keeping stuff secret and hiding the truth for so long, remains, in my mind, a crime against humanity. And the fact that they are still up to those old tricks, they seem to have a cure right now, a vaccine for this H7N9, while it's ravaging our country, France and the rest of the world is equally despicable.

"The fact that this vaccine came to us through a backdoor, instead of direct from the Chinese government to our country's leadership, speaks volumes about the Chinese government sleaze taking place here."

Harding took a moment to think, "I see us having two problems here. Your primary mission is clear. You're our expert at getting this possible godsend of a vaccine to our people. You need to proceed to make that happen. We may need to do some subterfuge of our own about how we came to get this vaccine ready so soon. I'll get you some expert help on that as soon as I can. On a second track, we need to protect Dr. Zhao's confidence. For now, I agree with your action to keep the China-connection classified. In fact, let's assume that the fact this vaccine came from China is classified as Top Secret SCI and NOFORN. That is, a matter of the highest national security and information to keep away from any foreign individual or government. It cannot be discussed outside of official channels, the highest official channels. You're right that the corporate types at HeptImun, other than your local people, don't need to know. Consider that an order from me. Until DNI assumes control of this information and compartment, my office will strictly control access to this information

"I want you, right now, tonight, to take measures to strip and segregate the physical evidence we have of anything relating to China. Get the Chinese labels off of everything. Switch to our containers—uniquely marked so they can be identified. Lock that box of documents up. Nobody else sees it. I'll get you some security help ASAP.

"Also, immediately get the process started to make sure we are right about the new vaccine and get it in production. That cannot wait. Until we think of something different, just go with the story that you and your team created this new VLP vaccine."

Karen cut in, "But, sir, the vaccine is not approved. We do not have FDA clearance to put it into production. Testing and release of a new vaccine still take time. It's highly regulated."

"You can't expect government regulations to guide you in an event unique in human history. You need to do what is right for humanity. That is what you're ordered to do. Besides, you and I have a friend at the top of the food chain, above FDA, who can clear the way for us."

"Uh, sir, I'm not sure what you mean there." Karen sounded uncertain.

Harding gave a little laugh, "Well, Captain, I guess you have been too busy today to watch the national news. That fiasco at the White House that caused the Cabinet to catch this Parisian Flu crap had its first casualties today. Seven Cabinet members are sick with the flu, but they lost the Budget Director and the Secretary of Health and Human Services today. Both dead. An acquaintance of yours and an old military medical colleague of mine from the Ebola days, Stephen Royce, was named, by the President, as Acting Secretary of HHS this afternoon. A call to Steve will be one of my first things to do after I get off this call. I'm sure he will agree on the priority of saving lives, not following regulations."

Harding finished with, "Expect some visitors from DC tomorrow morning. Are you clear on your marching orders, Captain?"

Karen answered Harding, "Yes sir."

———

Thousand Oaks Defense Pharmaceutical Plant (TODPP)
Thousand Oaks, California
10:05 PM PDT August 5th

"I wanted to get together before we call it a night. I've talked to each of you, and it seems we have accomplished all we can tonight." Karen looked around the group assembled in the conference room. "Let's just go around the room and do a quick recap on what we've accomplished, so everybody is on the same sheet of music. It looks like we will have some visitors tomorrow. I don't know who just yet. Tony?"

Tony Chen motioned to a woman sitting next to him, "For those who have not met her, this is Marissa Connors, the team leader for the VLP research group from HeptImun. Marissa and her people have confirmed that the H7N9 VLP appears to be remarkable. I don't want to get too technical here, but the first reports are that the genetic copies in this VLP are even more complete than in the successful H5N1 VLP we are currently producing. In short, at first look, the Parisian VLP looks like the real thing. Antigen testing will take some time."

Sonya sat next to Marissa, so she went next, "We ran full QA on the vaccine vials, as though it was our own product. It passed every test: purity, formulation, packaging, everything meets our production standards. We have an accurate assay of its contents, its exact formulation, and it is easily reproducible. Those vials of vaccine meet American medical standards. And, although the outside packaging container was marked in Chinese, the interior packaging on each vial and the ten vial boxes are printed to WHO standards. That is, it meets HeptImun shipment standards, you know, multi-language but primarily French/English, so there is no way to tell it's Chinese. There is no 'Made in China' anywhere. Whoever did this followed the HeptImun factory manual. Kerry?"

Kerry Weathers shrugged, "Same goes for the raw vaccine and the VLP sludge. It looks just like what we would expect. We don't have our cell-based line in operation yet, but we have done run-up testing using Sanofi's Perth strain cell-based raw product, and this seems to be fully in line with expectations. And, as per instructions, all of the Chinese containers have been replaced by our own HeptImun containers for both raw vaccine and

VLP sludge. The packaged vaccine product and materials are now in plain HeptImun logo boxes, all marked as 'QA Lot 29.' The Chinese printed stuff was turned over to Ross."

Karen turned to face Ross Tanner, who said, "My little part of this conspiracy is that the box of Chinese documents and all shipping documents and containers indicating Chinese origin are now in an 'undisclosed location' marked as Top Secret NOFORN in accordance with General Harding's instructions. All personnel who are aware of the Chinese connection have been given and have signed written warnings per 18 U.S. Code § 798 that disclosure of that knowledge to anyone is a crime."

Karen turned to George Marquardt, "Do you have anything for us, George?"

George shook his head, "I have nothing to add except to confirm that all HeptImun people are aware of the disclosure rules, both my·staff and Marissa's crew. I'd like to return to that issue in the future, but for now, we are good with only local HeptImun employees being in the loop. Even if it's a somewhat uninformed loop. You military types obviously know more than we civilians know."

"I understand," Karen said. "I'm sure we will get more guidance on that from up above. Probably rather quickly. Rest assured that there is a critical reason for this classification. And the reason behind the classification is classified, too. Isn't red tape marvelous?

Karen stood up and looked around the table, "So, everybody, good work tonight. See you all tomorrow morning. Early tomorrow morning, as I am sure there will be people back East unwilling to deal with the three-hour time difference."

———

Chapter 46

Camino De La Mimosa
Camarillo, California
5:05 AM PDT August 6ᵗʰ

The cellphone buzzed and vibrated on the nightstand. Karen groggily flopped her hand out of bed to find it.

"Hello?"

"Captain Craig?"

"Yes."

"Are you awake ma'am? I'll give you a few seconds to wake up."

Karen swung her feet out of bed and stretched, "It's OK; I'm awake."

"Yes ma'am. This is Major Sarah Morton, General Harding's adjutant. Good morning."

"Yes, good morning.

"Ma'am, I realize it's very early there. But, I figured you would want a head's up as soon as possible, but I gave you a couple of extra hours to sleep. We also called on your Iridium line and talked to Major Sands, giving him this information, too. I just got back to Fort Detrick from putting General Harding on an Air Force C-40B jet at Joint Base Andrews. They were wheels up right at 6 o'clock our time. Their ETA at Naval Base Ventura County is around 0830 hours your local time."

"General Harding is coming out here?"

"Yes ma'am. After he and Acting Secretary Royce talked, and then conferred with Royce's attorney and the people at DIA, they decided they wanted to be there for a full briefing and make their decision in person after talking to you and your staff. I understand Secretary Royce also contacted the White House. I'm supposed to make arrangements with you for the transport of the Acting Secretary, his agency counsel, the general, Colonel Kessler from USAMRIID, a brigadier general from DIA, and seven other staff people. That's twelve persons for transport from the airfield at Naval Base Ventura to your location. That's apparently fairly close to you."

"Yes, it is."

"And, the general asked you to be ready to fully brief everyone on the same issues you spoke to him about last night, plus whatever you have found out since then."

"I understand. What else?"

"Colonel Kessler wants Lieutenant Colonel Craig, his response team commander, at the briefing, too. Can you get word to him?"

"Yes, he is right here."

"Hmm, that's handy, huh? Do you have any more questions, ma'am?"

Karen thought a moment, "Yes, what uniform is the general wearing?"

Karen heard Sarah Morton give a light chuckle. "Both General Harding and Colonel Kessler, plus the two from DIA are all in short-sleeved service uniform with the bi-swing jacket. The secretary was in a blue HHS logo jacket with a polo shirt, sorta casual. Good question, ma'am. I remember our first meeting when you were just getting your first taste of Army protocol. You're learning."

"Yes, I am. Thank you for the head's up call, Major.

Karen set the cellphone on the nightstand.

From behind her in bed, she heard Marty say, "Did I hear that right?"

"Yes, you did. Time to get up. You need to get someone down to the LA Jail and get the little passenger bus back. I need it here for VIP transport at eight-thirty. And you need to switch to your summer service uniform. The brass who are coming will be in theirs for the briefing, and your attendance is requested . . . no required. Oh, and the acting secretary of Health and Human Services is coming, too. It's showtime in Thousand Oaks."

"Damn, I was hoping we'd have some time together this morning."

"We will, in uniform. Get up."

———

Training/Ops Room
Thousand Oaks Defense Pharmaceutical Plant (TODPP)
Thousand Oaks, California
10:25 AM PDT August 6th

When Karen had thought about twelve VIPs coming from DC plus her people that she would need to help with a briefing, it had become clear that the conference room near her office was too small. She decided to use the training room for the briefing Harding had requested. That would also give them a good, big screen for any PowerPoint slides or pictures that needed to be shown. When Tony, Sonya, and the others arrived that morning, she told them to be ready with their best executive briefing on their areas of expertise. George had been forewarned that the VIP group from DC had been on the plane all morning so they would probably be hungry, and their internal clock said it was lunchtime, not breakfast.

As promised by General Harding, one of the people coming in from DC turned out to be a female U.S. Navy officer from DIA, Lieutenant Maris DeLoit, who introduced herself and took charge of handling the classified aspect of the briefing. After consulting with Karen and Geof Sands, Lieutenant DeLoit separated those with need to know the intimate details of the China connection from those who were needed to brief the VIPs on a particular area of expertise. Thus, the division between military and HeptImun remained with Karen's military staff sitting in on the full briefing, while the key Heptimun personnel were asked to wait in the conference room until needed. The people not invited into the main briefing were, nevertheless, given instructions about not mentioning the Chinese origins of the shipment.

DeLoit started off the briefing in the TODPP training/ops room with a classification warning to all of the VIPs and military present, explaining that there were certain parts of the briefing that would be of the highest Top Secret–Sensitive Compartmented Information due to classified sources and danger to unnamed personnel. She announced that the Director of National Intelligence (DNI) had designated the appellation 'LOTUS' for the sensitive compartmentment information involved in the current matter. Hereafter, the classification would be known as TOP SECRET—LOTUS. She explained that only those who either already had actual knowledge or who had a defined need to know would be allowed to have access to the entire briefing, or any sub-element or subset of this information. Then, true to her word and her duties, Lieutenant DeLoit left the room, as she, herself, had no reason to know the details of the most sensitive information, which Karen and her officers knew involved Zhao Xiang, her bizarre phone call and its aftermath.

Now, nearly an hour later they were ending the briefing. Karen had led off with her report on her background with Doctor Zhao and the cryptic phone call. Karen had showed the background photos of Joan, including the one with her diplomat father in London. A staff officer from DIA followed Karen with a more detailed report on Zhao Xiang. Karen was interested to note that the DIA report on Zhao Xiang included a photograph of Karen, Jared Bentley and Doctor Zhao at the French restaurant in Maryland. The two CIA guys had used a secret camera.

Kerry Weathers was then called into the room and reminded of the classification issue, as each HeptImun employee was, in their turn. Kerry gave a complete report of what had arrived in the shipment, and he included the cellphone photos of the crate contents that Karen had thought to take. Kerry explained what each component in the shipment was for.

George Marquardt had come in next and reported that they had already put one of the raw material containers of H7N9 VLP sludge into their cell-based VLP production lines in the Camarillo factory the previous evening. It appeared to be proceeding just as designed, and they should have the first home-grown batch of H7N9 VLP in about thirty hours. A flask of the raw vaccine was being processed into the finished vaccine product for testing as he spoke. They had analyzed the components of the finished vaccine from the shipment to get a recipe for adjuvant, preservative, inactive ingredients to come up with a match of the original Chinese version of the H7N9 vaccine.

When George had mentioned "Chinese vaccine" he was reminded by a DIA officer to call it the 'Reference Vaccine.' Nobody was to use the word 'Chinese' in regards to the shipment or its contents, in any mention that was not Top Secret SCI. George had not been in the room for the really sensitive information about Zhao Xiang, but this reminder made sense to him.

George continued his part of the briefing, that each of the 108 flasks of the raw, concentrated 'Reference' vaccine could produce about 10,000 doses of finished vaccine, or just over a million doses total. Marquardt gave an estimated schedule of when the TODPP factory could be up to full production of the Parisian Flu vaccine. A few weeks. The other plants in Illinois and North Carolina, slightly longer.

Major Chen started the scientific briefing, but his part was just an introduction before Sonya Hayburn and Marissa Connors were invited into the room. They gave a presentation consistent with their corporate backgrounds. They gave the acting secretary and the generals a complete PowerPoint presentation on the history and science of virus-like particles and the recent success of creating a vaccine for the Egyptian Flu by the North Carolina plant and CDC. It seemed like Marissa had previously prepared her flashy PowerPoint VLP presentation for some other use at HeptImun. Sonya finished with a quality control report card on what she had found in the 'Reference' shipment. She got the new name right. They did a full gas-chromatograph of the contents, there are no unexpected additive chemicals, that is, no Trojan Horses in the mixture. All components and the finished vaccines were top quality and something their plant in California would be proud to have produced.

After Sonya finished, Sonya and Marissa left.

Karen stood up and moved to the front of the room, "Mr. Secretary, General Harding, General Hollister, that's the core of our briefing. We are ready to answer any questions you or your staff might have, or discuss any input you or they might have to add to the discussion."

The Army brigadier general named Hollister, who had been introduced as being a deputy director at the Defense Intelligence Agency, cleared his throat and stood up. Karen had noticed him getting a note from his assistant and working on his laptop all through the scientific briefing.

Hollister turned to look at Harding and Royce, "I need to point out that while we have been sitting here, there has been some very disturbing news starting to dribble out of China. There are first news reports and a flash report from our Defense Attache in Beijing that the Parisian Flu has hit several members of the ruling political elite in Beijing. The Chinese president and premier both seem to be in the hospital, and the heads of two ministries, both very important in a crisis such as this, Defense and Health, are reported as deceased. There are also reports of a massive vaccine program in progress and some sort of high-level controversy regarding the vaccine. That information obviously leads to the obvious question. Why would this Doctor Zhao, who works for the Health Ministry, have sent this goldmine to Captain Llewellyn-Craig when her own ministry was in dire need of protection from this flu virus that's just now hitting major Chinese cities?"

Everyone was silent. Karen turned to look at Royce and Harding.

At last, Stephen Royce spoke, "That's an excellent question, General Hollister. But it's obviously a question far beyond our ability to figure out with limited information. However, it may be a sound reinforcement of our need to keep the connection with China out of the equation of what we do with the vaccine we have been handed. The answer to your question may simply be that Doctor Zhao takes care of her friends, like Captain Llewellyn-Craig, before she takes care of the communist leadership. Or, it could be much more complicated in the secretive labyrinth of Chinese political intrigue. Those national security issues will need to be looked at, as we are able to look at this whole thing deeper. What we are here for today is to help me and General Harding decide how we save as many American lives as we can as fast as we can. Those are my orders from the President. Yes, someone needs to get a handle on this geopolitically and figure out what happened to the Chinese Politburo. My job is to deal with thousands of Americans dying of this disease, probably millions dying. That Chinese geopolitical national security issue does not change my problem. Saving American lives is the paramount national security issue."

The civilian executive from the Food and Drug Administration now stood up. "Mr. Secretary, on your point there, it is probably obvious to all, given the horrific death toll we have and will have from Parisian Flu, in every quadrant of the country, that we need to get a program approved to get this vaccine on the street as soon as possible. You have Secretarial Authority to direct FDA to issue an emergency use authorization for the use of the vaccine. But, it would be foolhardy, and frankly illegal, to set a massive release of an untested vaccine in motion without some level of testing. Now, the Egyptian Flu testing took the better part of six months, which we don't have. What we need is an immediate, large scale test of both safety and efficacy. The quicker, the better. The question is how and where."

"I think I have an answer to that." Karen was surprised when Marty stepped forward from where he had been leaning on the back wall of the room.

He had not been introduced as one of the briefing participants, although he had been allowed to stay in the room.

"And you are?" Royce asked.

Colonel Hal Kessler spoke up, "This is Lieutenant Colonel Martin Craig, USAMRIID's Response Team officer-in-charge, who did the great job in Santa Barbara that we talked about on the flight from DC."

Royce nodded, "Proceed, Colonel."

Marty took another step forward and continued, "Yes sir. My team is currently deployed at the Los Angeles County Jail, trying to help them with a massive outbreak of the Parisian Flu within their facility. They had almost 10,000 prisoners when this started. They are nearing a thousand dead, and have another 2000 sick and being treated. But they still have around 5,000 adult male prisoners who are theoretically flu-free, still locked up, and in danger of catching this flu.

"They are all in one place, controlled population, and we are already putting them under a testing regime and administering the Egyptian Flu vaccine. You have 10,000 doses of the Parisian Flu vaccine in the shipment. If you give my team half of the vaccine in the shipment, I can have a full-scale efficacy and safety test underway by late afternoon today. It will not be a double-blind study, because giving a prisoner a placebo when he is in an influenza death trap like that jail would be unthinkable. But, you would have your field testing done and antigen reaction tests from thousands of men rolling in after maybe a week's time.

"In that week, Karen . . . Captain Llewellyn-Craig can have your first vaccine ready to distribute to America and more raw VLP material ready to send to the other defense pharmaceutical plants and any commercial vaccine producer who can make use of it. You can be producing millions of doses of the Parisian Flu vaccine in a few weeks with full testing."

Secretary Royce looked at the guy from FDA, "Does that do what FDA needs?"

The FDA representative said, "Yes sir. A good idea."

Secretary Royce turned to General Harding and raised his eyebrows.

Harding nodded and turned to Marty Craig, "Lieutenant Colonel Craig, you need to get back downtown. You have work to do at the jail."

Harding turned to Karen, "And Captain Llewellyn-Craig, you need to give Mr. Marquardt a contract change order to cover those millions of doses of vaccine we need."

—

Chapter 47

Centre de Protection Infantile Saint-Saëns
Paris, France
11:14 AM Local Time August 18th

Inspector Michel Dormer opened the passenger door on the Renault sedan. His wife of twelve years, Bernice Dormer, took his hand and got out. After she stretched to stand up, she rubbed her sore upper arm. It still hurt from the two vaccinations they had gotten earlier from Michel's employer.

Bernice looked at the building, then to her husband. She asked him, "You're still sure about this?"

Michel smiled and nodded, "As long as you agree."

Bernice smiled back, "Of course, I agree. How could I not? I thought we would be waiting years for this chance. I don't believe you have been able to cut through the bureaucracy."

"I know some people; I'm part of the bureaucracy. The magistrate read my report and inserted my name into the temporary orders he issued when I asked him. He knows me. And this was a unique case, too."

Michel held open the front door of the children's center for Bernice to enter. After a short wait, the social worker Michel had talked to on the phone took them upstairs. At the far end of a hallway with many doors, many youngsters at play, and many caregivers at work, the social worker turned into a room. Each corner of the room had a crib in it. The social worker pointed to the crib in the far corner, by the window.

Bernice and Michel Dormer walked over and looked into the crib. A beatific smile from a baby girl greeted them. She was still very thin and fragile for her age, six months. But her smile was wide, and those piercing deep-brown eyes were the same ones that Inspector Dormer had been entranced by as she lay there on that filthy raincoat in that horrible apartment. Michel Dormer had fallen in love.

Bernice Dormer bent to pick up the baby. The baby cooed and reached to touch Bernice's face.

"What's her name?" Bernice asked.

"She doesn't have one," the social worker explained.

Michel gave the full explanation, "I never found any paperwork on her. She had been born there in that flat. Her Kurdish refugee parents had never filed her birth documents. There was no evidence anywhere of her name. The medical examiner decided the woman, the dead woman in bed nearby, was her mother. So, she has nobody . . . had nobody, that is."

Michel reached with his finger to twirl a ringlet of the baby's curly black hair. He said, "I thought we could name her Marguerite."

Bernice looked at her husband and smiled. She understood.

——

Main Lobby
Thousand Oaks Defense Pharmaceutical Plant (TODPP)
Thousand Oaks, California
2:05 PM PDT August 19th

Everyone was in the lobby saying good-bye after Shaysee O'Neil's third visit to this plant and her fifth to the local area this year. The television crew accompanying Shaysee this time was bigger than her earlier visits. This time she had a senior producer, two technicians and several writers with her to produce a full-hour special on the breaking news about the new vaccine against the Parisian Flu. It would be broadcast in primetime this evening. It was a big break for Shaysee's career. In fact, as she thought about it, the two avian flu pandemics this year had lifted Shaysee O'Neil to prominence at the network. She expected an offer of an anchor position.

Shaysee shook hands with Marissa Connors, PhD. The vivacious corporate scientist with her ready-made graphics had contributed much to the network's news story. With Marissa's sidekick, Sonya, the two young women made a photogenic, woman-powered-science narrative for Shaysee's report. Their boss, Karen Llewellyn-Craig, simply rounded out that feminine narrative. Shaysee also gave a quick handshake to the other staff at TODPP. Social distancing rules had retreated somewhat with the news of the vaccine putting an end to the pandemic.

Finally, Shaysee faced Captain Karen Llewellyn-Craig. Shaysee had made sure the network got the captain's name right on the onscreen graphic this time. With this being Shaysee's fourth report involving Karen this year, she was getting to know her as a friend. But, there was one thing still unresolved between them. Shaysee decided to make one more try with Karen as she said good-bye.

"Well, Captain, it has certainly been interesting working with you. This has been an amazing year for both of us," Shaysee said.

"Yes, it has. I remember those first reports of yours from Cairo," Karen said with a smile.

"Yes ma'am. I'm getting much better at my journalistic duties. And, I can tell an evasive answer when I see it."

"Oh really. What do you mean?" Karen had a reasonably decent poker face.

"I can read all of the Department of Defense press releases and background stories expounding on how you published your graduate thesis on H7N9 genetics way back in 2013 and how Doctor Marissa Connors is an acknowledged industry leader in virus-like particles and has been somewhat famous for that for years. All that serendipitous background leads to this great vaccine advance. But the fact remains that your team seemingly came up with the solution to this worldwide H7N9 pandemic almost overnight. I was here the last week of July, and you gave me your beautiful, hopeful speech about how you would strive to complete your work in six months or maybe less. And now, I'm back, three weeks later, and I'm doing a story on how you finished everything in those three weeks. Millions of lives will be saved, as if by magic. The world is singing praises of the fantastic effort, but it's too good to be true. Isn't it?"

Karen shook her head, "No, Shaysee, we just had a stroke of fantastic luck, and we had the faith of Secretary Royce in us to allow us to move forward, and the hard work of many people coalesced into a fantastic breakthrough. And, the Army Medical Department requested the Department of Defense Public Affairs Office arrange for your network to send you here to tell our story. Nothing evasive at all. We are doing our best to be transparent, at every level."

Shaysee smiled and shook her head, "So, you're sticking with that story?"

Karen smiled back, "Yes, I am. And, with your primetime special tonight, so will you. It's your story as much as it's mine. Casting doubt on the good news story of the century serves no purpose. Not that there is any reason to cast doubts."

—

Chapter 48

Foyer, Main Auditorium
World Health Organization Headquarters
Geneva, Switzerland
9:30 AM Local Time October 28ᵗʰ

The greeting between the two women started as a handshake but mutually moved to the cheek-to-cheek embrace common in diplomatic circles. They quickly moved to get out of the crowd, somewhere where they could talk freely. The WHO Global Partnership Conference would start soon. They found a quiet corner to speak to each other.

"Joan, it's so good to see you. Needless to say, I've been waiting many months for this." Karen Llewellyn-Craig said.

"Yes, Karen, our short conversation by phone in September was nice, but insufficient to say much of importance."

Karen nodded, "I saw in the news and now, on your nametag, your promotion, Madame Deputy Minister. You seem to have come out of these 'interesting times' on a positive note."

"Yes, my old friend Cao Jinghui, was moved up to fill the vacant Minister of Health position and he rewarded our friendship and our success with the vaccines by putting me in his old spot at the ministry."

Karen intentionally spoke quietly as she asked, "And there have been no repercussions from what you did . . . uh . . . your assistance. I don't know what to call it. You were fantastic. You saved millions."

Joan laughed at this, "No, no repercussions at all. And there won't be in the future either."

Karen was confused, "None. The way you spoke to me on the phone. I assumed there might be problems."

Joan nodded, "There could have been, but the world has changed, at least inside China."

Karen frowned, "I know about the deaths. That was quite perplexing, how those very senior people died when there was a vaccine available." Karen assumed she ought to stop talking on that subject.

"You had some deaths in your Cabinet, also." Joan smiled and thought for a moment. "I realize it may be difficult for you to keep the information I give to you from others in your government. But I think I can enlighten you a bit as to what happened without disclosing anything that could be bothersome for either you or me. Let me explain some of what happened."

"Of course." Karen leaned toward Joan to allow a quieter conversation.

"It was Jinghui, my friend who is the new Health Minister, who helped me arrange for the air freight shipment to you. You must meet him later, he is in Geneva, too. I have, of course, told him about you. Jinghui and I had been waiting for word from the senior leadership on how and when we could send word to the West that we had the H7N9 vaccine. That word did not come, and people were dying. Some areas of our country and some people in government also desperately needed the vaccine and were not getting it.

"It became clear to Jinghui and several of his close associates in the Defense Ministry whom he had worked with to do the vaccine trials amongst the troops and to deal with the initial problem in Baodi, that the extreme hardliners saw this as an opportunity for a powerplay, both internally and with the western powers. They would punish the West for how they treated China in the aftermath of coronavirus, they could damage the West irretrievably like happened with coronavirus, only worse, and they would use the opportunity of the chaos from the Parisian Flu for a power grab, or rather a consolidation of power within China. I cannot say exactly what happened, and I can say I'm happier not knowing. Still, it seems Jinghui's peers and cohorts over in the Defense Ministry outmaneuvered the hardline leadership and played the vaccine and disease cards with a 'better hand' than the hardliners. Things were touch and go for a few days there in early August. That is not a very well-kept secret."

Joan finished with, "Just as a silly mistake caused your American Cabinet members to get sick and some to die from the Parisian flu. So too, something occurred in early August, and the hardliners had problems with the flu, not getting the vaccine in time. I cannot say more about that."

Karen was wide-eyed at this disclosure. "So, your sending me the vaccine was an outgrowth of those political moves?"

"Yes, in part. And everybody in power now in China is quite happy about how things worked out. I have been congratulated for inventing the Chinese vaccine and saving lives, and I have been given a promotion. Nobody wants to hear anything more about what Jinghui, or I, or his confederates did with the vaccine . . . or didn't do." Joan Zhao smiled at Karen, "So, you did a wonderful job of following my rather cryptic instructions in those difficult days. Your taking credit for the vaccine worked perfectly. Karen Llewellyn-Craig can rest easy as the heroine of the American vaccine story. Zhao Xiang can rest easy as the heroine of the Chinese version. We can all rest easy. That is, until the next virus appears."

———

Beaumont Family Ranch
Santa Ynez Valley
Santa Barbara County, California
Late February

The six Northern Pintail ducks were restless in the Santa Ynez Valley farm pond. The instincts of their breed told them all it was time to head north toward the Arctic breeding grounds. Already they saw others of their breed flying north in formation high above them, having started their journey farther south in Central and South America. With a lifespan of twenty years or more, both the drake and the hen would make many more annual trips north and south and could wind up over the years anywhere on the northern half of the planet. Alas, the instincts of the breed also told them to find a new mate every year, so the drake and the hen would find new mates up in the Arctic. The Pintail drake, hen, and four yearling ducklings would, thus, start the cycle of life over again. But some of them would remember this lovely pond with the horsefly larvae and the fertile worm-rich vineyards. It was a beautiful place to live.

—

End

Afterword by the Author

As I worked to finish this novel, in early 2020, I found myself in a rather eerie position of being able to use real-life news stories of the coronavirus pandemic to reinforce and smooth out the fictional story that I started years ago. I was working on this story in earnest for several years and started collecting reference files for the idea back in 2013. In July 2017, I had brought the project to the point where I thought it a good idea to prepare for a website for the novel project, and I reserved the internet domain ViralNovel.com. To say that it is eerie to see things I have imagined and possibilities I have researched for these past years coming to fruition on the evening news does not cover my wonder at what has transpired in real life.

It was not entirely happenstance that I placed my epicenter of the pandemic in a smaller urban center in China. Prior occurrences like SARS and earlier avian flu incidents pointed to China's habits, its marketplace, and particularly its government, as being a probable Achilles Heel for the start of a pandemic. None of the epidemiologists who study pandemics were surprised when coronavirus started in China. I chose Baodi and Tianjin province years ago and scoured their streets on Google Maps for locations for the start of my story, whereas Mother Nature chose Wuhan city and Hubei province as her Chinese epicenter. I chose a newly mutated strain of Avian flu for my villain, but Mother Nature had the resources to invent a new coronavirus for hers. As I write this, there are news reports that it may not have been Mother Nature that made these choices, but rather an errant Wuhan virology laboratory. I had long ago chosen my hapless wild ducks from the Mekong as my animal vectors; the real world seems to have used bats from Wuhan.

When I first wrote about the events I place in Egypt, France, and California, I was wondering if mass quarantine and cessation of international trade and travel were believable. I know better now, for Iran, Italy and New York, and many other places, are living the real story. And, the real-world situation, in some ways, made writing this story easier. My readership doesn't need the book's characters to explain some things, like face mask rules, social distancing, contact tracing, and quarantining in place, that I earlier thought I might have to introduce my readers to in detail.

I think my story in this novel still has importance as we proceed through the real fears of the worldwide coronavirus pandemic. Avian flu is still out there and could replace coronavirus, or join it, anytime. Sadly, learned scientists expect that avian flu is still on the human agenda. When Bill Gates warned of a world-wide pandemic in 2015, I am pretty sure he was thinking about avian flu as the likely danger. The difficulty and time frame to prepare a new crop of vaccines for emergent viruses may advance a bit as we learn from past and current mistakes. I have worked on the story of virus-like particle vaccines and the concept of my government-owned vaccine plants for most of my time working on this novel, relying on the emerging virus-like particle industry and my personal experience with a similar U.S. Government process in armament production. As I write this, the current news stories about creating a vaccine for coronavirus indicate that corporate production and vaccine creation timelines are still a sore point. Maybe my fictional solution has merit. My novel is set a few years hence and pretends we have learned something from coronavirus. I hope that is true.

So, thank you for reading this story that once upon a time came from my imagination. I apologize if my fiction strikes a little too close to home and reality. This fictional novel was meant to be creative, not prophetic.

Kevin E. Ready
Solvang, California
April 2020

About the Author

Kevin E. Ready

Kevin Ready studied Government and Politics at the University of Maryland, University College in Berlin, Germany and received his Juris Doctor degree from the University of Denver. He had four decades of experience as a U.S. Navy officer, U.S. Army officer and government attorney. He has twice been a major party candidate for U.S. Congress. Kevin E. Ready lives in the Santa Barbara County, California with his wife, Olga and children. He is the author and editor of several books.

———

Visit Kevin's website at http://www.KevinEReady.com
Kevin produces a blog on Politics and the Law at
http://www.LawfulPolitics.com and
http://www.Twitter.com/LawfulPolitics

VIRAL

by

Kevin E. Ready

Published by
Saint Gaudens Press
Phoenix, Arizona — Santa Barbara, California

http://www.SaintGaudensPress.com

Saint Gaudens, Saint Gaudens Press
and the Winged Liberty colophon
are trademarks of Saint Gaudens Press
Copyright © 2020 Kevin E. Ready
All rights reserved.
Print edition ISBN: 978-0-943039-57-2
eBook ISBN: 978-0-943039-58-9
Printed in the United States of America